P9-CFC-049

THE ROMANCE READER'S GUIDE TO LIFE

ALSO BY SHARON PYWELL

Everything After
What Happened to Henry

THE ROMANCE READER'S GUIDE TO LIFE

SHARON PYWELL

FLATIRON
BOOKS
NEW YORK

This is a work of fiction. All of the characters, organizations, and events portrayed in this novel are either products of the author's imagination or are used fictitiously.

www.flatironbooks.com

Designed by Steven Seighman

The Library of Congress Cataloging-in-Publication Data is available upon request.

ISBN 978-1-250-10175-4 (hardcover)
ISBN 978-1-250-10174-7 (e-book)
ISBN 978-1-250-16109-3 (international edition)

Our books may be purchased in bulk for promotional, educational, or business use. Please contact your local bookseller or the Macmillan Corporate and Premium Sales Department at 1-800-221-7945, extension 5442, or by e-mail at MacmillanSpecialMarkets@macmillan.com.

First Edition: April 2017

10 9 8 7 6 5 4 3 2 1

To Todd

Faithful friend. Hapless protector.

It is what you read when you don't have to that determines what you will be when you can't help it.

—OSCAR WILDE

A FEW WORDS FROM LILLY:

Where She Is Now

If you're reading this, then you aren't where I am, which is dead. I was delivered here a little prematurely courtesy of some mistakes that might, if I'm going to be totally honest here, have something to do with Vixen Red lipstick and the feelings that cluster around it. I've been told I have bad judgment but that's ridiculous. I have excellent judgment—just check the profit margin from Be Your Best Cosmetics.

See? Excellent judgment.

I call my current location Where I Am Now. It's hard to be more specific because I myself am not real clear about my location. It's relatively new to me. If I were you, I wouldn't find that very satisfying but it's all I've got. More on this later but you might want to know—I'm not alone here. The dog was here to greet me when I arrived.

My sister Neave is in control of a good deal of what you'll know, and not know. The thing you should keep in mind the whole time you're listening to her is that Neave is relentlessly, sometimes dully, honest. Also, she thinks that we live in one place and one time. I now know that isn't the case. My friend the high-heeled dog explained what he could to me and we left the rest to faith. But Neave, the only relief she gets from this limited view of time and space is books, because when she's inside a book she goes wherever it says to go.

Neave believes in stepping into a book the way I believed in stepping into the Ritz. Things in the Oak Bar are solid and beautiful. You can smell the leather and the gin and after a martini the men are all more lovely. Lovely, lovely men. At five o'clock Henry rolls around the hors d'oeuvres cart that the Ritz bought from the *Oceana* after its final cruise, and he arranges a few pickled mushrooms and a smoked oyster on toast for me. Love that man.

I don't think books did Neavie as much good as the hors d'oeuvres cart did me. Books made her both cynical and dreamy at the same time, which is not in my opinion a useful combination. Look at his suit, she'd say, not in a way that means the suit is a good thing, but in a way that said what kind of man spends a fortune on a suit? I'd say a very interesting man. Then I'd note that it was possible she was out of her depth. Here it was, right after Armistice Day, I'd say to her, the streets flooded with newly sprung, often handsome soldiers looking for company, and she was spending her Friday nights bent over a cash flow at work or padding around her kitchen making a pie. Reading a book. She's not ugly but she's bookish, which is not a real enchanting characteristic in the world I lived in. Nobody writes love poetry to their bookish mistress while she shlumps around making pies.

I can see inside Neave's head from where I am and I know what she'd say to me even now, even after I died, if she heard me giving dating advice. What do you know? she'd say. You're dead.

And she'd be right.

NEAVE

Lynn, Massachusetts—My First Job

Lilly and I were Irish twins, born in 1924 and 1925 in Lynn, Massachusetts. She was a sunny, unsteerable, reckless girl and she grew up to be exactly the same kind of woman. I followed in her wake, sometimes smoothly and other times just bumping along behind her in the chop. It didn't matter—wherever she was going, I was going there too. We grew up kicking each other's feet in the same bed, eating the same food, taking each other's side in every scuffle over the occasionally limited resources in the house we grew up in. Long before we launched Be Your Best Cosmetics together we were each other's first confidante, most inventive playmate, best defense against every evil. But here's maybe the most important and wonderful thing about her: Lilly didn't really think evil existed. Of all the reasons I wished I were her, that's the big one. That blindness was her doing and undoing; mine too, maybe, but not in the same order. That's why I'm here telling her story and she's not.

In 1936, I was eleven years old and oblivious. I didn't know that Hitler had just gotten production of the People's Car under way. I didn't know that some of the dirt I dug in the backyard to make roads for Snyder's toy cars had blown there all the way from Oklahoma in the great dust storms. I didn't know that the civil war in Spain had been launched, or that the Yellow River in China had overflowed at levels that were about to cause millions of people to starve. The whole world was going to hell, and I was making dirt roads for Snyder's metal cars. I was enjoying myself.

Janey was youngest, only six years old in 1936, and Snyder was oldest and the only boy. This made him feel like the odd man out but the fact is, he was odd—not the kind of brother you'd wake up for company in the middle of the night if you had a nightmare. The four of us functioned as a sometimes cooperative group. I knew that if Lilly and Snyder and I pooled our resources we could get a loaf of bread for seven cents and eat the whole thing in the backyard with slices of Daddy's tomatoes. Daddy loved his garden and hated his job at General Electric doing something with boilers that we didn't understand. He'd come home looking flat and dark, go to his garden, and walk back into the house a little lighter. The boiler room made Daddy unhappy but overall I'd say that it was his nature to be irritated or squashed by a good deal that went on around him. It wasn't just the boiler room.

We knew he wouldn't miss a few tomatoes as long as we didn't leave any big bare holes. We foraged in Daddy's garden and Mom's pantry like stray dogs. Snyder once stole a jar of our mom's jam, which he shared when we caught him and threatened to rat him out. We didn't want to spoil Janey's dinner, so we didn't tell her about it. Also, she can't keep secrets. We made a bread-and-jam picnic in the far back of our property when she was taking a stroll to the end of the block. We love Jane, but she has to be managed. She's overly transparent, overly cheerful—characteristics you wouldn't think could get in the way of trust, but the fact is, they can.

That year the bubble around my life extended just as far as jam and tomatoes and the seven-cent loaf of bread, and at the time I found that a very workable amount of room in which to live. I was just at the lip of knowing about other bubbles, other worlds, and my brief glimpses outside my little universe were changing me. My schoolbooks were full of tiny-waisted unopinionated mothers making dinner and brothers who were always pleased to lend you their bikes. At a certain point these stories started to feel wrong. This cheerful primer-book world was clearly what the grown-ups believed I saw or wanted me to see, and I was beginning to feel duped. Worse, I knew I wasn't supposed to feel duped. I was supposed to feel just like the children in the primers, which was scary because I didn't. There had to be something wrong, and it seemed to be wrong with me.

I started nosing around for stories about stubborn siblings and disappointed fathers. I'd look around my classroom hoping to find my fellow students raising eyebrows, looking worried. Nothing—only bent heads, jiggling feet, and moving lips, apparently at peace with the view from the school primer serving eleven-year-olds. No company here. Of course, I had Lilly, whom I loved completely, and Snyder and Janey, whom I would step in front of a bullet for, but someplace deeper down, I was alone.

I did what lots of people like me do: I started haunting the local library. One day I found a book in the Children's Room about a boy who lived with his parents in an ocean of Wyoming prairie grass. They raised horses. The boy was happy because all the company he needed in the world was his horse. But in a brief scene buried around page 320 where it might go unnoticed, his mother went running into the dark Wyoming winter night after a fight with the boy's father. She ran miles and miles until she reached the railroad tracks. There she stood, waiting for the night train to shoot through the Wyoming prairie, where she lived with the things that weren't enough, with the cold husband and the boy who was obsessed with his horse. She saw people in dining cars lifting glasses of wine, beautifully dressed people in brightly lit car after car, all of it rushing by so quickly. She watched them with her whole heart. I could tell that. I couldn't entirely decode this moment in the story, but I knew it was true and real and important. I'd stumbled onto a secret message from the adult world that had slipped past the gates of the Children's Room. I was scared. I was thrilled.

I hated the Children's Room. Our town library was a converted two-story house riddled with wood rot and mediocre donated castoffs. Its Children's Room was cobbled out of what was once a nursery. The grown-ups who thought that children had smaller feelings and needs than adults had put the "children's" section in the building's darkest little rabbit warren. A stuffed dog who looked like he'd known happier times slumped on one of the bookshelves. He was alone, no other animal friends or posters of puppies to back him up. A table with a small pile of books was wedged against a wall. *Peggy's Pokey Puppy*, *Snow White*, *Cowboys of the Wild West*, *Mommy and Me Make Cookies*, *Lizzy and the Lost Baby*, *Adventures in Our Back Yards.*

A wasteland.

The librarian thought it was morally important that once children stepped into the library they should be shuffled into this room and made to stay put. She kept her eyes on me, smiling in a cheerful, threatening kind of way and making sure I stayed where I belonged in my little desert of happy endings and cheerful relations with talkative animals. I made three separate attempts on the living room, home to Adult Fiction, and I was turned back every single time.

Mrs. Daniels changed all that. It was Snyder who brought her to me, or me to her, which is more accurate even if it didn't feel like that. Sometimes after school Snyder delivered groceries and five-dollar bags of coal for Mr. McGarry's grocery. The only customers who bought five-dollar bags were rich people who didn't care what it cost and poor people who couldn't scrape together enough cash to get half-ton deliveries. Mrs. Daniels was one of the rich ones. She was so old that the skin on her arms was sliding off her bones and her eyes weren't cooperating with her anymore. She needed somebody whose eyes still did their duty, because Mrs. Daniels was a reader. That's how she came to offer Snyder five cents an hour to read to her after school.

Snyder was only vaguely interested in working and not at all interested in sitting for hours with a bony old lady. "I've been in her house," he told us. "She reads trash like *The Sheik* and *Office Girl*. She gets Love Pulps with people kissing on the covers." The idea of getting to read whatever was in a Love Pulp made something in me come totally alive, never mind the unbelievable sum of five cents an hour.

"Tell her about me," I said. "Tell her I can do it."

He did.

"You're no bigger than a potato," Mrs. Daniels said when I got there. Snyder had walked me over and bolted the moment my feet hit the porch. "What was your brother thinking of to send you to me?"

"He was thinking I would do just fine," I said. "I'm little for my age but I'm eleven," I added. She gave me a long up-and-down look and handed me a story by Ernest Hemingway in *Cosmopolitan* magazine. "Sentences are short in this one," she said. "Try it out for size."

I tried.

"What do you think of Mr. Hemingway?" she asked when I was done. The reading had gone briskly sometimes; lumpily sometimes.

"I think this man who goes fishing in the start of the story is in trouble. I don't think he's gonna get out of it either."

"Cynical little creature," she observed. "You mispronounce something in every line."

I glared.

"Very well," she said. "Perhaps you only mispronounced one or two things."

"I'll read for free until it's better if you want. It'll get better fast with practice, Mrs. Daniels."

She looked me up and down again. "What if I pay you nothing for weeks?"

"If I'm not reading good, that's fair."

"Well."

"Well what?"

"'If I am not reading *well*.'" She sighed.

Mrs. Daniels called out to her cook, Violette, and told her to bring cookies. She offered me one. I reached eagerly and then I thought of Snyder, Jane, and Lilly, all cookieless.

"What's wrong, girl?"

"At home if there's not enough for everybody I shouldn't take anything."

"There's no one here to share with but me," she replied. She reached forward and lifted the largest cookie from the plate and took a bite. "And I eat what I please."

"You took the biggest one," I observed.

"Of course I did. I like cookies."

"That's rude," I told her. "The first person to pick should pick the smallest one."

"Who says?"

"My mother."

"Indeed? Well, I stand corrected. But since I've taken a bite out of it I don't have to put the damn thing back, do I?"

"Swearing's rude too."

"I imagine it is. What did you say your name was?"

"Neave."

"Well, Neave, I thank you for your reading efforts today. I will pay you your five cents and give you a bag with enough cookies in it so you will be able to share with your siblings. How many are there?"

I didn't answer because I didn't know what a sibling was, which was embarrassing.

"Your family's vaguely Irish, isn't it? How many are there? Twelve?"

"How many what?" I managed.

"Brothers and sisters," she said, and her voice was friendlier.

"There's me and Lilly, Jane, and Snyder."

"We can manage that many cookies."

She gave me a nickel and told me to go to the kitchen and ask Violette for a paper bag of cookies. I stood motionless.

"What is it now?" she asked. Her eyes had drooped closed but she talked to me as if she could see me still standing there shuffling from foot to foot. I studied a hair on her chin. Her fingers drifted to it as if she could feel my eyes on it, and, her own eyes still closed, she plucked it out while I stared.

"Am I coming back?" I managed.

"Do you want to come back?"

I nodded. The skin on her neck crinkled like a turtle's and one of her eyelids wasn't doing the same thing as the other one, which I did not like but I wanted to read *The Sheik* so badly that I stood my ground. When I want things, I want them badly, and Mrs. Daniels wasn't the first scary thing I'd stared down. "Very well. Come tomorrow if it's all right with your mother."

We lived only four houses away, and I ran the distance as if a wild animal armed with machine guns were at my heels. I banged into the house calling for Lilly, and when she came to see what the matter was I made her sit down right there and read something hard with me, something as hard as *The Sheik*.

"What are you doing for Mrs. Daniels?" Mom asked me that night at dinner. "You went over there today?"

Something dinged in me, warning me off the subject of books, which could lead to a discussion of my gaining access to *White Collar Girl*.

"Carrying things. Sweeping."

Snyder looked up from his meat loaf but kept his mouth shut.

"Sweeping and carrying what? I thought Mrs. Daniels had a cook in the house who could help her."

"Well, Violette's a Protestant. And Mrs. Daniels likes someone who knows the rosary to say it with her."

That whipped my mother's head around. "Mrs. Daniels is a Catholic?"

I nodded. "It's just not easy for her to get to church, so you don't see her there." I could feel my mother's assessing toe-to-hairline sweep of me. I smiled mildly and looked right back at her. I knew what she was thinking. Rosaries? None of her children took church very seriously, but I was the only openly resistant member of the family. I'd been a cranky First Communion candidate, complaining about the classes and the memorizing and the idea that now I was old enough to get in real spiritual trouble. I'd resisted the white gloves I was supposed to wear to Mass now that I was old enough and the doily that got pinned on my head every week. I was a pew kicker and a malcontent. My mother had used those particular words to describe me and they'd stuck in my mind.

"You're over there for longer than it takes to say a rosary, missy."

I'd overreached. "Well, sure. You know I think she really just likes company. She's very lonely." This didn't seem like too much of a lie—simply a different way of looking at things.

My mother considered a little longer. "It's a worthwhile thing to do if the poor woman's lonely. You be nice to her. But take no money from Mrs. Daniels unless you're making yourself useful doing something that needs doing in this world as well as the next. Nobody on Earth should pay another person to say a rosary with her. Do you understand?"

I did understand and I indicated this with a puppety nod. Maybe our mother wouldn't have stopped me from going to Mrs. Daniels's house if she knew I was heading hip-deep into the land of Adult Fiction, but I wasn't taking that chance. Such a small little lie and besides, I could find something to dust the next time I was in her house and so it wouldn't even be a lie at all.

I was a bad Catholic but I still had some uneasiness about all this lying. I took it, like I took most of my uneasy feelings, to Lilly.

"Oh, don't be a ninny. Who cares if Mrs. Daniels likes hearing rosaries or not? Mom's never going to walk over there and ask her."

"She's not?"

"Nope. She thinks Mrs. Daniels is a little scary. I heard her say it to Mrs. Seifritz."

"Really?"

Then Lilly said exactly what I needed her to say. "You didn't do anything wrong. If she gives you more cookies, ask for extras."

The first afternoon I worked for Mrs. Daniels, we ended with Mrs. Roosevelt's "My Day" column, and then she said that was enough reading for today. "I need to stretch. I'm going to tell Violette to bring us a little something," she said. She stood up and started toward the kitchen. I stood up too, and drifted to the part of her bookshelves that held the titles like *Paris Spring*. Mrs. Daniels stopped in her tracks. "Move along, child. Leave that section of the library alone."

"Will we ever read one of these, Mrs. Daniels?"

"One of the romances? No."

"Why not?"

"You are young, and impressionable."

"Does something happen to you if you read them?" A rhetorical question—I assumed that something happened to the people who read them, or Mrs. Daniels wouldn't be shooing me away from them.

"The first thing that might happen to you is that people mock you for reading them. They think that women who read romances are idiots. I assure you, they are not."

"No?"

"No. They are people who trust that love exists and that it is more powerful than bad logic or bad writing."

"Why would anybody be against love?"

"On the surface, a reasonable question."

"I'm not against love," I offered.

"So you are a devotee of love?" Mrs. Daniels said drily. "One wouldn't assume that to look at you. But the world is full of hope, isn't it? It appears in the most unlikely of places."

The next time we met she set me to *The Odyssey*, not going in any order but picking out parts she particularly liked. On my first day with Mr. Homer I found the Sirens busy trying to draw Odysseus and his men onto the wreckage-strewn rocks around their island, luring the sailors to destruction with their beautiful voices. Of course, Odysseus survives to fight another day, out-tricking the singers by plugging his crew's ears with wax so they couldn't hear him howling to be taken closer, closer, to the Sirens in their ring of broken boats.

I knew I was supposed to hate those damn Sirens, but I didn't. I figured that a person takes his chances with Sirens because he wants to—maybe has to. He crosses his fingers and ties himself to a mast and says, Keep going, everybody—I'm not missing this—and that made sense to me.

NEAVE

Mr. Boppit, Wonder Dog

That summer we came upon Mr. Boppit waiting patiently outside George's Sweetheart Market for a person who was never going to return to him. This kind of thing happened to dogs back in 1936 if feeding them got too expensive. Bop was there at ten a.m. when Snyder and Jane were sent to the store for milk. He was there at five p.m. when Lilly rode her bicycle by. He was discussed at dinner, and all of us trooped back to see if he was still there at seven. Yup—alert and patient, attending his betrayer. I suggested that his owner maybe had suffered a heart attack in aisle three and the dog hadn't actually been dumped. Lilly mocked this hopeful view. "The mutt was ditched by somebody who lost his job or left town. He hasn't even gotten his full growth yet and he probably already eats a pound of dog food a day. Look at the size of those paws."

We walked slowly home, but once everybody seemed to have gotten busy with something else I snuck an enamel pan out of the kitchen along with what leftovers I thought I could liberate without drawing any attention to myself and I walked back. He was still there, and pleased to accept the meal. His manners were good and he greeted me civilly—not a jump-on-you-chew-everything kind of dog. He watched as I set the food down and he looked up at my face for permission before he ate, though when he did tuck in it was clear that it'd been a long time between meals. A good dog. I asked George if I could use his tap and an old pan and I set out some water for him. When I walked away I kept looking back to see if he was watching me. He was. The tail would lift and sway when I turned toward him, droop when I started to turn away.

The next day I went back with a ham bone and some vegetable-cheese casserole. He was still there, still polite, and pretty cheerful considering his situation. I sat down next to him this time as he ate, and when he was done he sat down next to me and set a paw on my knee. I described my day. He listened attentively. If I walked away right then I thought maybe George would drive him off and we'd come upon him in a week trying to tip over trash cans behind the Breakfast Nook Spa. Boys would attach things to him or drag him around with ropes tied to his overly loyal furry neck. He would be hungry, maybe scared, all alone.

I took a few steps away, but I looked back at him and his tail lifted. Our eyes met—the tail swayed a little. "Well, come on," I said. He looked at the door of Sweetheart Market. He looked at me. "I'm not going to try to explain ratfinks to you," I said, "or back doors. But I don't think your owner is coming back, no matter how long you sit there." He stood and I swear he sighed. Then he fell into step by my right knee and we walked home in companionable silence.

Janey fell on the poor dog like he was her last friend on Earth, and he didn't object when she climbed on him and yanked at his ears and tail. She named him Boppit, and I added the "Mr." because he just looked too sober a creature to give him a name that called up the sound a cartoon mallet made hitting a cartoon head. Mr. Boppit's manners were elegant, not something you'd expect from a goofy style of dog. But dogs don't always match their looks any more than people do. I've seen three-pound lapdoggish ones attack a horse and giant fang-toothed ones hide under porches when the ice man's bell goes by. Mr. Boppit was neither. When Jane got calmer and stepped away from him, Bop sat down quietly and held up one paw for her to shake. She took it and he didn't budge until she was done pumping it up and down. Mom saw that and it decided her in Mr. Boppit's favor.

He was initially my dog, not because anybody discussed it but because I'd brought him home. He was also partly Janey's by default because she was the baby and he'd given her his paw to shake. Snyder wasn't usually moved by animal magnetism, and Mr. Boppit wasn't the kind of dog who imposed himself on you if you weren't interested. Lilly outright disliked him. She claimed he smelled like a dog, but then, he was a dog. Exactly what was he supposed to do about that, I asked her. He also shed and liked to sleep on our bed, which Lilly hated, but his major offense was what he did to Lilly's shoes. Bop could push any door in the house open easily, even manipulate a simple latch, so getting into our closet was not beyond him. Lilly'd find him there sitting in a pile of chewed-up remains and she'd whack him. He'd stand there and take it, tail down, looking as ashamed as any dog ever looked, but the next week he'd do it all over again.

Aside from his feelings about shoes, he was a perfect dog. He let Jane tie bonnets on his head and sat at her doll table with her for tea. He walked by our sides and guarded us on our trips to the end of the block to buy penny candy at the corner spa. The winter after he came to us, he was walking with Lilly and me through some marshy fields by the beach. A little whisper of snow that had just fallen made it hard to see what was underfoot, and I was skidding along on the icy skin that had frozen over some standing water. I broke through and got a foot jammed in the shattered ice, which didn't put me in any danger but Mr. Boppit couldn't tell that from the volume of my yelling. The water was icy, only seven inches deep, but it sloshed in over the top of my boot. Worse, when I yanked the boot up it caught on the edge of the hole I'd made and pulled the boot right off my foot, which sank in the still unfrozen muck as I struggled.

Lilly yelled directions at me from the dry path along the marsh. She'd just gotten a new pair of boots that week, her first new boots in three years, so she was not stepping into any slushy goop to offer help unless there was more at stake than wet feet. She stayed put and yelled helpful advice. Not Mr. Boppit. Ears up, tail streaming out like a flag, Mr. Boppit charged to my unnecessary rescue: He got a big mouthful of my jacket, braced himself, and yanked me right off my feet and through a good five feet of ice water before I stopped yelling. As soon as I was quiet he released me and stepped up to lick my face. That's the kind of dog he was.

Of course, Snyder used Mr. Boppit's nature against the poor animal. I think Janey was the only creature on Earth Snyder loved, but still he'd pretend to hurt her just to torment Boppit. He'd grab our little sister and make-believe whack her. The dog got positively hysterical—whining, barking, trying to push himself between Snyder and Janey while Snyder fake-yelled at her and windmilled his arms around her head, fake-attacking. That's the sticky little dark place where Snyder lived. Boppit was helpless in these situations—too sensitive and good to imagine what Snyder really was.

At night Boppit slept on the floor between our bed and Jane's cot. He would have climbed into bed with us and wedged himself between Lilly and me if Lilly had let him. I would have let him. My sisters were sound sleepers but sometimes I'd wake up anxious and confused, climbing out of some bad dream. I'd look over and there would be Mr. Boppit looking across at me in the dark all calm and alert. He would watch me as I'd try to remember what I was dreaming, fail, and calm down. Sometimes he'd step up to the bed beside me and lay his head on my pillow until I told him I was all right. I'd say I was fine and he should lie down. I'd shut my eyes to convince him I'd fallen back asleep, but when I opened them again to see if I'd fooled him, his eyes would be shining at me; his tail would thump on the floorboards. He was on guard, shielding me from whatever it was that had woken me.

NEAVE

The Pirate Lover

Mrs. Daniels regularly sent me home with paper bags of Violette's cookies or brownies. In our backyard a sweep of birches stood between the rock and the kitchen window so we were invisible to our mother, who said charity was for the weak. Uncertain if this idea extended to free cookies, I distributed them in secret. In bad weather we met in Snyder's bedroom; in good weather we met on the big rock at the back of our property. The first autumn afternoon that the air turned crisp Mrs. Daniels had Violette put a huge pile of coal in the grate—as much coal in one fire as my family used in a day. We toasted bread and slathered it over with jam during breaks from reading. My whole life wasn't heaven, but those parts of it were.

I'd been waiting for the moment when I could get an up-close look at the forbidden shelves of her library, and it finally came one afternoon when Mrs. Daniels excused herself for a slow trip to the facilities. She turned the corner into the hallway and I was on my feet and across the room in a flash. I told myself that I was going to take only a quick look, but that didn't last a second longer than it took to see the first cover: *The Pirate Lover.* Well, I told myself, I would borrow it for a very short amount of time and just skim a few chapters before returning it. By the time she got back, *The Pirate Lover* was jammed into my book bag and I'd rearranged my face into an innocent blank.

I took my stolen book to the bedroom closet that Daddy had built as a storage space for old snowsuits and clothes waiting for the next kid in line to grow into them. At the back was a perfectly usable if very tiny space that was out of sight and sound of family life. It actually had an electric socket, which made it easy for me to read with the help of a yard-sale lamp our mother had bought and abandoned in the garage. I dragged in a stolen pillow and a borrowed blanket and settled in with *The Pirate Lover* as soon as I could do so unobserved. The first afternoon I hid there I folded the blanket into a fat square seat, flicked on the yard-sale lamp, and just sat regarding my kingdom. It was raining and the drops hit the shingles just inches from my head with a soothing *rapraprap.* Thus began the part of my life that was lived in book romances.

All I can say in my defense is that I was just looking for the truth.

Also love, which I hoped was a true thing.

THE PIRATE LOVER

Electra Gates was a young woman so beautiful that she had commanded the attention of the men around her from the age of twelve, and though she had been an obedient and proper young woman, or perhaps because she had been an obedient and proper young woman, she had yet to taste passion herself though she had inspired it. She had hated no one, desired no one, loved no one. So when she encountered Basil Le Cherche, her feelings were a revelation to her.

She first encountered his coolly assessing gaze in a Parisian drawing room in the spring of her eighteenth year. Electra's mother was French, her father had been British, and when he was alive they had moved easily from one world to the other. But upon his death his widow had been shocked to discover how far beyond their actual means they had been living. His creditors swarmed their home and picked it clean, and the world they had known evaporated in a matter of weeks. It took only one social season in London for her mother to see how utterly their new poverty had changed her world. Where once she had known only flattery and smiles, now she met an endless stream of small humiliations. She took her daughter and withdrew from the London rooms they could no longer afford. They would take what they still had and go to Paris, where she could live more cheaply—and discreetly. Her mother had lived there in her youth with distant relatives, so this world felt familiar to her as well as far from their current difficulties. There she would bide her time, waiting for her daughter to reach the full flood of a beauty that could secure the attention of Paris society—and its wealthiest men. Two years had passed in this manner. Now the waiting was over.

"We have saved every sou in preparation for this last chance," her mother had said to Electra. "We must play out our hand now."

Even as they were reduced to worn cotton and broken shoes from seasons many years past, Electra's mother had studied the little dolls dressed in Paris's latest fashions that made their way to every small village and major capital where women owned mirrors. She had sold their sticks of furniture and every jewel she owned to pay for the Chinese silks and extravagant carriage fees that would provide her and her daughter a kind of disguise—the trappings of wealth and security, neither of which did they actually possess. She bet her future on this last gamble.

Electra did not regard herself as a hand to be played, but she was an obedient daughter. Thus in the spring of her eighteenth year she found herself drinking tea in a Parisian drawing room on the day that all the talk was of a woman who had been found on the steps of Notre Dame, her clothes sliced away from the desecrated body, her throat cut cleanly at the artery. A picture had reached the newspapers and fascinated all of Paris—the victim's head thrown back, lips white and parted, her face alabaster and her eyes wide but utterly empty now.

In a corner of Madame Cirque's Tuesday salon she heard a soft suggestion from the Viscount Pronauge that the victim looked like a mythic virginal sacrifice. "A draggle-tail homeless creature, a prostitute, apparently," someone in the little cluster around the viscount added. "No, no," another said, clearly agitated. "We've all passed her in the street—she's the baker's daughter. A simple, good girl!" Electra turned away from them, covering her fear with a practiced smile, and at the crest of her turn she saw the face that changed her life forever—Basil Le Cherche, standing out in the select gathering like an obsidian shard in a bank of snow. All evening she struggled to keep her eyes from him, and all evening she failed. Each time her eyes found him she met his gaze. No matter the quickness of her turn or the interval between searching glances—he was waiting with a stillness deeper than any she had ever observed in man or woman.

She drifted toward Madame de Lac, a woman who would know the worst of anyone in the upper social circles of the city. "Who is that man?" she asked, dipping her chin in the dark stranger's direction as quickly and unobtrusively as she could.

"Someone to avoid at all costs, my dear. His name is Basil Le Cherche. He is brother to a judge on the highest courts—Monsieur Henri Le Cherche. They say that his brother's influence is all that keeps his neck from a noose now. Basil Le Cherche is rich, but his wealth, they say, is rooted in piracy and smuggling. He is also a noted swordsman."

"But duels are illegal in the city!"

"My pet, the sword he wields is not brought to the battlefield but the bedroom."

Madame de Lac laughed to see her young companion flush crimson.

Electra was still taken by surprise in this place where one's clothing and connections mattered all; one's character and intelligence not a whit. "I heard of tiresome difficulties after your father's death. But you and your mother seem to have had a change of fortune," Madame de Lac observed, her eyes tracing the French seams of Electra's kidskin gloves. Electra merely nodded. She refused to tell the lie her mother had invented to explain this new wealth if anyone asked pressing questions—a departed long-lost relative from England who had left them this inheritance. No such thing or person existed, Electra had argued, and one lie will only demand ten more to prop it up when it totters. But her mother had not hesitated. "You have no idea how easy it is to lie," she sniffed. "And you will be moving in a world where lies are legion—it is easier to identify a liar if you are one yourself, Electra. I suggest you learn the skill."

Electra's mother had moved them by now into a more acceptably fashionable address on Île de la Cité. From their windows they could see the river parting as it reached the island. They could see the falcon family that waited patiently beneath the roof balustrades of Notre Dame, see them carry up the rats and pigeons they hunted and delivered to their young. Electra watched them dismember the rodents, shredding them into pieces small enough for their fledglings.

"They keep the city rid of vermin," her mother would say when Electra grieved the little animals' deaths, imagining their terror and pain as they were carried upward in the falcon talons. "All things die. All things must hunt to live. If you did not learn this lesson during our time in the country, you will learn it here in the city."

Perhaps. Already she was finding similarities between some of the people she encountered in this sophisticated city and the falcons that had made Notre Dame their home. Already she was vowing to herself that she would be carried in no raptor's talons.

And now in this Parisian drawing room she once again turned to find Basil Le Cherche's dark eyes upon her. She met them, straight-on, and was shocked to see that this made him smile. So forward and rude! She knew enough of both London and Paris etiquette to feel that she was being tested as well as assessed, and she resented it. When she and her mother arrived home at last she found herself in a most unsettled mood.

"I will not be ogled," she whispered to herself. "Not by anyone!"

Who was this dark creature whose presence made the rest of the world so much less important? Why did he distract her so? Was what she felt anger?

Her mother noticed none of this shift in her daughter. She was taken up entirely with preparations for the Grand Ball, which was only a week away. On this night young women were shown to the world in hopes of attracting a bidder who could offer the girl's weight in gold.

Marriages to the most powerful men in Europe had begun in evenings such as this.

Electra's mother had endeavored to discover all there was to know about a certain Monsieur X. Did he prefer women in modest gowns or daring ones? Upswept severe hair or something looser and more flirtatious? What topics did he most enjoy discussing? And Monsieur Y, worth ten thousand a year—did his attention run more to breasts or ankles, either of which could be safely exposed without severe judgment? Electra mocked her mother gently at first when she pressed these topics, and then, rebuked, sighed and did what good young women did: practiced certain topics for discussion and traveled from the tenth arrondissement to the Île and back in search of the right shoes.

"Mother, surely shoes will not determine the course of a lifetime," she said as she sighed from her seat at yet another shopkeeper's establishment.

"Do not patronize me with your naïve romanticism," her mother said drily. "Your future lies entirely in the hands of the man who chooses you. The rest of your life could depend upon this night," she insisted as she pressed a beautiful frock against Electra's lithe form to test its effect. "The sooner you understand that, the better."

Electra had followed her mother from shop to shop, taken lessons in dance and locution, agreed—sometimes with nothing but her silence—with her parent's strategies and perspectives. But something happened between the day her mother selected a dress for her to wear to the ball and the date of the ball itself: Basil Le Cherche.

From the moment she had turned to see if Viscount Le Cherche was still in that crowded drawing room and found him seeking her eyes, she was changed. The silent, obedient daughter was still visible, but so, if an observer cared to look closer, was something less predictable. Brazen man, she thought to herself. Disrespectful ogler! And his dark clothing, his distant hooded assessment of the others in the room—as if he watched them from a cool and bottomless distance—a raptor's gaze. Well, she was no passive dove waiting for the talons. Perhaps she had talons of her own.

She came home from that initial meeting and held the dress her mother had chosen for her against her perfect breasts, swirling before a mirror and letting the reflection take its time with her, letting her own feelings about what she saw take shape. Electra knew that its clustered roses and cool paleness showed her freshest features to advantage—the firm, creamy skin, the mirrorlike eyes, the thick tumble of silky, pale hair. Yes, she was what Paris fashion regarded as lovely. But was it the kind of loveliness that appealed to Monsieur X, Monsieur Y, or Monsieur Le Cherche? The anger that had had its origin, she believed, in her reaction to the Viscount Le Cherche spilled over and into her cool gaze in the mirror. She would not be forced to be a particular kind of woman by anyone—not her mother, not Monsieur X, not the harpies who clustered around Madame de Lac. She would not be costumed for their regard. If Monsieur X and Y disliked what they saw, that would only leave her freer to go her own way. And Electra Gates suddenly, unaccountably, wanted to be free.

She threw the gown her mother had chosen aside. She went, alone, into the city. When she finally found the reflected image she'd sought in a tiny alley in the Marais, she felt a kind of excitement that was entirely foreign to her. The deeply cut bodice exposed her breasts almost to the nipple. The waist was tightly cinched, the skirt full of movement, almost diaphanous—and when she was still the material lay on her thighs like a caress. Perhaps most satisfying to her was an uneasy glittering feeling marbled through this new mood—the mood of a huntress who, at the same moment that she understood herself to be engaged in a blood sport, felt that she was the hunted as well as the hunter.

Six days now to the ball.

I set the book down, startled to find myself still in my closet. I looked up at a green winter coat that Lilly had passed on to me the winter before and I knew right then that I wasn't going to return this book to its shelf the next time I went to Mrs. Daniels's house.

The grown-up world, from what I could see on these pages, wasn't exactly what I'd thought it was. How could glittering feelings and raptor talons have anything to do with my mother or my father, or Mrs. Daniels? Either I didn't understand anything, or their world was even stranger than I'd imagined. I climbed out of the closet, jammed *The Pirate Lover* under my mattress, and told myself, again, that Mrs. Daniels wouldn't miss one book from those crowded shelves if I kept it just a bit longer, which could possibly mean forever.

She didn't seem to miss it at all. She set me to a few pages in *The Odyssey* the next Wednesday afternoon. On and on I went, listening to Telemachus whine about how he was too little and weak to fight the suitors and how his dad was maybe dead and who was going to help him blahblahblah. When Athena finally told him to get off his rear end and go have an adventure, I'd already decided he wasn't worth my attention. Mrs. Daniels sensed my mood and took the book back, flipping to another section: Odysseus—stranded on Calypso's island and kept prisoner as her lover. I perked right up. "Is he in love with Calypso?" I asked.

"I sincerely doubt it. They amuse one another, but his destiny is elsewhere. He must return to his home."

"Because he's in love with his wife?"

"Perhaps."

"But that's what he says, Mrs. Daniels."

"In his world, little girl, being able to lie well is a desirable skill. And he lies very well. All the most attractive characters in this story are accomplished liars. It's a good skill in a dangerous world. Wait until you meet the woman he hopes to return to—she is his match in every way. She is a particularly gifted liar."

"They read this book in school but not until ninth grade."

"Are you saying it's too hard for you to read?"

"Oh, no." I straightened up and got my face looking like it belonged to somebody who could read anything a ninth-grader could read. I could even read stuff I didn't understand. That was my job and I was going to do it.

"Good." She took the book from me and flipped through. "Perhaps I should have taken you to Circe's island. I suspect Circe would amuse you."

"What happens on Circe's island?"

"She turns all the men into pigs."

I must have looked stunned, because she shook her head a little bit at me. "Don't worry. She turns them all back into men in the end."

"Why did she do that to them?"

"Because she could, I imagine."

"The ladies in these stories don't like men."

"Which ladies?"

"The Sirens sing songs that make the sailors come so close they crash into the rocks and die. Circe turns them into pigs. And you told me that General Agamemnon's wife and her new boyfriend clubbed him to death when he got home from Troy."

"Keep in mind that the stories are made up by men, for men, about men. What they have to say about the ladies is perhaps not entirely unprejudiced. And we do not have the ladies' perspective. Would you like a cookie, child?"

Yes. I would like a cookie. And I decided, mid-cookie, that when I got home I was not going to think about the Sirens or Circe or any of it. But I couldn't help myself. I did anyhow.

LILLY

Where She Is Now

Neave thinks that Snyder and I didn't know she squirreled herself in the back of the closet with those books she stole from Mrs. Daniels. Of course we knew. We didn't tattle because it would irritate Mom, who would try to make her quit it, and then they'd fight. When she and Mom fought, everybody's concentration went to hell and dinner ended up burned.

Neave would tell you straight-faced that she's reasonable, but that's not even within screaming distance of the truth. If she feels pushed around it's easy to accidentally jab an elbow into her dignity because it sticks out in all directions. I liked that about her, but maybe I could enjoy the vinegary side of my sister because I was her Lilly. She loved Jane and Boppit and I guess even Snyder, but she loved me most. I say that as simple fact, nothing I earned or did anything special to get.

The way Neave is made hasn't always served her so well. She's stubborn. She gets mad pretty regularly. To be fair, when she does get mad it's usually for a good reason, but she doesn't try very hard to tamp it down. This is a mistake on her part. She never learned to just look thoughtful and nod if somebody was irritating her. She didn't know how to let whatever Mom or Snyder were saying just bounce off her while she paid no attention to them and considered whether or not she should go to that Filene's sale and stand in line for stockings. That's what I did and it always worked for me. Neave would have been a happier woman if she'd been more interested in, say, Chanel, than the stuff she found on Mrs. Daniels's shelves. Books can get you in more trouble than a little black dress can. You always know where you stand with a good suit, and Vera Maxwell was enough of a guiding light for me, though she never satisfied Neave.

You love according to your nature and when I was there, alive, my nature wasn't that solid, steady thing that Neave's is. The way I loved Neave was more flexible, less dogged, more shiny than the way she loved me. My kind of love could catch a breeze and blow away in a fight over a burnt pork chop, blow right back in at the other end of a pretty box from Tiffany's or a little joke. That, according to my dog companion who was here to greet me when I got Where I Am Now, sums up my limitations as a mother as well as a sister. I wasn't gifted in the parenting department, a lot of which involves just being there, which is boring. I loved my Annie, but I couldn't stand being bored.

Neave and Janey made it easy for me to be a mediocre mother. There they were, always at the ready. "Oh, I'll take her for an overnight!" or "Lilly, there's a cartoon reel this Friday at the Hollywood Cinema. Why don't I take Annie?" Annie adored them and they did the same right back at her.

Neave's love was immovable in hurricane, flood, or fire, as steady as a line of mountains. She would throw herself between Annie and a pack of feral dogs any day of the week. And the way she felt about me? I knew I could do whatever I wanted, even if she hated it, and I'd always be forgiven. She forgave me for not being the best mother in the world, and she loved my little girl like she was her own. She forgave me for Ricky Luhrmann, which shows you that I could do anything at all and still stay in Neave's good graces.

Ricky: she hated that man almost as much as he thought she did. I can't change what happened between me and him, even for her, because nobody on Earth had ever made me feel as powerful as Ricky Luhrmann made me feel, or as helpless. My future was shackled and bound to him as soon as he followed me to the ladies' that night at the Ritz and got my telephone number. We had business together, and we played it out right to the bitter end. Even if I'd been able to see everything that was going to happen, I bet I still would have given him my number.

Oh, well.

Right up until the end I felt so confident, so completely safe. I was an idiot. I could blame some of that inaccurate view of myself on Neavie, though that's unfair. She treated me like I was the most beautiful, capable, powerful woman on Earth, and I ask you, why would I disagree? I didn't know anybody more honest or smart than Neave. If she said I was that woman, I was. I felt equal to any man, any moment, any chance. It made me reckless. Isn't it a joke on us that the power she gave me might have been what attracted Ricky.

Who is now looking her way.

Like I said, Neave. I'm so sorry.

NEAVE

Monsters in the Movies

Early on in his life, comic books got Snyder Terhune by the throat and he never even struggled. We often don't, when the thing we love finds us.

My brother's favorite magazine was *Monsters in the Movies*. In 1938, Mr. James Moses, writer and publisher of *Monsters in the Movies*, put an announcement on its back page: *Looking for local clubs to host me on my coast-to-coast tour!* Right then and there Snyder Terhune, ninth grade social outcast and friend to no one, determined to create a local fan club and host Mr. James Moses on his tour. He sat down, wrote to Mr. Moses, and let him know the Lynn, Massachusetts, club would be pleased to host him. He dropped it in a mailbox and set out to create a Lynn, Massachusetts, club. He didn't ask our mom if it was okay. By the end of two weeks he had found six other kids who thought *Monsters in the Movies* was the country's most important publication and they headed to our basement to puzzle out some secret handshakes. Members ranged in age from Snyder (just barely fifteen) to Billy Upton (thirteen but big for his age). Snyder was their leader but fourteen-year-old Arnold Strato was their strategist. The pack of them trooping down into our basement looked as serious as if they were heading off to dismantle a bomb. Only Arnold Strato seemed to have any sense of humor about the whole thing. The first meeting they had, he was the only one who even glanced my way to see me sulking at the head of the stairs (I wasn't allowed to go down there or bother the boys in any way) and he threw me a wink and grinned. I liked Arnold. He didn't have any of those dominating habits that older boys tended to exercise around younger ones. His own inclinations and his large family had given him diplomatic skills that came in handy for groups like this one. By the end of the meeting he and Snyder seemed to be sharing presidential duties and honors, Snyder deadly serious and Arnold looking like he'd found an interesting game and was happy to play it for a while.

The club had surprised our mom but pleased her. It looked like a big social breakthrough for Snyder, that's for sure. The boys pooled their money and ordered member buttons and a member whistling coffin. The instructions in the magazine for club formation suggested that all meetings begin with the coffin opening and a reading of club rules. From my perch on the stairs I heard the first suggestions for rules lean toward bloody bonding rituals that were sure to send somebody home crying if not to a doctor. Then Arnold suggested musical armpit fart combinations to start every meeting and that set them in a safer direction. By the time of Mr. Moses's visit in June, five other boys had joined them, all friends of Arnold's. Even in this fanatic subgroup of the still-gangly boy population, only Snyder had a budding fantasy comic collection. Only Snyder invested in an untouchable backup copy of every comic he loved. Scantily clothed Martian women with interesting radioactive parts hung all over his walls. The alien women in his pictures pursued men with lassos and Radiation Project Heat Ray guns or stood over them from craggy moonscapes, their balloon-like breasts and tremendous thighs either beckoning or threatening. Maybe both. Sometimes they fell in love with handsome scientists in white coats. Sometimes they became slaves or admiring colleagues of Earth Men.

But back to Mr. Moses, who wrote to Snyder to say that if the host group was amenable, he'd be there on June 14. He would love to meet with the local fan club, and appreciated the offer of a place to rest his head that night. Mom wanted it to be a success for Snyder. She hated visitors, and hated spending money, but she loved Snyder and she suffered when he was unhappy. She bought a roast in the middle of the week, which meant something in our house, and baked what looked like hundreds of cookies—an impulse that only Christmas itself had summoned before that afternoon.

Mr. Moses had called from his last stop (Hartford, Connecticut) to say he expected to be at our house around four, and by two o'clock most of the members of the Lynn, Massachusetts, *Monsters in the Movies* Fan Club were standing in our driveway, staring down the road. Also me. Janey was too young to be interested. Lilly stood around in the front yard for a while and imitated them, craning her neck and making mummy noises, but when they paid no attention to her she drifted off. I was the only non-club person keeping watch and staying as close to Arnold Strato as I could. Mom came out after about an hour to give us lemonade and encouragement—I think she doubted Mr. Moses and was starting to dread what it was going to feel like when he never showed up.

Every minute past four o'clock was agony. At five fifteen, when the dusty Ford station wagon holding Mr. Moses and half a ton of back copies of *Monsters in the Movies* turned the corner, the little group went off like a bunch of sparklers. The man had to force his car door open against the bodies pressing up against it, but when he got out and onto his own two feet, his manners were perfection. He greeted the jiggling club members like they were the reason he'd been born, which they probably were. He asked to be taken to the grown-ups in exactly the same tone an arriving alien would say he wanted to be escorted to their leader, and they pulled him into the kitchen. Mr. Moses swept my mother's hand to his lips and thanked her for her hospitality. It's a cliché gesture, a little piece of melodramatic trash, but it's amazingly effective if you can get just the slightest hint of irony in it, which Mr. Moses managed. He was a smart man even if he did make his living by writing a magazine about movie monsters. She smiled and told him there was roast beef for dinner, and he said, "Superb."

He was everything a fan could hope for. He was collegial with Arnold and Snyder, more playfully goofy with the younger boys. Every single member received a poster—a Virgil Finlay illustration for *Masquerade Digest* with a one-eyed Martian removing a fake human mask (Virgil Finlay, value in 1955 set at $10,600, which I know because Snyder owned the original when it went to auction). And then, even more wonderful, Mr. Moses distributed one-eyed monster masks (all missing by 1955, and probably valueless even if they hadn't been).

Being a girl and thus an eternal non-member, I was banished from the club's secret after-dinner meeting even though I'd read every copy of *Monsters in the Movies* from under Snyder's bed and examined them page by page before returning them in pristine order to the places Snyder was sure I would never find. Mom saw me hanging around the doorway leading to the basement—down to the place where what really mattered was happening—and she swatted me away. "That's all nonsense anyway," she said. But if it was so nonsensical, why was she breaking all her rules about waste and sugar and roast beef on vegetable dinner night? When she got busy elsewhere I crept as far as the third stair down and sat myself down just out of everybody's sight.

At the time I wouldn't have put it this way because I was thirteen years old, but I look back now with a clearer idea about what was radiating from all these little boys. I felt it then but I didn't understand it. Those pictures of decapitated humans and creatures with eviscerated trunks—they kicked off a kind of anxious, thrilling, physical, dark sweetness. I wasn't old enough at the time to call that sweetness sexual, but I felt something even back then that I might have called desire. I didn't know what it was desire for, but I guess the *Monsters in the Movies* club members were confused about that question as well.

The visit from Mr. Moses temporarily changed Snyder's life. He went from solitary weirdo with a pile of magazines under his bed to King of the Comic-Book People. Other human beings wrote down his telephone number and then actually used it. They asked him what he thought about *Princess of Mars* and *Space Girl and the Masked Monkeys* and listened respectfully when he told them. I think our mom hoped this would happen, and that was why she baked cookies and passed them out like they were loaves and fishes. She wanted Snyder to have a Sermon on the Mount moment. Everybody has a hope, and this was our mom's hope—that Snyder would be happy. It's the burden we lay down on the people we love, but there's nothing else for it—they have to bear it.

WHAT WE CALL ROMANCE:

The Pirate Lover

When I'd asked Mrs. Daniels what exactly the word "romance" meant when it referred to books, she said it just meant an adventure story with travel and monsters and "Triumph in the End." But most people nowadays, she said with a sigh, think it just means an adventure for girls that leads to a wedding. Like mixing up Nancy Drew and Odysseus? I asked. She thought about that and said no, she didn't think that was quite right.

I'd only just met Nancy Drew. The sports car seemed like it was there to make me admire her for being rich, which I didn't. The pleasantly chubby sidekick with "unruly hair" just seemed to be there to make Nancy herself look prettier, which it did, and which I resented, being myself a little unruly and maybe even to some people's way of looking at girls, a little chubby. I expressed these reservations to Mrs. Daniels, who said she understood completely and threw *The Hidden Staircase* into the fire. It was mostly a symbolic gesture. We dug it back out before it burst into flame because the truth is we liked Nancy Drew mysteries even if we had occasional doubts about Nancy herself.

I had not given up *The Pirate Lover.* In fact, I had reread it three times. The secrecy, the scuttling if I was called to dinner or chores so nobody would go looking and find me in the closet—it gave the illicit story more power over me. I read slowly, lived it over a much longer period of time than I would have if I hadn't been hiding it. A person thinks about the interrupted story in ways that a straight shot through doesn't invite. *The Pirate Lover* had my complete attention, as it should have. A story that could hollow out a stomach or set a little tingling current up a neck deserves your respect. I gave myself over to it.

THE PIRATE LOVER

The Dance at Last

Electra had not informed her mother of her change in costume, and when she appeared at the bottom of the stairs on the evening of the ball in her Marais gown, her reception was icy. She was ordered to change her clothing. She refused coolly.

"You can flaunt this little independence now, my girl, but when you step into the ballroom you will do as I have told you to do! You will follow the order of your dance card and step out first with Monsieur Y and last with Monsieur X. I will say to you only once more that I hope you conduct yourself more circumspectly than this new fey and willful attitude makes me fear you will conduct yourself. Electra, you must not finish the season without an offer, and both these men are eminently desirable. You risk everything by appearing in a dress so clearly immodest. Every single girl in Paris envies you for the names on that dance card, and if you throw away this chance at security for us both . . ." Her mother did not finish this sentence but stumbled on, near tears. "I remind you that we are poor, Electra, and you do not have the right to behave like a girl who is anything but what you are."

Anything but what she was. And what was that? Electra mused. So different were the feelings she had experienced in the last weeks that she could not be sure what she was. Typically when she stepped into a room she attracted the warm approval that a pretty girl will attract. But that night something in her caused every head to swivel in her direction and the gazes she drew could not be accurately described as warm or approving. It was not simply the provocative dress that had accomplished this change. When she passed a mirror she was startled herself at her new carriage, the sweeping energy of her movement. Something had changed, and it left her indifferent to the gossip that she heard flowing around her. Parisian social circles at this level concerned themselves very little with a powerless young woman's feelings. No one cared if she overheard words about "knowing one's place" or "draggle-tail dress" so why should she herself care? The women kept their distance; the men did not. Electra kept her shoulders square and her expression amused as she took Monsieur X's hand, and then Monsieur Y's, and then any number of eager young men's hands as they argued for the few empty places on her dance card. But they fell away when Basil Le Cherche stepped to her side. "Mademoiselle?" he murmured, bowing slightly.

"I do not believe you have the next dance, sir," she said mildly, lifting her dance card toward him just the slightest bit.

"Monsieur W and I have spoken about his place on your dance card and he has generously yielded it to me." He took her hand and led her to the floor. "You are looking ravishing tonight."

"You are too forward, sir."

"Am I?"

"You ask as if you did not know your reputation as a rake." The words flew out of her mouth before she could withdraw them, and she found that after an instant's shock at her own indiscretion she did not care what he thought.

"Truly?" He smiled. "How kind of you to take an interest in my reputation. But I tell you, on my own behalf, that I only seduce or am seduced by women who are themselves rakes. They understand what they wager with me," he said, taking her hand and then drawing her into the dance, moving as close as custom allowed. Perhaps a little closer. "You have been told that I am wealthy? And so you assumed I was the target of these ambitious young women's plans?"

"You speak carelessly of young women whose choices are very

narrow, sir, and whose path calls up judgment on all sides. You know nothing of being a young woman."

"This is true. However, you may rest assured that these young women regard me as unmarriageable, as I am."

"Is this because you are a pirate?"

"I am no pirate, my dear, but a privateer. I carry a letter of marque, which gives me permission to act as a ship of war against our enemies. It keeps my men safe from ships whose captains would enjoy pressing them into service."

"Why are you here?"

"Here at this cotillion instead of at sea?"

She nodded.

"I was born into this world. And it suits me to observe it on occasion. I am regarded as interesting, and that, along with my wealth, is why I am admitted here and anywhere I choose to go. I move in circles here, in Venice, in London . . . in certain Far Eastern ports."

She did not say, though she thought, that his beauty also made him welcome at these superficial gatherings where the ability to carry off the latest fashions mattered perhaps more than one's goodness. Le Cherche seemed to move in the crowded ballroom with complete unselfconsciousness—possessed, distant, fluid, quick. He turned her gracefully, a perfect partner if he had not been a seducer and pirate as well. At the dance's end she pulled away.

"This next dance is already given," she said when he kept her hand firmly in his own.

He smiled and slipped an arm around her, his hand set firmly at the center of her back. Le Cherche brushed aside the man who tried to take his place as Electra's rightful partner for the next dance. She began to protest, but Le Cherche's authority was so complete that she found herself being guided smoothly to the center of the room for the *Valse a Deux Temps*. Ballroom dancing was relatively new to Paris, and opinions were still divided as to whether it was too immodestly intimate. Older guests were still uncomfortable with the sight of a roomful of women being held in men's arms, faces so close that one's lips might accidentally brush a strand of the partner's hair. Electra had been prepared for this new fashion at the balls, given lessons not only on where to place her feet but her eyes, taught how to gently repel advances that could possibly make her vulnerable to charges of immodesty. In Le Cherche's arms, however, she found herself led by a man who was not accustomed to resistance in his partners. His hands, the set of his shoulders and torso, the quick shift in the position of his hips in relation to her own—her lessons had been with an inexpensive, second-rate dancing master whose lumbering exactitude had demanded concentration on her part—but this partner was effortlessly nimble. He seemed to not only guide her movements but anticipate them. She felt herself stepping perhaps too close, inhaling the scent of his hair when a turn brought her into contact with a tendril. Worse, she felt him feel her pleasure, felt him respond by offering new chances to test the limits of the dance's illicit opportunities. Midway through the dance she became aware of stares, unfriendly and coolly assessing stares that presaged gossip linking her to this arrogant man. She pulled abruptly away. "Thank you for the dance, Monsieur Le Cherche," she said hastily, and turned her back upon him as she retreated. "Momma, it is time to go," she said quietly when she reached the room where the evening's midnight repast was just being laid out and her mother lingered at the edge of a circle discussing new matches being made that night. "Call the carriage. Please." Something about her daughter's expression led the older woman to make her apologies without hesitation.

"Did something happen?" her mother asked when they were alone in the carriage.

"Nothing, Mother. I am simply tired."

But they both knew this was a lie.

On my next reading afternoon with Mrs. Daniels I found her flipping through a much, much handled book. The pages had swollen with damp and then been awkwardly pressed again, leaving the whole thing lumpy.

The spine was broken in so many places that some pages were threatening to flutter out and away. She handed it to me.

"Start in the middle of the page," she told me. "Our main character and her employer are talking to each other after she's just saved his life by smelling smoke, running into his bedroom, and putting out a fire." She jabbed at the line she wanted and handed over a thick book. I read:

> *'I knew,' he continued, you would do me good in some way, at some time;—I saw it in your eyes when I first beheld you: their expression and smile did not—did not—strike delight to my very inmost heart so for nothing. People talk of natural sympathies; I have heard of good genii—there are grains of truth in the wildest fable. My cherished preserver, good night!'*
>
> *Strange energy was in his voice, strange fire in his look.*
>
> *Till morning dawned I was tossed on a buoyant but unquiet sea, where billows of trouble rolled under surges of joy. I thought sometimes I saw beyond its wild waters a shore, sweet as the hills of Beulah, and now and then a freshening gale wakened by hope, bore my spirit triumphantly towards the bourne; but I could not reach it, even in fancy,—a counteracting breeze blew off land, and continually drove me back. Sense would resist delirium, judgment would warm passion. Too feverish to rest, I rose as soon as day dawned.*

"What's wrong with the lady?" I asked.

"She is falling in love with the man whose life she has just saved. In these kinds of stories it is a requirement that someone's life be saved."

"What was the good thing she did for him?"

Mrs. Daniels sighed the sigh she sighed when she thought my question was tiresome. "The man, unknown to the young woman who is too feverish to rest, has a wife. That wife set his bed on fire, trying to kill him."

"Why would his wife set him on fire?"

"Who knows why any wife wants to set her husband on fire, my dear, but in this case it's possible that the wife knows that her husband is falling in love with another woman—our heroine. Also, he locked the wife in his attic and hired a woman named Grace Poole to keep her prisoner there. Perhaps this too disturbs her."

"Why would the man lock up his wife?"

"He argues that his wife is intemperate, wild, impetuous, unfaithful. Crazy."

"Is she?"

"Possibly. But then again, those words describe the husband himself to a tee, so perhaps he misreads the lady."

Mrs. Daniels put on her glasses and turned to the last third of the book, checking margins and dog-eared pages. She found a spot, hit it with her pointer finger, and passed it back to me. "Here," she said, "I give you the attic-bound wife."

In the deep shade, at the further end of the room, a figure ran backwards and forwards. What it was, whether beast or human being, one could not, at first sight, tell; it groveled, seemingly, on all fours; it snatched and growled like some strange wild animal: but it was covered with clothing; and a quantity of dark, grizzled hair, wild as a mane, hid its head and face.

"Mrs. Daniels, this lady looks definitely crazy to me." I had heard Arnold Strato use the word "definitely" on Tuesday and had used it myself about seven times since then. "Definitely." Eight times. I set the book down. "Is she okay in the end?"

"I'm afraid the things that happened to her destroy her. She is not saved."

"Oh."

"Oh, indeed." Mrs. Daniels nodded.

"How could she have been saved?" I asked.

"She needed to be beheld, seen by someone who loves what he or she sees."

"Mrs. Daniels, have you ever saved a man?"

"Perhaps. The man in question believed that I had."

"What did your husband need to be saved from?"

"The man in question was not my husband."

"Oh."

"It isn't quite as simple as Miss Eyre would lead us to believe, but she does manage to touch on some of the salient feelings. That is why I read her every now and then. Also, she reminds me."

I wasn't sure what she was thinking of, but I determined right on the spot that I too was going to have things I wanted to be reminded of. Whatever they were.

NEAVE

Christmas

In 1939, Daddy was relieved of his job at the General Electric boiler room. Fired, in other words. They'd lost a contract, they said. I'd never had much interest in what Daddy did when he left in the morning but life was certainly easier when he was busy and away. Now he was around, frowzy and irritable. Our mother got quieter and quieter. Roast beef disappeared from our lives and was replaced with vegetable casseroles, ground chuck, and the less glamorous parts of pigs.

No one told Jane that when your father doesn't have a job at Christmas that you should dampen down your hopes, present-wise. This didn't discourage her. Disappointment and disaster have never been more than the drama that precedes the happy ending to her. Then and now, Jane believed that in the end your wishes come true, and if something besides the wish showed up, then you must have made a mistake about what you thought you wanted. That was how Jane Terhune managed her life.

But back to 1939, a year with carefully parceled-out coal and lots of vegetable dinners. We told her that ponies don't fit in Santa's sleigh and they made reindeer nervous, but she went ahead and wrote PONEE on her Christmas list anyhow, all capitals and an illustration of the kind of pony she wanted directly below the list: a little piebald stocky thing with ears that looked like a rabbit's. She picked out a name and had a serious talk with the ice man, who had a gray gelding named Bonehead, about hay and grain and stabling. When once again there was a package with home-knitted mittens under the tree instead of a PONEE, she stuffed them with paper, had me help her sew button eyes on them, and arranged for the two mittens to fall in love by supper and be married by bedtime. By Epiphany she'd dressed empty thread spools in ribbons and toilet paper and made them the mittens' children. I helped her.

In 1939, Santa was still expected to bring the tree as well as the presents, and that was the way our parents did it. That year Daddy waited until well after dark, into the bargaining hours when buyers were thin and the trees would be worthless in just a few hours. Stockings went up after dark as well, and everybody but Jane got to stay up long enough to switch our oranges out of our socks and into Jane's. She loved them more than we did; we loved her more than we loved our own oranges.

If anybody had asked me what religion I was I would have said "Christmas," and the Bible of my Christmas was the *Sears Wish Book*. It arrived just after Thanksgiving and lived on the kitchen counter beside the meat grinder. People nowadays forget how small a person's life could be before the war. Before every boy in our neighborhood shipped out for France or the Pacific, nobody on our block had traveled more than forty miles from Lynn, Massachusetts. We expected to marry somebody we met in high school, exactly the way our parents did. We figured getting to college was as likely as picnicking on Mars, and spittle-bent copies of *National Geographic* held the only exotica I ever expected to see. The *Wish Book* was a plate-glass window onto any number of faraway lives in which we would wear the mink stoles (page 287) and consider ordering the optional let-out skins (as soon as we figured out what a "let-out skin" actually was). We'd wear the gold watches (page 125) and live in a complete Arts and Crafts house (kits from $1,250, starting on page 368).

There were no monsters in the *Sears Wish Book* universe. There were tools for welders, short-throw lever-action rifles for hunters, and baling equipment for farmers. If a potato farmer appeared in an illustration, he was as neat and blond and purposeful as the characters in a *Dick and*

Jane primer. Nobody in the *Wish Book* lost his job. There were no Snyders in the country of *Wish Book*—Snyder who had made Jane cry by hiding her favorite plastic horse and telling her that it had died in the night. That was Snyder to a tee, senselessly mean in very little ways. I say it was a senseless meanness because being mean didn't make him any happier. If you're going to hide a plastic horse and tell its owner it's dead, you should at least get some pleasure from it. Otherwise what are you doing? That was my enduring question—what was he doing?

Why was our mother letting him get away with this? Where was justice! I told her what he'd done. She said it was none of my business. I said yes it was, and she said I was to butt out and mind my own business. MYOB, she said. Then I said something about it being her business to whack him good, but she wasn't taking care of business and so he got away with tormenting every last one of us.

I was told that cleaning out the coal bin might help me remember what MYOB meant. It was a long, dirty job and it didn't warm me up to the idea of minding my own business at all. How can you mind your own business with your family trampling all over it at every opportunity? This question was still on my mind an hour later when I walked into the empty midafternoon living room and approached the record collection. *You're a Sweet Little Headache* was our mother's favorite, played so much that every one of us knew right where the scratches were. I sifted through until I found it. I brought it to my secret reading place at the back of the closet and I brought *You're a Sweet Little Headache* down hard against the floorboards and left the shards where they lay. Maybe I half hoped that she had heard the sound of cracking vinyl and would come and find the remains. I know I felt a keen, gusty swoosh of satisfaction as the record broke. Then that feeling drained away and I felt what I imagined was how you feel when you're poisoned, like something inside you was dying. Or had done it already. I didn't speak to my mother all the next day. She pretended not to notice, which I minded.

I hated how much she was in Snyder's power. His unhappiness made her worry over him. A few times she made us let him have the

Wish Book even when it wasn't his turn. Sometimes it's like that with awful people. You give in resentfully because the largest person in the room says you have to, but then you don't mind so much because you can see it kind of works. And really you don't want them to be miserable. So even though it was my turn I'd watch him sit there with Jane on his lap, looking down at diamond rings with her because that was what she wanted to see and he loved her. Mean or not, Snyder loved Jane. He just couldn't control himself when the impulse came over him to tell her that her plastic horse died. If I was trying to see it from inside his head I guess I'd think it caused him some torment, but I'm not so inclined to try that.

The only fly in the *Wish Book* ointment was the fact that everything in it cost money. Besides the previously mentioned pony, Janey the Hopeful had her eye on a sled that could be hers for $4.30—a pretty much impossible sum, we thought, but Jane didn't. Snyder didn't either, apparently. All along he was thinking very seriously about that $4.30 (plus shipping). In mid-November the *Monsters in the Movies* group started shuffling into our basement two or three times a week as well as the regular meeting time. And the shuffling thing got my attention. They actually looked a little shady, ducking their heads and keeping weirdly quiet until they got into the basement, and even there the chatter sounded muted. Gradually I saw that Snyder and Arnold Strato were the forces behind the extra meetings, and something involving cash was going on.

Though Arnold was fifteen, he could talk like a grown-up when he was with grown-ups and he could mix with everything and everybody down to the youngest Monsters member. He was tiny, barely more than five feet five and fine-boned, and even though he was the kind of guy who would go to a *Monsters in the Movies* meeting, he had never been bullied in his life. Bullies just pinged off him—they approached him if they were new to him, and then after a little conversation, they'd veer off.

I was pretty mesmerized by Arnold Strato. At first I thought he came to the *Monsters in the Movies* meetings just so he could be near

Lilly. They said hello and she batted her eyes at him the first time or two he came over and I could see him heat up. Lilly did that just as a kind of reflex whenever she was near a boy who thought she was interesting, which was most boys. It didn't mean anything and Arnold Strato figured that out quick, but miracle of miracles, he kept coming to meetings even after he stopped looking for her.

"Were you guys counting money just then?" I asked him one afternoon after a meeting had broken up. The other members had scattered, and I found him for a moment by himself adjusting a pack on the back of his bicycle. It was a gratuitous question. I'd been sitting on the stairs going down to the basement, peering around the wall in my usual position and I'd seen Snyder fold a little pile of bills and put them into a tin box.

"Yes."

He swung onto his bike.

"Did the club get a job? Or something?"

"Sort of." I just waited then. He wasn't peddling away, which is what any other member of the *Monsters in the Movies* club would do. He was looking right at me as if I were as human as any of them, which I suddenly realized was not the way most boys looked at me, and he was cheerful and calm, which made me feel the same things. He had that kind of power. "We're selling some of our collections," he said.

"To who?" I thought every boy in school who would buy that stuff was already in the club.

"We took out an ad. Put up flyers in other schools. Mailed some stuff around."

I shouldn't have been shocked at this proof that Monsters boys were everywhere, but I was. "Whose idea was that?"

"Your brother's."

"No, it wasn't."

"Well, we needed some Christmas money so we came up with an idea. It's just fun. What does it matter whose idea it was?" Arnold Strato pushed away. He was one of those boys who treated machines like extensions of their bodies, everything clean and smooth, the bike skimming along like an animal with wheels. I stood and stared as he made his way to the end of the block, tipped to the left, and vanished.

I went to find Snyder. "So Arnold helped you figure out how to make some money?"

"Well, I was the one who knew which ones were the most valuable," he said.

Hah. So it was Arnold's idea. He saw the look on my face and his chin stuck up—its defensive posture.

"Arnold just helped come up with ideas for finding guys who would pay for them. He was just helping me with a special project of mine. That's all."

Arnold, it turned out, had been the one who designed and distributed flyers (his older brother had a car). Arnold had fronted the money for the ad but been paid back in full. Arnold had, it looked like, done just about everything except make a lot of money. I brought the story to Lilly, who wanted to know what Snyder needed the money for. I didn't know. I hadn't even asked, which she said was just like me.

Christmas morning, all was revealed. There under the tree was a Sears sled with "To Janey from Snyder" on a tag tied to one running board. It took all of us by surprise but Janey, the girl who accepted it as the kind of thing the universe dropped at your doorstep whether General Electric had laid your dad off or not. She hugged Snyder and yanked on her snowsuit right then and there.

The person most affected by the present was my mom. The sled made her cry—actually need to leave the room and find a handkerchief. Snyder Terhune had bought Janey a sled with money that could have gone to any number of comic books—and hadn't. We all knew that something about his unhappiness flowed into places inside Mom that none of the rest of us reached. The mystery was how once all that trouble got inside her head it turned to love.

That sled was magic. It looked like proof that the universe can come around and drop your heart's desire right under a candle-lit tree. Snyder had been generous and kind. The world was better than I'd thought. We had oatmeal and hot chocolate for breakfast and then we all ran outside to follow Jane up and down the nearest hill. She got so much water in her ears from melted snow that she spent the next week in bed with an ear infection. She insisted that we bring the sled inside and prop it by her door so she could look at it from where she lay. All that week, evenings drew to a close with the murmuring from her room—Snyder reading her *Sheena, Queen of the Jungle,* or Lilly or Mom bringing her a cookie.

I loved that Christmas. Most of us only know we were happy when we look back, but that week I was there inside it.

That February, General Electric got a big contract and started hiring again. The men who'd been let go first were the first to be rehired, and Daddy once again packed his lunches in the early morning and walked purposefully away to contribute to the world's needs in his own small and mysterious way. Mom got calmer. Vegetable dinner only happened on Wednesdays now instead of Monday, Wednesday, and Saturday. There was roast pork the first Sunday after he returned to work. I'd watched my mother pull out flour and butter and precious eggs and line them up on the counter just to look at them for a minute or two before she was sure she could indulge in the spectacular luxury of a cake. She saw me so still there in the doorway and asked me if I wanted to bake with her, and the invitation felt almost illicit—intimate and just a tiny bit wild. I nodded, and we spent the next hour beating and separating and whipping. I was happy.

Spring was close enough that we could smell dirt under the snow on warmer late afternoons and the sun stayed with us all the way to dinner. We felt safe again. We didn't listen to reports about what was happening in Europe. We didn't imagine that the world we lived in now had only had a few more months of life left in it.

MRS. DANIELS AND ME, AGAIN

The Pirate Lover

Mrs. Daniels and I moved in and out of *The Odyssey*. She'd pull it out of my hands whenever I stopped reading too often to ask questions or comment, which irritated her. "For heaven's sake, girl—stop asking about Penelope! The wife is in the story but it isn't, essentially, her story. Enough of that." She rummaged through the pile at her side. "Let's return to the modern world." She handed me some copies of *Good Housekeeping* and we made our way through several marital advice columns and a few of Mrs. Roosevelt's contributions. I thought Mrs. Roosevelt was a very sensible woman, but her teeth frightened me. Just a little.

"We'll mix it up a bit," Mrs. Daniels promised me at the end of that afternoon. "You needn't worry—I'll have us read the chapters where Penelope takes her ascendant place in the adventure and gets to set Odysseus to his last tests, but we can read several stories simultaneously. When you come next I'll have winnowed out some possible titles."

On my next visit, we sat down beside a stack that included *Leaves of Grass*, *Candide*, *The Adventures of Huckleberry Finn*, *Frankenstein*, and *Black Beauty*. She pulled *Candide* out of the mix just as I was reaching for it. "That was an error," she said. "There are things there that perhaps your mother would object to your reading." So *Candide* vanished, but I paid attention when she put it back on the shelf so that if an occasion to slip it into my school bag at the end of a reading session popped up, I'd be ready. I pushed *Black Beauty* forward as a likely candidate. I liked the picture on the cover.

"Well, that was a mistake too." She sighed, tossing it aside. "I don't think I can sit through the trials and tribulations of a horse. I object not to the horse itself but to the fact that I am supposed to be sentimentally outraged over the sad parts of its story. Noble abused animals. Crippled children. Insufferably manipulative claptrap. Perhaps I can find something more acceptable to both of us." She rooted through the pile and handed me *The Call of the Wild*. "How do you feel about dogs and dangerous climates? This one isn't so sentimental." I said I was enthusiastic about dogs, and off we went into the Arctic wastes.

At home I kept on reading alone in the closet—an activity that satisfied me in ways that I didn't really understand. I knew that according to the standards of my mother's world, Electra Gates's adventures were bad. I knew I was thrilled by their badness at the same time that I sometimes hid the book under my mattress, not trusting that the back of the closet was safe from discovery. My mother might go rooting around for an old snowsuit, after all. In the meantime I would close the wall of abandoned leggings behind me and go with Electra Gates while she discovered where the dangerous dress from the Marais would take her.

THE PIRATE LOVER

Soon after the ball, Electra and her mother received an invitation to a private summer house very near Calais. "My dear, it is better than we could have hoped!" cried her mother. "An invitation from Mr. Z! A country-estate weekend! I hear he keeps this summer retreat on the coast so as to more conveniently enjoy his yacht—that it has dozens of rooms and an enormous staff!"

After so many hours spent in Parisian gatherings, any reserve that once might have kept Electra from repeating slander was quite gone. "They say Mr. Z keeps this country house in Calais, Mother, so that he can continue his illegal smuggling back and forth from England. He is British, is he not?"

"Many people are, Electra. They cannot help it. As to how the man has acquired his wealth, what do you care what is said? Who knows who will be present this weekend."

"So, Mama, we are to care nothing of what is said about illegal smuggling, and to pay close attention to what is said about Mr. Z's yacht and Mr. Z's friends."

"Impertinent creature. You know very well that this invitation could be the result of one of those friends specifically asking for your presence. Perhaps that horrible Marais dress did its work after all." Her mother moved through their rooms quickly. "Mr. Z is sending a carriage for us. He has arranged everything—a true gentleman."

They were swept off in a coach-and-four. A broken wheel delayed them halfway there and they arrived long after dark, dusty and hungry. They could hear laughter and music from somewhere else in the enormous house, but were told by the servants who greeted them that the other guests had retired. They were ushered to a private suite, where a meal was laid before the fire. None of the servants who poured their wine, drew their baths, and turned down their beds spoke more than a few words. "Breakfast in the dining room whenever you choose to rise, ma'am," said the last as he slipped out of their suite.

"How wonderful!" Electra's mother cooed. "How luxurious."

That morning found them still oddly alone.

"It's strange," Electra murmured. "Mother, didn't you hear others last night?"

"Of course not. The servant said they had all retired."

"Are there not other guests?" Electra asked the pigtailed fellow who served them as they sat in splendid isolation along the long dining-room table.

"I couldn't say, miss."

"You are American?" she asked, surprised at his accent.

"There's a lot of different types wash ashore here in Calais, miss. The quays are just down the road, you see, and I was one that washed ashore. Mr. Z found a use for me."

"Where is our host?"

"I couldn't say, miss. But I'm told to say a recently arrived friend of Mr. Z is asking to speak to your mum when she's done with her breakfast. In the drawing room."

Electra rose. "I am done with my breakfast. I'd be happy to see this person."

"Just your mum, miss. Those were the orders."

Electra's mother dropped the bit of toast she had just spread thickly with marmalade and rose to her feet. "Just me? Of course. I'm with you entirely."

Electra sat frozen in her place for a moment after her mother was led from the dining room. Then she rose and made her way back to their suite, as uneasy as she had ever been in her life. She would insist they leave here the moment her mother reappeared. The minutes ticked by slowly. They had become an hour before her mother returned.

"Oh, my dear! It is as I had hoped! An offer from a man of rank who saw you at the Paris ball and has become entranced—enslaved by the memory!"

"Which one was it?" she asked flatly. Would her fate be the balding, potbellied X, with his twenty thousand a year and his deer parks, or Y, with his shipping company, his crooked teeth, and his strange smells?

"It is Monsieur Le Cherche!" her mother gasped.

The shock that went through Electra at that moment jolted her upright and out of her chair. "But Mama, how could an offer from such a man interest you?"

"You misunderstand, Electra. The proposal is from Judge Henri Le Cherche. Not his disreputable brother the viscount Basil Le Cherche. He has asked permission to come this evening to make his offer to you in person."

Henri Le Cherche? The dark figure dressed in expensive black silk and fine leather boots? A judge? Had she even danced with him? No—she had not even been aware of his noticing her at the ball.

"Does the man's family relationship with a thief and seducer not give you pause, Mama? Basil Le Cherche is his brother!"

"Not a moment's pause, my dear. Years of disrespect and poverty will be washed away in an instant. All you must do is make your way to the altar, where you will say 'I do' and we will be admitted into every circle in Europe!"

But what Electra knew, more clearly than she had ever known, was that she did not wish to be admitted to every circle in Europe. She wasn't sure where she wanted admittance—but something in her was awakening, something that pressed for its own concerns to be shaped and addressed. The creature inside her was only just in its infancy, but it had a pulsing vitality.

"He has asked for a private audience this afternoon," her mother chattered. "We must hurry!"

"Why?"

"There is so much to do! You must be at your most beautiful, and there are but a few hours to prepare." Her mother called in servants, who helped her truss and curl and bejewel her daughter without protest or question. They were, in fact, unsurprised by the extravagant grooming rituals, as if they had been expecting them. At the appointed time Electra was called to the parlor for the meeting with her suitor. He was not waiting for her. "Have a seat, miss," the servant said. "He'll be here direct." She sat upon one of the only two chairs in the room to await her fate. A moment later Judge Henri Le Cherche entered. She did not rise.

"My dear," the judge greeted her, sweeping off his hat and making a leg. "Thank you for honoring me with your time upon such short notice."

Indeed, it was the finely dressed man she had seen across the ballroom. "We are pleased to receive you," she replied, nodding and retaining her seat. The judge took the other chair before he was invited to do so and turned a smiling face upon her. "You were perfectly mesmerizing at the ball. The dress . . . such beautiful breasts."

"Pardon me?" She stiffened. Never had a man addressed her so vulgarly.

"Do not pretend to be so missish, my pet. I observed you with my brother—not the ideal match for any woman, and I'm sure you knew it when you accepted him as your dance partner. A woman who would wear such a thing, move with the . . . shall we say the carnal sensuality . . . with which you moved . . . that woman is ready for the kinds of things that I have to offer. And I am here to offer them."

"I am afraid you mistake me, sir."

"I do not. Your mother confirms your eagerness to marry me, and I am here to lay out my expectations."

"My mother speaks only for herself. Not for me. I am not interested in your expectations, and I do not give you any kind of assurance or consent."

"You needn't. Your mother is your guardian and she has the legal right to sign documents on your behalf, including a marriage license. She is eager to sign such a document. So I will proceed. Let me make my preferences in love clear. I enjoy the hunt, sometimes the spirited resistance, and the release that domination provides. My sense is that you will not only accommodate these tastes but will perhaps be talented at satisfying them. On occasion I have enjoyed companions that could be regarded as very young women. Very, very young women. Control is important to me. I enjoy the theatre of submission. Do you understand?"

Electra was young and she had been sheltered, so the specific images that this conversation called up were vague. They were, however, horrible to her, as was this monster sitting across the room from her now. His enjoyment of her discomfort was clear. But there was another sensibility bubbling directly beneath the man's thin veneer of amused contempt—hostility toward her, a woman he did not know and had come to bend to his will. And perhaps . . . was she right about the hesitation just before the raised eyebrows and curled lip? She had a sudden and very certain sense that this man was afraid of her as well, and therefore terribly dangerous.

"You will not have my hand in marriage or any other part of me," she said coolly. "Please leave."

He continued smiling. Not moving.

"I asked you to go!"

"That is of no consequence to me. Your mother and I will have a final tête-à-tête and settle the financial details. She knows nothing of my . . . proclivities. But my dear, I suspect that if she did, she would still sign you away. And I also imagine that if you attempt to describe the details of our conversation to her when I leave that she will believe nothing you say. She will see you as willful, attempting to avoid your adult responsibilities in order to continue an indulgent childhood. So you see, there is no point in struggle."

He rose, moved to her, and pulled her to her feet. He slid his hand inside the bodice of her gown and firmly tugged it downward, then stepped back to inspect what he had exposed. Her hands flew to her breasts, but he restrained her. He smiled. "They are perfect. As I expected."

Enraged, she covered herself again the instant he released her. "Did you ask Mr. Z to invite my mother and me here specifically so you could stage this ridiculous charade?"

"It is not a charade, and yes, Mr. Z knew your mother would be pleased to come here—so far from the opinions of her vulgar little acquaintances. We conduct a great deal of business here, Mr. Z and I, and he knew I preferred to manage this transaction with your mother far from anyone who might intercede with rude gossip. Or worse."

"We are leaving as soon as we pack."

"I doubt that. Mr. Z's loyal staff will not help you leave for any destination at all but one that I myself name. And at the moment I name none." He turned on his heel and left her angry, disgusted beyond measure. Dumbfounded, she stood exactly where she was and listened to the distant, polite sounds of the judge's departure and her mother's simpering goodbyes.

"Electra!" her mother called. "Come and say goodbye to Judge Le Cherche." Electra adjusted her bodice, walked woodenly to the door, and nodded slightly as he bowed. The door closed behind him.

Electra's first words were icily flat and crystal clear. "I will cut my throat before I enter a relationship of any kind with that man. He is not human. I do not know what he is, but he will never touch me."

"The matter is settled. I have spoiled you! And I will stand for no disobedience here, young miss!"

The two women each strode angrily away in different directions. When Electra reached her room, she drew a bag from beneath her bed, stuffed it with the sturdiest, most practical clothes she had with her, and opened a window. She would be as far away from this place as she could be by morning, nowhere to be found when Judge Henri Le Cherche sought his intended plaything.

Fate had forced her to become mistress of her own future. She swung her leg over the sill and jumped.

The day after I read this section of *The Pirate Lover* I sat in Mrs. Daniels's living room, again, reading a column from *Ladies Good Housekeeping*. I closed it. "Mrs. Daniels," I said, "have you ever run away?"

"Of course. Anyone worth their salt runs away from home at least once."

Well, no. I hadn't. And I was certainly worth some salt. "When did you do it?"

"Twice. The first time I was angry with my mother, I was perhaps six. She had spanked me to impress some lesson upon me, now lost to time, and I actually put a handkerchief stuffed with apples and two snickerdoodle cookies on a stick and marched off down our road. Very picturesque. I got as far as the first big hedge, where I sat down and ate all my provisions. Then it got dark and cold and, having run out of cookies, I returned home. No one noticed I'd been gone."

"Where did you run to the second time?"

"France."

"France?!"

"I was running from my second husband. It seems I hadn't outgrown the old strategy, though I packed more intelligently."

"What did he do to you to make you run away?"

"That is a mature subject for a much later date."

I'd tried to imagine what a mature explanation for a runaway wife might be, and the exercise was difficult due to youth and inexperience. Now, sadly, I know more and I can imagine lots of reasons for a wife to run away. But when the questions first popped up, I'd read between a few of the lines in the more explicit monster and fantasy comic books under Snyder's bed. I had read marital advice columns touching on intimate subjects. Still—nothing that I imagined made sense when it was applied to the woman across the tea table from me: fleshy wattles and wide waist, dark circles under both eyes and ankles like popovers. She'd watched me scan her from hairline to toes, and one of her eyebrows popped up. "It isn't all pretty bows and tiny waists, my dear—other things command men's attentions if you are interested enough in those attentions to cultivate and use them."

"Other things like what?" I'd asked.

"If you ask the question in such vague terms, then you are too young for the conversation. Now—I have a short story here by Mr. Fitzgerald called 'Bernice Bobs Her Hair.' Ready?"

I had been ready and I said so. Mr. Fitzgerald's story made perfect sense to me. Maybe I'd never run away from home but I knew what it felt like to wake up in the middle of the night burning with the desire to chop off all of someone's hair because they did me wrong by day.

"That'll show her," I said when we reached the moment when Bernice clipped Marjorie's beautiful long hair and ran into the night with the braids dangling from one hand.

"Yes. I thought you'd like that one. Go to the kitchen and tell Violette to fetch us brownies." Mrs. Daniels's cook was a wizard at brownies. I ate mine thinking about all the terrible thoughts and actions in the grown-up world, a place jam-packed with lusts and betrayals.

"Mrs. Daniels, can I ask Violette to show me how she does it?"

"Does what?"

"The brownies. The other things."

I thought Mrs. Daniels looked disappointed in me but she sighed and said, "You may ask her. Never let it be said that I stood between a child and her capacity to bake brownies."

That Saturday I came very early and learned to cream sugar and butter. Violette was patient and free with the kitchen's startling wealth. The room was saturated with light, orderly, calm, smelling of chocolate and melting sugar. I loved it so much I worried, just a little, if it was wrong to bake with Violette in Mrs. Daniels's kitchen. Was it petty and silly? Electra Gates would never concern herself with how much lard should be in pie dough, I thought; but then, I was not Electra Gates. I wanted pie, something that didn't seem to interest romantic heroines.

The next week Mrs. Daniels and I read passages from *Leaves of Grass*:

Through me the afflatus surging and surging, through me the current and index. . . . Through me forbidden voices, Voices of sexes and lusts, voices veil'd and I remove the veil, Voices indecent by me clarified and transfigur'd. . . . If I worship one thing more than another it shall be the spread of my own body, or any part of it, Translucent mould of me it shall be you! Shaded ledges and rests it shall be you!

I can't say I understood what I was reading, but I had the uneasy sense that these words had something to do with Electra Gates's dress and how that dress made men feel. Also made her feel. But I couldn't turn to Mrs. Daniels to help me figure out why they seemed so connected because, of course, she didn't know I'd stolen *The Pirate Lover* and I wasn't about to let her know now. The air was dry and cool and the sugar cookies were as big as soup plates. I ate three and was offered a bag with four more to take home for Snyder, Jane, and Lilly.

"Mrs. Daniels, did you like being married?" I asked.

"I wouldn't have done it twice if I didn't. Though no two of them are alike, and you can't know going in how it'll turn out."

"What happened to your husbands?"

"They died."

I must have looked stricken, because she added, "Everyone dies, child."

I received this information in silence. The men in the pictures of the Great War had died. I knew that. The newspapers were full of people who were shot or strangled or who fell off buildings. But I hadn't imagined that this had anything to do with me. This was the first time in my life, listening to Mrs. Daniels with *The Pirate Lover* and *Leaves of Grass* all tangled up in my head, that I felt the truth of this—everybody died. Such a dark discovery, but also so wild and satisfying. There was a pull toward dark things in the poem and in the romance, both. What did it mean that there was this terrible, sweet pull?

When I got home I crawled under Snyder's bed again and pulled out another *Marvel Mystery Comic*. A miniature alien riding on what looked like a huge ant was being held under a clear glass bowl by a pair of giant hands. It was going to die. I flipped to the advertisements on the back page: *EXPLODING HAND GRENADE. This menacing hand grenade looks and works just like a real one. All you do is pull the pin. Throw the grenade and watch the fun as the caps explode!*

Little boys were going to pretend to make things die. I understood this even as I also knew that if I tried to explore this sudden and strange feeling I had right now with a grown-up, I'd be told that there was something wrong with me. Maybe there was.

HYPNO COIN. In just moments your subjects will follow your commands while hypnotized by this powerful visual tool.

THE INSULT THAT MADE A MAN OUT OF ME. The Charles Atlas dynamic tension program will change your life.

I opened the bag of cookies that Violette had given me. She had included a Hermit Bar for each of my sisters and Snyder as well as one for me. I ate Snyder's cookie. Then, because I couldn't explain why his cookie was missing, I ate Jane's and Lilly's. A spider skittered across the floor. I caught it, put it carefully between the cover and first page of Snyder's comic, and squashed him. This made me feel better, then worse. I went out to play.

The next time I went to the library, I asked the librarian if I could use the poetry section—it was a skimpy little shelf with maybe twenty titles, most of them there because the local high school assigned a poetry paper every year for the twelfth-graders and they had kept asking for titles that weren't in the school library. There sat *Leaves of Grass*, which I slid off its shelf and opened.

The smallest sprout shows there is really no death, And if ever there was it led forward life, and does not wait at the end to arrest it. All goes onward and outward, nothing collapses, And to die is different from what any one supposed, and luckier.

For reasons I could not explain, once again that made me think of Electra Gates's dress.

NEAVE

What Happy Women Do

In the months leading up to Pearl Harbor there was no barrier, no domestic happiness, that could keep the coming war from saturating our daily lives–movie newsreels, newspapers, radio shows, talk on the street and in living rooms and diners and churches. Then Pearl Harbor and we were in the fight ourselves. Only Janey was untouched, protected by her naturally sunny nature and our habit of turning off the radio when she came into the room. If she asked anything about it, we told her everything would be fine. I don't know if she believed it. Being sunny does not necessarily make you stupid.

Rationing made turning to the relief of making a pie or a tray of cookies almost impossible. Mom and I hoarded sugar and traded Daddy's tomatoes for a neighbor's eggs, and we scraped together a cake about once a month. I still read for Mrs. Daniels, who didn't seem to live in the land of rations. At Mrs. Daniels's house, cookies still came floating out of the kitchen; crusty pumpernickel bread still got slathered with butter. I didn't know how and I didn't ask why. I just begged her cook to let me come early some days and bake with her. She said yes and at least once a week I would come an hour before Mrs. Daniels expected me and I'd sit in her kitchen getting a ball of perfect pie dough ready to roll out. I loved that kitchen.

At home it felt like the war sat down with us at the dinner table every night. Snyder was turning eighteen. The draft notice would be in the mail any day. All around us were boys who were begging parents to sign release forms to let them get in early, boys who talked about not wanting to miss their war. Snyder, I'm pretty sure, wanted to miss the war. He was restless and thin-skinned and just about impossible to be around. He was frightened.

I know it started with a scuffle between me and Snyder, but I don't remember over what. We got in a lot of scuffles that year. Whatever the argument was about on that particular day, some of it happened in the driveway behind the car. Snyder grabbed my collar and yanked, hard enough to make me choke. This upset Mr. Boppit, who flung himself between us. Snyder kicked Mr. Boppit, which made me slap Snyder. He stamped over to the car and turned on the ignition, yelling about going away, going far, far away, and not looking behind him at all. *Ha.* That's what I said. *We wish.*

I heard the brake being pulled free and the ignition cranked but I wasn't making connections, looking ahead at what could happen but failing because I was busy thinking about how much I wanted to hurt him. I didn't really believe that Snyder would unlock the brake. Then he did and he and the car started backward with me right in its path. Snyder's intentions weren't clearly murderous, because as I said, he was still yelling "far, far away" and I honestly don't think he was in his right mind. I just happened to be in his path.

It was Mr. Boppit who saved me. He charged in, barking like he thought that noise alone could stop the car, and when that didn't work, he flung himself directly onto me, pushing me aside so the car just missed me on its way to the end of the driveway. The rear bumper caught the side of his silky head. Only on the one side, though, so when he fell, the broken half of his face was on the ground. He looked asleep until we turned him over. A dead dog is stiller than a barn in a field or a chair in an empty room.

Snyder got the car to a full stop. I opened the driver's-side door and dragged him right out onto the dirt. He was bigger than me but I was angrier, and faster. I pulled him to his feet so that just before I slammed my elbow into him he could see my face. I heard as well as felt the elbow drive directly into his left ear. By the time I whirled around to swing a closed fist into his nose, the ear itself as well as all the flesh around it was already swelling. Snyder and I had often fought but we had never fought like this. Before this, whenever we got near to anything that could lead to a broken nose, our mother could feel it happening. She'd materialize out of nowhere and she'd come to Snyder's defense. A young lady controlled her feelings, she'd say. You should be ashamed! Look at yourself, she'd say, as if a good clear view of myself could be enough to stop the kind of feeling that had me between its thumb and forefinger.

On this occasion, no parent was there to come save his bacon. Snyder and I fell away from each other, me satisfied for a full eight seconds or so before a darker feeling took over and I felt terrified by what I'd done to him; by what I'd felt when I was doing it. Boppit lay on the ground at our feet. I don't know what was in Snyder's mind, but he backed away from me and headed into the backyard, holding his ear with one hand and his nose with the other. If I could have disembodied myself, been me and not-me, I'd have backed away from myself too.

Watching him retreat I had a black tar-blot kind of feeling, like I was behind his eyes instead of mine, walking unsteadily away with blood running down my face. I spun away and ran into the house, up to my bedroom on the second floor, where I propped myself in the windowsill overlooking the vegetable garden. I heard the kitchen door slam and looked down and there was my mother with a washcloth, following Snyder, sitting beside him and handing it to him, talking softly. He held the washcloth against his nose. I saw her put her arm around him. I thought, One of us has to say what happened to Mr. Boppit. One of us has to tell Mom and take her to his body in the driveway. I was breathing as though I'd just run a mile, fast.

Snyder's hand slowly dropped away from his face. The next day his nose would start to change colors, maybe to brown and purple. In about three days it would shift to green. His ear would swell to three times its normal size. His head drooped down and his whole body sagged. My throat closed. All along I'd thought I was desperate to see Snyder feel as bad as he looked right now, but here I was discovering that I hadn't had any idea what I wanted. Poor Snyder, I thought. Poor Mr. Boppit.

Mom left him. She climbed the stairs, walked into my room, and found me looking down at Snyder. "My, my," she said, tilting my head to get a clear view of me. I had a few swollen places of my own, which I saw her taking note of and deciding not to talk about. She reached out a hand to touch me though and said, "Well, I guess you'll clean up all right by your wedding day." I pulled my head away, which surprised her. Hurt her, I'll bet. That made me satisfied for the briefest little moment before it made me ashamed and sad. She stood studying me for a while before she went to the window to look down.

"Neave," she said finally, "I feel like I need to warn you about yourself. You think I don't know, but I do, because I was like you. When I married your father, I was a person with real high highs and real low lows. Some days I see you dancing with that dog in the backyard when you think nobody's looking, or getting silly with Lilly and I know you've got the highs. An hour later I see you in some rage about some nothing little thing Snyder might have done, clinging to a grudge like it was a life raft."

"They're not 'nothing little things.'" I admit I sounded sullen.

"See? Exactly like that. If you could see yourself. Don't get comfortable with a grudge. Don't be the eternally aggrieved."

"I'm not!"

"You're sixteen years old and it's time you listened to me say it. Happy women aren't like that, Neave. They understand that others depend on them and they shape themselves to others. You're just going to make yourself unhappy by insisting on your own way. Smart women don't do that. I can see resentment on your face right this minute, and I've got some news for you—resentment is the poison we drink ourselves, hoping it will make the other fellow die. You're going to have to start damping yourself down. You'll do yourself mischief if you don't. You'll end up alone. You'll be too hard to love."

She wasn't looking at me while she talked. She stood by the window and looked down at Snyder and I understood when she got to the part about damping down that these were not words she was going to say to my brother. But neither would she be saying them to my sisters. Jane and Lilly would never be found sitting on a bed in the late afternoon covered in dirt and blood. That was more my role in the family.

"Maybe facing up to your own nature wouldn't make such a difference if you were beautiful, but it won't help to sugarcoat the situation, because the fact is, that's not the case," she went on. "No matter, really. We all just work with what we have and that's not tragic. Pretty girls lean on their looks so much they end up more stupid than God made them to begin with. Better to be on the sidelines watching. It's a blessing to you even if it doesn't feel like one now. But if you don't want to end up alone, you'll have to rein in a bit of what you are. Sweeten yourself. Do you understand me?"

I have thought that if my mother had touched me or looked at me when she said these things that I would have received them very differently. It wouldn't have burned so much. There would be no record shards at the back of my closet. Just the feel of her hip against mine would have cooled the bad news about my future, but she stood apart. Of course, I have also thought, if a child whipped her head away from your hand the last time you tried to touch her when she was in an agitated state, you'd hesitate to touch her the next time. Here I was in the next time, and we stood ten feet apart with her looking out the window and me looking at her and it could have been different but it wasn't. She left me there to consider myself. That's the expression she used.

I considered myself right into a state where I wondered if my feelings could kill me. It felt like they would, so I guessed maybe she was right about the work that lay ahead of me. There was never going to be a way out of it. I would be alone.

I got up. I peered out at Snyder, who had pulled himself together. I saw Mom go into the yard again with a new washcloth wound around some ice. They talked quietly while he held the ice against his ear.

Standing there with Snyder in my sights I felt the purest most overwhelming hatred I had ever suffered in my life.

I was afraid for myself then.

There was Mr. Boppit's body to deal with, lying in the driveway behind the car's rear wheels, and I couldn't bear it. I left the bedroom with its dangerous view of Snyder and Mom and I got Lilly, who is good in messy situations. I led her to Mr. Boppit's stiffening side and we wrapped him up in my sweater and an old quilt. Lilly threw him in the trunk of the car and told me to get in but I just could not. She told me to get away if I couldn't do what had to be done and she climbed into the driver's seat and cranked the engine. Off she went. To this day I do not know what happened to the body of Mr. Boppit.

But I know what happened to his reputation. That afternoon Lilly and I sat down with Jane and explained that Mr. Boppit had volunteered for the army dog corps and that he had shipped out for training that morning. She cried, but she was proud. She'd seen the newsreels of Dogs for Defense. All through the war she told everyone about Mr. Boppit's contribution to the Allied forces, the sacrifices he was making for our freedom. I began to believe it myself. We imagined Mr. Boppit on patrol, his nose to the wind to capture the smell of Nazis, saving the sleeping soldiers whose lives he tirelessly protected. We could see Mr. Boppit sniffing for bombs and carrying medical supplies to men so deep in the thick of combat that other soldiers could not penetrate the rain of bullets keeping them from hurt buddies. But Mr. Boppit could.

Lilly and I didn't know she'd written off to the United States Army Dogs for Defense program to ask after Mr. Boppit's assignment because she'd gone to Snyder for help and he gave it to her, keeping Mr. Boppit's real fate from her for sake of her feelings. He wrote the letter with her but thought if he only gave her money for the stamp or an address to mail it to, that the letter would sit in her bedroom until the war was over. But our mailman loved Jane and helped her get the address. I don't know how she got the envelope and the price of the stamp, but she did. And she made her way, all alone, to post the letter.

Snyder was the one who answered the telephone when the apologetic lieutenant called, saying the army had no record of a canine Mr. Boppit Terhune's service. Snyder made a decision on the spot—he laid it all out for the man. The lieutenant's name was Jerry Hall. He listened carefully and said that he had a little sister himself. Then he wrote a letter to Jane on official army stationery, describing the heroism of Mr. Boppit and the gratitude our country felt toward him for locating over forty bombs before one detonated and did the courageous Mr. Boppit in at last. Janey sat right down and cried. So did I.

Jane wrote a three-page description of the life and death of Mr. Boppit and mailed it off to the *Herald*. She included a picture of her and Bop on our front steps, the dog with what looked like a grin on his face and Jane draped over his unprotesting head. It ran on page one over the line "Mr. Boppit, Wonder Dog." The AP wires picked it up and it ran all over the country. Letters and offers of new puppies came at us from all directions for weeks—people telling us about their own dogs, many of whom had actually served overseas.

Daddy put the kibosh on the idea of a new puppy so that was that. Jane was unhappy about this, but in the end she accepted his decision with a lot more dignity than I could have mustered. She was content with the glory that she'd managed to secure for Mr. Boppit.

LILLY

Cape Ann. High Tide. Goodbye, Dog.

You try lifting a fifty-pound mutt and dumping him over the side of a slimy dock. His head was still bleeding when I got to the back of the car and saw the body, so I pulled Neave's sweater right off her back and wrapped him in that. It wasn't her best sweater but I probably would have wrapped the bloody dog in it even if the thing were spun from gold. She just stood there and let me wind it around him. I could have told her to chop off her hair and wrap the dog in that, and she would've run for the scissors. So there I am, holding a dead dog wrapped up in a pilly sweater because Neave and Snyder were no use at all, thank you very much. Neave at least should be on this work detail but no, that wasn't gonna happen. I stuffed him in the trunk and climbed into the driver's seat. I was going to have to deal with the dog alone. I backed out of the driveway looking back at Neave's poor face. That chuckleheaded dog and her were each other's best company.

I myself am not charmed by dogs. They smell. They shed. They pee on stuff and they find ways to break into your closet and, if they're this particular dog, they chew your shoes. I didn't expect to feel so strange, sliding the body into the water an hour after I drove away from our house. Just for a tiny little window I felt like everything good and beautiful had gone dark and something black was drifting over me. I looked down and there were his furry legs still looking like he was running in the water even though he was definitely dead, and the way his one remaining eye looked up at me—like he was really seeing me. I didn't like it.

I sat there for a while after he floated off. Then I got up and walked back down the stone quay to the car. I wadded Neave's bloody sweater up and pitched it into the nearest trash can. I thought that was the end of my relationship with Mr. Boppit, the dog who jumped behind a moving car because he didn't have the good sense God gave turnips.

But it wasn't the end of my relationship with Boppit. He was here when I got to Where I Am Now. I recognized him right off even though he wasn't, strictly speaking, a dog—slurpy thing going on with the tongue, goofy cocked ears, a rear end that looked like it was wagging even though there wasn't a tail. He was dressed in navy whites, which seemed right. So did his high heels. Here's the surprising thing—it was like we'd had this meeting between our two dead selves a dozen times before, only we'd been different on the other occasions. We knew each other.

"Well. Finally," he greeted me.

The thought that I should be frightened drifted by, but it was distant—a balloon thought floating over my head. I wasn't frightened. "I'm dead?"

"You are."

"And you're dead?"

"You dropped me over the side into the water yourself. So I'd say yes. I am."

I'd always thought that the one way to find out where you go after you die would just be to die, but apparently that wasn't the case. Here I was, dead, and still I had no idea what was going on. Nothing around me was clear except Boppit. There was no horizon or foreground, no gravity.

"It'll clear," he said, watching me look around. "Be patient."

A chair materialized behind me and I sat down. I stopped squinting and the air around me started to take on different thicknesses. Now there was a marble floor under my feet, and then a counter, a table, a row of shining spring sandals.

"See it now?" Bop asked.

I did! "Filene's! We're in Filene's third-floor shoe department!"

"Isn't it beautiful?" A chair had popped into being behind Bop as well as me, and he sat down. "It's a dream setting, my dear, a dream that you and I both share and cherish. Call it common ground. That's why we find ourselves in it now when we're first getting acquainted. You know it from firsthand experience. I'd only heard of it but I always knew it was here! I should tell you that I don't think this little scene is going to last for long. Enjoy it while we're here."

"It isn't real?"

"It is what it is."

"And what are you? I mean, I know who you are. I don't know what you are."

"You know what I am. I'm Mr. Boppit. And the other common ground that's most common between you and me besides our feelings about shoes is Neave. I'm Neave's protector, and now she's in trouble. Your job here is to help me help her."

"But we're dead."

"Where we are and where she is are much closer than you think. There are even places where they occupy the same spot. You have a lot of Neave in your head, and she has a lot of you in hers. Shared, common ground. Cherished ground. That's why I'm here to collect you. Also, the kind of trouble that Neave's in right now is trouble that you put her in. It's your trouble, slid over onto her life."

I knew what the dog meant. He meant Ricky.

"We're going to put ourselves between her and him," Boppit said.

"So . . . what do I do?"

"Well, while we're here, why don't we look at those silver strappy numbers by the first display table? Then we're going to sit down and think about Neave."

"Just think?"

"That's usually the best start."

LILLY

Arnold Strato's War

Oddly, 1942 is much clearer to me from Where I Am Now than it was when I was in 1942 itself. Snyder reached his eighteenth birthday, reported for the draft, and was discovered to be almost entirely deaf in his left ear. Maybe Neave did it when she clobbered him. Or his hearing in that ear might always have been bad or absent, and he'd just gotten used to it. He was designated 4F, and Daddy was furious. Mommy told him that there was no one to blame. But he did blame. He blamed Snyder.

My brother joined the thousands of women and older men working in munitions factories, and in his free hours he disappeared inside his comic books. The entire population of his comic book world was fighting the war and the BLAM!BOP!BANG! on the pages Snyder read always meant victory for the Forces of Good. Just a little inconvenient resistance to make the ultimate victory meaningful and BLAM!BOP!BANG!

We'd sit in dark movie theaters and watch the newsreels, good-looking pilots with girls dangling from their elbows, beautiful uniforms and devil-may-care expressions, cigarettes dangling from their lips, hearty laughter. Very sexy.

War, the newsreels, the prospect of brave boys dying to defend our homes. Girls who the month before would slap a boy for slipping a hand under a waistband now allowed liberties to heroic young men facing death. Our parents' idea of the future—the far-away place with a family gathered around a meat loaf and a good mortgage rate on the house—it just shrank away. There was more Now, less Later. Love (In These Times) got a lot of people between its teeth and shook them hard, and that's how it got Arnold Strato.

I knew that Arnold had come to those first stupid *Monsters in the Movies* meetings because he was interested in me. I'd let him kiss me behind the gym one Friday afternoon after school just to test-drive the experience. Arnold was at a point in his life where girls took up lots of the room in his head, but he didn't see them as people. He saw them as romantic objects, which is sweet but dumb. I brushed him off. After all, cute as he was, he'd still showed up at a *Monsters in the Movies* club meeting. Not sexy.

Then in his junior year Susie Brink caught his eye and he fell like a bird shot out of the sky: Susie Brink, who was as pretty and empty as a Christmas ornament. Having no personality of her own to speak of, she was perfectly happy being some boy's standard factory-line romantic object. Arnold didn't know that when she leaned over his desk in advanced algebra class to tell him she so much needed his help with problem number seven that she was making sure he had an uninterrupted view of her new brassiere's lace details. Pitiful cliché move. Any boy smart enough to get my attention would have seen it for exactly what it was and been merely amused. But Arnold was pure and stupid. The girl poleaxed him.

When Pearl Harbor put all those boys in uniform, Susie B made it clear that boys in uniform truly deserved a girl's respect and attention. Susie B couldn't name more than three American presidents, and if you asked her where Oregon was she'd have trouble finding it on a map, but she knew how to brush by a boy in a way that left him a little breathless. Off she went to express her patriotism with several other young men, and Arnold couldn't stand it. He convinced his mother to sign a paper that said he could enlist before his eighteenth birthday, and he got himself in uniform as fast as he could. He was just a few weeks short, he'd argued when his mother tried to slow him down. If local gossip was accurate, the uniform worked. Susie Brink awarded Arnold the final favors, or so whispers in the high school hallways reported. In the old world, the world before the war, that kind of whisper would make Susie Brink an outcast. In this new world, she was a patriotic and heartbroken young woman in love. She had given in to her feelings, which were understandable In These Times.

Neave had had a crush on Arnold since forever. She'd have denied it, but that would mostly be because she didn't recognize what she had as a crush. My sister was as dopily romantic and inexperienced as Arnold Strato. In a heaven where looks and gawkiness don't matter, Neave would have snagged Arnold Strato easily. But she wasn't living in heaven and those things matter in life.

Then, war. Most of the guys who might have been interesting enough to date were enlisted. So when the USO had dances for the guys, we girls went to them as a kind of public service to the troops. At first it was fun. Then they started coming back from postings—overseas stuff as well as from training—and they were different. Rough. They didn't pay attention to you when you told them to get their hand off your ass. They laughed, and put the other hand up your blouse. No class, no money, no manners, so as far as I was concerned, no reason to keep going to USO dances. I was not the kind of girl who thought a uniform gave you the right to keep your hand on my ass. The movies say that war turns raw material into noble men, but from the dance floor at the Charlestown navy station USO, it looked like it just turned a lot of them into pigs.

It did less than that and more than that to Arnold Strato. Before he shipped out he got a diamond on Susie Brink's finger. Neave and Snyder went with his family and Susie the new fiancée to stand on the train platform and see him off. Neave was there because of the crush she didn't know she had. Snyder was there for his *Monsters in the Movies* colleague. Arnold gave Susie a deep, long movie kiss. She waved a handkerchief and looked mournful and poetic.

We kept going to school, even though it didn't seem important anymore. All the younger male teachers had enlisted the week after Pearl Harbor except for one, a history teacher we called Mr. Quaker. He told Neave's class that war was just a struggle for limited resources, like land and women—part of an ongoing battle that the male of a species wins by expanding the size of his holdings, both geographical and genetic. Not so different, he said, from what dragonflies or wild horses do. That night at dinner Neave delivered almost the whole lecture, right down to imitating the teacher's habit of clearing his throat every three or four words. He was, she reported, a conscientious objector.

I listened but I just did what I do, which was to let Neave step in it while I stepped aside. She had to know how Daddy would react to talk like that. It was like he was a hornet's nest and she'd whacked it. He said he was going to call the school superintendent and have that cowardly, godless commie homo asshole fired. "We are not monkeys or bugs! Man is made in God's own image! What kind of man uses a lot of big words to back down from a fight?"

"He said horse. Not monkey," Neave corrected. Stupid girl. To which Daddy slapped his hand down on the table again, hard, and very close to her plate.

Mom whispered, "So many young men," and you could hear the concertina wire in her voice. She wasn't thinking about species survival or monkeys or bugs. She was thinking about the flags in neighbors' windows. She was thinking about where Snyder might have ended up if that ear had been in working order.

"Exactly what do you think is the making of those young men?" Daddy was talking low but sharp. "You go to war a boy and you come back a man. Every man understands that. Women don't understand because women never face it."

It took Daddy only about three weeks to get the Quaker teacher fired. Still conscientiously objecting, the guy drove an ambulance in France, where he ran over a mine and exploded himself the first week he was there. At school they held an assembly to honor his brave service.

Arnold Strato got himself posted onto a submarine when he found out that sub assignments paid better than topside service, and sent his money home to his parents along with letters to Susie Brink about their wedding, which would happen the moment he got home from war. Susie's love and the promise of his life with her, he wrote—these were what got a man from day to day. Eight months later arcing battery charges on Arnold Strato's submarine blew the engine room into flames. The navy sent a letter saying he was getting great care. It said Arnold was a hero, and they were discharging him. Fiancée Susie was with the family when they went to collect him at the train station, little tears seeping prettily as she clutched a lace handkerchief. Neave was there, still with the crush on Arnold, still unaware of the fact that she had a crush. She described Susie in particular detail when she gave me the blow-by-blow later that afternoon. We hated Susie.

Arnold's family walked right past him, sweeping the crowd for something that looked familiar. Everybody was met, the platform was empty, and Arnold was still waiting for them to recognize him. When I went to visit him at home I got a close-up view of what his family saw. Half of Arnold's face had melted away. What was left of his right hand looked like the business end of a club. The way that hand hung threw his whole body into a crouchy twist.

Susie Brink didn't last out the month. When she told Arnold that she could not love him anymore, when nobody in town could think of a job for him to do where he wouldn't scare away customers or other employees, he went home and sat on his parents' back porch. Neave, being Neave, started bringing him comic books, *Superman*s at first, but Superman was spending all his time nowadays fighting Japs and Jerrys, so they switched to comic book westerns for peace of mind. Daddy went to the Stratos' once to pay his respects to the returning decorated hero, then came home and sat in the living room for a week without talking to anybody.

Mom said that the church told us to visit the sick and that it was my duty to visit Arnold Strato, so I walked on over one Saturday morning and knocked. Mrs. Strato looked surprised to see me but said that she thought Arnold would be happy to get the copy of *Laredo Law* I'd brought. Neave had told me that Arnold hardly ever spoke, that they just sat side by side and read comics until she left. Sometimes, she said, he didn't even say hello or goodbye. I figured I could deal with that.

But he wasn't silent with me. The second I stepped onto the porch, he started talking and he didn't stop. "Lilly. Lilly, Lilly, Lilly," he said. Half his mouth smiled, his lips all puppety and a line of drool on his chin. "I'm so glad you're here." No chitchat, no preamble. He launched in like he was just continuing a conversation that'd gotten interrupted for a second. He said, "You know what my CO's favorite expression was?" I shook my head. "'Faint heart never fucked a pig,'" he said. "He was a piece of scum."

I knew that inside this person was the Arnold Strato who'd kissed me behind the gym, the Arnold who'd come to Snyder's dumb club meetings and been nice to Neave. But that Arnold had been replaced by this monster boy who sat on the Strato porch and scared people. Maybe the two Arnolds had always been there inside him and we just hadn't seen the dark, shadow Arnold inside the light, sweet Arnold. "The fucking boat's going down and he stands there and watches us hanging on to the rail in sixteen-foot waves, half of us burned and out of our minds with pain, and he says, 'Hang on! Faint heart never fucked a pig, boys,' and then, thank God, he gets washed over the side himself. We couldn't get to him through the waves." Arnold's lips twisted up into the closest thing he had to a smile. "The son of a bitch finally drowned. And you know what I thought when they hooked his body and dragged it aboard? I thought, Tough shit, man. Faint heart never fucked a pig."

I didn't go back to visit Arnold Strato again. Neave did, and I'd ask her what they talked about and she always said the same thing: nothing. Did you talk about anything when you brought him *Laredo Law*? she asked me. Nope, I said. Not a thing.

Arnold died of a heart attack at the end of that autumn. They said it was stress from respiratory problems—nothing to be surprised about in a man who'd breathed the fumes in a submarine fire. But that's not true. Arnold Strato died of a broken heart. Love killed Arnold Strato, love and the desire to pass his own genes down to the next generation, like a monkey or a bug. You don't think of it as something that can kill you, but I tell you, it can. If anybody knows that, it's me.

NEAVE

Jenna Louise

Lilly got her first job at Mr. Case's corner store. Elly the counter woman had to quit because she couldn't commute from her farm on their rationed three gallons a week anymore, and Lilly happened to be looking over some mascara wands when Elly gave her notice. Lilly stepped right up to offer her services. We lived within walking distance. Gas was no problem. Along with household needs, candy, personal hygiene products, and a lunch counter, Mr. Case's spa had the largest selection of cosmetics in town.

Lilly didn't know anything about cleaning products, and she hated the penny-candy customers, but she could sell a tired farm wife or a baggy-socked secretary twice the Lash-O-Lizer the woman could afford then get thanked for taking her money. Her makeup aisle was a kind of tropical oasis of romance blooming in a desert of cleaning products and nail clippers. Every woman in town found some reason to drop by that spa and ask if she thought they were using too bold a lipstick color. They never were. Most of them left with a little package under their arms and higher hopes for themselves than what they'd had when they came in. Maybe they hadn't put red meat or a frosted cake on their tables for a month, but that didn't stop them from leaving with a new Lash-O-Lizer wand.

One of Lilly's best customers was Jenna Louise Bowles. Jenna Louise was in Lilly's class, one year ahead of me. Lilly thought that girl was a genius. Jenna Louise knew how to get an eyeliner pencil line up the back of her leg perfectly straight, an invaluable skill when all the silk stockings in the world had sacrificed themselves for the war effort and become parachutes. Jenna Louise knew more about eyebrow pluckers and strategic placement of folded Kleenex than anybody in the senior class. Boys got stupid around her. Mr. Dextin in the science department once walked directly into a door after she'd breezed by in her cashmere pink sweater. She wore Chanel No. 5, a grown woman's scent.

Lilly probably remembered Jenna Louise for her beauty expertise, but Jenna called up something else in me, something scaly and dark—the kind of feeling Lilly would say I shouldn't bother myself about. If Lilly Terhune had paid a little more attention to the scaly dark things, she might still be alive.

One day I was at my locker, invisible in my saggy bobby socks and white cotton shirt. Jenna Louise walked by, unfurling herself as she blew past the football-team members who were clustered across the hall. Every boy's head rotated around to follow her. The team captain made the sound first. It sounded hissy to me, but I knew it was a real word and not a hiss. He was a fat sixteen-year-old with pimples on his nose and a peanut-butter sandwich in his hand, team captain only because his father donated the money for the uniforms. He said it whispery but with sharp edges. The word was *cunt.* The boys' eyes had been glassy and their feet were jiggling, and then I heard a soft *b* sound and then the scratchy twist at the "itch" before they saw me standing there and then all the energy just went cold. They drifted off in different directions. I looked on past them to Jenna Louise, who was just reaching the end of the hallway, that seam line running up the leg and vanishing at the skirt hem, the pretty little tip-and-roll that her high heels gave to her hips as she walked. Her skirt snugged in just below her butt to show her figure to best advantage. I went to history class.

I tried to describe the way it made me feel uneasy and clammy to

Lilly, who told me to ignore a bunch of stupid little boys showing off for one another in a high school hallway. But I couldn't. That night after dinner I found myself holding *The Pirate Lover.* I opened it at random and the book fell open to Judge Henri Le Cherche, coolly assessing Electra's breasts. I snapped the book shut.

In the spring of her senior year, Jenna Louise disappeared after a school fair. At first the girls in our class whispered that she had run off with an older boy, maybe the mechanic from Peabody who somebody told somebody that she might have been dating. I'd read the newspaper account and put the paper down because the words describing the body that was found in a swamp behind the school had words in it that felt like they'd been made of razor blades: *violated*, *burned*, *bound*, *nude*. I'd never seen the word "nude" in print before in my life. At school the word "rape" was passed along the hallways like a dead snake. Then some of the bobby-socked girls said that she had brought it on herself, those skirts and the sweaters and the Chanel. Her own fault. Fast girl. *Whore*—that word was used too.

The words seemed to protect them from what happened to Jenna, like an incantation that had to be said before they were able to move on to talk about algebra or hair spray. It seemed to work for them; it didn't work for me.

THE PIRATE LOVER

Runaway

Electra Gates fled the marriage that would destroy her. If a curving waist, a glittering jewel at the ears, and a dance all had worked to draw the repellent Henri Le Cherche's attention to her, then better she were hideous, better to be poor and invisible! What was beauty to the one who was beautiful if she could not control its effects? No doubt her clear dependence upon her undependable mother had also drawn him to her. The Marais dress, the physical pleasures of dancing—she had experienced them as a source of power, but they too had betrayed her by attracting this monster.

She hurried, panting, toward the sea in the darkness of a moonless night. At the quays she would find a boat that was just about to slip its anchor. She would put the sea itself between her and the monster Le Cherche.

Two loiterers pointed her to a handsome black vessel with a new suit of sails a half mile out in the harbor. That one, they said, is the only ship in the harbor with its water and victuals already on board and a Blue Peter flying to signal its imminent departure. A British crew, for the most part, they said. She'll be off at the next tide, they told her. Perhaps the captain would take a passenger. Who knew? But she must hurry if she wanted to let her destiny take this turn. For a fee, a very small fee, they would be willing to row her out this very minute.

Her eyes swept the harbor, the deep-green water and then the disk of the horizon arcing so far away. No carriages or coaches leaving the city were safe. Henri Le Cherche could stop any of them. But the sea— there was freedom. Yes, she said. Yes, take me.

So they did, taking from her first the few coins she offered and calling up when they reached the ship's high tumbledown. "Hello, the *Cat*! Hello, the boat! Young person seeking passage asking to come aboard. Handsome piece too, mates!" The speaker turned to a blushing Electra. "Pardon the language, miss. No offense meant."

A row of grizzled faces looked down at them, all grinning to see the handsome piece. "Send her up!" called out one.

One of her rowers hooted back, but the other turned to reassure her. "It ain't no navy ship with navy rules, miss," he said, "but you won't do better than this ship here. It's a handpicked crew of volunteers and they sail with the *Cat* because it's got the best fighting captain among all the privateers. You don't want to cross him, but he's always got more volunteers than he can take. Only the best sail with him."

"What is his name?" she asked.

"Le Cherche. Viscount Basil Le Cherche. A fine seaman and a cunning sea wolf. No storm's sunk him yet, nor no ship could take him with less than eight hundred pounds of metal to throw at him. Nobody's forced his flag down, never."

Just then Basil Le Cherche himself appeared at the rail. His expression remained impassive and he looked down calmly. "Permission to come aboard," he called at last. "We'll drop a line."

Electra froze. Had she run from one predator directly into another's grasp? She looked behind her at the port, considered her options, and stepped into the rope cradle. She allowed herself to be swung up and over the rail, greeted with hoots and then, under Basil Le Cherche's cool and silent stare, respectful becks and nods from all hands. Le Cherche led her to his cabin, the only private space on the ship. A bank of windows at the stern reflected candlelight from tapers set on an enormous desk. The room was beautiful, even luxurious in a masculine way. It had the look of a country gentleman's study, lined with books and furnished with Turkish carpets, polished wood chairs, a massive desk. A cello sat on its stand by the bookcases. He nodded to a chair and she sat.

"I had not expected to see you so soon, Miss Gates."

She reddened, more in pride and anger than embarrassment. "If I had any idea that this ship was yours, you would not have. I am under duress. In fact, I am under duress from your own brother, who has convinced my mother to give me to him in marriage."

"He is a rich man. You are a poor girl."

"He is an animal, and poverty is preferable to allowing him to lay his hands on me."

"I would agree," Le Cherche said mildly.

The steward interrupted with a knock and entered bearing a tray with little glasses of gin and a plateful of biscuits. "I thought the lady might need some refreshment," the steward said by way of explaining an entirely invented intrusion whose only goal was to get a better look at the captain's passenger. Le Cherche let him set the tray before them and fuss with cloth and decanter before he dismissed the man. He poured her some gin, which she held uncertainly.

"Ah," he said. "Tea would have been the more expected thing in your world, wouldn't it? But this is a different world. A pity we had no opportunity to prepare, but we did not expect you." Electra met his gaze, tipped the glass to her lips, and drank. She coughed. "You will no doubt be served any number of things you didn't ask for by everyone from the bosun to the bosun's cat." He smiled. "They don't see many beautiful women."

"You are a Frenchman, but your crew is English?"

"For the better part. I find they're excellent sailors." He poured the clear liquid into his own cut glass. He drank. "But now that we are alone and since you already seem to have decided to reject my brother's advances, I can tell you what I know of his proclivities and tastes."

"You needn't. He described them to me himself."

"How unwise of him to reveal them to you before he had you securely in hand. He must have been very confident of your malleability. The better strategy would have been to conceal his own nature until you were a wife and had no legal rights."

"Your brother described his expectations of me because he does not believe that my acceptance or rejection is relevant. He informed me that my youth makes my mother my legal guardian and she can dispose of me as she will."

"And your mother would give you to him?"

"She would."

"So the woman is either dull-witted or venal."

Electra held her head a bit more erect, tried to make her expression wooden, but she was not indifferent to his words. They were painful and they were true—or rather, they were painful because they were true.

"Unfortunate," he said softly. "So you fled?"

"I was forced upon the water, sir. I would surely have departed the city by carriage or horse had I not been sure that your brother had the power to keep a watch on all roads."

"You are quite right. He dislikes being thwarted and would have spent whatever was required to secure you. Let me answer your questions before they are posed: No, I will not return you to him. And no, if you remain aboard I cannot tell you our destination. Do you still wish to stay? We slip anchor at the next tide."

Electra nodded.

"Strange creature." He smiled, but not with his eyes. "The twisting currents of fate gave you the mother and circumstances that would draw my brother to you and then send you fleeing to this very vessel. I seem to be a part of your revealed destiny, and I am not a man to do battle with destiny." He turned away from her. "Trotter!" he called. "Find Miss Gates a berth near the surgeon's in one of the cabins by the gunroom. Stow her things and see to it that she is fed. Dismissed."

Apparently he meant this last command for both Electra and Trotter. She hesitated by the door. "Sir? I am entirely prepared to supply a fee for my passage, though I may need to beg for patience in payments. . . ."

"You assume I care about fees, mademoiselle." He brushed past her on his way out the door. "I do not."

So began Electra Gates's first sea voyage.

NEAVE

Mrs. Daniels Decides to Go

Mrs. Daniels decided to die in the winter of 1943. I was still reading to her once or twice a month. We checked in on "Can This Marriage Be Saved" and revisited favorite scenes in favorite novels. We still read Mrs. Roosevelt's "My Day," and returned to *The Odyssey* every now and then. At this point in our acquaintance Mrs. Daniels and I communicated in the kind of shorthand that I'd only known with Lilly. More and more when tea arrived, she pushed it away. Then one afternoon she mentioned speaking to her husband.

"Mrs. Daniels, I thought your husbands were dead."

"That does not always silence them, particularly if they have something to say."

"What did he say?"

"He suggested it was time to come along."

"Ah." I just nodded. "Which husband was this?"

"Oh, the first one, of course."

"Mrs. Daniels, was this in a dream?"

She looked me over, considering. "All right," she said finally. "We'll call it a dream."

"Dream or no dream, you should eat, Mrs. Daniels."

"I'm a grown woman, Neave Terhune," she said kindly. "I'll do what

I want about my own dreams. I had Violette especially bake this crusty pumpernickel you love. And this butter?" She held it up. "Irish butter. The best in the world, though how the Irish do anything so fine as this butter is a mystery to me, given their attraction to self-destructive, pin-headed, backward habits. Have one of those little cucumber things. Those at least are English."

I tried to eat the little cucumber things but failed. Violette set a half dozen slices of aromatic bread before me, and for the first time in my life the siren call of toast failed to move me. Mrs. Daniels and I sat across from each other, the table between us piled high with every delicacy I had ever greedily sought in her house. It all sat untouched. In the next weeks Mrs. Daniels actually shrank, physically, but that didn't diminish her. She just got concentrated.

"Neave Terhune," she said on the last day I saw her alive, her voice pure and hard and very small, "I am grateful to you. And I have loved you."

I already knew that, and the knowledge cut into me so sharply I didn't think I could stand it. I said, "Even though I'm a kind of unlovable young woman."

"Yes," she nodded. "Particularly so."

I began to cry.

"Don't cry," she said, a terrible kindness in her voice. "All will be well. I'm sure of it."

She died just before sunrise. That week a sunny young man improbably identifying himself as her son showed up with a lawyer and went to work selling everything under her roof. He knocked on my door one day to tell me his mother had left me her books.

"She knows I'm no reader, and most of these are for ladies." He shrugged. "You know. Novels. Stuff like that."

I thanked him. When the boxes of books came into my house courtesy of some chunky young men that her son had hired for the job, I went through them looking for the Forbidden Shelf of Romances. None were there. I had "borrowed" several of them, meaning I'd jammed them into a book bag when Mrs. Daniels left the room for even an instant, but I'd returned them all, all except *The Pirate Lover*, which I hadn't ever been able to give up.

I took *The Odyssey* and *Jane Eyre* under my arm and climbed up to my bedroom. There I sat on my bed and looked out into the backyard. In Daddy's garden the carrots and cabbages were long gone, but I watched a rabbit nose around hopefully until a neighbor's terrier flushed it into the next yard, the dog howling along behind the poor floppy-eared thing, intent on ripping it apart. It made me cry again, the stupid dog. The rabbit.

There are people who think that every experience offers you a lesson, but I'm not one of them. Mrs. Daniels died. What are we supposed to gain in the way of comfort or wisdom from that?

That afternoon, Lilly knew where I was and she had a feeling for what I was feeling. She came and sat next to me. *The Pirate Lover* lay on the floor by my bed. She picked it up, asked me if I wanted her to read to me. I said yes. She kept on until the moon got high enough to throw shadows that moved when the curtains blew, which was pretty. There was the runaway Electra at the captain's table in her first hours on board the *Cat*, skimming rapidly across the black surface of an ocean, sailing away from all that threatened her. Love, courage, generosity of spirit, adventure—all triumphant. Surely this was the truth, somewhere. The awful feelings seeped out of me. When Lilly stood up and stretched and said let's sneak downstairs and fry up some eggs, I realized I was hungry. So that's what we did and the day ended all right after all.

THE PIRATE LOVER

The Fool's Game

Had she found herself on a pirate ship? Electra Gates was led to a cabin that had room in it for no more than a modest cot, over which hung a single lamp. "The surgeon's mate was the last one to use this cabin and he liked a bunk better than a swinging hammock but I can ship you either one, miss," Trotter said as he swung the door open and let his lantern shine to the farthest edge of it—five feet away. A rat skittered out of the light and into some hole invisible in the dimness. Electra stepped into the coffinlike space. "Unlucky bloke. Copped it last trip."

"Pardon?"

"Ship's surgeon. Fool took a swim in shark-infested waters. Just as useless in the sick bay—was afraid of blood—so I'm sorry to say he ain't much missed. I myself prefer a hammock to a bunk. Most find it an easier berth in the workings of the ship. When at sea, like, if you know what I mean, miss. And it's drier should water happen, which is frequent."

"A swinging hammock, then, would be perfectly lovely, and I thank you." He turned to leave but she stopped him. "Mr. Trotter, am I aboard a pirate ship?"

"Oh, miss, never in life! You must not use that word before the crew or captain, for it's a low word, miss! We're a letter of marque! The cap'n's got the letter set careful like in oiled leather in a waterproof tin chest and I've seen it myself. We sail at the pleasure of the queen."

"You mean king."

"No, ma'am. I mean Victoria, our queen. I see the confusion. The cap'n's got a French name and a French brother, but he's no friend to either. This is no Frenchie Louis-Philippe ship. He's his own man, miss, a man with connections on both sides o' the Channel. We hunt Spanish and Dutch prizes—as do all the French and English afloat at the moment. I should tell you that there's still a half a glass before the tide and a person who found she wasn't where she wanted to be could disembark now if she hustled. Should you want to hustle. If you take my meaning."

"You don't want me aboard, Mr. Trotter?"

Mr. Trotter blushed a deep pink. "Well, some say women aboard are bad luck, like parsons, but I find they lighten the people's mood. Not that we aren't a happy barkie, which we are, but they do. Unless they cause fighting. Then they're no good to man or beast." He waited for her to absorb this information. "Normally, miss, you'd mess with the midshipmen and keep an eye on the young gentlemen as a person of a more refined nature but as we're a privateer there're no young gentlemen so you're a member of the gunroom mess though the cap'n invites you to dine with him tonight, you being a kind of guest."

"I'm very tired. . . ."

"A cap'n's invitation is an order aboard that cap'n's ship, ma'am. Now, don't you fret. We'll accustom you to our ways. I'll leave this light, but you must remember that fire is the barkie's worst enemy besides a Spanish man-o'-war and you must never leave it unattended."

He withdrew, leaving her in the dim cubicle whose tiny light threw a hundred flickering shadows. She unpacked what she could, dressed in what she hoped would be appropriate for the captain's table, and sat still, a bit uncertain, waiting to be summoned. She had pulled a new cotton doublet over her shift, sought out and located her rouge and kohl, but looked in vain for a mirror. There was none. How strange it was to prepare oneself for public judgment without the aid of that reflective surface. There were probably no mirrors at all on board. She was in a world where one's reflection meant very little—a man's world.

She heard the sounds usual to departure, but because she was new to them she could not read them. Still, foreign to her or not, they proceeded in the time-honored order: the cable being wound aboard, the anchor being catted and fished, the pinnace being run up to the davits, the halyards in their blocks. She waited on. The entirety of her cell tilted to one side and she braced herself against the walls of her little quarters, feeling the living wood around her vibrate against the pressures of sea and wind—they were moving. Still she waited uncertainly, sitting silently. She heard the turning of the glass called, heard the gunroom members surging through their shared mess and back to their posts, and then finally, finally, a banging on the door and Trotter's voice, shrewish now and a bit anxious. "Ain't you ready, miss? You mustn't be late!"

When she swung open her door Trotter took her by the hand and pulled her through the ship's narrow passages toward her appointment, lecturing on when various messes messed, and how to tell the time from the unvarying routines and noises on ship, and how lateness was never, never countenanced on a well-run ship like the *Cat*. They reached the doorway to the captain's cabin and he pushed her forward, gently, over the doorway and into the beautiful space with its stern rising up from a steep counter in a wall of glass. Light glanced up off the waves in their wake and into the shining room. A table glowed with silver and crystal. Behind each seat stood a nodding, smiling, clean-shaven man dressed in his best coat in the stifling heat of the close room, waiting for her. Looking at them watch her approach she understood that these eyes would be her only mirror aboard the *Cat*. She took a deep breath, smiled as warmly as she could, and thanked them all for the kind invitation to their dinner. She was rewarded with unguarded admiration.

The captain seated her at his right and lifted his first glass to her. "To my special guest, Mademoiselle Gates. A glass of wine with you, my lady."

She raised her glass to his and drank. On this ship, her value, her rights, her safety, all rested on the captain's authority, and she saw that his authority was total. Had Le Cherche hosted this dinner with the particular purpose of establishing a protected status for her?

"A beautiful Sauterne, Captain," she said when he filled her glass again.

"I had five cases brought aboard before we sailed. I served, in youth, in Her Majesty's Royal Navy, and there I came to a deep appreciation of what private means can supply in addition to what the grateful nation provides a man during wartime."

"Sailors are not well provided for?"

"They are if a pound of bread, pounded dry peas, a pound of salt beef that's made its way around the Horn three times before it hits your tin plate, and a quart of beer satisfies you utterly. War is not about cuisine, however. Or glory," he added.

"Not glory, sir?" she asked.

"One might stumble upon glory. But war is not glorious in and of itself. It is simply the great contest for resources."

"Like a crown?" she said, her tone gentle but challenging.

"Incidentally perhaps," the purser joined in. "But a crown is merely the key to what matters."

"Which is what, sir?"

"Land. Silver. Wheat. Women."

"Women?" Electra smiled thinly, remembering that she was a guest at this table and in this world, but finding it difficult to curb her own tongue. "Surely we are not something that would appear on a purser's list, sir, like a case of Sauterne or a plot of land to be squabbled over—a mere possession."

"I mean no offense, ma'am." The purser blushed. "I was merely speaking."

The captain broke in. "As to squabbles and mere possessions, I could ask you to remember Helen of Troy—a stolen possession who caused quite a squabble. But pardon me. We border on discussing politics, which is not a suitable topic for a captain's table. Mr. Davies—I believe the bottle stands by you."

The mood lightened with each bottle. Deep into the fifth course a somewhat drunken young lieutenant was holding forth with a story that threatened to become inappropriate before a mate kicked him under the table and he changed the course of the narrative, making it virtually incomprehensible. Electra glanced at Le Cherche, catching him in a moment when he thought he held no one's attention. She expected to find an arrogant man among those he considered his inferiors. Instead she saw a man who sat at an enormous silent distance from those around him, a man with a face whose lines and battle scars showed suddenly in stark relief—a sad man. She turned quickly away, and when the little story had ground to an illogical conclusion Le Cherche clothed himself again in good cheer, calling for toasts all around and a good night. Hours later as she lay in her swinging hammock she heard his cello begin to speak through the thin cabin walls, unaccompanied, the loneliest sound she believed she'd ever heard in her life.

In the days that followed, Electra ventured enough into the life of the ship to come to know its routines, to know her gunroom fellows, and to be invited several times more to the captain's table.

"So you are a letter of marque and you hunt the Spanish?" she asked on one evening when they were alone except for the bustling presence of Trotter, who waited upon them.

"We are and we do. But if you were of any value at all to my brother, we are now the hunted as well as the hunters."

"I doubt this. Your brother might have gone to the relatively controllable expense of having local roads watched to stop me as I fled, but he would not set out upon the boundless ocean to find something as insignificant, in the end, as a woman."

"Ah." He smiled. "Remember Helen of Troy."

"I recall your example of Helen of Troy, Captain—but I am no Helen of Troy, and your brother is no Menelaus."

"You need not be a Menelaus to be made unreasonable under the influence of pride or of a woman. And your looks are not so unfortunate, Mademoiselle. There are all kinds of charms that can give a woman the power to bewitch a man. I have seen but little of you, yet even in that short time I can see that your arsenal has weapons beyond physical beauty."

"Weapons? Surely love is not a battle, monsieur."

"Not if the players remain cool and reasonable—each understanding that passion is a fool's game."

"Is it? I hadn't been told."

"I suspect you have. You forget—I have met your mother, a woman who wages her marital campaigns as if they were great fleet actions with life or death at stake, which they are. Yet I doubt that love itself was ever the prize she sought. Not for herself, or for you."

Electra blushed. This was true—not only had her first encounter with this man been in the drawing rooms of Paris, where he no doubt had heard every bit of gossip about her that could be had, he had also heard her admit that her mother would gladly surrender her to Judge Henri Le Cherche. "Your brother feels no love for me. I am merely an object to him, and surely he can find another one in the drawing rooms of Paris. He will not pursue."

"My brother feels no love for anyone. That is irrelevant. And as for the things about you that might interest him, you combine a certain naïve freshness with sensual boldness. You have no frilly mannerisms; there is none of the tiresome simpering and rouge so common among husband-hunters. And there is the natural grace, the almost feral ease, with which you carry yourself. You are lovely, Electra Gates. In some moments, like this one when you are a bit confused and a little angry, you are ravishing."

"You are too forward, sir." Electra looked directly at him, no turning aside, and he met her gaze completely and laughed, throwing his head back with the full-throated unselfconsciousness of a boy. Looking at that muscular neck, Electra felt her own throat close, her own skin heat.

"My dear, in this room, on this ship, I am the only one with the power to say what is forward or not. But you needn't fear me. I am immune to you, even as I recognize your charms."

"You are not . . . drawn to women?"

"I have spent more hours in women's beds, my dear, than the most expert husband-hunter has spent in dress shops and balls. I am simply a pragmatist. I have seen what people call love and I am not interested in it."

"If you expect to shock me, you will find yourself disappointed, sir."

"I do not wish to shock. Merely to be clear about both my own position, and yours. If I know my brother, Henri, your resistance has inflamed and enraged him, and in such a state he can be dangerous. He has great wealth and influence, and he is perfectly at ease using them to get what he wants. If your story of his proposal and your rejection is true, you have made the mistake of doing one of the few things that could make him determined to find you—you defied him."

"My story is true, sir."

"Then we will be running out the guns for practice tonight because we need to be perfectly ready when he catches us. And he will catch us."

"Knowing that he would pursue you, you still took me on board?"

"My brother and I have worked at aggressive cross-purposes our entire lives. His sexual habits and business practices are known in certain specialized circles, Miss Gates, and I abhor them and pity him. Helping you hurts him. That is sufficient satisfaction for me. Do you know how my brother made his fortune?"

Electra did not respond, not having the words for what she knew. She stayed as still as she could, attempting to betray none of her feelings, for this unbreachable, powerful, sad man across from her had stirred something in her and she wished to hide this from him—to reveal none of the tingling, alert channels opening in her body as she watched him lean back against a chest, a crystal wineglass in his hand and his liquid gray eyes still and clear upon her.

"His public persona as a judge provides cover for the actual source of his wealth—the very wealth with which he purchased his judgeship. My brother specializes in providing certain clients with sexual delights in the way of a diverse group of specially trained young boys, girls, and women who do what they are told. The ones who do not are sometimes disposed of in ways that amuse another very special subset of his clients."

"Who would allow herself to be so used?"

"They are not asked, my dear. They are abducted and controlled. There are many ways to control another human being, and his network is made up of men who, like him, take physical delight in exercising those many ways. Once subordinated and diminished beyond the ability to be interesting, they are sold or leased out to the highest bidders. You would be shocked to learn who seeks his services."

"Perhaps I would not be."

He leaned forward, looking at her more closely. "Perhaps you would not. You are an interesting woman, Electra Gates."

"Captain Le Cherche . . ." She stopped, unable to shape her question into words. He waited patiently, so quiet and attentively focused that she felt a flush of heat rise from the center of her body and spread. "There was a feeling I had when he stood in the room with me and told me he would take me as a wife. What he was feeling toward me at that moment . . ." She stopped again.

"Hatred?" Basil Le Cherche said mildly. She nodded. "Yes, Electra Gates. Your understanding of him was quite accurate. No wonder you interest him."

"But he doesn't even know me. Why would he feel hatred? And hating me, why would he propose marriage?"

"You inspired hatred because you attracted him beyond his ability to be indifferent to you. That is all that was necessary. Had I left you ashore he would have plucked you up in a matter of hours. And I am firmly against my brother's habit of plucking things up."

A call down from the masthead: five approaching ships. It took only a matter of minutes for Basil Le Cherche to leap up to the highest crosstree with a glass, to train it on the lead ship, and return to Electra. "Our time is come even before I expected," he said, smiling faintly. "My brother approaches."

NEAVE

How Be Your Best Begins

Lilly was twenty and I was nineteen when the returning servicemen got us fired by needing our jobs. Since she'd started at Mr. Case's spa she'd tripled his cosmetics sales. Women drove thirty miles for Lilly Terhune's advice on how to handle problematically thin brows. I was baking at the Bigelow Diner and successfully tripling the number of customers on Tuesdays and Thursdays, which were pie days at the Bigelow. But in 1945 we were supposed to marry a returning hero and have kids and dinner parties that ended with Cherry Surprise Jell-O cups, recipe available on page 52 or on the side of your Jell-O box! Lilly must have turned down five proposals that summer and fall. She was looking for romance, which she saw as something related to but not necessarily the same as marriage. I was looking for romance too, but in my mind, in a corner too secretive and dimly lit to actually admit existed, romance involved pursuits and captures, heart-stopping dangers and erotic escapes, the abandonment of the self to the other. In other words, I had a very limited social life.

She dragged me along with her on an odyssey to the best furrier on Newbury Street and talked the both of us into four-year credit plans for two raccoon coats. "A girl's got to bait her hook," she said, spreading them out on our bed for us to admire when we got home to Lynn. Lilly Terhune was surely a baited hook if ever there was one. She was double-booked every weekend. I wasn't, but that wasn't the fur coat's fault.

We lost our jobs just after we bought those coats. Lilly turned to me with perfect faith, convinced that I could come up with something wonderful for us to do that also generated cash. We lay side by side in bed at night and talked about desire. Not Jell-O. We wanted adventure, risk, diamonds, travel, love. Not Jell-O. Lilly slept like a log all night and spent all day certain I would figure out a life full of diamonds and big cars. She didn't bother to strategize beyond that herself—she was sure I'd manage to make it happen, whatever it turned out to be.

I made an inventory of our talents and found more of them, of a more interesting kind, in my sister's possession than in mine. How many women had come to her in that corner store and learned how to turn every head in a room with a dab of red glycerin, a line of kohl, some turmeric powder, and a snug skirt? I'd watched, transfixed, while every single one of them had left with a package in her hand whether she could afford it or not. Lilly could turn a dumpy jam-smeared housewife into a pagan goddess of love, and if you don't think that draws women like ants to sugar on the sidewalk, you don't know anything.

Mr. Case hadn't even apologized to Lilly when he told her to turn in her apron so he could give it to a guy who'd spent the war in San Francisco, putting Coca-Cola and cigarettes onto cargo ships.

"He's useless," she'd fumed. "Mary Lou Evans came here last week and there he was, ringing up a high-beam gloss for her when she very specifically needed a matte. He didn't ask her about her evening plans, or her outfit. You know high beams smear like crazy. It was a dinner date with a new prospect beau! Smearing, messy . . . and that high gloss doesn't do anything for her skin. Totally wrong."

No matter. Lilly was fired.

I followed her into unemployment soon after. I'd started at the Bigelow right after high school graduation, waiting tables. Waitressing is not like baking. There's no satisfaction in waitressing, and you have to interact with sticky children and the occasionally hostile or stupid customer.

When I'd alienated one customer too many, Mr. Bigelow told me to help the baker, a seventy-year-old heavy smoker with bad eyes who dropped ashes in the bowls as he mixed. During the war years the Bigelow family had an intimate and vaguely illegal relationship with the local members of the rationing board. They'd cultivated friends who sold things that fell off trucks so the Bigelow kitchen had always been awash in lard and sugar, giving it a steady customer base through the rationing years. Late in 1943 the baker came down with a bad case of serial hangovers and I found myself basically in charge of all the Bigelow's baking. My first week I turned out a raft of blueberry and peach pies. They were gone in an hour. Word spread that something had happened to the pies at the Bigelow, and customers lined up for them. Mr. Bigelow fired his baker and gave me a raise.

My first week as the Queen of Pies at the Bigelow Diner I was in the kitchen by five a.m., fanning whole bananas sliced lengthwise into crescents over butter-yellow pools of custard. I laid them out like pinwheels, and over that I slathered a sheet of chocolate custard. Big hit. I would sit happily in that diner kitchen on Friday nights, looking at what there was to work with and doing some prep work for Pie Day. The smell of baking pies called up afternoons in Mrs. Daniels's living room and Saturday mornings in Violette's kitchen. I'd sit in my little calm, orderly paradise, going about the business of snickerdoodles and hermits.

Lilly mocked me. "Another dateless Friday night," she'd say, shaking her head at me. "If you're putting the guys off on purpose, go ahead, but if you want to learn how to change your social life, I'm around for consultation." I ignored her.

The first pie that I considered truly my own was a banana butterscotch. Next came a plain butterscotch with sweet-cream ganache. I had learned about ganache from Violette and I loved the sound of the word. I'd hum it under my breath as I melted semi-sweet chocolate into heavy cream: *ganacheganacheganache*. Jane and Snyder polished off the test-drive first pie in an hour. Jane got almost hysterical about it. We had to cut her off at piece number three before she made herself sick. Jane ended up helping me brainstorm pies, which led to what I came to think of as the Jane pies: M&M's pie with little rivers of M&M's running through them; banana pinwheel and peanut butter cream pie (with nuts and without); s'mores pie with crushed graham-cracker shells and thin sheets of melted chocolate under broiler-toasted pillows of marshmallow. People stood in line for Jane pies. No matter: I was replaced by a guy who'd spent his war playing poker in Newport News. He knew as much about pies as he knew about lipstick. Mr. Bigelow said he'd love to keep both me and potato-peeler boy, but there wasn't enough cash in the cash flow. At Mr. Case's spa, where Lilly had once ruled the cosmetics department, the lipsticks disappeared and an underwear display popped up. At the Bigelow, standard berry and pumpkin things got baked, but the long lines for Pie Day dwindled, dwindled, vanished.

So we found ourselves unemployed, in a world that seemed designed to keep us that way. I lay in bed at night and tried to plot a way out, but I only looped back to the reasons that Lilly and I were trapped and would never lead the lives we were born to lead. This kind of thinking gets you nothing but deeper into the weeds, and besides that, it isn't restful. Finally I slept.

I dreamed of burning beds and fog. I dreamed of a little sleeping cabin as small as a coffin, no mirrors anywhere, and in the dream I found this terribly troubling. I wanted a mirror. I had vanished inside myself as well as in the dream world. I was nowhere. I was no one. I couldn't remember what my eyes looked like, or my lips! I was gone, but not gone. In my dream mind I suddenly knew that if I had mirrors I could look in them and see what I was. I could build a house with mirrors, glassy surfaces reflecting like light on water! Inside the house all was safe. Outside the house all was danger. There were dogs in the house—dozens of dogs, all baking cakes. I woke.

The next morning I stood before the bathroom mirror and looked at myself very carefully. I stayed there long enough to make other members of the family bang hard on the door and demand that I hustle it up. I drank four cups of coffee, and took the idea that had shaped itself in me to Lilly. "Cosmetics," I said to my sister. "You did all the cosmetics invoices and ordering at Mr. Case's. I don't see why a couple of girls with cash on them couldn't buy blusher in bulk as well as he could. We've got a little cash, me from the diner and you from Mr. Case's. The most important thing to have when you start a business is customers. And you've got customers." This was true—all the regulars looking to fix their lives with foundation, concealer, eye shadow; all the women who opened like flowers when someone told them that yes, they would profit from a lip liner as well as a stick—they all needed Lilly. There was nobody in Mr. Case's store now to tell them these things but the useless Mr. Underwear. Mr. Case, guilty about firing her, let her leave her card at the counter, and her ladies began picking it up and calling her.

That's how Be Your Best was born. We looked around and found out that setting up a storefront of our own was out of our cash flow's range. But there had to be a better way. Why, I asked my sister, couldn't we sell cosmetics right in customers' homes? Who needs a store?

We gave a party at our house and invited all the ladies from Mr. Case's who'd ever bought so much as a tiny badger brush from Lilly. We got $10 worth of orders, which translated to $3 of profit. I considered that enough of a sign to sink a good part of our savings into a bulk order of cosmetics. Ladies needed Spring Breeze Eau de Cologne more than they needed a plastic bowl and if they didn't, they bought the cologne anyhow. We had solid proof.

The second Be Your Best party was at Ellie Goertling's house, and four ladies showed up. We'd promised Ellie a hostess gift and she swore she'd get us at least eight women. I brought a blueberry pie. Lilly applied makeup, gave advice, swore eternal friendship to everybody there. We spent seventy cents on the pie, fifty cents on Lilly's hostess gift, and made thirty cents that night. We thought we were sunk. But when Lilly called each of those ladies to see if they wanted to host their own parties, she got four yeses on the condition that we brought a pie. We decided to keep going.

We'd learned about credit and we used it to buy stock and turn our bedroom at home into a storage facility for future orders. Blush and liner and matte finish and Romance Glow were stacked ceiling-high. Mom was quiet at first and then kind of mad. She started making comments about pride and waste and lessons, never directed at us but always in the air. Ask the woman directly what was on her mind and she'd say rump roast. Why this circle, circle, circle around what was really on her mind? Speak up! I wanted to cry. Come out in the open and fight like a man! Lilly called me an idiot. "You don't want to know what's on her mind," she said. "Easier to deal with *circle, circle, circle*."

Maybe it was easier for Lilly, but it made me crazy. I said as much to Lilly, who told me lots of things made me crazy so what was new? Boo-hoo, she said. Get over it, Miss Prickly, Miss Sensitive. This made me rude at the dinner table, which led to Daddy reaching out and delivering a quick slap to my shoulder, which nobody, nobody at all, commented on the unfairness of, since it was Daddy doing the slapping.

Boo-hoo. Get over it.

I marched up to our bedroom, squeezed between the stacks of foundation and brushes, and sat on the bed. I felt sullen. Trapped. I looked around me and tried to imagine a way out. There was no doorway into my future visible from that little crowded room. I had to flee. I had to summon the nerve to plunge into the possibly fabulous (possibly horrible) unknown: to leap. Every story in the world that I loved told me that this was so.

The next day I emptied everything from the savings account that held all my pie-baking earnings and I rented Lilly and me a warehouse space as well as the couple of huge rooms and the kitchenette on the floor above it. I committed us to a one-year lease and arranged for a telephone line. I bought two mattresses and made Snyder help me move them into the rooms above the "office." We dragged a desk up the stairs, then all the cosmetics we'd stored in our childhood bedroom.

Jane cried, because she thought everything should stay exactly the way it always had been, and even Snyder looked a little anxious as he helped us move. "It's just so strange," he said, looking around. "I mean, it's just some rooms and a stove. Weird."

"Think of it as my superhero lair," I said.

Lilly and I weren't the only ones who had to rethink work after the war. Snyder had lost his job at the munitions plant along with everyone else when it closed to refit itself for peacetime appliances, and he hadn't gotten a toe-hold on the world since then. The returning vets hadn't just taken our jobs—they'd taken the ones Snyder might have had. He trudged from day to day, still the boy who lived in his childhood room to the left of the landing at the top of the stairs. Snyder looked so small, so young, standing in our dusty warehouse with his hands drooping at his sides, watching us move on and away. "It'll be all right," I said, not because I believed this but because his unhappiness suddenly made me feel protective. "Thanks for helping with the move."

"I could come back tomorrow," he said. "I know a store that's getting rid of shelving. You could use some shelving. Let me have the extra key and I won't even have to bother you to get it in."

Nothing we said could keep Snyder and his shelving from coming back, several times. For those first weeks when we were trying to settle into the warehouse we'd return from a cosmetics party or an appointment with a cosmetics supplier to find him perched in the single comfortable chair in our living space.

"Leave him alone." Lilly shrugged. "He needs someplace to go besides that firetrap bedroom of his. He isn't bothering anybody."

True and not true. Our old contentious habits with each other weren't going to vanish just because I felt sorry for him and he needed someplace to hide from his life. The first time he left a cup and three dishes in the sink I told him that if it happened again I'd take back the key we'd made the mistake of giving him the week he helped us move in.

"Why is he hanging around here so much?" I complained to Jane.

"Daddy. Daddy's been giving him a terrible time. He says it's time Snyder grew up."

"Well," I said. "It is."

"Daddy says that he was helping support his family when he was in ninth grade. He says Snyder should leave the nest."

"Daddy let Lilly and me live there after graduation even when we both lost our jobs. Why isn't he letting Snyder have some leeway?"

"Snyder's a boy. Girls stay with their parents until they go to a husband. Don't pretend like it's news to you that that's how Daddy sees things, Neave. If this gets bad, you and Lilly are going to take him in."

And we would take him in. Jane would make us do it. Lilly and I had a brief meeting on the subject. The only solution we could come up with was to find our brother a job so Daddy would leave him alone. Lilly found a fruit-and-vegetable store that was looking for help and willing to hire a non-vet. Snyder didn't want to sell oranges and potatoes, but Jane made him do it. He took the job. Daddy backed off somewhat, and a fragile peace was achieved.

Meanwhile I got us a party line with dozens of ladies on it who might be tempted to rock a receiver out of its cradle to eavesdrop away a spare ten minutes. As soon as it was installed I called everybody I knew and sprinkled the date and time of our first cosmetics party into each conversation. I don't think I'd ever met a woman, besides my mom, who didn't rely on their telephone party line for the occasional distraction. They spread news almost free of charge, whether you wanted them to or not, and I was going to make sure every single call that Lilly or I made included our phone number, along with cheerful descriptions of glowing skin, luminous eyes, and free pie. I didn't stop at telephone calls. I pursued well-dressed strangers on the street. I invited a neighbor in the middle of a condolence call the day after her husband died.

The lease had been a terrifying motivator—one year at $23 a month. Lilly might have the glamour and the sales touch but there was something to be said for a willingness to be terrorized, and I was better at terror than my sister. That first party cost us $3.28 in pie ingredients, lemonade, and coffee. The office did not show to advantage at the time and I told Lilly I was sure we would have done better if the walls hadn't had some holes and the room hadn't looked so enormously empty with just us, all huddled at one end of the warehouse. We sold enough to make $13.98 profit.

"Lilly," I said, "Half those women came to this party because they haven't gotten out of the house since the war ended. Four of them lost their jobs just like we did."

"Vets took 'em?"

I nodded. "You could teach them to do what you do: make women up, make them feel better. We could turn them into salesgirls."

"Why would we do that?"

"We would do that because it's how we're going to make money. We find salesgirls, show them how to run a party and do makeovers, show them how to sell product . . . we make them buy their sales kits from us and when they get rid of their first kit, we keep supplying them. For a percentage. We have to stop thinking of ourselves as selling makeup and start thinking of ourselves as selling sales positions. We talk to everybody we meet who looks lively and restless—talkative waitresses who know what to do with lipstick, moms in the park trying to start conversations with strangers, women who look like they pay to get their hair done standing next to us in line for a movie—we tell them there's money to be made in sales."

"Is there?"

"Who knows? But there won't be any if you don't pretend you believe it's out there. We can make them successful. We co-host their first parties, coach them if they're having trouble, treat them like they matter, and then let them loose on the world with our blessing and our makeup."

"I don't know," Lilly said. Then she said, "We need some cash to prime the pump."

And who would loan us a nickel, two girls with a warehouse lease and big plans? It turned out Mr. Case, still feeling guilty about firing Lilly, would, to the tune of $500. "You were a good worker and a smart girl, Lilly," he said when he counted out the bills. "And I know you'll pay me back." We took $200 and created new kits in pretty blue cases with "Be Your Best" printed on the side. Then we went out in search of hungry-looking young women who would listen to us tell them about what their lives could be. We pulled out our pencils and figured out just what they could make in a week if they sold five kits; we told them anybody with determination could do twice as many as that.

About fifteen of them bit, and we invited them all to the warehouse for an introductory tea. We put a robin's-egg-blue box with an ivory cloth bow on every one of their seats. When they opened them there was a picture of a watch that any salesgirl who moved a certain amount of merchandise in a quarter would receive. The watches had already been ordered, COD, and we were counting on the salesgirls' profits to help pay for them.

I made chocolate pie, raspberry supreme pie, and lemon chiffon pie—the prettiest ones I knew. Lilly made little cucumber sandwiches exactly the way they said to do it in *Ladies' Home Journal*. The tea settings came from the same going-out-of-business hotel sale that the chairs did. We borrowed tables and linens from Mom's church, signing them out under her name. I'd stripped Daddy's backyard of flowers, which he grew as handily as tomatoes, and we filled the robin's-egg-blue training corner of our office with blooms for what we were calling our first Be Your Best sales conference.

"Someday," Lilly said to me as we cleaned up afterward, "there's going to be a ring of real diamond chips around that watch face and not just glass ones. Someday there's going to be a real pearl necklace in that little blue box. And then robin's-egg-blue cars. Also fur coats," she went on. "Then incentive vacations to tropical paradises." She spoke lightly, but there wasn't any joking in the tone. There would be cars and coats.

"Silver-blue mink coats," I repeated. She nodded. "We're going to have ourselves a time, Lilly." We sat down on the floor at the end of that day, popped open a bottle of beer (we'd looked at Champagne but the last nickel in what I was calling our training event budget had gone into cucumber sandwich ingredients) and passed it back and forth. It felt wonderful. We'd been knocked down but there we were, wobbling a bit but back on our feet. For my money, that day on that floor with that can of beer was the real beginning of Be Your Best.

NEAVE

Problems Arise, Solutions Appear

By the end of our second year we had more than thirty salesgirls, some selling like mad and some just sitting on their sales kits doing nothing. Problems arose. Some husbands did not like having their wives at evening sales parties. It disrupted their dinner and they were alone with their own children, who didn't want to eat their vegetables or go to bed. We held cooking and freezing demonstrations so ladies whose husbands didn't want them to work outside the home could continue to look like they didn't. We sent letters on robin's-egg-blue stationery to the husbands, thanking them for their support for their wives and quoting fake husbands who wrote to us to say that their wives looked so much better groomed, were so much happier and peppier now that they were cosmetics representatives. "If we can convince them it'll spice up the bedroom life, they'll handcuff their wives and deliver them to our doorstep," Lilly said. "Talk up the 'pep' benefit." I worked on the prose. She edited it.

The salesgirls had some bad parties. Five caved to their husbands' demands for hot dinners at regular evening mealtimes and quit. Six others cried when parties didn't go well. They got mad at us when we offered suggestions. What did we know? they protested. We were children—kids who didn't understand what it meant to have an angry husband and toddlers with colds. Three salesgirls gave up when their children began to cry whenever they saw their mothers dressed in heels and makeup to go out to a sales party. Then a leak in the roof let in enough water one weekend to soak through a quarter of our unsold product, all of which had to be trashed. Bills and rage and self-doubt all week, and then the leaky roof.

We went to a little bar near the office and sat in a booth with two beers in front of us. "You'd think somebody with three-year-old twins would leap at the chance to put on some decent shoes and go talk to somebody taller than a milk box," Lilly said with a sigh, referring to the first mother whose children's tears had convinced her to quit. "Mom will just love this. She and Daddy just live to be able to say that lipstick is vanity and we were in over our heads."

"We're not in over our heads and we're not just selling lipstick," I snapped. "I've seen you sit down with a woman and talk about her face. We sell the way lipstick makes her feel. Daddy doesn't know that feeling exists and Mom's afraid of it. Forget them," I said.

Plunge ahead, I thought, no matter what wastes of unknown space are ahead.

"That's right," Lilly said. "It's sink or swim and we're going to paddle like mad."

Of course, the old reverse-roles thing was going on. I was struggling with a secret belief that Mom was right and we would fail, while Lilly didn't believe a word Mom said. Nobody in the world had yet convinced Lilly Terhune that she was a fool. She might be a grasshopper but she knew I was an ant, and I was with her. She had faith in me, and I was going to get us back on our feet and lug more than my own body weight as I marched. We would get more salesgirls. We would rally. Women with gumption who wanted a job and some control over their own destinies were everywhere and we would find them and make them brilliant representatives of Be Your Best Cosmetics.

And then just when we needed it to happen, the winds of destiny got behind us in the form of Ruga Potts, recent émigré from the skeletal postwar remains of her part of Europe. We found her at a Be Your

Best party, dragged along by her landlady, who thought her foreign renter needed some American influence, meaning neighbor ladies and a piece of pie.

I took one look at Ruga Potts and the rest of the room fell away. Her skin was poreless and her black hair fell in waves as far as her shoulders. She was perfectly, if a bit boldly, made up, an exotic bird in a room full of pigeons. She looked bored.

I sat down next to her. "I made the pie myself."

"How nice for you." She lit a cigarette and sat right where she was, ignoring the chattering groups of women around her waiting for an eyeliner-application demonstration. She clearly didn't need any instruction in the eyeliner department. Everything about her looked like a pacing animal even though she was at rest. I pushed myself into the narrow space beside her.

"I'm Neave."

"Ruga. Potts."

"You're interested in makeup?"

"Not this makeup."

"Really? Why not?"

Ruga Potts leaned forward and plucked a lipstick out of my hand. I'd been demonstrating its smearlessness. She slipped her hand into her own purse and produced another—an Elizabeth Arden in an elegant little gold tube. She twisted both open and held the first one under my nose. "Smell," she ordered. I did. "Now feel." She drew two lipstick lines down the back of my hand, one from Be Your Best and the other from Arden.

"The Be Your Best is creamier," I said proudly. "And it smells better than the Arden. Coconut."

"That is why your lipstick is junk."

"It's what?"

"Junk. It goes on too smooth, like I think perhaps there is too little ceresin. Some people would say pine bark might fix all." She shrugged. "I say ceresin wax. But this lipstick you sell, if you leave in car, in sun, just a puddle. Also it is rancid in ten weeks no matter what. That is what I think."

"I don't agree, Miss Potts. We ordered those lipsticks from the same manufacturer who produces for many top cosmetics companies." I sounded stung because I was. "Are you a cosmetics manufacturer? A makeup artist?"

"I am a drone. I color in airplane-engine drawings for engineers at your General Electric plant."

"Why do you do that?"

"An agency for refugees arranged all—job and landlady. So I am now in the land of ice cream and steak, coloring pictures."

"Did you work in fashion before the war?"

"In Warsaw I was a chemist."

"Did you make cosmetics in Warsaw?" I asked.

"No," Ruga Potts replied. "I learned about cosmetics in my mother's and grandmother's kitchens before the war. Every little village and town in Hungary and Poland had a woman who knew how to do this and sold to neighbors. My mother was known everywhere for parsley skin tonic. For moisturizer she used evergreen found only in Carpathian forests. She called it Krakow Cream and women came from Vienna to buy. Vienna," she repeated, her tone reverential.

"So your mother was the Helena Rubinstein of Poland."

Ruga Potts smiled at me for the first time, amused. "And where do you think all those Helena Rubinsteins came from? They came from Krakow, from the Australian bush, from little Polish shtetls. You know why cosmetics now all use lanoline? I tell you—because Chaya Rubenstein, also known as Madame Helena Rubinstein, lived among greasy sheep on a ranch in Australia. Sheep grease? It is lanolin. It stinks, but so good for skin. So she hides the stink with lavender and water lilies. Voilà. Expensive skin cream. Sheep grease and lavender." Ruga Potts turned away from me to survey the room. She sighed. The guests were seated in little groups, two getting massaged with Soft Touch Moisturizer for Hands and the others around samples of the cosmetics.

"Would you like to try our new rouge?"

She stared. "You joke with me?"

"Is everybody from Warsaw as rude as you?"

"My manners deserted me sometime in the spring of 1939. I keep watch for them but they have not returned. Why do you care? You do not seem like a woman who worries too much about manners. You call me rude to my face."

"Because you're rude."

She shrugged. "Better than stupid. Or dull."

"Why aren't you working as a chemist if you're a chemist?"

"I am a refugee with a Polish accent that sounds, to ignorant people, German. A bad accent for these times. I am a woman. What combination could be worse here? No engineer's license and here one must have a license. They ask me always how fast I type. Also, at the moment, I am tired."

"But you hate the job at General Electric?"

She nodded. "Boredom is so exhausting. I am tired now all the time."

"I'll bet you could double your salary selling these cosmetics. You're glamorous. You know how to use them."

"Don't be foolish. I am rude. These women are stupid. The ones who are not stupid I would tell to go buy Madame Rubinstein's cosmetics, or better yet, I would tell them how to go home to their kitchens and make their own creams and not to waste their money on yours." Ruga Potts leaned over a sales kit and pulled out a moisturizer, took a dab from the jar, and applied it to the back of her hand. "A moisturizer is mostly water. Then mineral oil. A bit of citric acid to lighten skin perhaps and hide lanolin smell. Little bit white paraffin and acetanilide to soften." She shrugged. "Unremarkable. Women who pay so much for this kind of thing are fools."

"You look like you use moisturizer, though. In fact, you look like you use lots of cosmetics. Does that make you a fool?"

"Do I look like a fool?"

"No. So tell me, Ruga Potts, whose makeup are you using?"

"My own and my mother's formulas. Sometimes a little something from Arden. Arden hires good chemists. This"—and here she held up a jar of Be Your Best demonstration moisturizer—"I make for maybe seven of your pennies. I do not waste what little money I have on pretty jars." She shook my hand. "Here," she said, digging into her purse and producing a bottle and a small tin container. She handed it to me. "A gift. This is my mother's toner and her moisture cream. Use it. Then you see." She stood, told Mrs. Brightman that she could easily walk home, and she left the party.

That night we made $29.85.

I went home and described Ruga Potts to Lilly, who was less interested in her history than in the toner and moisturizer she'd given me. After four weeks with it, Lilly declared the concoctions revolutionary. Even at two weeks, she'd said in amazement, there were actual visible changes, something that few honest cosmetics producers actually expected. "We need to buy the toner and moisturizer formulas from this Ruga woman," Lilly said, "or we can do it the same way everybody else in the business does it and steal it. We just need a smart chemist."

"Is that the way they do it?"

Lilly snorted. "How can you be so smart and so clueless? I think this Ruga Potts, whoever she is, might be just what we need. Let's get her on board."

Lilly was buoyant heading out the door to Mrs. Brightman's rooming house, where she fully expected to find a malleable and grateful Ruga Potts. An hour later she was back, angry, empty-handed.

"She called me shiny and vapid, can you believe it? What's 'vapid'? She said she wanted to talk to the rude one."

"The what?" I asked.

"She meant you, of course."

"I'm not rude," I insisted.

"I know that, sweetie. People misunderstand."

I dragged my feet on the Ruga Potts thing, not sure at all that I wanted or needed her. Then we got a call from a salesgirl who reported that one of her customers had returned a tube of "After Dark" lipstick and demanded her money back. "Rancid!" the salesgirl cried.

Just what Ruga Potts said would happen.

We pulled every tube of that lipstick from the kits we had pre-made in the office and I called in any tubes that the salesgirls had left. Then I went to Mrs. Brightman's rooming house after dinner and asked her if she would please tell Ruga Potts that I hoped to have a word with her.

"Does she owe you money?" Mrs. Brightman demanded. "She owes me money."

"No, Mrs. Brightman. In fact, I hope to buy something from her. Tell her that."

Ruga Potts let me wait a good ten minutes before she came down. "Not here." She sniffed, looking around Mrs. Brightman's parlor. "We sit on front steps." Ruga Potts didn't have much conversation to spare and she said nothing more as she led the way to the front steps and sat down. I told her I was interested in buying her mother's moisturizer and toner formulas. She stood up and headed into the rooming house, waving me back down when I scrambled up to follow. When she reappeared she had two shot glasses and a bottle. She filled them, held one out to me. I hesitated. "You're here to do business, yes?" I bobbed my head up and down. "Neave. You are Neave?" I nodded again. "Neave, if you want to do business with me you should accept my vodka." I held out my glass. She poured shots for both of us. "You should ask me to make cosmetics for you. That would make more sense. Be smarter."

"Why? It's cheaper to buy a formula from you and take it to a manufacturer than hire you."

"Your manufacturer has already produced one rancid product. Give him another formula and he will cut corners and make you another rancid product. You need a chemist to oversee the process."

"We don't have a chemist."

"I am a chemist. I can do some good for your other products as well, not just my toner and moisturizer which you would like to steal. You may find a bad chemist who understands nothing about the product, and who will make you bad moisturizers. Your lipsticks, they also need someone to correct. It would be helpful to you, I think, to have a knowledgeable person overseeing your manufacturer's work. Correct?"

"Doesn't matter even if it is correct. We can't afford that. Even my sister and I aren't on a payroll. Not yet."

"If you want my formulas, maybe you have to hire me. I can cost very little."

"You can't stand that job at General Electric, can you?"

"I cannot."

"So you would cost very little?"

"At first."

"Do you have to get permission from your family to sell them to us, seeing as these are family formulas?"

"I have no family. The formulas are mine to sell or not. To make or not." She set the glass and bottle down beside her on the step. "All those years of study at university and what I have that the Americans want is what my grandmother cooked on her stove. So strange."

"I have to talk to my sister."

"Tell your sister that I will maybe accept a monthly retainer for at least one year. And we talk about a raise after three months." I knew that she was looking at Be Your Best as an escape hatch, a way out of the dingy rooming house and the stool where she perched at General Electric and colored in fighter plane engine designs.

"I think we need her if we're going to go to the next step, Lilly," I said.

"Well then. Go tell the witch she's on retainer and we want that moisturizer now. Also the toner, and after that we need to get the lipstick right. We're already on the roller coaster. Let's let the ride go on."

Lilly threaded an arm though mine and bumped my hip with hers. I went back to Ruga Potts's boardinghouse and we sat down side by side on the porch steps again. She accepted the piddly retainer figure on the condition that I promised to renew every month for at least a year and we would talk about a raise after three months. "Also," she insisted, "I want at least one of the lipsticks to be packaged in little glass jars. My grandmother loved little glass jars."

I held out my hand. Ruga Potts shook it. That was how Be Your Best Cosmetics got scientific.

NEAVE

What Technicolor Did for Us

Over the course of that year we whiplashed between being sure we'd be tycoons and sure we'd be bankrupt. Ruga Potts had to go for two months without her full retainer fee but she stayed with us in order to escape the alternative, which was a drawing board at General Electric. Then a miracle happened, and it seemed to unleash a whole little stream of happy things.

The miracle was Technicolor. Movie actresses started to appear on magazine covers in aquamarine eye shadow, rose-tinted cheeks, ivory skin, Chinese red lips, and a black slash of eyebrow. For a while Veronica Lake's face was everywhere, creamy and pink, more blond than possible, more like a tropical bird than a human. Images like this unleashed a river of imitators who had no idea, really, how to get that flip at the end of the eyeliner. Back in 1937 everybody looked at cartoon Snow White's Technicolor face and held their judgment. That was a children's movie idea of prettiness on a cartoon princess. Also there was the feeling, persisting still in some circles, that only actresses and prostitutes put that much color on their faces. But the door had opened. In the war years the first starlets began being photographed with the exact same blue eyelids and rouged cheeks as Snow White, and the game slowly changed. Women flocked to department store cosmetics counters, the older ones uncertain and the younger ones delighted, everybody looking for the New Look and that look still so new that a whole lot of women were walking around with faces that looked like children's crayon drawings of women rather than women with their natural charms accented. Well, Lilly said—we can help them with that.

Lilly showed the salesgirls how to teach women to put a matte start on the lips, then the lipstick itself, then fixer powder, and a final color in pencil or angled tiny specialty brush: five products, each one presented as a necessary component of a coordinated regimen that had been formulated by Ruga Potts, who was proving to understand sales as well as ceresin. We had each and every one in stock. Lilly taught the sales force how to apply false eyelashes and put a foundation fixer on the face that was lighter than the natural skin before contouring with other brushes, deeper shades. Technicolor seemed to give everybody a sense of confident freedom with color. They wanted more and more of it. Gone was the norm of a single eye shadow lasting five years. Gone was the single tube of lipstick. We were in the money.

The biggest sellers were lipsticks and nail polishes. Our packaging was beautiful—perfect little robin's-egg-blue boxes bound up in blue cloth ribbon. Our bags were high-gloss blue, visible from a block away and very, very pretty. I painted every room in the warehouse offices the same pale blue. I bought two more desks and moveable walls to divide the workspace. We advertised for an assistant.

We'd built up a head of steam and I was determined to use it. These kinds of moments didn't last forever. They were windows of opportunity and we were supposed to fling ourselves through them before they closed.

That fall Lilly decided that what I'd been wearing at salesgirl training events wasn't up to our ever-improving company standards. Nothing that a shopping trip with her couldn't correct, she said. She marched me through Jordan Marsh and then into Filene's, then onward into smaller shops below Chinatown that carried warehouse-direct sales, me reluctant and she hunting methodically. Then she found it, an aquamarine sheath with a tropical-flower design so detailed that the blossoms seemed to have been photographed onto the fabric. She pushed me into a changing room. It slipped on effortlessly, yet I could feel where it clung to my breasts and rear. When I stepped out to inspect myself in the mirror, the thing made me feel like there were bubbles in my chest. Lilly inspected me.

"Fabulous! Good lord, girl, you should see it from the rear! It fits like . . . what was her name? You know, that girl who I always said was the best-dressed thing in the senior class? Sexy girl. She bought all those cosmetics from me back when I was at the spa? Who was she?"

"Jenna Louise Bowles."

"Right. This dress makes me think of her, and she was the master at the head-turning effect. That dress, trust me, will turn a head or two."

Apparently my sister did not remember Jenna Louise's fate, only her fashion sense. I felt my throat tighten around the image I saw in the mirror—someone who was me and not me, a piratical young woman in a Marais dress.

I bought it.

The next morning I told Lilly I wanted to test some new lipstick names. "Let's switch out Night in Paris to something more like Wild Paris Night."

Lilly shrugged. Why not?

Wild Paris Night outsold Night in Paris. By a lot. So I tried Silly Girl, Beautiful Fool, and Tomboy, and those did better than Camellia Lady. Most of the Tomboy buyers were high school girls, giggling fifteen-year-olds sneaking makeup into the school bathrooms to put on before homeroom. We priced it low and we manufactured it with less glycerin than the lipsticks we sold to their mothers. Nothing a fifteen-year-old girl loves has to last longer than a few weeks, and it had to be cheap enough to buy with babysitting money. We could do that.

I kept going, pulled along by the feeling I'd had when I looked in the mirror that afternoon and thought of the Marais dress. I wanted to come up with something windblown and a little scary, something that sounded like the way Jenna Louise's rear end had looked as she swung down the high school hallway in a snug cocoon of skirt. Something so powerful it could swing a line of heads toward it in its wake. I'd felt those bubbles in my chest. I knew what was what. That quarter we put out Dangerous, Witchcraft, Fast Girl, and then Vixen. Three of our salesladies' teenage daughters showed up one day asking to be trained to sell. All by themselves, they quadrupled our high-school-girl sales in their first month. They held parties in classrooms after school or, if the school booted them out, they'd meet in somebody's bedroom on a Saturday afternoon and make each other up. This crowd wanted Vixen and Fast Girl, not their mother's Blush Rose. We launched Tough Broad Red, Vamp.

Sales on what Lilly and I called our "Hussy" lipsticks were twice what we used to get for the old Pink Dawn stuff. We started noticing Vixen on older women.

"We're on fire!" Lilly said to me. "Let's put out something called Tramp and see what happens."

Tramp didn't work, but for some reason Trampy Lady flew out of the kit bags and into every high school locker in town.

"How about Unstoppable!" suggested Lilly. "Outlaw. Catch Me If You Can. I like that—the thrill of the chase. The bad girl! What do you think?"

I considered. "How about Runaway?"

We sold Runaway and Catch Me If You Can so fast it was hard to keep it in stock.

Just a few short years ago we'd thought a brand was something you put on a cow. Now Be Your Best was moving from a kitchen-table-in-a-warehouse business to a recognizable New England brand because it turned out there were lots of girls who wanted to be seen as Fast Girls even if they didn't want to actually be one. We started to be known as what to wear for a riskily sexy look. Mom and Daddy noticed the shift in our fortunes. One afternoon a neighbor stopped our mother in the hardware store and asked her if her daughters didn't sell that lipstick called Prostitute? Or maybe White Trash? I can't recall. Even hours later she was so mad that her lips were like little pencil lines and spit came out the sides of her mouth when she said the *p*.

We assured Mom our balance sheets would prove that the trashy-young-woman market was a chunk of the business but not most of it. We promised her that we did not sell a product named Prostitute or White Trash. We were not the trashy-girl cosmetics company, we told her. In fact, several ladies in her church group had recently agreed to give parties. We were in their living room at the time, asked to come over, supposedly, for tea on Sunday afternoon. Jane and Snyder sat woodenly on the couch. Nobody but Lilly looked relaxed.

Daddy's face was a white blank while Mom told us that she didn't care what the other church ladies did, it was cheap, and though she didn't like to bring it up, it was the kind of thing that would put a man off. Not the playboy men—the serious marrying men. Daddy nodded.

"We're making money, Mom. I think that makes us attractive." Lilly smiled.

"Attractive to weak men. Parasite men," my mother went on. Daddy nodded again. "Men who want to use a woman instead of take care of her. I worry that you girls are looking . . . hard."

"Trashy," Daddy added in a flat, dead tone.

"Daddy!" Jane broke in. "That's ridiculous, and you know you don't mean it." She crossed her arms, crossed her legs, and addressed us firmly. "Don't talk to each other like that." Out of the whole pack of us, Jane was the only one with enough moral authority to stop the conversation cold.

I was mad for three days. Lilly had forgotten the whole exchange before she closed my parents' door behind us on our way out. Our parents had never hurt her and never would. That was my territory. I was the one lying awake at night wondering about whether what Mom said was truer than I wanted it to be, wondering if my fate was sealed, thinking about Jenna Louise. *Fast girl. Whore. Bitch. Cunt.* Lilly was going to keep putting on her respectful and attentive face, but nothing, nothing my mother said mattered to her. Also, she'd turned down more than a half dozen proposals of marriage over her dating career and she'd been wearing Vixen when the last one happened. So much for men not taking fast girls seriously enough to propose to them.

"They're not actually hussies, the girls who wear this lipstick, Mom," Lilly had said. "They wear the lipstick because they think men want hussies, and the fact is, men do. They pursue them like mad. You can't blame the girls."

"And what do the girls want besides wanting the men to want them?" our mother had demanded. "Do they want a home and a man who respects them? Then they'd better rethink their behavior, because that's not what that kind of woman gets in the end!"

"Actually, getting caught at last can be more fun than being chased." Lilly laughed.

"What are you saying?" The color rose up a bright, angry pink on our mother's face. "What do you mean by that?"

"Oh, Mom, come on. It's harmless fun. A little lipstick, a great dress, and guys chase that rippling skirt right into a beautiful restaurant, where they tell you how stunning you are looking this evening."

"This is very serious, Lilly. It is not a game. Things happen to girls."

Lilly rolled her eyes in my direction and I knew she was thinking but not saying that *of course* things happened to girls; that was the point: to elude, to entice, and finally, to be captured. And then have something happen to you.

My mother's idea of proper courtship was a measured, chess game–ish affair. The breathless, twisting pursuit had no charms for her because she didn't see the chase leading to a candlelit room, pleasant flattery, or a cinematic seduction. Her idea of a chase leaned more toward the baying hounds, the pinned animal finally on the ground, its body gripped in the teeth of the captor. And who will marry such a girl, she was thinking. Imagining what was in my mother's head put those images firmly into my own. I struggled back to the more pleasing images that were in my sister's mind.

"Some of those dresses I see, and some of that paint on their faces, they deserve what they get," our father said. Which made me really mad.

"We've got to go," Lilly said, pulling me toward the door before I could collect myself enough to speak. "We'll come for dinner on Sunday, Mom. We promise."

I stayed upset, of course, but Lilly whacked me on the rear and said, "It never occurs to Mom or Dad that not all the girls are thinking about a kitchen with linoleum counters. Some of us have other things on our minds." She rolled her eyes. "Momma and her church ladies, forever lost in the garden of primrose boredom. Daddy and his Neanderthal ideas. I mean, so, so dumb."

Plunge ahead, I said to myself. Paddle fast.

THE PIRATE LOVER

Pursuit

Five ships in pursuit of one; five swift ships with a combined force of 2,128 pounds of metal against the *Cat* with her 488. Basil Le Cherche spent an hour at the masthead with one arm coiled around the rigging and the other training his best glass on the approaching ships. He ordered the *Cat*, with her shallow bottom and experienced crew, into a foggy series of sandbanks and islands close to the coast, treacherous to the hulls of the larger pursuers. There he had a lead thrown every hundred yards to mark depths and he set the crew to build a raft designed to hold lanterns spaced at exactly the intervals of the *Cat*'s cabin lights. When night was thick about them he used the starless dark to cloak them as they slid past the last in the sweeping line of Henri Le Cherche's ships. Safely beyond them he ordered the decoy raft dropped over the side. While it was lashed at the *Cat*'s side they unfurled its sail, lit its lanterns, and cut the whole floating deceit loose while they darkened their own lights and headed briskly into deeper waters. The judge's forces saw the raft's carefully placed lanterns and pursued the flimsy little decoy. Before the *Cat* was an hour away they heard the rending cracks of a mast going overboard—one of the pursuers hitting a shallow bank and coming to a halt that cost them masts, as well, hopefully, as her hull. They heard cannon fire and saw the raft's twinkling lights vanish one by one as its attackers' cannon fire reached it.

"We will have enough room and time to vanish for now," Le Cherche said to Electra.

"And in the morning, when they see they have lost us?"

He answered this in a tone that seemed both resigned and faintly amused. "Earlier today I saw my brother aboard the flagship. He leads the chase himself, an entirely invested opponent. He will chase on."

Electra stepped closer to Basil Le Cherche—as close as she dared. His calm, his intelligence, his electric physical presence all drew her into his orbit and held her like a planet holds a moon. Now only a palm's span from him she could feel the heat of his body. The smell of his sweat, the warmth radiating from his chest in the cool night air—these pulled at her in ways she did not choose to question. She sought his eyes, so alert, so keen and cool. What was the other light she saw in those eyes but could not name?

"Mademoiselle, you seem so intent. What is it you see?" he whispered.

His question summoned up its name. "Sadness," she said. He turned away from her abruptly. Drawn to him, powerfully moved, she stepped close enough to feel the moisture of his breath. "I have placed you in danger by coming aboard this ship. I am sorry, Captain."

"I do what I please," he replied, more than allowing her to come so close—in fact, moving just the slightest bit closer to her. "Not what pleases my brother." She saw the vein below his jaw pulse, rapid and hot, and restrained the hand that began a journey toward that face, toward a caress down that cheek. He took a deep breath and stepped away from her. "You should leave me now, mademoiselle." And when she did not leave him he said gently, firmly, "A captain's suggestion on board that captain's quarterdeck is an order, my dear." And so she left him.

The next morning's light showed that, miraculously, Henri Le Cherche had found their trail. Two of his reduced convoy were hull-up on the horizon. "How could he do this? Is the man a warlock? Has he made some pact with the devil?" She stood beside Basil Le Cherche on the quarterdeck, both their eyes trained on their pursuer.

"I believe he has, mademoiselle." Basil smiled. "But the answer is simpler than that. Henri and I learned the sea together, from little boys in our tiny sailboat on the marshes to men captaining our own yachts and ships," Basil said to her. "Perhaps more importantly, our instincts were similar even before we learned side by side. They were woven into an almost inviolable single force in that childhood, and now sometimes it seems we sail with each other's minds. I try to imagine him imagining me. He does the same. Sometimes we cannot escape one another's minds. Or one another." He said this last in a thick tone, his hands clenched.

Judge Henri Le Cherche's flagship approached, three battleships behind him, all headed directly toward the *Cat*, all fast and heavily armed. Outrun, outmanned, outgunned, Basil Le Cherche knew that his best tricks had been deployed and failed. He waited on his brother's approach.

Henri Le Cherche ordered the *Cat*'s white flag raised and named conditions, which were simple: Basil Le Cherche and Electra Gates were to surrender themselves. No one else mattered to the convoy surrounding the *Cat* with its guns trained on her hull. The *Cat*'s sailors massed around their captain to argue their case. They could still fight their way free, they insisted. But Basil Le Cherche drew up to his whole height and made his orders clear: they could fight their way free, perhaps, but it would cost them half the lives on board. They were to do as they were told, take their freedom and use it to stay in hiding in and out of the many harbors along this coast. "This is not over," he told his crew. "Speak to every fishing craft, every soul afloat you meet in the next weeks asking for news of our fate. Have faith in an escape. We will do everything we can to send some message naming a time and place to rendezvous. If in three weeks you hear nothing, you are to sail on without us. Do you understand? If you hear of an escape but have no message from us, search us out—but only as long as you are safe. You will not place the *Cat* and all your lives at stake beyond that." Basil Le Cherche's crew nodded and fell back.

"Do not think that we are lost, Electra Gates. I will move heaven and hell before I let him have you," Basil whispered in an aside to Electra. "I will find a way to make you free. Have faith in me." And strangely, against all the evidence of the crowded ships of an enemy bearing down on them, against all the logic she could bring to bear, Electra did.

NEAVE

Snyder's Universe

Snyder lost the job that Lilly found for him with the fruit-and-vegetable-store owners. He'd done what he always did, scooting out on Fridays to get to the back alleys of New York so he could root through Dumpsters behind comic-book publishers before the garbage trucks got them. He made mistakes whenever he had the chance, undercharging for oranges and overcharging for turnips, mindlessly accepting deliveries of rotten potatoes. Our father did exactly what he'd said he would do and threw Snyder out. He was on our doorstep that night, Janey at his side and a suitcase in his hand. I resisted, of course. Jane told Snyder to go into the kitchen area and make us coffee and off he went, leaving her the room she needed to work on us.

"Use the womanly charms God gave you," Lilly said to her, "and talk Daddy into letting him come back. You can do it."

"I probably could, but Snyder and Daddy are never going to be at peace with each other. It's a terrible thing to say, but Daddy just seems to hate him. Snyder needs to move out."

"That doesn't mean he has to move here," I protested.

"And where else is he going to go?" Janey asked, but it wasn't really a question. "The money he made, what little of it there was, went to fantasy art and books. He can't afford an apartment of his own, or even a room in a rooming house. You have space, and you're starting to make money. You're his sisters, and you know it's the right thing to do."

Janey was not somebody who would stare you down; she'd give you an openhearted meet-my-gentle-gaze kind of thing, which was much, much worse than a stare-down. I looked away from her.

The next day Jane, Snyder, and I drove back and forth a dozen times, staggering up the warehouse stairs with posters (some framed, some in cardboard tubes, some flat), boxes of comics, and fantasy books. Lilly had managed, characteristically, to be too busy to help.

"I'm hiring a carpenter and dropping more walls in this warehouse today," I said to Lilly when she reappeared. "We're going to put him in the back corner by the fire escape, and we're plumbing another bathroom because I have shared my last soap dish with Snyder Terhune."

Construction started the next week. We told him to start looking for another job but I didn't see any sign of effort. He was stuck. And he was living in my space.

"Send him to that drugstore on Weiller Avenue that has the giant comic-book section," our little sister suggested. "Tell him to find the guy who's ordering all those comics. They'll understand each other."

Jane was, as usual, right. Where Lilly had aimed only at getting Snyder employed, Janey was interested in making him happy, which she suspected might finally make him competent. At the drugstore he developed a following of the comic-book people. They adored him. The store owner noticed the heavier foot traffic when Snyder was around but got less enthusiastic when he realized that none of Snyder's fans bought anything but comics. He kept our brother on a part-time schedule at an embarrassingly low hourly wage.

"That's not a real job!" I despaired. "He'll never earn enough to leave."

"Oh, calm down," Lilly said cheerfully. "Who cares about what Snyder does or doesn't do. Look at us! We have outrun, out-tricked or outsold every trouble! We've got the Technicolor look nailed down fast and hard. Good lord, we have two bathrooms!"

And so we did. The next thing I was going to do was get a decent stove to replace that piece of junk that had burned my last cake into a doorstop. Then shelving and something that could work as a butler's pantry. Then a counter surface big enough for rolling out dough. Time passed. Snyder made little or no effort to move out.

Then one afternoon I walked upstairs from the "office" space to our loft living space, and found my older brother with my copy of *The Pirate Lover* propped in front of him at the kitchen able, eating a bowl of cereal at four in the afternoon.

"That book was by my bed. In my room," I said grimly. "Which is not your room."

He ignored me. I pulled the book out of his hands.

"Don't touch my stuff. Stay out of my room."

"'*Don't touch my stuff*,'" he mocked. "What are you, ten years old?"

Someplace deep inside me the answer was yes, of course I was, *and you stay out of my room!* Snyder's superpower was that he could drop me through a rabbit hole right back to third grade.

He pointed to *The Pirate Lover*. "You used to keep this book at the back of the closet, right? When we were kids."

"What were you doing in the closet?"

"It wasn't your personal closet. We all knew you had stuff hidden back there. Big deal. I mean, I know you went into my room and got into my comics. You did, right?"

This was true. I had.

"You know, this story's not so great. Nothing important happens except the sea fights. And ending with a wedding? Lame."

The book in front of him was lying open where he'd stopped. "How do you know the ending? You're not even halfway through."

He shrugged vaguely. "I've read it a couple times."

"Really? How many times?"

"A few." He shifted uneasily.

It felt so strange, imagining Snyder stepping quietly into my room, sifting through the books on the nightstand or the floor, plucking this one up.

"I think it's weird," he said, "how you keep reading this thing over and over."

"It's not half as weird as *you* reading it over and over. Why do you do that? Is it the pirate stuff and the guns?"

"It's . . ."—his feet shuffled under the table and he tugged at a hank of his own hair—"the deciding who's in charge stuff. It's the contest."

"What contest?"

"Between the pirate guy and the electric girl. Whatsername. Electra. The contest about who's the most powerful."

"What are you talking about?" Electra and Basil had each seemed to me to be engaged in the same struggle—the challenge of abandoning control; the challenge of opening themselves with complete trust to the other. My brother had turned the same pages that I had, but read an entirely different story.

"He's terrific but the girl's really limp. What makes her special? What's her superpower? Getting the right dress for a ball?" He snorted.

"I wish you could hear how stupid you sound right now. Stop jiggling your foot."

"It's not jiggling. And what if I feel like jiggling? What could you do about it?"

"I could throw you out of the apartment."

"Jane won't let you. Lilly won't help you. And you can't do it alone."

This was true. It would be useless now to break his nose or throw his books and clothes out the window and into the parking lot. Jane and Lilly would be very unhappy with me, and I would hate that. They'd lug his stuff right back up the stairs.

It was so clear. My idea of the universe and my brother's idea of the universe were at war. In his universe, control meant everything and the players used whatever power they had to achieve it. In my universe, relinquishing control was the goal. Love was the prize.

Calm down, I heard myself saying to myself. *Snyder Terhune is a dummy and you shouldn't waste any time trying to make him less of a dummy.* Something in the way I looked at him then caught him up sharply. He closed the book.

"I was going to put it back before you came upstairs but you were early," he said. "You wouldn't even have known." It was clear that this didn't soften me any. "I'll stay out of your room from now on," he added. "Really." He set book down and retreated to his corner of the apartment.

Time went by. Then the drugstore owner sold out and moved to Florida, and the new owner announced that he was gutting the building and opening a restaurant. Snyder's little trickle of part-time work ended, and he was once again entirely unemployed, a man with nothing in the world to do except wander around our warehouse and rifle though our personal things, a man who contributed not so much as one box of Wheaties to the group larder.

If Snyder wouldn't take care of his own destiny, we would have to do it for him. I called a meeting: me, Jane, Lilly. "We have to get Snyder a life," I said, "because he has to get out of this apartment."

"He can't go back home," Jane insisted.

And he couldn't, not as long as Daddy was Daddy. Snyder was diffident and retiring, a 4F boy who thought comic books were important. He made our father nuts.

I hadn't made this warehouse into my home just so some of the things I'd come here to avoid could follow me, and that included both Daddy's temper and Snyder's dumbness. "Snyder's got to figure out how to make money, and the only thing he's good at is knowing which comic books and fantasy junk all the other comic-book boys want. So," I finished, "that's what he'll do."

By this, I explained over the rest of that meeting, I meant that Snyder would buy and sell comic books and sci-fi/fantasy art. Jane had a friend who had an uncle who had a gallery on Newbury Street. She was given the job of prevailing upon him to let Snyder have a show. I could make him give me the list of all his old corner-store customers who'd come for his comic-book advice. Lilly could throw the party for the opening night. We put Jane in a blue dress of Lilly's that had an interesting neckline and sent her off to see the gallery owner.

She succeeded. After a two-hour lunch the man agreed to offer us his only unbooked week in mid-September in exchange for 50 percent of sales. Now all we had to do was get Snyder to cooperate. Again, we knew that Jane was our most effective negotiator. She resorted to her toughest strategy with Snyder: she cried. He gave in. In a rush of confidence she went back and renegotiated the gallery owner down to 40 percent. We took Janey out for her first beer. "Good girl," Lilly said, tipping her mug against Jane's. "You're on the road to womanhood."

LILLY

We Launch Snyder's Career

After Janey worked her magic on the gallery owner and Snyder, we got down to work. Neave rustled up a mailing list that included all the customers from the old drugstore that Snyder could name, all the old *Monsters in the Movies* members, and a list she bought from a mail-order house that sold back issues of *Batman* and *Tales from the Crypt*. Then I did what I did best: the gallery opening-night party.

I got a little resistance over the Manhattan fountain rental. Jane said it would be vulgar and I said, "It's alien invasions, for chrissakes. We're gonna have a wall full of blow-up breasts and ray guns and we should worry about vulgar?" Neave sided with me. We got the biggest fountain they rented. All the salesgirls from the Lynn office came, as directed, with dates. They were told not to bring the men of their dreams but the men who dreamed about them—specifically, the ones who didn't have much hope of actual success with them. The gallery was packed. Jane forgave me for the Manhattan fountain when she saw its supernatural powers. People with no previous relationship with the Princess of Mars were handing over wads of money for the poster-sized book cover art that featured her, with and without ray blasters or much in the way of clothes.

I saw all this like I was in the center of the room in the middle of the moment, even though I was really here with Boppit, Where I Am Now. I was dead, and I knew in the logical part of my mind that all this was in the past, but here I was watching the former Monsters club members refill their cocktail glasses.

"You made this happen?" I asked him. "You got me here?"

"Oh, no," Boppit said. "You took us here. I'm just in your tail wind."

It was truly, impossibly, the Snyder Terhune Fantasy Art collection's first sale. I was standing next to a man wearing what looked like his father's bunchy pants. He turned away from the enormous seven-eyed thing on the wall he'd been examining and walked right through me to get to the next picture. "Oh my God," I gasped.

"You'll get used to it," Boppit said. "Or maybe not."

I was the invisible Dead Lilly me, and I was also the Lilly who had gone to that party in a pale-green silk, clinked my glass against the ice in the Manhattan fountain, and laughed at our success. Back then it all looked cheerful and bright, the big posters full of muscular half-naked heroes wearing red capes and blue stars, the outsized monsters and energetic space travelers protecting or attacking pneumatic heroines. But now . . . so many sharp blades! So much blood and so many breasts! It was a weird parade of chains and nipples and explosions.

"Why didn't I see it then, Boppit?"

He knew what I meant. "You were a girl. This is the world that little boys live in. Some little boys, anyway."

When I was here in life, this party was nothing but a good time, a reason to be proud of ourselves. It made me laugh then. Now I feel a clammy something.

"It's the Ricky thing that makes it clammy-feeling," Boppit said. "You hadn't met Ricky yet. But now you've experienced him. Your perspective is changed."

It was. I had experienced Ricky, and Ricky had enjoyed what he'd done to me. I'd felt it even as it was happening, but I could only say I knew it as the truth from Where I Am Now. And I could feel it in the guys staring at the fantasy art now. More than half of Snyder's choices for the show were covers from the war years: knobby-kneed Japanese soldiers with filed black teeth, snarling as they bent helpless American women over tanks or trucks and jabbed their rifles at them; Nazis shackling American women with chains; Superman ripping the deck off an enemy cruiser to free American WACs. Back then I'd laughed at the stuff on the gallery walls.

"It's okay," Boppit said to me. He offered his hand and I took it. People flowed all around us, pointing at particular pictures and getting more and more excited as the Manhattans and the images on the walls worked on them.

"I want to be back the way I was," I said. "Everything just light and funny. Not clammy."

"It's a loss." Boppit nodded.

"Oh, look, Boppit, it's Ruga Potts. Ruga!"

"She can't see you, Lilly. Not the dead you."

"I know. Good lord, I didn't see what these pictures looked like then. I wasn't paying attention."

"One of your strengths when it isn't one of your weaknesses. Look over to your left: Neave steering that six-year-old away from the picture of the just-about naked woman wrestling the just-about naked man?"

"What the hell is she hitting him with? And what's that thing behind them?"

"A space pod. And she's not hitting him; she's paralyzing him, and then she's going to roboticize him."

"How do you know that?"

"I'm familiar with the issue."

You know, Charles is better looking than I thought he was when I was alive. That night I'd found him standing in front of a Frank Frazetta illustration of the woman with snakes wrapped around her and an enormous, muscular rope of a creature swinging its fanged head toward her. The woman and her snakes were arranged to draw the eye to her cantaloupe-sized breasts and rounded rear. I thought she looked great, standing there facing the monster with real moxy.

"Charles Helbrun III bought that print," Boppit said. "His advisers told him to buy Frazetta because they expected it to get more valuable. Helbrun had no feel for that image at all. He only thought of it as an investment."

"If Helbrun didn't care about the art, why is he here?"

"To meet Neave. He'd read an interview with her in the business pages, and all of a sudden he was seeing the little blue Be Your Best bags everywhere. He was curious. He was impressed. Look," Boppit said to me, pointing across the room. "There's Helbrun writing the check for that print. Now he's asking her for her phone number."

I turned and followed the direction of his stare. "Yes," I said. "It's clearer from here. Is everything I thought I saw back then wrong?"

"Of course not," Bop said. "What you saw from where you stood then was true, just like what you see now is true. It's all true."

"Helbrun had a good walk. People turned their heads to watch him go by. Nothing's as attractive as a beautiful man who couldn't care less about looks. He cared about business, and winning, and getting what he wanted. You know I love Neavie to death, but I was surprised that a guy like Charles Helbrun was interested in her."

"You shouldn't have been. He saw her as the businessman's perfect partner."

"Well, just goes to show you how little I saw back then. That event was the jumping-off place for Snyder. All those years we thought he was incompetent, but really he just wasn't doing what he was supposed to be doing."

Boppit said, "That huge studio that Neave found him after the show gave him storage room, a place to mount art, his own telephone line . . ."

"The answer to the Snyder problem was right there all along but we didn't see it."

"You weren't really looking at him, Lilly."

"Maybe. We were careless about lots of stuff, weren't we?"

"You were careless. Neave wasn't. Jane wasn't."

"It was great, being alive. I mean, look at me in that aqua number! I looked fabulous. But I was stupid."

"That's why I'm here, doll."

"Really?"

"Well, partly," Boppit said.

So we were able to take our considerable proceeds and help move our brother into a studio with enough square footage to store his prints and books, a workstation where he could mount posters and cut glass, and most important of all, a telephone so he could stay in touch with the first wave of customers he'd found at the gallery opening.

He was launched.

NEAVE

My Romance

It took forever for Charles Helbrun III to move from asking for my telephone number to asking for anything that could be called a date, but eventually it did happen. He had stayed in touch after Snyder's gallery opening. Typically he had a practical reason for the call. He wanted to ask advice about hostess gifts for the wives at a client conference; a friend in a different business had asked him a question about packaging and he thought I might have valuable insights to pass along. Then, finally, at last, I returned from lunch to find two dozen roses and a card asking me to dinner. To thank me for all my help, the card said.

"Is this a date?" I asked my sister.

"Of course it's a date. I think it's a date. I mean, does the man ask an accountant who he hires for occasional advice out for dinner and send him roses? No. He sends him a check. It's a date."

I called his office and his secretary said she'd be happy to take him a message. I said tell him yes. She called back to ask if Saturday at eight was acceptable. I said yes. He arrived in a six-year-old solid black Ford, which surprised me since I knew what he'd spent on that print he'd bought at Snyder's gallery and it was an astonishing figure. He didn't expect the downstairs door to Be Your Best to be the first-floor entrance to my home, and he stood there knocking for a full five or six minutes until I heard him and ran down the stairs.

"This is the right address, isn't it?" he asked. He was carrying another two-dozen roses and held them toward me when I swung the door open. "I didn't realize you lived directly above the business."

You wouldn't expect that a few flowers bought by a man with enough money to buy the store where he found them would flatter me, but they did. I was new to flowers. "This is where we lived when we started out," I explained, leading him into the warehouse's living area. "We've put in a kitchen. Bathrooms. Sectioned off a couple bedrooms. I kept adding things instead of leaving."

"'We'? I thought your sister was married."

"Just recently married. Lilly and I were here together at first."

He followed me silently. This wasn't someone who felt awkward with conversational lapses. Generally I wasn't bothered by them either, and it was surprisingly easy to watch him look around. "Lots of light. Who decorated it?"

Decorated? "Me," I said. "I guess."

"Rather bohemian." He walked through the front sitting area and into the wider spaces of the kitchen. "You didn't strike me as a nesting kind of woman."

"I'm not in this particular nest a lot. I work long hours."

"I'm the same. If you want to get things done, it's what you do."

"What's your house like?"

"People describe it as formal. I hired an interior designer. I need the house to be presentable for business entertaining. It has to look purposeful. Tasteful."

"Controlled?" I suggested. He nodded. "How much entertaining do you do?"

"I host a Christmas party. Two or three dinners a year for specific client cultivation."

"You had your house professionally laid out for one party and a couple dinners a year?"

"Entertaining is not what I love best about my job, but it's necessary. It builds trust among the people I do business with, and at my own dining-room table I can control who's sitting next to whom. It's easier to manage a lot of variables."

"You sound like your dinners need a stage director more than a good cook."

"You of all people should know that some things in business are theatre. I've read about your conferences."

"Lilly does the theatre in our business. Not me."

"Well. Theatre." His head made a dismissive little twist and dip. "Not the real point of any business that matters, really."

"Don't underestimate theatre, Mr. Helbrun. The stuff Lilly pulls off is the beating heart of our business." I started to pull on a coat and he took it gently from my hands, stepped behind me, and eased me expertly into it.

"Charles. Please. You look very lovely tonight, Miss Terhune."

"Neave. Please."

"Neave and Charles it is, then." He smiled and dipped into a tiny and very endearing bow. I bowed back. The tone of the evening softened.

Even though my early training for Be Your Best parties had given me some competence with makeup, I'd still let Lilly give advice on wardrobe. She'd been disgusted that I hadn't asked him where we were going. "The ladies' room at Locke Ober needs an entirely different look than the benches at Durgin Park. I don't think this is a clam-shack kind of guy, but he could surprise you and nobody wants to walk into a high-heel kind of place wearing flats." She'd compromised and put me in a pair of pleated wool slacks with a white broadcloth silk blouse and low heels. She'd stuck diamonds in my ears. "There you go—very Marlene Dietrich."

"Not Rosie the Riveter?"

"Absolutely not. The diamonds make the tailored slacks look tongue-in-cheek: smart. The blouse is expensive and, more important, it looks expensive. A classy combination. Put those pearls down. Too conservative."

"But the outfit's conservative," I pointed out. "Diamonds jump out at you."

"Exactly. That's what they're supposed to do. You've got to get the knack of being two contradictory things at once and selling both, honey. Makes people look twice. Wear this necklace of mine. Small stone, but it's a good one. He'll know the difference. There you go. That's an outfit that can straddle different worlds." She sighed. "Better on a first date to under-dress than overdress. Keeps you from looking eager."

"You mean I'm trying to sidestep stupid or trampy."

"That's what I was trying to say. And you're borrowing my fox coat. You'll walk outta here looking sexy and when you whip it off in the restaurant: the most confident outfit in the room. You'll see."

It turned out he was more a men's club than a clam shack kind of first-date man—a white tablecloth, heavy cutlery, and cut crystal kind of room that specialized in steak. I was in a sea of black dresses that threw my pearl-gray slacks and ivory blouse into sharp relief. But I could feel Charles Helbrun III's satisfaction in the contrast when he slipped off my coat to hand to the maître d'. He made a point of stopping to introduce me to several tables on the way to our seats. Lilly's judgment had been dead-on accurate: he was perfectly pleased with the unfrilly look of me. He ordered our drinks with only a quick glance at me for contradiction. And when I didn't contradict, he went on to order for us during the rest of the evening. Instead of feeling irritated, I felt flattered. I felt taken care of. I was in his world, and I was happy to sit back and watch while he navigated it gracefully. I settled back in my seat and looked around. It had begun to rain and the city streets reflected the lights from passing cars as if they were skimming along on black mirrors. From where I sat the outside world seemed far away, and we were in a fire-lit room full of tinkling crystal and glittering silver.

"This is lovely," I said, and I meant it, entirely.

"Tell me about your company. Please. I'm really interested."

He was. Unlike most listeners, Charles Helbrun didn't fidget or interrupt with observations and leading questions. He was patient. I told him about Lilly's early days at the corner spa and her faithful following. I told him about the first salesgirl conference—a half dozen young women eating pie in a warehouse on folding tables and chairs we snagged from our mother's church by forging her name. But I left out what had distinguished us from competitors and doubled our sales: the "bad girl" lines—the Vixen lipsticks and Fast Girl eyeliners.

The effect of concentrated interest is very powerful. I forgot myself, talked on and on to this handsome man in the expensive suit who gave me his complete attention. When the evening ended he walked me to my door and held out his hand. I took it. No kiss. And I realized when I closed the door behind me that I'd been thinking hopefully about that kiss for the last half of the evening.

"So how was it?" Lilly hadn't waited for the next day—the telephone had rung about ten minutes after I got in.

"What do you have? Date radar? How did you know I'd be back yet?"

"Just guessed. I figured a nice place, slow service, eight o'clock reservation, fairly reserved good-night scene . . ."

I told her where we'd gone, and she declared the restaurant choice a victory for me. "You can tell how serious a man is by where he takes you on the first date. If he's pretty sure he's going to want to see more of you, he tries to impress you."

"Wouldn't that just depend on how much money the man has or whether or not he thinks you'd like a clam shack?"

"Could. Usually doesn't. So how was the kiss?"

"No kiss."

"Really?" She considered. "So he's taking things very slow. Being a gentleman. That could also be a good sign. Or a bad sign. Sweetie pie, you just may have gotten yourself a serious boyfriend."

And so it seemed, for that was the beginning of Charles Helbrun III and me. He'd call on Wednesdays and ask for Friday or Saturday—the serious nights. Before Charles, I thought of wine as the drink that came in two colors. After Charles, I entered a whole new universe, a place where I put clothes out on a bed and thought about their effect on a man whom I very much wanted to interest. My whole center of gravity leaned over and tipped onto a nipped-waist skirt with fifteen yards of fabric in it. It was new, and heady.

"You got it, girl." Lilly nodded when I tried on the new skirt for her to inspect. "That's the spirit."

"He says these disparaging things about women he thinks fuss about their looks," I told my sister.

"Yeah, well, that just means he's lying, or he's not paying attention. All women fuss with their looks. The smart ones just look like they didn't fuss. Men like to think they pick and choose what they notice, but that's hooey. We do the picking and choosing. Don't listen to him. Listen to me." It was true that seeing myself in the mirror in heels, snug waists, and costume jewelry was startling, but startling in an exhilarating way.

And I could feel Charles reacting to the heels, the Shalimar, the tinkling accessories, no matter his stated distaste for "fussiness." The first time I swung the door open to greet him after Lilly and I had put me together for a purposefully provocative effect, I could feel the immediate spike in interest as well as a little surprise. I think I actually stood back a bit and tilted my head, ready to be admired. I was in the hands of something I could only call desire, though at the time I didn't know that I wanted to be desired more than I desired the man himself.

"That's a beautiful woman," I said to him one day as we waited in a movie line. I was watching a tall, composed brunette across the street slip her arm around a man and pull him closer until he declined his head. She kissed him—a serious kiss.

"She's well dressed, elegant. But she's vulgar." He shrugged. "The woman's on a public sidewalk! Forward women think they're attracting men because of how bold they are."

"Well . . . they do attract men."

"Men who use women. The wrong men."

The kiss at the end of that evening, like the few kisses that had preceded it, was brief and direct. I brought the question of kissing to my sister.

"You've got to be kidding." She was sincerely amazed. "He's never so much as gotten his hand on your ass? Do you think he has an idea of gentlemanly behavior that says you should make the first move?"

No. I didn't think so.

"Are you sending some kind of 'Go slow' signal?"

I didn't know. Had I? I entered every evening with Charles in a slow burn of anticipation for . . . something. But what? When I tried to imagine the something I wanted, it was tangled up in the idea of a kiss but it wasn't exactly a kiss. I wasn't a child, but my knowledge of adult sexual love came from places like Electra Gates's life rather than my own. I didn't have any of my own. Somewhere deep in reflected imaginary thirdhand experience, Electra was ripping her skirt away so she could force herself through the narrow break in the wall that separated her from Basil Le Cherche. Such ferocity! And then the two lovers left silenced and stilled. I had never been silenced and stilled; nevertheless, I believed in it. All of it.

I set *The Pirate Lover* aside and picked up my battered Walt Whitman, scanning the strange words about leaves of grass for the hundredth time. *If I worship one thing more than another it shall be the spread of my own body, or any part of it. Translucent mould of me it shall be you! Shaded ledges and rests it shall be you! . . . You my rich blood! Your milky stream pale strippings of my life! Breast that presses against other breasts it shall be you! My brain it shall be your occult convolutions!*

The first time I met these words, they summoned up the dress from the Marais. Now I spread a beautiful skirt out and considered its effect myself, but there was still a mystery here that Electra Gates had figured out, and I hadn't. I felt fairly sure that whatever I felt about Charles, it wasn't the feeling that Electra knew.

That Saturday, Charles invited me to a party at his firm that he described as a key business event. Lilly approved. "It means he's really confident about you. Ready to have you looked over by his most important audience."

I was pleased and then surprised that I'd felt a little spark of relief when he'd invited me. Why wouldn't I be able to be looked over? I was the co-owner of a successful business, an independent and, with some help from Lilly, a very well-dressed woman. So what if I was also a boiler-room worker's kid from Lynn whose claim to fame before lipstick was M&M's pie? I wasn't hard to look at. A big law firm party was not over my head. But still, there was that spark of relief to be admitted into the deeper recesses of Charles Helbrun III's world.

I dressed myself and just checked in with Lilly to see what she thought. She changed the shoes, the purse, the skirt; she kept the hat and gloves; she added a necklace. "Now you're fine," she said. "Go forth."

On this date the care I'd taken didn't seem to have any effect on Charles, who was focusing on cultivating two possible new clients. He'd given me a quick glance at the door and only said, "This won't be something you'll need the hat and gloves for." I left them behind. There were only four other women at the party, and they were, as he'd somehow known they would be, hatless and gloveless. I asked him who they were. Two were wives, he said; two were models, hired to make the event more glamorous. He excused himself, said he was sure I'd do fine, and strode purposefully to the other side of the room, where a tight circle of men was jabbing the air with the drinks in their hands. As I watched, he inserted himself into the conversation and then, with a deft turn, he cut one of the men out of the herd and drew him to two comfortable chairs in an area apart from the thick of the party.

"Got him," he said with satisfaction when he rejoined me. "That's twenty thousand in billing for next year."

That night we had our first serious, serious kiss. It left me breathless and hollowed out, but not, to my surprise, more enamored with or attached to Charles Helbrun. I closed the door on him that night, both satisfied and not.

LILLY

My First Husband

The dog didn't criticize everybody when he was an actual mongrel, but now that he's a military man, and dead, he spends some time making judgments from the high moral ground. This is an unattractive feature, and it occurs to me that one of the reasons we all like dogs is that they're a totally judgment-free species.

"You used to be nicer," I said to him. "You used to like everybody."

"I was a dog. And I'm nice now. And I'll tell you that even as a dog it bothered me that humans didn't learn from experience. It's very frustrating to watch you people. Alarms should have been going off in all directions."

This is true. I'd married Peter Winthrop in 1950. Neave and I had turned the apartment into something that looked like a home. I was twenty-six and Be Your Best was getting real traction. Twenty-six was an old maid in the world I lived in but I wasn't worried about that. I'd just woken up one morning thinking that marriage was an interesting idea. Peter Winthrop was a dream on paper: an Ivy-educated doctor, a good looker. And unlike a lot of guys who thought that a working wife was an embarrassment—a clear sign that they didn't make enough money to support the family—Peter Winthrop was not going to get in my way in that department. He said he thought money was sexy. If I wanted to make it, he said he'd be happy to spend it. So when he pulled out a diamond one night, I said yes. He wore a tux. I wore a white suit. Neave was my maid of honor. Mommy cried. I moved out of the Be Your Best studio and into a suburban house. Annie was born nine months later.

"First husbands aren't like training wheels that teach you how to steer a husband."

"They should be. How could you have been married to Peter Winthrop and not come out of it knowing that people lie?"

"Look, Boppit, the man was a dream: the way all the nurses at St. Elizabeth's treated him like a god, the Harvard diploma, the great teeth. And what person doesn't lie? Really."

"Neave does not lie. Jane does not lie."

"And that's not always been a very attractive or useful thing for them."

"Neave would never have looked twice at Peter Winthrop."

"That poses no problem. He would never have looked twice at her. But I sure caught his eye."

Boppit sniffed. "You didn't even know him when you married him."

"What wife does? Here's some irony for you—Neave's responsible for me meeting him. I stepped on a nail and she dragged me off to get a tetanus shot. There he was, running St. Elizabeth's emergency room that night, cool as a cucumber. I took one look at him and I felt like a man in a desert who's just spotted a watering hole."

"Or a mirage."

"Maybe. But think how pretty those mirages are."

"A little skepticism when he started working eighty-hour weeks would have come in handy."

"I wasn't going to be one of those pathetic, insecure women who go through their husbands' pockets and call him at work every hour to make sure they're there. Doctors' wives expect them to have long hours. How would I know he was at the track?"

"If you'd looked in those pockets you would have eventually found a stray betting ticket or an IOU from the poker games. You wouldn't have been so surprised when the bank called and told you that you were losing your house because he'd taken out three more mortgages without mentioning them to you."

"Legally, my signature on that first loan might as well have been made by a chicken. Then he made the mistake of saying what he did with our money was none of my business. I said it was so my business but I was going to make it not my business as soon as I could. I was going to divorce him. Annie wasn't even three years old but that was not going to change my mind. If I'd been able to dump him on the grounds of being a liar and a thief I wouldn't have had to invent some proof of infidelity. He cooperated with the girl and the photographer because I threatened to go to his chief of staff to discuss the hours he'd signed in but was really at the track or in the basement at a poker game. He knew I'd do it."

"Still. He could have given you a lot more trouble."

"Maybe. But he knew that if he gave me trouble, it could cost him his job. Maybe his medical license. He gave me the divorce. Annie and I moved back in with Neave for a while. The whole Peter Winthrop adventure lasted three years, diamond to divvying up the furniture. I agreed not to ask for alimony. He agreed to leave his mitts off Be Your Best. Besides Annie, the best thing to come out of it was that it made Neave hire a lawyer who knew how to incorporate Be Your Best so that no future husband could get his hands on it. For my little sister, me and Annie living there was like one long pajama party full of Monopoly and popcorn. We came up with some of our best ideas for the company during that time. She was like a dog who'd been handed the biggest ham bone on Earth."

"She was lonely," Bop said.

"She was lonely," I repeated, and suddenly I could see her sitting in front of me with a popcorn bowl on the table and Annie on her lap, both of them so happy. I saw how bereft she was when I told her it was time for me and Annie to get our own place. "I hadn't been paying her much attention. I wasn't thinking of her."

"True," Boppit said.

Suddenly I felt very small, very selfish. "Neave loved us. I moved us out anyhow so I could do what I wanted without having her looking over my shoulder. I dragged Annie after me. I told myself she was too little to be upset by all the changes."

"You did." He nodded. "You were a solid C-plus mother."

"Take me back in time. Let me be alive again. I'll do it different."

"Lilly, if you played it all out again you'd still be you, so you'd still do the same things. Let's be realistic."

I looked at this dead dog in navy whites and high heels and I snorted. "Realistic. That's rich."

"You can't do everything, Lilly, and you were doing a lot more than most women ever dream about doing. You created and ran a successful business. Not everybody's born with this maternal engine driving them around all day, chuffing them off to PTA meetings and coffee klatches and sledding hills. You loved Annie and you did your best."

"I loved her according to my nature. Which was shallow." It was the first time I'd seen this as the kind of serious deficiency that can ruin a life, ruin somebody else's life. I'd generally thought that my nature was simply light and carefree, traits that most people value over sober self-awareness.

"Maybe a little shallow, but very beautiful," Boppit said.

"I don't like how things look from here, Boppit. It's . . ."

"Broader?"

"Yes."

"I know, sweetie," he said. "I'm sorry."

THE PIRATE LOVER

Capture

A barge from the black ship bearing Judge Henri Le Cherche splashed down, rowed over, and carried the two captives to their fate. And so Electra Gates found herself once again facing Judge Henri Le Cherche, this time on the deck of his flagship with his brother at her side.

"The lovely Miss Gates and my troublesome brother," Judge Le Cherche greeted them. "How convenient for you to have run away, mademoiselle, since it made it easy for me to describe you to the world as a fool who placed herself in the hands of the vermin that hang about the Calais docks. So sad, and so easy to convince them that you were probably taken by slave-traders, probably dead." He smiled. "No one need search for you now. How unfortunate for you to have so few powerful connections and friends on shore. You see, I have always known how vulnerable you were . . . how alone in the world. Only that desperate mother to push you one way and another, a woman without a single powerful friend." He smiled. "And now I needn't even bother with a wedding ceremony or any public scrutiny of our relationship. So much better than my former situation. I thank you for delivering yourself into complete anonymity. I will use it well. And dear brother," he continued, still smiling, "how satisfying to put you in chains in the hold. You never appreciated the charms of chains. Pity. They do have charms." Their captor lifted an eyebrow and three brawny members of his lower deck dragged Basil Le Cherche off. "Come, my pet," Henri Le Cherche said, taking Electra's arm so firmly that it was ringed with bruises within the hour. "You must be made ready for me."

He led her to an airy chamber with windows overlooking the sea, a room as beautiful as Basil's quarters on the *Cat* but without a single book or instrument. Instead of Basil's cool teak floor and walls, here every surface gleamed black except for one wall which held an enormous mirror. There he left her in the care of three frightened young women, each holding boxes. "Sit still for us, mademoiselle, or he will make us all so sorry. Please." Electra looked into their terrified eyes and nodded, submitting while they washed and perfumed her, laced her breasts into a bodice, drew silk stockings up to a filmy garter, swept her hair first up and then down in a mass of curls (Would he prefer curls or a bound mass? Curls? We will try curls . . .) and finally, for what seemed like an eternity, they painted her lips and eyes, brushed blush and color between her bound breasts, hung glittering jewels from her ears, and finally stepped back to critically assess their work.

"Will he be pleased?" one asked the others nervously.

"He will be impatient." With this they turned away as if Electra herself had been a doll or mannequin and bustled out, leaving her alone before the mirror. She regarded herself. The image reflected there glittered. Her eyes traveled over the smoothed, scented, blushed, bound breasts. She drew herself to her full height and glared at her own reflection fiercely. She would allow no one to touch her, least of all the monster Judge Henri Le Cherche! Then, in part to banish thoughts of the judge, in part because she could not control the direction her mind took when she turned it away from this room and that man, she imagined his brother. She imagined Basil Le Cherche's gray gaze, his cool authority, his hands touching her. Heat pulsed down to the world between her legs and she drew her own hands up and around her breasts. The touch sent a thick surge of feeling downward from her belly. The door opened. Before she could resume her indifferent perch on the locker Judge Le Cherche caught the last of her self-inspection.

"Yes, you are quite lovely. You will be even lovelier when I rip away all that careful work done by my young handmaidens. I hope you will be lovelier then. If not, there are other uses for you."

"You disgust me! I know how you made your fortune, sir!"

"A person must make his way in the world, my pet. We all must make our way. Selling something that others want—that is all I do. I am a merchant of sorts. It is the buyers who make the market. Not the sellers. It is business. There is nothing personal involved."

"Nothing personal perhaps for the buyers. Very personal for the sold."

"Well then the trick is not to be one of the sold." He approached her, lifted a hand and grasped her chin. She ducked her entire head quickly to break his hold and when he tightened his grip she sank her teeth in the palm of his hand deeply enough to draw blood.

"Unmannerly bitch!" he spat. "You perform such an act when you are told to perform it—not in response to any impulse of your own!" He wrapped the hand briskly in a linen handkerchief and the swift-flowing blood pulsed through, red field on white. "You should be more careful of your own safety, Electra Gates. Perhaps a night in the same conditions as my brother will make your position here clearer to you."

Within moments she found herself dragged roughly to the hold and shoved into what seemed to be an animal stall, an enclosure full of stale hay and the smell of pig. The door slammed shut and the clank of a lock followed. She struggled to see in what seemed to be total darkness.

"Electra?"

The voice came from the wall to her right. She pressed herself against it in the darkness and found rough boards, many of them loose. "Basil?"

"Are you all right?" His voice was so close! He was just on the other side of these ill-fitted boards—some quite thin. She struggled with more determination and power than she had imagined herself capable of, finally pushing two planks aside—just enough space for a slender woman if she weren't wearing these voluminous skirts. She shed her outer garments, untying the long petticoats and struggling out of the yards of silk around her hips. Clad only in the bodice, the chemise, and sheer stockings that the frightened young women had forced upon her, she wriggled through the opening into the stall next to hers. Her eyes adjusted to the dim light of the interior and she could make out the form of a figure prone, chained to bolts driven into the hull itself: Basil Le Cherche. His face was swollen and bloodied, his clothes torn, his chest exposed and in the tiny shafts of light entering through cracks in the wall behind him his skin gleamed with sweat. In the narrow shattered rays she made out his expression—he was smiling.

"Smiling! Are you mad?" she hissed.

"You move like a cat," he said. "So fierce and focused. You are a welcome sight, Mademoiselle Gates." His expression became less amused, his eyes shone with something that once again sent sweet pulsing confusion through her. In his eyes, which were now full of desire, she could see something she had sought her entire life without even knowing. "You are beautiful," he said softly. She reached him where he lay in the dim light and touched his face with a searching hand. It caressed the broad forehead, the cheek, the square jaw. She felt his hands find the silk garters and begin to move, exploring in the dark. She pulled back instinctively, then, slowly, pressed herself into the hand. He pulled away. They had both been startled by what he had done—both swept open.

"Forgive me," he whispered. But she did not want to forgive him. She took his hand and placed it at her waist, drew it downward just a small bit, then a small bit more.

"Do not play at this game, Electra Gates," he entreated thickly. "You do not know me."

Electra felt herself skimming along on the feelings that had begun the first time she had seen this man—feelings that had been intensified and focused as she saw his authority and power, the conflicted heated contradictions beneath the cool gray-eyed gaze. She remembered the feel of her own hands on the scented breasts she had seen in the mirror only moments before.

"I am deadly serious, Basil Le Cherche." She drew his hand upward again, across one breast, around its pebbling nipple.

"This is unwise. We could be discovered any moment!"

"All the more reason to act now . . . to be who we are now."

Who was this passionate creature saying these things? It was herself—a self she was only just discovering, and this self pulled closer to the man chained here in the darkness beside her, lay her thigh against him so it gave his own feelings away. She gasped at her own reaction to it.

"You cannot say you are not moved," she whispered. "You cannot say you do not wish me to do this." She took his face in her hands and even in the dim shadows of their prison she saw the intensity of his desire, the depth of her power over him at this moment. She drew his lips to hers and they fell into a deep kiss.

"I do not intend to be turned aside, and I am not engaged in a game," she moaned. She placed his hand over her heart, which beat hard and fast. "What is happening to me is beyond my ken," she whispered, "but I do not fear it. I seek it. I seek you. You say a woman has never moved you. But I say you are a liar."

"Witch! Sorceress! I am not a liar—only a man whose mind has always controlled his impulses. But now . . ."

"Now?"

"Now I am controlled." He placed her hand on his own chest, which pounded an answering cadence to her own, an insistent pulsing demand, and he pulled her against him. His chains draped across her back, her chest. He circled her with his arms, found the long laces at the back of her corset and loosened her bodice with the dexterity that only experience could give. The cloth fell away, the perfect breasts stunning in the low light, chains circling them, chains crossing her body and tangling it with his as he wound her more tightly in his arms. Basil Le Cherche had had many women but always before he had been distant, protected, cold. Now his body, the body that had always done his bidding, was entirely out of control, breathing hard, pushing aside linen and lace. When he realized that among his feelings at this moment there was fear, he was astounded. He had never experienced this before—neither the unbridled need nor the fear of that need. He rolled aside in an excruciatingly difficult act of discipline. "Stop! Electra, we will find a way to freedom and you will return to the world you have left. You will be sorry for this moment."

"I have lived in that world and I know exactly what residence there is worth," she answered. "I have no use for it. And I will not be sorry." She slipped the last of her clothing away.

"They could open that door in a moment. You risk your life."

"I might have but a very little life left to live, and nothing in my life has made me feel alive as you do—as this moment does. If we live, Basil Le Cherche, I could never go back to where and what I was when I first saw you. I have traveled too far to ever be able to live in the world I once inhabited. You have shown me that. Tell me again that I am beautiful, Le Cherche. Say it again, for now you will meet no resistance when you praise me. Or touch me."

"You are the most beautiful woman I have ever known," he said, lowering her beneath him, giving up any control he might have had over his own body, his own mind.

She had barely set the loosened planks back in place and returned to her own space before footsteps descended, guards appeared, and Electra Gates was pulled out of her cell and taken back to confront her captor once again—but it was not the same Electra Gates who had been dragged down only a matter of hours before. She was a more formidable opponent now—a fiercer creature more aware of her own powers. Her own capabilities. Her own joys.

NEAVE

And Then, Ricky Luhrmann

When the divorce from Peter Winthrop was final, Lilly started dating again. Long ago we'd set up a daytime roster of babysitters to help us manage both Annie and Be Your Best, but evenings it was always one of us. Jane and I, both smitten with Annie, were always happy to be left with the little girl while Lilly made her way back into the world of romantic adventure. Maybe that eagerness of ours put my sister on too long a leash.

When she announced that she'd fallen in love again, it was a surprise. It shouldn't have been. Ricky Luhrmann was fiery, poetic, volatile—traits that made the man a mesmerizing date but should have given her pause about his husband potential. I said as much, which did less than no good. Right from the start he made her ecstatic and he made her suicidal. She'd come home from every date with him looking drugged—so glassy and heated I'd thought she was ill. Asked if she felt all right, she'd laugh. Not a funny ha-ha laugh.

He wrote love letters, which is enough in some cases to clinch the deal. I don't know why more men don't take advantage of this simple truth about women. Love letters can turn the most stubborn case around. He told her she had a wild heart, and I said that wasn't exactly the way I would say it, but I kind of knew what he meant. She did have a wild heart, and the fact that he saw it and loved it delivered her into his hands.

"He says he dreams me," she murmured one slow afternoon as I tried to interest her in a few shifts in the budget lines. "He says I'm a doorway, a sacred space like all doorways, and he thanks God he found the country I lead to."

How many good women have been snared and skinned with a little poetry, even bad poetry? *Run!* I wanted to say, but Ricky was like a scent or taste that shook all the reason out of her head. My sister's mood made me appalled and envious in roughly equal measure.

"*Love is as strong as death, and I want you to know my love is as strong as death,*" he'd written to her. "*I want to be destroyed by you. I want you to be willing to be destroyed by me.*"

This particular piece of poetry must have scared her some, as well as made her feel other things. I know it made me uneasy. She'd folded it up and stuck it in a box that she'd buried in a drawer. Three months after they met they had a terrible fight—something so bad it gave me real hope that she'd break it off. I never knew what caused the argument, but it seemed to be of a sexual nature. When she got home to Annie and me at her apartment that night she was enraged, her wrists darkening and one shoe without its heel. I told her it didn't look right—any of it.

"I know that," she said to me. "I let him know that he has to remember I'd leave him in a New York minute if I didn't like how he was treating me. Maybe I scared him some. I don't know. I scared myself."

"Why?" I asked.

"Because the second I said I could walk away from him any minute, I knew it wasn't true."

"Sure it is, Lilly," I'd said at the time. I'd seen Lilly walk away from a dozen men twice as rich and good-looking as Ricky Luhrmann. My Lilly could take care of herself. My Lilly could walk away from any man. Couldn't she?

She said, "Ricky has this troubled place in him. He can't change that. It's what he is; maybe it's things that have happened to him."

"Oh, come on, Lilly—look at yourself spouting sentimental crap about his troubled past. Look at this thing on your wrist." I reached out and touched the plummy bruise. The way I felt when I touched it ran up from my fingers and into my head: whatever this "dark place" was, it gave him his hold on her, and she wouldn't or couldn't see this. So she was powerless.

"You've got Annie to think of," I reminded her. "Lilly. Walk away."

"He won't do it again. I'm sure of it. He's sorry. Annie's never seen anything but what a kid should see, Neave. I'm making sure of that. She's fine. And he'll get to love her. How can you not love Annie?"

"I don't know, but I imagine it's possible. And what about whether or not Annie likes him? Doesn't that matter?"

"We're working on it. It'll all work."

But what I heard was Lilly deciding that it was all going to work and forgetting anything that might contradict that fantasy. Granted, for months after that, Ricky Luhrmann was a model suitor. He made good money working for a contractor who renovated houses, and he liked to spend it. Yellow roses were his signature courting flower. He took my sister dancing, bought bottles of Champagne, and made reservations at the kinds of restaurants that had tablecloths and candles. It was as if he'd opened her skull and gotten a direct sightline on her fantasies. He might spend his days with a tool belt on his hips, but he knew how to wear a smart suit and order a Rob Roy. He could lead a woman across a dance floor and rivet every eye in the place on them. I'm sure he had other talents as well.

By the time he proposed, the memory of the fight, and the darkness about its cause, was far away in Lilly's mind if not mine. She came to my apartment the morning after she took a ring from him. "He pushed me against the wall," she said breathlessly, "and I said, 'Luhrmann, let me loose,' and he said *Not until death do us part, kid*, and he kissed me. Hard. Neave, it was like a ball of electricity moving through me. It just has to be right. Otherwise I know it wouldn't feel like that." She hadn't even said the word "yes." Apparently she hadn't had to. He'd just handed her the ring, and she'd slipped it on her finger and come to show it to me so I could admire the shine.

"What about Annie?" I asked.

"She'll wear patent-leather shoes and ten layers of petticoats. She'll be adorable."

"I wasn't asking about her party dress, Lilly."

"She'll be so excited! And she loves sleepovers with you and Jane. You can take her for a couple days for our honeymoon, right? And when you and Charles are going out, Janey can take her, right?"

Of course. I shut up then. There was no point in trying to make Lilly Terhune dig at a situation to find its broken or cranky parts. That was my job.

He told her she was going to marry him before the month was out and that is exactly what happened. The wedding was small. I wore a navy suit. Lilly's dress was a pastel rose silk. Annie wore one of those frothy things that make children look like cupcakes. There was no groom's side or bride's side—we huddled together like people trying to stay out of a cold wind.

"How could she do that?" my mother murmured sadly.

"What?" I looked around, genuinely befuddled. My mother approved very deeply of marriage. In her mind it ended the nerve-wracking dating period and settled things. Daddy's feelings on the subject weren't so clear. He'd avoided any talk at all of love with his children as being somehow inappropriate. He sat woodenly beside our mother, his expression detached and his thoughts, like they were so often, a mystery.

"It's not white," she said. "This is a wedding."

"For chrissakes, Mom. She's been married before. It's close. Just a whisper away from white."

"In matters like this, it is not possible to be close. Even if it's a symbolic gesture. White. Not-white. That's that."

I looked at Lilly and Ricky Luhrmann standing side by side in front of us. His hand brushed her hip and the upper part of her body responded, snakelike, in a smooth little twist that brought her almost facing him. His hand moved to her collarbone and he whispered something to her that closed her off completely to everybody in the room but him. It gave me a rattled kind of feeling. I couldn't name it.

Annie sat at the end of my row. She craned her neck to see something directly behind her. I followed her sightline to a man who looked remarkably like Ricky Luhrmann.

"Who was that man?" I asked her when the vows were done. "The one you were looking at."

"That's Max." She waved discreetly.

"And who's Max?"

Annie scooched over closer to me. She was almost but not quite whispering. "Ricky says no talking about him."

"I see. Is he a friend of your mommy's?"

"Ricky told mommy he's a son of a bitch," she whispered. "Max does go-search. He goes on the sea, and he searches."

"What does he search for?"

"He said 'Son of a bitch,'" she giggled. "He looks for snarks."

"He searches for snarks? Honey, I think Ricky's brother might be pulling your leg."

Annie looked momentarily stricken, then thoughtful. "No, Aunt Neave." The little girl shook her head vigorously from side to side. "He's nice."

"So you and Max are friends?" I asked, speaking confidentially after looking around to make sure no one was paying any attention to us.

"I can't be his friend because Ricky says we can't. But I think we are anyhow. He came to our house and Mommy and Ricky yelled." I nodded and kept quiet, waiting for more. She rooted around in the folds of her dress and came up with a tiny boat. "Grandma says no toys allowed because weddings are serious," she whispered. "But I brought my boat."

"I won't tell."

"Max gave it to me." She craned her neck again to get a view of my mother and reassure herself that she couldn't be seen, and then she sailed the boat across her lap. "While they were yelling in the kitchen. Max and me ate cake in the living room."

"Annie."

My tone was serious enough to make the little girl alert, mildly apprehensive. She set the boat at rest on a fold of skirt and looked up at me.

"Annie, are you happy that your mom is getting married?"

She shrugged, more evasive than noncommittal. She said, "I like my boat."

"I do too. Do you like your mom getting married?"

Annie craned her neck around to catch Max's eye. He lifted a finger and crooked it at her; she crooked a corresponding finger back at him. She settled back in the seat and sailed the boat across a fold of skirt. "Mommy says I can't be alone with Max."

"Why not, Annie?"

Annie heard the alert uptick in my tone and she tipped her face away so she didn't have to look at me when she answered. "Can we make a pie when I stay with you?"

Yes. We would make pie. I repeated my question. Annie shrugged.

Back at the reception at our house I climbed the stairs to our old room to help Lilly change from her wedding gown into the next of her day's outfits. I started in on the thirty-eight pearl buttons running down her back, one by one. "So Ricky has a brother," I said to her. "And he has go-searches."

"Max. But Ricky hates him." Lilly's third glass of Champagne had pinked her cheeks and compromised her skills at self-editing. "And it's *research.* He does ocean-current tracking or something. He and Ricky aren't exactly part of each other's lives, so you won't be seeing much of him, believe me. I insisted that Ricky introduce him to Annie and me before we got married because I had this stupid idea that family was family and hating each other was no reason not to introduce a brother to a fiancée and ask him to your wedding. I set up this one little dinner with him and Ricky acted like I'd asked him to eat a live grenade."

"Why don't they like each other?"

"Sometimes people just don't like each other, Neave."

"People don't like each other for reasons."

"It isn't worth digging some things up and poking them."

"Lilly, why would you tell Annie to never be alone with Max?"

"I don't remember saying that."

She'd twisted away from me with the same half drop of the shoulder that her daughter had used earlier. "Liar, liar," I said. "Pants on fire."

"The truth is, I don't know. Ricky just said that he wouldn't trust his brother with anything precious to him. I don't know what he meant. But the way he said it . . . I got nervous for a minute, and I might have said that to Annie."

"Why wouldn't Ricky trust his brother?"

"I didn't ask him," my sister said, and I knew she was actually, amazingly, telling me the truth. Lilly didn't ask questions that could have bad answers. "It looked like we were never going to see Max again. No reason to know details. Right?"

"Lilly . . ."

"Not today, Neave. Not now." My sister lifted her glass and drained it. She smiled at me. "Right now the world is a wonderful place, and I've got nothing to worry about except how long I've got to wait for you to get me another glass of this stuff."

She handed me the empty glass. She smiled a wide and authentic and mildly drunken smile. Lilly Terhune felt perfectly safe in the world, and this little matter of a brotherly rift was irrelevant to her present and future happiness. This is another way Lilly and I differed. The only place and time on Earth I had ever felt entirely safe was in front of Mrs. Daniels's fire with a book in one hand and a cookie in the other: a child's place and time. And now we weren't children.

"Trade you." I made my tone playful, light, and I held up her empty glass. "Another glass for more info on this brother."

She shook her head like an animal that's had something it dislikes pushed in its nose. "What do you care about his brother?" she demanded. "You've got this habit of caring about everything. I don't know how you drag yourself from day to day lugging it around with you." She swished her skirt. "All I know is there was a little sister who died when she was really small. Some kind of accident, and that seemed to be the start of all the bad feeling. Ricky doesn't like to talk about it, because it was bad and it was somehow Max's doing, whatever it was. She had some flower name. Daffodil. Daisy. But I figured Ricky said what he did about keeping Annie away from him because of whatever happened to the little sister. So. How about that drink?"

"I've changed my mind. You've had enough to drink." I set her glass down and moved to help her slip off the shimmering wedding dress.

"You don't know about people from looking at them," she continued. "The guy looks like such a solid citizen, but Ricky says when they were kids, Max was a terror with the girls."

"What does 'terror' mean?"

"Look, I only know what Ricky was willing to say. He said once that Max got a girl's dress slammed in a car door and dragged her—" She stopped. "Who knows what really happened." She made a quick turn to make the skirt blossom out again and raised her chin, dismissing all dark considerations. "Come on. What do you think this skirt's got in it? Fifteen yards? I'm gonna knock 'em dead." She smiled as she headed for the stairs. "There is nothing in this world like a dramatic entrance." She looked at my face and sighed, irritated. "Come on, Neave—you've got to keep what's long ago and far away right where it is—far away. The past is over."

"The past isn't over. It isn't even the past."

She stopped right smack in front of me, and pulled me into her arms. "I love you, Neavie. Always have. Always will."

I snorted at her and pulled away, but as I followed her down the stairs, her skirt a line of shining runnels all tumbling toward Ricky Luhrmann, my throat closed. Something in our lives was over now, forever, and the new place where we lived felt more dangerous. We were almost side by side when we got back to the party, but I doubt anyone actually saw me. Lilly looked as if a hundred lightbulbs had all been flipped on inside her. I scanned the room to find the brother and spotted him already heading for a door. I trotted along to place myself by his side and stuck my hand out. "I'm Neave. Awkward that we didn't meet until now, isn't it?"

"Yes. Nice to meet you." He had a cool, firm, solid-citizen handshake.

"Also odd I didn't know you existed until today." He kept standing there, not bothered by the silence, not acting like it was his job to make friends. "So what have you heard about me, Max Luhrmann?"

"That you're more intelligent than your sister. More awkward. Not social. Apparently as a child you used to hide in closets. You have a particular relationship with a childhood book called . . . I don't know. Something about sea travel and sadism. . . . You're interested in naval history?"

"Not much. If Ricky's the source of any information about me, you might question it."

"You don't like Ricky?" he asked in the same kind of tone you'd use if you were asking how somebody felt about lamb chops.

"I don't really know Ricky very well. But I hear that you don't like him. Or he doesn't like you. Or something like that."

"A bold statement from a woman who didn't know I existed until twenty minutes ago."

"A ridiculous rebuttal from a man who tells little children that he hunts for something called a snark."

"I do. A snark is a dense packet of water that moves through water of lesser density and often different temperature. Sonar can't penetrate it, so it's of interest to the navy." I looked blank. He added, "Submarines hide behind them."

"Oh." I considered. "Mr. Luhrmann, you don't seem much like your brother."

"Miss Terhune, I don't know what you've heard about me, but if I were you I wouldn't give it much thought because I don't think we're going to be seeing a lot of each other. I'm not very involved in my brother's life. He's usually unhappy with me, most recently because I told him not to marry your sister."

My tone wasn't half as offended as I actually was. "Your brother is lucky my sister even looked in his direction, much less agreed to marry him. She's probably the best thing that's ever happened to him."

"That's very likely. I wasn't trying to protect my brother." He smiled but just with the bottom of his face. "I don't think your sister has any idea who my brother is."

"That's a traditional starting point for most marriages, isn't it?"

He looked at me more carefully than he had a second earlier, then turned away from me. "I should go. I don't want to upset the groom, who looks unhappy every time he checks and sees that I'm still here." Max smiled past my shoulder and waved at Ricky, who did actually scowl. "See? I wanted to be here out of respect for the bride, who is lovely, by the way. As is her Annie. And it was a pleasure to meet you, Neave Terhune."

An hour later I was helping Lilly jam the last of her going-away things into a suitcase. She'd had several more glasses of Champagne. We snapped it shut, sitting on it side by side. Jane and I had a schedule for Annie between us while Lilly was on the honeymoon. Lilly pulled the suitcase off the bed and clicked her way toward her new husband on new blue high heels. "You're going to have a great time!"

We did. Days, Jane introduced Annie to the stuffed animals that had traveled with my little sister out of her own childhood and into adult life. Now they sat on a shelf in her closet, still lined up according to their complicated, long-held grudges and rosy-tinted new love affairs and new marriages.

Nights, I sang Annie all the words to "You're a Sweet Little Headache," and "Warm Kitty." I had bought a phonograph and after dinner we danced in the almost empty warehouse space to record after record. Her favorite, which we played at least three times a night, was called "Make My Mistakes Again." I'd bought it because it had a picture of a beautiful sailing ship on the record cover, and Annie sang it out full-throated and then growled at the end, her idea, she told me, of what a pirate sounded like.

I think of the times past when I had it all
I toyed with men's wives and their daughters

And in my pursuit of this ill-gotten wealth,
I stabbed and I slashed and I slaughtered.

And for what? (HEY!)
The men that I've fought,
Are matched by the number of women I've bought.

And if I could go back and make my amends,
I'd make all those mistakes again.
And kill every last one of those bastards, my friend!

Before the happy couple got home we managed to have two picnics, one outside and one inside. Our last day we drove to Wingaersheek Beach and found five starfish. Then Lilly and Ricky returned home, which for now was a rented house in Nahant, and Jane and I packed Annie's bag. "Don't worry." Lilly laughed at us. I don't know if I looked as unhappy as I felt, but Jane certainly did. "She'll be back for lots of sleepovers. This is her second home. Right, Annie?" Annie nodded, uncertain. After she and Lilly left me I stood in the warehouse kitchen and rolled out two dozen classic sugar cookies, singing the Pirate song, alone.

LILLY

Janey Marries

Janey met Todd Blumenthal a week after I got married and he proposed to her about ten minutes into their first date.

"It was ten weeks," Boppit corrected me.

"You get what I mean, though. Fast. Janey said yes right off, completely sure of herself, completely sure of him. Mom finally got a daughter's wedding that she could plan without the daughter interfering! She was so happy. I hadn't let her put so much as a pinky finger on anything to do with my weddings. And Neave? Neave never even bothered to get married. That left Janey. When Mom started in with the lists and table settings, our little sister just smiled and said all her choices were wonderful. Janey had made the only choice that mattered to her, which was the groom.

"Mom stuffed our little sister into a blindingly white cupcake dress and perfectly awful shiny satin shoes. Jane smiled and smiled and let her do it. Mom chose daisies as the bride's bouquet. Unbelievable. Limp little stalky weeds, and Jane told her they would be very pretty. The reception was booked into the VFW hall, whose regular caterer was asked to produce his usual rubber chicken surprise. Janey paid no attention to anything but Todd, and Todd was too busy plotting out a future full of children and Christmas trees to pay any attention to a wedding. Jane walked down the aisle looking like an explosion in a bakery, the dinner was inedible, and the whole mood was incandescent. It was a happy wedding."

"You know," Boppit said to me now, "they're going to have two little girls of their own as well as taking Annie into the fold, and they're going to rebuild an old schoolhouse into a home and raise the girls in it. They're going to adopt a border collie named Jeffrey who will be their youngest daughter's best friend until she's eight years old and Linda Shouman moves into the neighborhood."

"Then what?"

"Then Linda becomes her best friend."

"How do you know all this?"

"How do I know anything? I told you that time-wise, things are much closer than you'd think, and not necessarily all moving in the same direction. Jeffrey, actually, I've met. This is his twentieth family."

"He gets reborn?"

"I'm not sure I'd call it that. He keeps coming around when he's called. He's a border collie, like I said."

"Is he going to protect the girl, like you protect Neave?"

"Better, I hope."

"But it's going to work, right? I help you reach Neave. You protect her from him."

"That's the plan," Boppit said, nodding. "That's why we're here."

"He's bearing down on her, isn't he? She's in his head."

Boppit nodded. "Yes."

"Neave's so vulnerable. People think she's capable, but in a little box in the back of her mind the girl still believes in nobility and salvation and magic animal helpers. You know that book she reread every year? The one with the pirate? She actually thinks that that book is the truth: good triumphing over evil, love triumphing over everything."

"But that is the truth, Lilly."

"Don't be ridiculous, Dog."

"Ridiculous? Aren't you right now sort of talking to a kind of magical animal?"

He had a point.

NEAVE

Our Mother Dies

Our father died quick and our mother died slow. It was the reverse of the way my parents did most things, but I guess the way you make meat loaf or change a tire isn't the sum of you. Dad was writing a letter to a local congregation suggesting that perhaps their (unmarried) minister had socialist leanings when he just tipped over and hit the linoleum. Mom claimed she knew from the sound that he was dead before the body hit the floor. Aneurism. I read some of the letter he was working on. It said even a minister needed to be a man among men.

"Man among men my ass," Lilly had said when I reported this. Lilly wasn't somebody who got reverent around death just because it was death, and she and Daddy had never really liked each other. "Every day he'd tell you that war was what turned boys into men. I think Daddy spent his war loading toilet paper and hamburger onto troop ships."

I didn't believe her. I went to my mother.

"Well, he ended the war that way. But he didn't start it like that. He was on one of those big landing ships. It was attacked and sunk. Some other boat picked up survivors. He ended the war in Newport News. We didn't talk about it, really."

I let myself imagine my father floating on a debris-choked ocean surface, maybe underneath planes still strafing the water, maybe with oil slicks burning around him.

"You weren't curious about what he did in the war?"

"A wife doesn't prod."

"But . . ."

"You are a prodder, Neave. You have a give-no-ground temperament and it scares me. A girl who wants men to be interested in her can't be aggressive. A person only gets to be more of what they are as they get old. You need to remember that. It wouldn't be a bad idea to consider your own nature. I don't want you to die alone. But the way you are . . ."

I figured she was right, of course, but I didn't have a handle on what I could do about it. It was just how I'd been made. And my mother was, truly, now alone. Jane had begun her married life and decamped to a snug Cape Cod in Swampscott with Todd. Snyder was making enough money to have moved into the studio where he ran his business and stored his books and prints, though he was still coming home for dinner at least three times a week.

Eleven months after my father died my mother got a cold, which became bronchitis, then pneumonia. She struggled to keep the house running without asking anyone to help. When Lilly and Jane and I visited and found the dishes unwashed, the refrigerator empty, and the trash piling up, we were frightened. Snyder was no help. A kitchen full of dirty dishes and leftovers looked perfectly normal to him. My mother and her concerns were a kind of mystery to him, and though he made some feeble efforts to cook or clean, she rejected them. Boys were not supposed to do that kind of work, she'd say. At first she even rejected Lilly's and my help, but we could see her drifting—staying in bed all day, and then not knowing what day it was. Then she stopped refusing help.

"Neave," she said to me one early evening when I was standing at her sink. "Put that sponge down. Come talk to me a minute. Please."

Her voice was so thready it gave me an ice-water-in-the-chest feeling. I dropped the sponge and my hand went to my breastbone. She was having a little trouble breathing. "I'll boil some water and we'll do that thing with the towel over your head for steam," I said. "To loosen your chest."

"Sit."

I did.

"Your brother, Neave, looks like a grown man but he isn't. All he knows about is comic books, which is not enough. How will he ever find a wife? He has what he calls his own business. But I've talked to him when he comes here for dinner, and the fact is he doesn't really know about the world. He can't say what he owes or who owes him. He has no business sense."

"He'll learn."

"Not on his own he won't. You and Lilly have business sense. Now you and the girls got him going on this comic-book-business idea, but you're not done with him yet. He needs more help. And he doesn't have anybody but you. Except for when I'm feeding him, the man lives on burnt toast and cold cereal. Tell me you'll show him."

"Don't be so dramatic. You have a cold."

"I have pneumonia and I am an old woman. And there's something else. Neave, your father didn't pay any taxes for the last ten years of his life."

"What does that mean?"

"It means the house will have to be sold to pay taxes. I was hoping Snyder would have a kind of net, some money to fall back on, but he won't. You and Lilly have each other and your little cosmetics business seems to be working. Jane has her Todd. Snyder has no one."

She'd started with cool detachment, but that unraveled as she went on and now, to my dismay, she started to cry.

"You're just feeling emotional because you've got this bad cold. You'll be fine." I said these words but looking at her sunken eyes, her papery face, and sandbag slump, I knew the thought of her dying was in my head. I'd just been thinking it behind my own back, but it was why I was here sitting by her side right now, letting her talk about what I needed to do for Snyder.

"Just tell me you'll help him."

"Yes," I said. "You don't have to worry, Mom."

Three days later our mother's lungs filled with fluid and she drowned, lying in her bed and surrounded by her children. Snyder got through a quiet wake and the graveside burial and then he began to unravel. He began to smell stale. He sat quietly in corners while my sisters and I cleaned out the house, sold it, met with an accountant who helped us pay off our parents' debts. I didn't believe letting him sit around and feel terrible was going to help much, so I started right in on him.

We began with cooking lessons. I told him that when we had lamb chops and chocolate cake under control we could move on to tracking sales figures and business costs. Snyder was grateful, which surprised me. The cooking lessons were a disaster but the columns of numbers, and the reasons to keep those columns, started to make sense to him. After all, he had filled out and erased and rewritten countless order forms from the backs of comics all his life. "I can do this," he said to me one night after a long conversation about mailing costs and advertising, cash-flow charts and taxes. Then he said he was hungry and he needed a shower.

We were going to be all right.

THE PIRATE LOVER

Why Do You Hate Us?

Electra's captor blindfolded her and brought her to a darkened chamber, where she could hear men hooting and grunting as he ordered her to stand still, arms at her side, and tolerate the blindfold until he himself removed it. When he did she gasped. There on a large bed were five men surrounding what proved to be a woman's body, her skirt rucked up and over her head, her white legs parted—pale bent wands on a rectangle of black satin. Her fists were clenched, her wrists bound and tied to the edges of the bed.

"They were a bit rough. It's what they pay for. If the girl can't manage, we'll have to find some other use for her. Our customers enjoy a variety of imaginative play—there are still many roles available for girls who have been slightly damaged." Le Cherche pulled Electra away then, into his own private chamber.

"Why do you show me this? Who is this poor woman?"

"I believe her name was Emelia Benelotte. Pretty name, no? She rejected the marriage offer of a man who had enough influence to make her disappear from her old life, and appear in this one. True, he was thirty years older than she. Fat. But he had a great deal of money. She should have said yes to him, don't you think? When she rejected him, he simply offered her parents a handsome fee for her and they gave her to him. Perhaps they actually weren't venal and cruel—he told them he would be kind. Then he delivered her into my hands—he'd already had particular men in mind who wanted to do particular things with her. We've given her a new name and a story that makes it clear that she has been a very, very bad little girl."

"You think this will frighten me into submission."

"If it doesn't, you are a fool. You see what your fate could be. Of course, you could be my own personal plaything—safe from the kind of casual group use that might be unpleasant for you."

"Why do you hate us?"

"I don't know what you're talking about, my pet. Purr for me." He approached Electra and stroked her head. "I said purr." She turned her head sharply away. "You will learn," he said dryly. "Be grateful that I am patient."

She heard the men's casual laughter as they left the bound and brutalized girl. Was resistance seen as sexually provocative behavior in this strange world—at best a waste of time, at worst exactly what her captor desired most? She bowed her head in as submissive a way as she could and whispered, "I understand, Judge Le Cherche. I will not be a fool."

"So much better. Do you see how pleasant this can all be?"

Just then cannon fire sounded above them. A sailor pounded into the room. "Sir—the *Cat* has cut out our xebec."

"How is that possible? Who was posted at watch?"

"They approached in small boats, sir, in total darkness and quiet. It was . . . we were distracted, sir. They swarmed over the side and took the xebec by surprise."

"You were drinking, you mean, and playing with some of my clients' castoffs! What about the xebec's crew?"

"Half seem to have joined the *Cat*'s number. I do not know the fate of the others."

So the crew of the *Cat* was at hand, active and interceding, never mind that it was a small frigate-size craft against Judge Le Cherche's remaining three ships.

"Whoever was at watch duty will answer to me!" cried the judge. "And when we take the xebec back, and blow the *Cat* into eternity, we will deal with the deserters as well. Take the wench back to her quarters and tell the first officer to report to my cabin."

The sailor into whose hands she was thrust was clearly shaken, more frightened of Le Cherche than of the cannon whistling over their deck. Sweat beaded his brow, and his grip on her arm as he dragged her toward her cell made her cry out at one point. "Hurry up, you stupid cow! If I am not back in three minutes . . ." The sailor never finished his sentence. He didn't have to. In a particularly close doorway Electra watched for her chance and made a point of losing her balance—directly onto her escort. He kept his feet, but in the tangle of skirt and legs and arms she had swiftly lifted his sailor's knife—a tool with both blunt blade and fid, each folded neatly into the handle. The man was so anxious he did not immediately feel its absence or see it folded into her skirt as he pushed her into her cell.

Within moments she had worked aside three planks and slipped into Basil Le Cherche's straw-covered prison. She flipped the marlinspike open, examined the links of his chains, selected what seemed the weakest, and drove the fid into its center, bracing and twisting to force the link open. With determined persistence she succeeded, and the captive took the fid from her and drove it into a link on the other hand's chains, saying, "The first time I saw you I knew you could turn the course of my life in some way, at some time. Electra Gates, I don't understand your powers but I am grateful to them because you have brought me alive in ways I believed were gone to me forever. This moment is proof that I was wrong."

His words flew directly to their mark and she met his gaze, both their faces alight. She contained the deep urge to touch him and sprang to her feet.

"The *Cat* is driving towards us as I speak! They have taken the little xebec that accompanied this flotilla . . ."

"They learned our location and have planned this distraction. I would bet my life that if we can reach the water, they will be searching for us. They are giving us our main chance. Come!"

He led the way to the head, which opened directly to the sea at the boat's lower levels. "Step lively, and step quick!" he called. "Trust me, Electra! Follow me!"

He plunged before her, out of the ship and into the black waters. She hesitated not an instant before she followed him into the darkness.

NEAVE

Gay Divorcée

Eleven months after the wedding to Ricky Luhmann, Lilly showed up at my door one rainy night with a suitcase to one side of her and Annie to the other. My sister had gotten quieter and quieter on the subject of her life. We could go for weeks without saying anything at all that wasn't about back orders or salesgirls or payroll. The woman who came to my door with Annie clinging to her legs that rainy night was barely recognizable as my Lilly. Her hair hung clumped and damp, her eyes were sunken, and her expression was as frozen as a ceramic doll's. Annie was very quiet, which scared me as much as Lilly's looks.

Before this night my sister had spoken in no specific terms about her marriage to Ricky Luhrmann, but from a few brief and sweeping generalizations it was clear that gradually things with him had changed. We got Annie to bed and I sat my sister down at the kitchen table. I asked her if she wanted a warm bath and she looked stricken in a way you wouldn't expect when you offered a shivering woman a warm bath.

"What's wrong?"

"I don't want a bath. That's all."

"Okay," I said. "Tea?" She said yes to tea. "Tell me," I said when I set the cup in front of her.

How had this lumpy, hesitant ill ease between us happened? It was one of the things that Lilly's marriage had accomplished. So thank God for Annie and the business, the shared countries where we both felt happy. They bridged the distance that had grown between the Lilly who was my closest ally and partner, and the Lilly who was married to Ricky Luhrmann.

"He climbed into the bath with me tonight," she whispered. "And he turned me around and he was a little rough and I was tired and I tried to put him off, laugh, say wait a minute, wait till later. But he just tightened his grip. He hurt me. He can be firm. Rough, actually. But something tonight scared me, Neave. I started to struggle, and that made things escalate. He liked it that I struggled."

She stopped talking. We both listened for Annie, wanting her to be far away and asleep because Lilly was going to take us someplace we didn't want Annie to know existed. "He wanted it a particular way," she whispered.

"What do you mean?"

"He pushed my head underwater, and I struggled. The more I struggled, the more . . . It excited him, Neave. He was like a kind of zombie, unreachable. And in another way he was completely there—I mean, more completely there than I'd ever seen him. I pushed back, tried to kick loose of him, because I was actually thinking, What will happen to Annie if he kills me? Until I listened to myself think those words, I didn't admit that it was that bad. But tonight I actually thought he could. Maybe I've thought that for a while, but I just couldn't listen to myself think it. But tonight it just shot through me and I got loose from him and pulled myself around. . . ."

"And?"

"I grabbed his private parts and I twisted." She laughed in a way that made the word "hysterical" pop into my head. "Can you believe that? It gave me just enough time to get out of that tub, grab the clothes off the floor, get into Annie's room, and lock the door. We climbed out the window listening to him banging on the door, screaming at us to let him in. I got us on the roof, and I pushed us off into the bushes. It felt like jumping off a cliff into a tidal pool a thousand feet below me. I told Annie it was a game."

"She couldn't possibly have believed you."

"I know. She kind of went dark, completely quiet. Neave, when I heard myself thinking I might die I got so scared. Not for me. I thought, Well, Jane and Neave will take care of Annie. Neave, if I die, you will, won't you?"

"You're not going to die."

"But if I do, if a truck hits me or I fall off a cliff, Annie will be all right, won't she?"

"I don't know if Annie will be all right, but I know that Jane and I will take care of her."

The laugh was thin and bitter, not a Lilly laugh. "So like you, sugar, to tell me the truth when anybody else on Earth would have lied."

"What lie?"

"That no matter what happened, Annie would be all right. I know I don't pay as much attention to Annie as *Good Housekeeping* says that all good women yearn to do in their deepest hearts. I never said I was Mother of the Year, but I love her. I might not stay home and knit her sweaters every Saturday night, but you know I'd throw myself in front of a bullet for her. You know that, right?"

"I know it," I said. "You'd step in front of a charging bear to protect Annie."

"Oh, shut up," she said to me, but she said it like she knew that the jokey tone was just to give us some kind of safe surface we could use to skate over this terrible thought: harm coming to Annie.

"Jane and I'll be right behind you," I nodded. "All of us taking on the bear."

We sat for a full five minutes in an aching silence before she said, "Why do they hate us?"

"Who?" I asked.

"Men."

"Only Ricky pushed your head underwater, Lilly. He isn't all men."

"But the way he looked, I've seen it before in other guys. *Guard yourself*, Mom always said, and I laughed but I knew why she was saying it. I'd been in the backseat of a car. I've been pushed against a wall or two. Not every man in a backseat gets that switch flipped inside of him, but some of them do and it's hard to tell, at the start of things, if he's one of the ones who could hurt you. Maybe wants to hurt you. It's harder to tell because they don't know themselves. They just want to . . . do things to you. For some of them, some of the time, it's not just sex they want; or if it is, the sex involves torn clothes maybe or a black eye. Or worse." Now she hardened herself. Straightened out her face in a wooden, icey-eyed way.

I'd never heard my sister talk like this—Lilly, the girl who'd been known to book three dates in a single weekend. The playful risk-taker, the woman in Chanel No. 5, the believer in Love.

"Maybe I know why they hate us," she murmured.

"Yeah?"

"They hate us because we make them feel," she said. "We make them feel all kinds of things, and they can't stand it."

That night Annie slept in the small bedroom that had been hers when she and Lilly last lived with me. My sister and I slept in my bed. When we were little girls we kicked and elbowed to demand more room in the narrow space we shared, and woke up most mornings spooned. On this night we started right out spooned, but it took a long time to shut down the whirring pictures in my head, damp down the feelings that I didn't want to be feeling, and sleep.

Luhrmann came after her the next day. We woke up to the sound of the downstairs door being banged on, a splintering sound of the aging bolt being snapped off the door, then feet pounding up the stairs. I dialed the cops. Luhrmann reached us and began pounding on the door to the apartment. I told Lilly to stay put, but she didn't. She marched right up to the damn thing and opened it.

"You stole my car," Luhrmann said—almost a whisper, eyes like a reptile with something in its prehensile sights. "I'm here to get it back."

"You don't own a car. That's my car! And you didn't have any trouble finding another one to borrow real quick so you could come over and threaten me."

"That car's in my name. Which makes it my car." Of course, everything was in his name except Lilly's half of Be Your Best Cosmetics, carefully shielded from a moment like this. He was her husband.

"Might be in your name, but it was bought with cash I made," Lilly said evenly. "So—my car."

Even as inexperienced in the world of love as I was, I knew this was not the right thing to say at this moment. I had come up behind her, carrying a copper pan. When Luhrmann stepped over the threshold and put his hands on her, I swung—a satisfying, thumping *whock*—and he was down, looking up at us from where he'd hit the floor, dazed but scrambling like a squashed spider, struggling to get to his feet and make something bad happen. I stepped over the threshold and swung the pan over my head, clearly focused on his face. "Don't do it," I said softly.

"You think you can get away with that?" The blow had left him vague and thick—slower but still dangerous.

"Yes." I kept my tone matter-of-fact because I wanted my ability to hurt him and get away with it to sound very much like a fact.

"Bitch," he said, the word coming out like a small metal thing with sharp parts.

"You bet," I answered. "Get out of here, Luhrmann."

Before the exchange went any further, flashing lights in the street below us from a police cruiser blinked up the stairway. "Up here!" I yelled. "Top of those stairs!"

Two patrolmen slogged up the stairs to where Ricky Luhrmann lay, now moaning and making himself as pathetic as possible. I heard Annie open her bedroom door and turned to see her behind me, hesitant and afraid but purposeful, standing her ground. "Go back to your room for just a little bit, sweetie," I said. "It'll be all right." She froze, uncertain.

"Go ahead, Annie," her mother called out to her. "Neave's right." The little girl turned and retreated. The police reached the door.

"Did you see her attack me?" Luhrmann cried. "You must at least have heard that fucking pan hit my head, even from the bottom of the stairwell!" He kept talking. The cops stood there long enough to hear him swear he'd never give Lilly a divorce and she had a few things to learn if she thought she was in charge of anything besides lipstick, and she wasn't in charge of him that was a goddamn fucking sure thing. "And if your sister thinks she can stick her nose in where it doesn't belong then she'd better think again. I knew you'd come running straight to her." The tendons in his neck stood out in a lizardy fan. Lilly silently held out her wrists to show the police the purple places spreading from what he'd done to hold her down the night before. There were marks elsewhere besides, she told them, if they cared to see them. Then they saw her spit right in Ricky Luhrmann's face. Later she swore she did it on purpose because she knew it would make Luhrmann do something outsized stupid with the cops standing right there, and it did. He stood up, lunged at her and got her by the throat. The cops pulled them apart.

"It's a domestic matter, ma'am. If they weren't married, maybe you could call it assault. But it's between a husband and wife." Then the bigger guy turned to Luhrmann. "Mister, I think you oughtta shove off until you cool down a bit." The cop planted himself directly between Luhrmann and Lilly and rested one hand on his billy club. "Lady, just make peace with the man," the cop said when Luhrmann had stamped down the stairs, out onto the street, and back to his borrowed car. "Better or worse, the guy's your husband."

"Not for long," was Lilly's reply. Lilly Terhune had watched me see Ricky Luhrmann getting her by the throat. There was no pretending it had been anything but what it had been, and I was not a person who could be persuaded that I hadn't seen something. And there was Annie, who had been protected from scenes like this in the past but who only a few minutes earlier had stood in a hallway and watched me threaten her mother's husband with a sauce pan.

Lilly didn't care if Luhrmann wouldn't cooperate. She didn't care to wait around for the Commonwealth of Massachusetts.

"Annie saw that," she murmured when Luhrmann had gone.

"Yes, she did," I agreed.

"She's not going to see it again. If you've got no objection, Neave, Annie and I are moving in with you for a little while. I'll wait till after the sales conference. But right after that I'm booking a flight to a dude ranch in Nevada and planting myself there for the six weeks it'll take to get the divorce legal."

Made sense to me. We bought a plane ticket to get her to Nevada the day after the conference. I told her that a divorcée dude ranch was probably no place for Annie, and she agreed. Jane and I could easily manage Annie between us when she was gone and she shouldn't look back. If I were going out with Charles or stuck at a business dinner, Janey would step in. In the weeks before she left for Nevada, Lilly and Annie and I fell into the habits of the early days of Be Your Best. We made vats of spaghetti, played Monopoly late at night when Annie had been put to bed, and plotted out new seminars for the conferences and more splashy sales incentives. We didn't so much as speak Ricky Luhrmann's name though the idea of him was everywhere.

The upcoming conference was going to cap off the best year we'd had since we'd started the business. Ruga Potts had done away with the melting lipsticks that went rancid, the colors that changed within three weeks of purchase. The pace-setting salesgirls were supporting whole families now, and this year for the first time we were giving these chosen few real blue diamond necklaces. Lilly and I had waited for this moment for years. We went to the jewelry exchange on Washington Street together, picked them out and went to the Parker House for a celebratory drink. We set them on the table between us so we could look at them while we congratulated each other. Lilly insisted on wrapping them in pretty blue boxes herself and then we put them in the office safe. She had rented a white horse to help with the presentation—she was going to ride him onstage at the moment the diamond-necklace winners were announced. "Remember Barbara Stanwyck on that staircase in *Double Indemnity*? That's the entrance we aspire to, baby."

The conference went off without a hitch. Lilly led the session on "Keeping Our Husbands Happy," which she'd invented when we lost three solid sellers to husbands who wanted their wives home every night instead of running cosmetics parties. The blue-diamond winners included, luckily, a beautiful twenty-four-year-old wearing a very low-cut dress that got us a picture in the *Boston Herald Tribune*. Thirty new salesgirls came our way within a week of seeing that picture. I sent congratulatory letters to each of their husbands, including stories from husbands grateful for the vacations and refrigerators their families had bought with Be Your Best income.

"Send them the 'You can expect more sex if they work for us' letter," Lilly called out. Lilly had perfected this one, managing to convey the idea without mentioning the act at all. "Send them the 'My wife is so much better groomed now that she sells for your company and she's lost twelve pounds.' "

"We don't need to do that. These women are making money you can see—that's enough," I said.

"Just shows what you know about men," she said back. She rolled her eyes.

"Next year," I said, grinning after the last of the conference was wrapped up, "it's going to be a powder-blue Cadillac as well as three diamond necklaces. Now—off you go to become a divorcée yet again."

"I'm aiming for 'gay divorcée.' I'd lay odds at about even."

That night Annie and I had a stuffed-animal tea party with sugar cookies and cucumber sandwiches, milky tea, and licorice. Annie suggested we add MoonPies at our next tea because the stuffed animals preferred them to cucumbers. I didn't blame them, I said. MoonPies it is.

Lilly came home from the dude ranch a blonde with a taste for cowgirl shirts and boots. It didn't last long, and I sort of missed the cowgirl shirts when they ended up wadded behind the Chanel suits. It took her a while to regain her mind. Annie clung to me when her newly platinum-blond mother barreled into the apartment. It hurt my sister, but I could see it from Annie's point of view as well.

"I scare her," Lilly said to me that first night after Annie had been dispatched to bed. "I'm the woman who pushed her out her bedroom window and told her to jump."

"That's true," I said. "You did. But I think the cowboy shirt and boots and yellow hair are more what she's reacting to now."

"Why is it that kids like everything to stay the same? I can't stay the same. I look at her looking at me like that, like I'm the Martian mother come home to push her out windows again, and it feels bad. Kids are so judgmental. Narrow. You know, I'd like to be what the child wants me to be but, then again, I don't. It's not going to happen."

"She'll adjust. What's that color you're wearing now?"

"The girls on the ranch called it Hell-Bent-for-Leather Brown."

"I like it. How about Lusty Wench Red? Night of the Ball Blush. Pirate Girl Pink."

"Snapping-Eyed Wench." She laughed.

"I'm not joking. What woman doesn't want to have a little piratical streak?"

"You don't," Lilly snorted. "Got any pie around here?" Lilly sighed. "Or bourbon?"

"She's a little louder than she was when she was a brunette," Charles Helbrun observed. People expected Charles and I to appear places together now and I was often at his side at his business events. He was a less reliable date for me at Be Your Best parties or Terhune family gatherings, but he showed up enough to be considered my own particular beau.

A little louder? I knew that in his language, "loud" was code for "vulgar," which was not a compliment. I'd invited him along on a walk with Annie and Lilly, and the afternoon had had some awkward silences—these might have made Lilly seem louder than she actually was when she tried to fill them in. Annie had started the day out being very charming but had gotten less so as her adult company got more awkward and she got hungrier, which made Charles impatient with her.

"Her daughter is very pretty, but she could stand to lose a little weight," he said at one point when we had fallen a bit behind the others. "She doesn't want those pounds to hang around when she gets older."

"Annie is not overweight." This was true. Annie weighed less than a full bag of groceries and was nobody's idea of fat. "And my sister has never been vulgar," I added. "Vulgar means 'common' which is not Lilly Terhune. At all."

"She might not be common, but she can still be vulgar," he replied. "And her stories about Reno—all horses and barbecues and divorcée man-hating pajama parties. She describes something like a summer camp with gin fizzes and lawyers."

"If she was that frivolous, her divorce lawyer wouldn't have congratulated her on how ironclad the Be Your Best paperwork was. Ricky got nothing."

"For that she has you to thank," Charles said.

"Your boyfriend doesn't like me," Lilly said when we got home from that outing. "Not that it matters what he thinks of me. How's it going in the romance department with him and you?"

"Pretty well," I said. She'd been so busy trying to return to something like normal that a lot of my moods were passing by her unnoticed. I hoped this uncertainty I felt about Charles Helbrun and me breezed by her now. I didn't have any other gentleman callers to compare him to. He turned every female head in the place whenever he stepped into the office. They thought I didn't know that they asked one another why a guy who looked and walked and talked like Charles Helbrun III was dating a woman who looked and walked and talked like me. This both pleased me and made me feel bad. "He's great," I said. "We're great."

"Amazing," Lilly said. "In the end I'm the idiot about men and my hermit sister is the one who gets it right and snags the rich, handsome, smart guy." She sat down, looking suddenly more like a sack of sand with a good haircut than a gay divorcée. "This is the last I'll say of it," she said. "Neavie, I've known men who made me a little nervous, but in the end Ricky was . . . more. I swear I didn't know there were men like him. And when I should have seen it, I didn't. Something about him was like a barbed hook set right through my brain, pulling me toward him. I'll never marry again. I'm bad at it. I've got the very worst kind of judgment about men and I've got Annie to think about. So I've decided to stop making mistakes. No more husbands."

"I don't think it works like that, Lilly. You can't just wave a wand and make yourself different. You love men."

"I do," she nodded. "Which makes the whole situation sad." She lit a cigarette and sighed. Her mascara had raccooned around her eyes, which shone like a child's with a high fever. "A little magic would help right now," she said. "Or a facial."

LILLY

Meat

I moved Annie and me out of the warehouse and into our own apartment a few months after I got back from Reno. I knew Neave wasn't happy to see us go. I said things to her like *I'm a grown-up and a mother to boot. I should be on my own. I leave dishes in the sink and wet towels on the floor and it drives you nuts. Me and Annie get in the way of your social life.* The truth is I wanted to live my life without Neave looking over my shoulder. I wasn't worried about Annie because I knew Jane and Neave and my little flock of daytime babysitters would back me up any time I needed help or just wanted some leeway so I could do a little coming and going. So I moved out and I did some coming and going.

When Neave found the bloody hunk of meat on the warehouse apartment back door I felt a kind of a thud, like something inside me had fallen off a shelf. I was really determined not to know what I knew, so I said things to her like, *Some idiot's idea of a joke*, but I knew it wasn't a joke.

She was pretending not to be rattled, but she was. That kind of surprise can make your blood feel like you got picked up and shaken like a cocktail. When I got to the office she took me upstairs and led me to the back door. The nail was driven through a section of marbled gristle and fat. I'd never noticed how much real blood there was in a piece of meat before you cooked it. A little stream of it had run down the door and puddled at the mat.

"I'm throwing that mat away," Neave said. "Who would do this?"

She pulled the bleeding meat off the nail and held it away from herself. The thing in her hands looked very much more like part of a dead animal than it looked like the main course in a good dinner. She stuffed it in the trash she'd brought out to the fire escape. "Get some bleach, will you?" she said to me. "And scrub brushes."

She did most of the cleanup. I was in a good suit and she hadn't gotten dressed for work yet. But I stood and watched while she worked, the two of us there, the brush *scrtchhscrtchh*-ing, and the traffic just beginning to wake up and move in the street below. It was cool and sunny, a beautiful day. When she finished scouring, she took off every piece of clothing she'd had on her and stuffed it all in the trash after the meat.

"People in the company come up and down here sometimes if I send them up to get something. People know I live here. Have we fired anybody recently who was kind of odd?"

I said, "Everybody is kind of odd. It was probably some drunk. Somebody who got the wrong door."

"Lilly, the door has the company name on it."

"Well. When you're drunk . . ." I said.

We were not right with each other all day at work. At lunch Neave said, "You know I'm walking around looking at everybody—our own sales staff, the accountant, the coffee-shop guys in the building next to us, and I'm thinking, *Was it you?*"

So when we were alone at the end of the afternoon I knew I had to do it. I told her that I'd lied when I said I had no idea who would hang the meat on the door. Neave can get real quiet and she was quiet now.

"I've been seeing Ricky. I didn't tell you because I knew what you'd say."

"Why would you do something that stupid?"

Which was exactly what I thought she'd say. Neave has always had a habit of looking at things and then telling you what she sees. I said, "Just before Annie and I moved out he called and said just a drink just for old times. I said no. Then I said yes. Then I said yes again. It's my own business, Neave. I'm a grown woman. The reason I'm telling you is that Ricky has been saying things. Sort of crazy things. And the meat, and the way it's waiting here on the door, it's Ricky all over. I think maybe it could be for you. From him."

"I haven't seen Ricky Luhrmann since before you divorced him. Why would I even cross his mind?"

The fact was that Neave crossed Ricky's mind quite a bit and what he said about my sister might, conceivably, have led to this piece of meat on a door: Neave had poisoned our marriage; Neave was jealous of me; Neave did what she wanted with the company and didn't consult me; Neave had hired a pack of lawyers to keep the company away from him though he was my legal husband and the company was legally his. Part his. The rants began to lead to the same place: she hated men.

"I don't know why," I said to her. This was both the truth, and not the truth.

Neave looked at the nail on the door. "So this is a threat?" Her face was pasty white and her lips were just two pencil-thin lines. "Break it off, Lilly. Get rid of him. Now."

"I can manage things, Neave. Calm him down."

"Lilly. Remember the night you and Annie jumped out the window."

"I can control him."

"Clearly you can't control him," she said.

Then Neave said she was going to track that lunatic down and I said that would be the dumbest thing to do when Ricky was in this frame of mind. I knew him through and through, I said, which didn't end up being accurate. Stay out of it, I told her. I'd talked Ricky Luhrmann down from all kinds of ledges and I could do it again.

I was still stupid enough at that point to think that was the truth. I was wrong.

Neave, I'm so sorry.

BOPPIT

Where We Are, Where I Want to Go

I'd discovered, in my time as a dog, that people don't take you seriously if you're a dog. They hit you with things, and abandon you, and take away your favorite stuff; but then, they do that to each other too. I was comfortable as a dog because my nature is loyal and steady and basically affectionate. It's like Neave's nature.

I am Neave's protector. As far as I know I'll always be her protector. Sometimes I fail at it, I know. I'm not confident that I can protect her now, but it's my job and I'm going to do it as well as I can. That's why I was sitting on the curb outside George's Sweetheart Market. I was there to follow her home. That's why I was here to greet Lilly when she became Dead Lilly. I was there to get Lilly to lead me to Neave, to get Neave to see us so we can intercede, advise. Maybe, I hope, save her.

Lilly and Neave share parts of their minds that overlap in ways they don't see or understand. It's this kind of powerful attachment that holds the universe together, and I am here to use it to save Neave. Their bond is very strong—flexible and porous and twisty in places where the connections are thickest. The fact that Lilly is dead is not as much of a problem as you might think. It could even be an advantage.

If Neave is going to save herself from Lilly's fate, she's going to have to be more like Lilly. I know that doesn't make perfect sense, given what Lilly's judgment has been like, but it's true. Lilly has to get mind-to-mind with Neave, cross over the distances between them and get in her sister's head. Lilly is there all the time even now, of course, but I don't mean her being in Neave's mind as a memory. I mean in Neave's mind as part of Neave. A grafted Lilly-Neave, a seeped-into-each-other new entity.

Neave needs to figure out how to stand in front of three hundred salesgirls and make them want to be her. Just like Lilly can. She needs to feel powerful, sexually confident, full of authority over Ricky Luhrmann, just like Lilly did. She can't be Neave-ish and stand there thinking about things.

Right now Ricky Luhrmann is stronger than Neave, but he might not be stronger than the two of them together.

That's the plan.

NEAVE

I Talk to Max Luhrmann

You aren't held to keeping promises to a person who's lost her mind, and I didn't keep my promise to Lilly to stay out of her business. I went to the police to report the bloody piece of meat being hung from my door. The police said *Do you know who did it?* and *Do you have proof?* and I said not really. They said that hanging meat on a door was not a crime, and no property damage had been done, and I didn't even really know who did it, did I? Could have been a joke, right?

"Why would a piece of bloody steak be funny?" I asked the uniformed man behind the counter.

He shrugged. "Could be funny."

The policeman saying these things wore a badge that identified him as PETZOLDT #4967. "Officer Petzoldt," I said, "that meat is a threat. And if it isn't a threat, let's say it's destruction of property."

"Lady, what does a nail in a door cost you? Some spackle."

"Let's say it's harassment. Let's say I want a restraining order. Or I just want you to talk to the guy. What do I need?"

"I can't talk to the guy or deliver a restraining order if I got no idea where the guy is, sugar."

"Well, you'll try to locate him, right?"

The officer rocked back a bit and lifted one shoulder vaguely. No, he was not going to try to locate anybody.

"If I find him, give you an address, will you question him?"

"Well, yeah, but nothing's gonna happen if we don't have the guy to talk to."

I looked in my rearview mirror all the way back to the apartment that day, certain that a blue Ford had made at least three of the turns I had and then fallen out of sight. That night the telephone calls started, all to my home number, all just before dawn or a couple hours after midnight. At first I picked up the receiver and talked to the breathing thing on the other end. I addressed it as Ricky and I told it I was going to track his ass down and get him in a world of trouble if he didn't leave us alone. More calls. When I didn't pick up the receiver they kept ringing: twenty rings, thirty rings, forty rings. I unplugged the telephone.

Lilly had sworn that she didn't have a telephone number or address for him. How can that be? I'd protested. You're meeting this man in hotel rooms but you don't know how to call him? Didn't she see how controlling that was? How perverse? I wasn't entirely sure she was telling me the truth, but it looked to me that even if she did have a telephone number and address for Ricky, she wouldn't give them to me.

I called the last construction company he'd worked with and the foreman said he'd had to fire him months ago. He wouldn't say why. The only Luhrmann I could track down was his brother, Max, who was listed in a university oceanography department. I wrote the number down and put it on my kitchen table. I didn't call it.

I took the problem to Charles. "Have you ever hired a private investigator?" I asked him.

"Once for an accounting scam. We hired a numbers guy, a specialist who knew how to tease stuff out of cooked books. Why?"

I told him. He shrugged. "I have no experience with that kind of problem. Are you sure her ex-husband is the one who nailed it to your door?" I said I was sure. Then I said I was 99 percent sure. I said Lilly was sure too, even if she said she wasn't. He said, "So it's a hunch. Maybe not true at all. Don't take everything personally, Neave. This might not be what you suspect."

I protested. He suggested that maybe there was some teenage prankster in the neighborhood, some fool who'd had a few beers. "Maybe he had a crush on Lilly. Or someone in the office."

"A crush?"

"You know—like an older guy's version of the way third-grade boys show a girl they like her—they hit her. Throw things at her. Are you dealing with anybody who might have a crush on you? Maybe that's why it was left for you."

I was already pretty sure that wasn't the case. I decided not to talk any more about the problem with Charles. If Charles understood anything at all about the impulses that could be expressed in a piece of raw meat nailed to a door, he had decided to pretend that he didn't. He was useless here. He wasn't a stupid or inexperienced man, so this willful blindness infuriated me. In what cramped corner of his mind must a man crouch in order to see nothing?

I drove to the university where Max Luhrmann worked. In the engineering building I threaded myself through what felt like a series of basement tunnels, following signs and arrows to "Oceanography" when I could find them nailed or glued to the cinder-block walls. I stopped a passing man and asked him if I was heading toward Max Luhrmann's office. "The smart guy?" he asked.

"Isn't everybody here smart?" I asked.

"Not like him." He pointed left.

When I found his office, there was no Max in it, but there were thousands of pounds of dismembered electronic equipment. I called his name but got no answer. The sign on his door listed office hours, one of which was right now. I sat down to wait. The room was beautifully cool, the light diffuse.

Thirty minutes later I woke disoriented and frowzy, sat as upright as I could until the confusion cleared, and found myself staring directly at Max Luhrmann. He was across the desk from me, quizzical and, for just a moment before he fully registered that I was awake, curious with a touch of pleased. When he saw I was awake his face quickly shifted to something flatter, more impassive. "How long have you been staring at me?" I demanded.

"Just for a minute. So, Neave Terhune, what brings you here?"

I described the telephone calls, the meat on the door, the renewed relationship with Lilly, who claimed she didn't know where Ricky Luhrmann was. "The police say they'll help but they can't do anything if they can't find Ricky. So how do I find Ricky?"

"You don't want to find him, Neave."

"Bullies stand down if somebody faces them," I insisted. "I'm going to face him."

"That's a charmingly romantic idea, but I don't think it actually works like that in real life."

"It's a time-tested technique."

"Maybe in second grade it is."

"Ricky's not going to hurt me," I insisted.

Max lifted his shirt, pulling it high enough to expose two white keloid lines running from his abdomen to his breastbone. "I bounced against a windshield trying to stop Ricky. He'd grabbed a girl's skirt, slammed it in the car door, and tried to drag her into mutilation if not death. So you see, Ricky is entirely capable of hurting someone. Say, you, for example."

I looked at the gnarled lines of white scar tissue. I thought about Lilly telling me that Ricky swore the mothers in the neighborhood were afraid of Max, who was rough with the girls.

He let his shirt drop. "It doesn't help to stand in front of some kinds of people. It can make them more determined to run you down. If you involve anybody else, like cops, it will only escalate. Ricky escalates. Resist him, he escalates harder. He doesn't care about rules as much as he cares about other things. Walk away from this."

"But Lilly . . ." I began.

Max turned away from me. "I have a lot of work to do. Please shut the door on your way out."

I stalked back to my car telling myself that he was wrong. I had an almost animal sense that backing away from this man would be seen as a display of weakness, a dangerous admission of fear.

I pulled the car door open. At first glance what was lying peacefully in the driver's seat was a sleeping dog. Who would have expected a neighborhood dog to jump through the open window and fall asleep in the front seat? The idea tickled me, though, and I was smiling as I said, "Come on, you. Out you go." The little form stayed still. I reached out a hand and stroked its head, which flopped to one side. It hung loosely from the body and now I could see that the dog's neck had been twisted almost entirely around, snapped before the animal was arranged peacefully on my car seat with its head propped on its paws. The body was still warm. I jerked upright and scanned the street. No one in sight. A trickle of blood had run down from the dog's muzzle and only just dried on the car seat to a purplish crust.

I walked slowly, woodenly, back into Max Luhrmann's basement office. He looked up from his desk, saw my face, and stood up. He fell in line behind me, let me lead him back to the car and the small body curled on the passenger seat.

"It's him, isn't it?" I asked.

"It's possible." Max leaned over and touched the dog, leaned down, smelled the dog's fur. He turned to me. "A woman's perfume. Your sister's?"

"Is it Chanel No. 5?" I leaned over and breathed in. Lilly's perfume. "How did you know to smell the dog?"

"It's something that he'd do."

"How do you know that?"

"It's just the way we are. Sometimes I can get in his head; he can get in mine. Doing this with the dog in front of my office, I suspect Ricky's saying a little something to me as well as to you."

"Like what?"

"That he's watching me as well as you. He doesn't like me talking with anyone about him and he knows that's the only reason you'd be here. He's telling me he doesn't like it."

"What would happen if you talked to anyone about him?"

"They might know him better."

Suddenly I thought of Lilly standing before me on her wedding day all wrapped up in a Champagne haze and sixty pounds of couture silk. *I don't know . . . there was a little sister . . . Some kind of accident . . . the start of all the bad feeling.* "Max, you had a sister? What happened to her?"

"She died."

"How?"

His voice flattened and the words came out like beads he'd been fingering for years and years. "She drowned."

"Lilly told me that was the beginning of the bad feelings between you and Ricky. Is that true? What happened?"

He turned and took a step away, said, "I'll get a box. Take the dog away."

"Don't touch the dog yet. I'm calling the police and I want them to see this exactly the way it is now."

Max shrugged, a gesture showing just how helpful he thought the police would be, and he was right. He waited with me for a cop to arrive. It was Officer Petzoldt, who actually rolled his eyes when he saw me.

"So somebody put this dog in your car? Is it your dog, Miss Terhune? Was anything taken from the car?"

We established that the dog was not mine, that no one took anything from the car, and that I firmly believed that Ricky Luhrmann killed the dog and put it there as a threat.

"People are funny, Miss Terhune. Have you found the mutt's owner?"

No we hadn't, though we'd walked around the immediate area while we'd waited for him to get here, asking anyone passing by if they'd heard of a missing dog. No one had.

"Well, Miss Terhune, I'm not exactly sure what crime you're reporting," he said with a sigh. "But as to the perfume smell, the dog is in your car and you wear perfume. We're probably just smelling your perfume."

"I don't wear that perfume."

The policeman turned to Max. "This guy she's talking about is your brother?" Max nodded. "So you didn't see him do this either? Nobody saw anything?" Max said he had not. "And can you give me an address or place of employment for your brother?" Max said he could not. Officer Petzoldt shrugged. "It's a dog, lady. And honestly, I don't smell much of anything. Maybe somebody didn't like the dog, or didn't like you, or maybe both, but there's no witnesses and you can't even get anybody on this block to claim the dog. It's not gonna go to the Supreme Court, even if we found the guy you think may have done it."

Max stood beside me on the sidewalk as we watched Officer Petzoldt drive off. He'd found a cardboard box and gently lifted the body from my car, set it in the box. "I'll take care of this." He started walking away from me, holding his box of dog gingerly to one side.

"Max?" I called after him. He turned around.

"You know him. What's he going to do next? What should I do?"

He turned his back again and took a few steps, stopped, and turned to face me again. "I think you should stay with a friend for a while."

"I don't have any friends." This was true, and it was the first time it struck me as odd. I had Lilly, and work, and Jane and Snyder. I didn't want Ricky Luhrmann sitting outside either of their homes, trailing me to either of their doors.

Did I have Charles? No. Charles would say he could not compromise my reputation by taking me in; Charles would tell me there was nothing, really, to worry about. If Ricky showed up at his door, Charles Helbrun would have no more idea what to do than Snyder would. I didn't want to see that. Nor did I want to even think of Ricky Luhrmann on my sister Janey's front steps.

That left no place. Before this moment my small circle had been enough, and now I saw that it wasn't.

"Well." Max stood and considered for another moment or two. "My department research vessel has a cabin that's pretty comfortable and nobody expects anybody to be sleeping in it. Slip four at the Charlestown docks: the *Rubber Duck*. You could use it nights. Stay there irregularly so you were hard to predict."

"I'm not afraid of Ricky Luhrmann."

"I know that. It's why I offered you the *Rubber Duck*."

"I'm not hiding on your boat, Max."

When I was no more than a block away I had to brace myself so I wouldn't look behind me in the rearview mirror. I looked anyhow, and was rewarded with the sight of him still standing there watching me, perfectly still with a box of dead dog in his arms.

I told Lilly about the dog, certain that it would end any connection that bound her to Ricky. I could see her withdraw inside herself someplace far from me. "Lilly, you aren't still in touch with him, are you?" I know I sounded alarmed when I said it, even though I was struggling to sound like a rational bystander.

"No." Then she added, "But he gets in touch with me. His old number's disconnected. He calls me from pay phones."

"He can find you, but you can't find him. Listen to yourself."

"I can handle him, Neave."

Were her eyes shining? Was it possible that the thing inside Ricky Luhrmann that had left that dog on my car seat lit something up in her? "Lilly. He put your perfume on a dead dog. Please."

She actually patted me on the knee. "It's going to be all right."

Then she smiled, not at me. It was a private smile and I knew it was for him, or for something that she was when she was with him. It was an in-turning thing, and as I watched it I knew I could have burst into flame right there in front of her and not caught her eye.

We were in the worst kind of trouble.

LILLY AND BOPPIT

How He Hates Her

He hates her in this weird, unreasonable way," Boppit observed.

"Well, I know that. It was like he had some raw spot inside him and every time they came together, she'd run a blowtorch over it. If she missed the raw spot he'd turn around so she could reach it better. Right from the start it was like that. Take the dinner I set up with her and Ricky to cultivate peace and harmony, me still thinking that was a possibility. Ricky brings up the subject of company ownership. *Well*, he says, *of course as the husband I'm a legal owner of Be Your Best.* Me, I would have let that just slide by. Who cares what he thought, because legally I knew that Neave and I had changed the paperwork after my first experience with a disappointing husband and locked every asset in the company into our names. Ricky didn't have any legal access at all. But Neave has always had this dumb idea that it's best to have everything right out on the table. She makes it clear to Ricky then and there: he's got no say in the company at all and the profits are his wife's. Not his. Bam."

"Very bad," Boppit agreed.

"Oh, it gets worse. She asks him if I'd ever actually spelled out the controlling parties in the business. *Just try it and see what happens, Mister*: that was her tone. He says he's sure he can legally arrange for ownership to include him. She says she doesn't think so. She doesn't hear his tone or else she just ignores it and she plows straight on. She says even if he got me to go along with that idea that it couldn't happen without her cooperating, and she was perfectly happy with the company ownership only including her and me."

"Ricky was always just the littlest bit scared of her," Boppit said to me. "That was coloring the conversation too."

"He didn't look scared at that moment."

"That doesn't mean he wasn't," Bop says.

"If only she knew how to flirt, put guys at ease. Not Neave. She wants somebody's attention, she waves a red cape. So she does this to Ricky, he snorts and paws and charges around, and when he's stomped out of the room I tell her maybe she could have been more diplomatic. And who does she get mad at? Me. She wants to know how I ever let Ricky Luhrmann think he'd ever have a say in anything to do with Be Your Best. I just hadn't seen the need to talk about it, I say. Easier to step over some subjects than go stubbing your toe on them. Why couldn't she do the same? Now I had to deal with foul-mood Ricky, and sure enough, we're getting ready for bed that night and I don't even have my stockings unsnapped from my garters when he starts in. *You're going to a lawyer and change things so I'm a legal owner of Be Your Best like any husband in America would be.* I rolled the stockings down real slow and I said Neave meant what she said. She wasn't giving that kind of control to somebody outside our partnership—somebody, I added, who shouldn't be burdened by all the work, the decisions, the responsibility. Just enjoy the profits, I said. Let me and Neavie do the work."

"Which didn't quiet him down," Boppit said with a sigh.

"Of course not. He said Neave was a controlling bitch who hated men. He said she needed a strong hand."

"He scared you," Boppit said, which was true but I hadn't wanted to admit that to myself at the time, so I hadn't. The kindness in Bop's voice made the taste of salt start in my mouth, made my throat feel like it was closing. He said, "That was something that had never happened to you before with Ricky Luhrmann, but it was going to happen sooner or later, Lilly."

This was true and I'd known it then, all the way back then when I was refusing to know what I knew.

Bop talked like he was in my head. "You weren't the only one afraid of Ricky. Max is afraid of him."

"No he isn't. I've met Max."

"Just because Max would stand up to him doesn't mean that Max isn't scared of him. It only means Max has nerve."

"Since when are you in Max's head?"

He shrugged. "We don't get to pick every place we end up." Boppit sighed again. "You of all people should know that, sweetheart."

LILLY

What I Saw in Him

You want to know what I saw in him, right?

The first time I laid eyes on Luhrmann he had his hand on another man's neck. It wasn't a fight—just a kind of tap to let everybody know who was in charge. Then he pulled a wad of cash out of a pocket and peeled off a Ulysses S. Grant and said the drinks were on him, real casual. The combination of the hand on the neck and the big drink gesture put me off. It's the kind of Big Man horseshit you see all over. He looked my way when he did it. Just a piece of meathead theatre.

I was at the Ritz Bar with some present and future salesgirls, the kind of girls Neave thought were silly just because it mattered to them that their shoes and purses matched. Which of course they have to. Neavie was back at the grinding wheel with her nose pressed real hard on some problem about the cash flow. She's happier with that kind of thing. I'm happier fishing for sales staff with a martini in my hand and a nice view of Newbury Street. The girls saw Mr. Grandstander focus in on me and smile from where he was sitting on the other side of the room.

"Take a gander at the table closest to the bar," one of them said to me. "That guy's looking you over."

"Let him look," I said. "That's all he's gonna get to do. I'm going to the ladies'."

Somehow I knew he'd do exactly what he did, which was find a way to get himself in my path on my way back, out of sight of his gang and my girlfriends. I wasn't drunk, so I don't know why I let him talk me into giving him my number, but he had it before I sat down with the girls again. Let him call, I thought. Doesn't mean I'm going out with him. Doesn't mean anything.

At first I gave him the bum's rush. He'd call. Leave messages. I'd ignore them. He kept it up for a full month before I said I'd have a drink with him. He said if I'd go for one drink he'd be satisfied and that would be the end of it, just one drink, which we both knew wasn't the real deal. How did we know so soon how to play each other's game, but still be able to surprise each other? It was magic, the way he made me resist him just enough to get a little friction going, and then find a way to make me feel like whatever he wanted was exactly what I wanted in the end.

I'm kind of shocked at myself. I mean, here's Boppit shaking his head saying, "So blind. So blind, and yet you saw . . ." Okay. I could see it from the start, but I didn't want to see it, so I didn't. I made fun of it at the Ritz Bar and then I let it make me say yes when he asked me for my number. I told the girlfriends he was a showy meathead and they said they thought he was sexy as hell, which he was. It was right smack in the center of him, whatever it was that made women say he was sexy as hell.

I was so confident. I could have any man who caught my eye and I could walk away from any of them too. Neave and I weren't Jell-O-cup-for-dessert women. We were the owners and directors of a fast-growing cosmetics company. I was the best-dressed woman in the room, and I paid for the Chanel suit myself, thank you very much.

I like men, really like them, even apart from the whole mating-dance thing. The truth is that most women like men. Ricky Luhrmann was not what most women would call likeable, though. He was something else. He moved like a big animal with lots of nerve. He could walk down any street and other men moved aside. He came at me like that, full of himself right up to the minute he was humble, treating me like I was the source spring of all good things, some kind of goddess he needed near him just to survive. If you've never been treated like a goddess, I'll tell you, it messes with your judgment. You forget, if you ever knew it to begin with, that lots of goddesses end up sacrificed on some altar or other.

NEAVE

What Does He Have to Do?

In the end I didn't find Ricky. He found me. Ricky Luhrmann showed up at my door acting like a bag of gasoline-soaked rags that had just met a match. It was about ten on a Friday night and Lilly had left Annie with me for the evening while she went out for a drink with some of the younger salesgirls. Any social life that didn't include Ricky Luhrmann looked like a good idea to me. Annie and I had sat on her bed and advised her on jewelry while she ignored us and picked out what she wanted. We'd waved her off and then driven to the apartment above the Be Your Best offices, played Monopoly until eight thirty, eaten large bowls of ice cream, then sat in bed reading stories until Annie had drifted off to sleep. I'd wandered into the kitchen and fallen back on my old friends: flour and chocolate. I'd imagined Annie and me eating pies for breakfast and the idea had made me cheerful. When I heard a knock I thought it was Lilly home early, knocking because she'd lost her key. I opened the door.

"Hello, bitch." The quietness of the words rattled me more than the words themselves. He threw his shoulder against the door as I tried to slam it shut. I scrabbled with one hand for the chain while the other pushed for all it was worth. He said, "You hated me from the get-go, which is fine with me because I can't stand you either. You go whining to my brother Max, you say things to him that aren't true. . . ."

I pulled in a deep breath to make my body puff up like an animal that fills its neck and chest with air to look larger. I imagined Annie sprawled out like a starfish in the bedroom behind me, probably drooling onto the pillow with her hair fanned around her. "Go away, Luhrmann. Lilly isn't here."

"I didn't come to deal with Lilly. I want to deal with you. Why are you talking with Max? What gives you the right to talk about me to my brother?" He jammed a foot quickly into the narrow opening I hadn't been able to close when he'd pushed against me with his shoulder.

"What is it with you and sticking your nose in my business? You think I don't know that you told Lilly I was trash? What do you know about what Lilly and I have? What would a dried-up old maid like you know? I've seen what you call a boyfriend. He's a busy boy, but he's clearly got no working equipment where it counts. Your sister and me, we've got what everybody on the fucking planet wants."

I looked at Ricky Luhrmann's blotchy face while he worked his knee into the doorway and tried to get it wide enough to pass through. I didn't smell any alcohol on his breath, which unnerved me. I had no explanation for what he looked like right now. I kicked the knee, hard.

"Son of a bitch!"

He reached down to touch the knee and I kicked his hand. He startled away and I got the door almost shut before he threw his whole body against it. I said, "I'm only a foot from the telephone and I can have cops here in five minutes. They want to talk to you about a piece of meat nailed to my door. They want to know about a dead dog somebody left in my car."

"Call 'em." His voice was unnaturally calm, like what was going on was exactly what he wanted to have going on. "I'll say you asked me over to talk about how sad you were about Lilly and me breaking up and how you hoped I'd come visit and in the generosity of my heart I agreed. Because you sounded a little unbalanced . . . a little crazy."

He took a deep breath and smelled the pie for the first time. "How sweet. Were you baking me something as a surprise, hoping I'd be here soon? That's the picture I'll paint for the cops. Here you are baking me something nice. A lonely, jealous woman making advances on her sister's ex-husband and getting violent when he rejects her, so in self-defense I had to subdue you. A nut case. What a whore. I only came over because I thought you might be a danger to yourself. I'll look so sad about it all."

Ricky suddenly twisted around, frowning. There were footsteps on the stairs. I peered past his shoulder down to the street. Jane's car. Jane—generous, perpetually cheerful Jane, dropping by because I'd told her I was watching Annie tonight and she'd decided to surprise me and keep me company because she believed everyone wanted company. The steps got closer and there she was on the landing directly behind Luhrmann. She'd been preoccupied with balancing the cake on its pink platter and the scene at my door took her by surprise. She moved toward us, very slowly, but she kept coming toward us.

"What are you doing here?" she said loudly, but we could both see that the cake was shaking in her hands. I could feel her fear feed something in Luhrmann, make him expand into a slightly larger, leering thing.

I said, "Jane? Thanks for coming. Is Todd right behind you?"

Ricky looked from her to me, from me to her, deciding. "Yes," she lied. "Just behind me."

Luhrmann looked me in the eyes. "It's not over," he whispered. "Women like you end up regretting how they act." He pushed off from the door and brushed by Jane, hard, purposefully swinging a shoulder and arm so that the cake and its pretty pink platter flew down the steps behind her, an arc of shattered glass and broken lemon cake. I closed my hand firmly around Jane's arm and yanked her into the apartment. We bolted the door and watched from a locked window as he made his way to his own car, got in, and drove off.

"Aunt Neave? Aunt Jane?" Annie, ruffled and sleepy, a good deal of her hair sticking straight up from her head. She had a stuffed bear in her arms. "What's happening?"

"Nothing," we said as one.

Annie considered this. "I smell chocolate!" she accused. "Did you make brownies?"

"Nope."

"I smell them."

"It's chocolate peanut-butter pie," I admitted.

"You made it after I went to bed!"

"It was a surprise. For breakfast." That was true, but I'd fully expected to make my way through half the pie tonight all by myself. Annie's face got accusatory. Stern. Certainly Jane's presence was suspicious.

"Aunt Jane came over to eat pie with you."

"You promise not to tell your mom if we let you stay up and eat pie?" Jane asked. Annie nodded, hard.

It is an absolute truth that having a little girl under your wing who thinks you can protect her makes you feel more powerful. That could be why we let Annie stay at the table until her face fell directly into her plate, at which point Jane plucked her up and carried her back to bed. We spent a half hour scrubbing cake off the stairs and sweeping up the shattered platter.

"What are you going to say to Lilly when she comes to pick up Annie?" Jane asked.

"The truth. That he's a psychopath and I'm furious with her for starting up with him again."

"Something's wrong with him. He's not normal. Neave, I heard what he said."

"He didn't say anything."

"He said it wasn't over. He said you'd regret something. He didn't come to see Lilly, did he? He came to say those things to you. He didn't even know Annie was here. I'm calling Todd and telling him to come over and wait with us until Lilly comes home."

"No, you will not. He's not coming back tonight. I'll bolt the downstairs and the upstairs doors. Besides, Lilly will be here any minute."

"Oh, Neave," my gentle and brave little sister said, her face darkening around lowered, worried eyebrows. "It's times like this I wish you were married."

When Lilly came to pick Annie up I described our evening. She got mad—not at Luhrmann, at me. "Why did you go talk to Max? Why would you do that!" she demanded. "You just went and got Ricky crazy. I told you he and Max didn't get along. That's all you accomplished!"

"How can you talk to me like any of this is my fault?"

"I told you not to talk to Max!"

"It wasn't Max who came here and threatened me. Neither one of us think Max left a piece of meat on my door. Do we? Or put your perfume on an animal and then broke its neck! You know in your bones that it was Ricky. What does he have to do? The dog in the car, Lilly!"

"I know this is hard for you to hear, Neave, but you don't understand."

"No. I don't." Lilly turned her face away from me. "Lilly? What are you thinking? Please tell me it's done; tell me if he calls you again you'll hang up!"

"Stop worrying," she said, and I don't know how I knew but it was clear and sharp and certain. She was going to see him again.

NEAVE

What Could Be Worse?

For the first time in my life I felt like I couldn't reach my sister, couldn't find any way to make her see me, listen to me. She said there was nothing to worry about, which was clearly a lie. I went to Jane, who had no advice or guidance to offer. It was surely a sign of how helpless and crazed I felt that I brought the whole subject up with Snyder. We had just gone over a month's cash flow for his business, which was doing so well that he'd had to hire an assistant and get a second telephone line.

"I knew guys like Ricky in high school." He shrugged. "That dog thing you're talking about, I knew two guys who had dead cats left in their lockers. That happens to you, you tell nobody or the next thing you find in your locker'll be worse."

"What could be worse than a dead cat in your locker?"

"Just the head of the cat."

"How do you know this?"

"I was one of the two guys."

After a moment of silence in which it was clear that I felt a little stricken on his behalf he added, as if to comfort me, "The head was just a threat. Never actually materialized."

But the dead cats had.

I tried to talk to Charles but took care to stop short of speaking about the things that really scared me. I told him about the threatening visit, but not the dog.

"You're overreacting again. This ex-husband of your sister's sounds shallow and a little stupid. Even if he did actually do these things—trying to scare you, playing pranks and yelling . . . those are the things a little boy does. They're childish. Doesn't your sister have a few other ex-husbands? I don't think there's anything to worry about."

I was of two minds about this reassurance. I was grateful, because I'd wanted to be reassured and he offered this; I was disgusted, because the reassurance felt so blind and dumb and cowardly, so far from the reality of Ricky Luhrmann at my door, whispering "Bitch" with white spittle at the corners of his mouth. Charles Helbrun III didn't believe in evil. What good was he when it raised its head and hissed?

It's a lonely thing to be the only person who sees what's sitting coiled right in front of you. So one afternoon when Ruga Potts and I sat over a row of sample lipsticks to compare color and texture, I told her about Ricky Luhrmann's visit. Also the meat and the dog. Ruga Potts had met Ricky Luhrmann on a couple of occasions when he'd come to the office to pick up Lilly. Ruga reacted with a shrug, like Charles Helbrun had done, but she had lived in places Charles Helbrun had only read about in the newspaper. "That kind of man," she said, "you try to ignore him he just comes back and lines your family outside your front door and shoots them. He only leaves you alive so you can tell others what he did. So he can poison their sleep as well as yours."

I nodded. That was more like it.

LILLY AND BOPPIT

Are You Made for Fire or Ice?

"Look at this Revlon advertisement, Boppit. This ad launched a million nail polish sales. It's the reason Be Your Best started to make money on the stuff."

"I know that."

We were looking at the "Fire and Ice" nail polish advertisement that changed the beauty business. There was a statuesque model in a skin-tight sequined dress, her gleaming nails fanned across her face and hip. A red cloak was gathered and draped through her arms and behind her shoulders, framing her. "That brilliant little quiz they included in the ad," I went on. "Look at this woman, all lit up like a silver goddess with red talons: *'Question one: Are you made for Fire and Ice? Question two: Would you rather have a cocktail with Mata Hari or tea with Florence Nightingale?'* "

"Well, of course the correct responses are 'Hand me that martini,' and 'Hello, Mata Hari,' " says Bop. "Did you know that Mata Hari was executed wearing a Creed suit?"

"The suit is not the point, Dog."

"Oh, but it is. She was Mata Hari, in part, because she knew what a Creed suit could do for her waist and because she carefully chose her execution outfit. That, my dear, is class. But the real point is that glamour has always required a little touch of tramp. It's why your 'Fast Girl' hot pink and 'Vampy Red' flew out the door. Every girl wants a little Pirate Lover in her life."

"A little what?"

"You know. Like that book. Evil threatens; people experience sexual adventures, some of a very sordid nature; love triumphs. All that."

"Damn book. She should never have stolen it."

"It wasn't really stealing. Mrs. Daniels knew she had it."

"Really?"

"Mrs. Daniels is a woman who paid attention. Actually, she was charmed when she noticed the book was missing. She knew where it was."

"This is all taking so long, Boppit. How are we supposed to get to Neave?"

"We think and think until we've got her clear in our mind. We concentrate. First she'll be like a picture in a frame; then the picture will start to move so it feels like a movie; then it gets its real depth and heft, like a hallucination."

"So it's imaginary. Not true."

"Don't be ridiculous. It's the most true. We get her firmly in our minds. At first she'll just feel us like a memory. Or a dream. We move closer. We concentrate. She thinks of us. We think of her. It's only a matter of time before she sees us, and we'll help her deal with her situation."

"Which is very bad," I said.

Mr. Boppit nodded. "It is."

NEAVE

I Am Not Alone

Going back to Max Luhrmann made no sense, maybe, but it was what I did. He was in my head. Actually, his throat, the part of the throat just above the collarbone that shows when a shirt's top button is open—that was in my head.

I found him sitting at his desk working something out with a slide rule. He went very still while he listened to my description of Ricky's visit: the smashed plate, the spittle on the lips. He stayed still for a full two minutes, which is a long time if you're sitting in front of somebody trying not to stare.

"He said it wasn't over? That you'd regret it? He used those words?"

I nodded. "He said that women like me end up regretting the way we act."

"Well, you wanted to find him so you could speak to him. Now you've spoken to him and you know how helpful talking to Ricky really is."

"You hate him."

"I wouldn't use that word."

"What words would you use?"

"Every choice I've made I've made because I thought that Ricky would not make it. It's given him a strange power over my life. He's shaped it because I made myself in direct opposition to him. We know each other so far under the skin that I feel a buzz in my scalp when he gets too close to me. Neave, trust me when I say that you don't want him to show up at your apartment again. Don't stay there alone. Reconsider moving in with your sister or your brother."

I ran through this idea again. Again, I imagined Luhrmann arriving at Janey's door, Annie answering his knock, Luhrmann smiling, the tiny girl alone there in the doorway with him for just a little window before anyone knew what was happening. I imagined Luhrmann at Snyder's door, towering over my brother, pushing past him into his apartment or studio, driving him into a wall with the force of nothing but his own bulk. I said, "I'm not going to their houses."

"Then you have to at least get harder to find. Take my offer to let you use the *Rubber Duck*. Don't be alone nights. Sleep on board until this blows over."

Things were not likely to blow over. The Ricky Luhrmanns of the world don't lose interest and stroll away. They slither out of sight under an abandoned car or wood pile, and next thing you know they're back, coiled in your bathroom sink when you go to get a glass of water in the middle of the night.

"Max, do you believe in evil?" I asked him.

He responded immediately, easily. "Of course I do."

My response was as quick and artless as his had been. "Thank God," I said.

Which made him laugh.

"You don't think things are going to blow over, do you?" I said.

"No." The word was frightening, but Max looked alert and calm. *Just facts*, his manner seemed to say. *You have to work with the facts.* "Neave, I grew up with him. We know each other. I didn't want it to get to this point, but here we are. Let me help you."

I felt a kind of cool rush move through my abdomen and up to my chest. It wasn't fear. It was something else.

"Just think about it."

"I'll think about it," I said, but I wasn't thinking about it. I was thinking about him. Max Luhrmann was in my head and Max Luhrmann believed in evil.

I was not alone.

THE PIRATE LOVER

Saved

The cold shock of immersion was so total, so encompassing, that at first Electra could not draw a breath. She sank down, struggling. Then she felt a hand around her body, another body rising up in the water beneath her and lifting her, pulling her to the surface. She gasped and her chest opened to accept the bracing air.

"You are strong, Electra. You can reach safety with me." His voice was so clear! It penetrated the deepest parts of her. A wind behind the change in the tide cut the water's surface up, a turmoil of foam around them and the waves building higher. Lightning again, and in its light she could see Henri Le Cherche's black ship behind them and the *Cat* half a league away and firing steadily toward their enemy. Waves broke around them in lacy confusion. But Basil Le Cherche's powerful body swam now alongside her, now beneath her, and she glided beside him, taking whatever risk there was with a high heart and more confidence in this strange man than she had ever felt for any other human being. She did not fear the future or consider the past—there was only this moment with this figure pushing through the waves, pulling her along with him.

He felt the change in her body, the fluid reengaging of thighs, arms, the coming to life in the water. Still he held her aloft and she let herself be held as he swam in steady great thrusts away from their captor's ship. They could see the silhouettes of sharpshooters in the *Cat*'s rigging, waiting for Henri Le Cherche's ship to get close enough for them to do their deadly work by light of cannon fire and lightning.

Electra felt her body pressed to Basil Le Cherche's, moving with him stroke for stroke. They moved in a dark waste of water while the world above and beyond them seemed full of fire. She felt something she could only call joy—a keen sense that she was thoroughly present and struggling for survival alongside a man who was thrillingly alive, whose touch had changed her irrevocably.

"Are you with me, little witch?" he called to her over deafening sounds around them.

"I am, truly!" she cried.

Another flash of lightning and she saw that Basil Le Cherche was smiling at her—smiling in this moment when they struggled through what might become their watery grave. She threw her head back and laughed. "Let Destiny take me where she will," she cried, "for she led me to you, Basil Le Cherche. If death is the price I pay for that leading, I shall tender Destiny what I owe her."

They met each other's eyes then in the enormity of the night sea as if there were only them, only these two beings in the entire universe.

A rending crash behind them and they twisted around together to see—the broad expanse of one of Judge Henri Le Cherche's convoy's mizzen sails was slowly, slowly, collapsing over the side, bringing a mass of spars and ropes with it as it fell. Electra and Basil witnessed the destruction, heard the screams of men pinned and broken beneath it, the shouts of others cutting away the rigging so the ship could make way again and not be turned to take the waves directly against her exposed starboard side, leaving her wallowing between troughs and in danger of capsizing. The other ships in the convoy let loose their sails, temporarily stopped their chase of the *Cat*, and made for their crippled companion.

"We will be within hailing distance of the *Cat* in but a few strokes! If they know their captain and their profession, they will be scanning for any sign of us," Basil cried. "We have but the narrowest window, and have no doubt about it, my brother will be shipping a launch over the side to search for us the instant he realizes we are gone."

No sooner had he said these words than Electra saw a darker shape in the water ahead: a barge, oarsmen pulling hard, every man scanning the waves in search of them.

"Basil!" she cried. "Ahead of us! Is it your brother's?"

Basil peered into the darkness and though she could not see it, the changes she felt in the body gliding by her side made it clear that he was smiling still. "It is the *Cat*'s launch—our own *Cat*." He bellowed out in a gale wind voice. "Ahoy, *Cat*!"

"Cap'n? Cap'n, keep up your calling, sir, in this flaming bloody dark so we can find you and get you aboard before those swabs sail around that goddamn mess and come to blow us to Kingdom Come!"

And so they were dragged, dripping and shaking, into the boat and swathed in cloaks as the barge crew pulled madly back to the ship. Within the hour they were on the quarterdeck of the *Cat*, the ship running for its life, skipping into waters threaded through with sandbanks and islands—places that Basil Le Cherche's somewhat piratical crew knew intimately but that would be death to the deep-bottomed ships of Henri Le Cherche's convoy. Anchor dropped, night watch set, Basil Le Cherche took Electra Gates's hand and led her to his cabin. He peeled the storm-soaked silk from her body and stood gazing upon her, and she let herself be regarded. In his eyes she saw things that made her feel feverish, urgent. She stepped toward him, wound herself around him, felt in his body the clear proof of his answering feelings. "Take me now, Le Cherche, or I will not be able to bear it," she whispered. "Now!"

And so he did. And though she was still new to lovemaking, he was a man who had learned from his numberless, nameless partners exactly what would move her, and he provided it. She could not have imagined any of the things he did to her before the actual moment when he did them. She could not have imagined herself doing what he urged her to do, and yet she did it, over and over. All through that long night they made love until they finally lay, spent and beaded with sweat, in the first light of dawn.

"Whatever you may be, little witch, you have me in your power and I am transformed. I did not know how strange and cold an existence I had before you touched me. I was dead and I did not know it. How strange to discover myself perhaps only moments away from my own death—for, beloved, my brother does not give up a hunt. It's possible, Electra, that he is more determined to capture me than you. Henri Le Cherche has long sought a reason to destroy me and now I have given him one. I have taken his property, his amusement—you, in other words—and provided him with the reason to kill me that he has always wanted."

"How could such a creature be your brother? How could such a monster as he be connected to you by blood!"

"Oh, my love, we are deeply connected. Why do you think there is such enmity between us? Only creatures who see themselves in each other could feel the kind of hatred we feel."

"That cannot be true."

His fists clenched and he took her face roughly in his hands, his voice suddenly gone wild, free of any restraint. "You do not know what was in my heart when I was a younger man! Why do you think I withdrew into a shell of myself, a creature who conducted his affairs with the world as if he had no feeling? In my youth I saw the danger I was in. I knew what I could become—I watched my brother become it, and it disgusted me. I withdrew into an icy numbness to keep myself safe from those feelings—all feelings—while my brother did the opposite and refined those feelings into elegant perversions. You have not seen his machines, his leathern toys. You have not been forced to play any of his particular games with him or his . . . clients. My brother has no experience of women as people—they are things to subjugate, humiliate. He fears them, and he has made fortunes by selling them to other, similar men and providing them with the perversities that satisfy their urgent compulsions."

She saw the depth of his horror and despair and cried out, flung the whole of her spirit and will between him and what so terrified him. "Basil. My love. That is not you!"

"You do not know what has been in my heart . . . my mind! My brother and I share more than blood. I have struggled all my life to make my nature the opposite of his! I have closed it off and now it is opened. You have opened it, and I fear as well as welcome what has happened to me now. I have only the love I feel for you as a beacon to guide me! Electra Gates, until you I had never met a woman I regarded as an equal. I controlled them, and so they had no power to move me. But now I have met my match, my savior! I am not talking to you now as one bound by custom or convention, Electra Gates. I speak to you as if we had passed together through the grave and into the next world, shorn of everything but the truth. And in that next world we would stand before God as equals. As we are."

"As we are!" Electra repeated. "I am not afraid of your past, Basil Le Cherche, or of what you have felt. I know who you are—be only that and I will be satisfied completely. Be the man I see before me now and I will move any mountain to remain by that man's side."

He swept her into his embrace, pressing her body against the length of his own, drowning them both in a kiss as sweeping and deep as the currents flowing beneath and around them, and they were carried.

NEAVE

You Should Be Married

The day after I refused Max's advice to sleep aboard the *Rubber Duck*, Jane called me to say that Lilly hadn't come to pick Annie up when she'd said she would. I looked at the clock: 7:07 p.m. What time did she say she'd be there? I'd asked. "Right after she left the office," Jane said. "She said she expected to be here at six. Neavie, when did she leave work?"

Lilly hadn't left the office, because she'd never come in at all. This wasn't that unusual, especially in the weeks before a conference. Lilly's work took her far and wide, to manufacturers and speakers and meeting planners and cosmetics events. She had a cavalier attitude about telling us her movements, and more than once we'd seen her disappear from the office for a couple days and return, triumphant, with a contract to rent five boats and an entire island for a scavenger hunt and an invoice for some kind of glittering prize to use at the end of the game. *Isn't that brilliant!* she'd say when she surfaced back at the office. *Won't we have fun!* I said all this to my sister Jane.

"Neave, you know she can be late for some things, but she's never, never been late to pick up Annie. And she didn't come."

I remember looking at a grease stain on a crumpled brown paper bag in my trash can and knowing this was all wrong, that everything was changed in an instant and my life might never be all right again.

"She'll call," I said.

Lilly did not return that night. We told Annie that her mom was on business and Aunt Jane was going to keep taking care of her for a little while. We told the girls in the office that Lilly had a migraine.

Four days later there was still no sign of Lilly, and migraines don't go on forever. Five days in, we admitted to Annie that we didn't know where her mom was. I looked at Annie sitting on Jane's living-room sofa, a quiet, pale face under a mop of black curls. Her eyes got greener when she was unhappy and bluer when she was pleased. They were very green now. "Don't be frightened," I said to her. "It'll be fine."

All my life I'd made a habit of not lying in general, but in particular not lying to children. I'd been especially careful not to lie to Annie, because I wanted her trust. But at that moment I wanted her to love me more than I wanted her to trust me, so I lied. I stood there and felt every muscle in my face arguing with me and I said, "It'll be fine." She didn't believe me, of course. Her little body was braced—she could feel something evil even if she didn't know what it looked like or where it came from. Or maybe that was me, bracing, feeling everything around me braced.

"It's all right, Aunt Neave," she whispered, and I turned my head to get a glimpse of myself in a mirror. Sure enough, I was wearing the kind of face that would leave poor Annie offering me comfort, offering me the very first lie I had ever heard her tell. I shouldn't even be in the same room with Annie if I wanted her protected. I was terrifying. "Maybe," Annie whispered, to no one in particular, "maybe he'll give her back."

At work I kept acting like there was an annual sales conference coming up and there was work to be done. The trapeze troupe that Lilly had hired called, looking for a final signed contract. "Lessons," their manager insisted. "Miss Terhune added a budget line for us to give volunteers from the audience a flying-trapeze lesson. She asked us if we could get a couple salesgirls up on the swings safely, do something easy but flashy and we discussed pricing. We need the amended agreement . . ."

She hadn't mentioned this part of the contract, but it was Lilly all over. Trapeze salesgirls: a sure bet for a picture in at least the Boston papers, maybe the AP wires, clear evidence to anybody with a lick of gumption that selling cosmetics at Be Your Best was the most interesting job in the United States.

We waited. Days passed. We filed a missing persons report with lots of photos of her. I went to work and pretended things were going to be fine. Jane asked me to move in with her and Todd because, she said, she thought I might want the company. I refused the offer. She pressed for visits—just dinner, she'd say. That was all. She'd call Snyder and we could all have dinner together, Jane and Todd, Snyder, Annie, and me. I tried to imagine the effect of putting all of our feelings around the same dinner table and refused again.

Snyder called. "Just do it," he said. "Do it for Jane. She acts like she's bravely optimistic, but I've been spending a little time with her and she's not feeling so optimistic or brave no matter what she says. If she wants us around her at dinner, I don't see why we can't give her that."

So I agreed to let him pick me up and we went, together, to Jane's house. Dinner was stiff and halting. Jane, a wonderful cook, had burned half the meal and forgotten the rest. We could feel the something evil out there, feel it pressing against us at a chillingly close range; feel the urge to huddle and eat out of the same pot. For dessert Jane had made Jell-O Surprise. I pushed a spoon into the wriggling green cubes and shoved it around a little. We put Annie to bed and sat together on the couch and I imagined what we might have looked like as characters in one of Snyder's comics, three stricken figures in a barren alien landscape with the indifferent universe glowing all around us—monsters approaching from the upper left corner.

Lilly would be ashamed of me, I thought. I would be damned if I was not only going to cower in my little sister's dining room but eat her Jell-O Surprise.

Annie got so quiet we sometimes were unaware of her sitting in the corner of a room. I did what I could to approximate my real life, but even though I was moving around at work looking exactly like I normally did, a part of my mind was closed down around the idea of Lilly. The dark feeling was like a wall around me. I'd peer out at the salesperson or accountant across the desk from me and wonder if they'd noticed I wasn't really there. They didn't seem to.

Finally there was some actual news. The police had found someone who had seen Lilly, identified from a company photograph, arguing with a man in front of a doughnut shop in Wenham, first on the sidewalk and then in their car: a Buick Skylark. Lilly's car. The witness remembered Lilly in particular because of her turquoise Chanel suit. The witness loved Chanel, she'd said, which is why she'd taken special notice. And something about the man made her feel strange. The man and the woman seemed to be disagreeing about something but no, they weren't yelling. No, there was no physical violence, though things between them looked very tense. *The man. I don't know what it was about him*, the witness said.

Then, nothing.

The fact that a witness said they seemed to be willingly in each other's company made the police interest lessen. "Ma'am," said the burly cop who'd told Ricky to get lost and cool off the night he came to my apartment, "women run away with guys—all kinds of guys. It's a fact of life. If you had my job you'd see it every day."

I tried on the idea that Lilly had been mesmerized, forced out of her sane mind, and hypno-controlled into running off with Ricky Luhrmann. Possible, I thought. Then, no.

No.

I had stopped talking to Charles about Ricky Luhrmann until now. Now I needed any trustworthy support or advice I could get, so I talked to him, leaving out any mention of Max Luhrmann. I discovered that I didn't want Charles offering any opinions touching on Max.

Charles had no advice about finding Lilly to offer. He said he didn't know why I lived alone, and I said I was a single adult and they tended to live alone, exactly like he did. But a woman, he said, should not live alone. See what it's exposed you to! See what happens when a woman is alone? His tone suggested concern about reputation as much as practicality or safety, and that took the conversation into an area that Charles and I weren't good at—disagreement. Angry disagreement, in fact. It turned out that, just as I guess I already knew, he loved my practicality, my independence, and my business experience, but he would actually be more comfortable if my independent, practical life were lived with a sister or some girl pal. Some arrangement that kept me less vulnerable. Because that, he concluded, was what I was: alone. Women should not live alone, he concluded again.

Should? What does that mean, "should"? I demanded.

You should be married, he finished. I should marry you.

THE PIRATE LOVER

Under My Protection

Women at sea on a ship of war were unusual but not unknown. Some captains took their wives or mistresses for comfort and diversion. Pirate vessels had been known to be crewed and even led by women. If there were squeakers aboard, a comfortable matron might be signed on to the logbook to see to the boys' manners and whooping coughs and home sicknesses—a mature someone with a figure that could be confused at a distance with a pork barrel. But a young, vibrant creature in skirts—she created tensions that could divide the tamest crew, and Basil Le Cherche's crew had come from the more distant edges of civilization. Electra Gates was not only young and vibrant, she was a woman in the throes of overwhelming passion, and this energy radiated from her. She had but to descend or ascend a ladder, cross the quarterdeck and lean upon a rail, lift a drink to her full lips before witnesses, for Basil Le Cherche to feel the masculine attention around her vibrate. He called the ships' company together.

"Mademoiselle Electra Gates is under my personal protection. I assume you understand me."

Silence greeted this short speech, but its effects were felt. Eyes were averted when Electra came on deck. Even Trotter, most unmannerly of personal servants, ducked and bowed and crept in her presence.

"What did you do?" she demanded.

"I protected you."

"From what? If a man on this ship did anything untoward, where could he run? I am safe here. Perfectly safe." She coiled herself around him, parting her legs and drawing a delicate line from his temple to his lips. He trembled in her hands but pulled away for a moment.

"Electra, do you know Joe Bent? Upper yardsman? A scar from cheek to nose on the left side?"

She nodded.

"Do you know why he's on board?"

"Riches. Adventure."

"Both true. Also rape. Four women in London. So easy for a man to simply slip away. The ship vanishes over the horizon and you avoid uncomfortable prison sentences or undesired trips to an Australian penal colony." She stared. He went on. "My seductive, mesmerizing creature—half the men afloat, both in the Royal Navy and in the privateers working these waters—are fleeing a woman. Sometimes it is a wife. Or perhaps the father and brothers of a pregnant girl, a girl who may have been induced to intimacy somewhat, shall we say, before she was ready to do so."

"You exaggerate."

"Joe Bent. Gunther Schmidt. Ahab Hummori. Peter Piper. One-Eye Bentham. Daniel Rose. The Davies brothers. Surely you saw something besides admiration in their eyes as they watched your arrival? Surveyed your charms?"

Yes. There had been a darkness in the gazes of these men in particular—some hunger. She had dismissed her observation. As if he divined her thoughts and was merely responding to something she'd said aloud, Basil added, "So you did indeed see it. My love, you were not wrong."

"I am in no need of protection. I am not your object."

"Not to me. Not to you. But to them, you are. The men I named will be encouraged to volunteer for the attack I plan on my brother's ship. In the event that I do not survive that attack, I do not want them here to watch over you. My first lieutenant and first mate will be briefed on your protection. They are steady, strong men. Good men. They can be trusted with your life. They will give their own to protect it."

"You plan a direct assault? Two ships like ours cannot attack your brother's convoy and survive."

"We will not fire a shot, my dear."

"Are you mad?"

"Only in my relations to you. In matters of war, I assure you I am no fool. The xebec will lead, but she will be tricked out as a perfect surprise—stuffed to the gunwales with powder and tar with the littlest fire left burning in her aft port—a fire that, if their own cannon does not reach her magazine and turn her into an enormous bomb, the flames we set ourselves will do the job. We will keep the *Cat* at a distance, appearing all the while to be moving heaven and earth to hurry her but actually we will have set a sail dragging behind her beneath the surface. We will point the xebec into the midst of my brother's convoy, set her mizzen to keep her on her course, and slip over the side into our tender to pull as fast as we can back to the *Cat*."

"And if you do not gain enough distance before the explosion?"

"Then I will die at the same time that my brother Henri does—but you will be safe. Now or later, my sorceress. He will hunt you forever if I do not stop him now. He must die in order for you to live."

"Do not do this, Basil."

"I know the danger my brother poses to you, my beloved. There is no other way."

"I will go with you."

"You will not. You have many strengths, my love, but setting sails in an instant and pulling a barge quickly through high seas are not among them."

Against every fiber of control and will, Electra's eyes filled with tears. The first one sprang free and coursed down her cheek. Basil touched it, gently, and swept it aside. "I do not believe I can live without you," she whispered. "I cannot imagine it, Le Cherche."

"Nor can I imagine my existence without you. So I must go to assure your safety."

NEAVE

Ponytail

Days and more days, and no Lilly. Jane and Snyder got quieter. Then I found Annie in the backyard one morning with a shovel and a shoebox.

"What are you doing, sweetie?"

"I have to bury William. He was sick and then he died," she answered, clutching the shovel so hard that the knuckles in her hand were white.

"Who's William?"

"My groundhog. Now he's dead."

"Really? Let me see."

Annie set down the box and lifted the lid. There lay William, still as a rock or a clump of earth, but that was because William was a stuffed animal and that had always been his nature.

"Are you sure he's gone?" I pressed on the groundhog's chest. She nodded soberly.

"Do you think he'll mind being buried, Aunt Neave? I thought about it, and maybe since he's a groundhog he won't mind being under the ground. But I don't know."

"Are you afraid that he's scared?" I asked.

She nodded.

"Let's consider that," I suggested. "Let's have tea and think a bit."

We did that, and in the end William was returned to life, though not to the same one he'd been living only a few weeks ago.

I went home to my apartment but couldn't settle anywhere. The kitchen was suddenly enormous and the light pouring in through the large windows felt hard and white. I moved restlessly from chair to table to sofa and back around again. I tried reading the first of the books that always sat by my bedside, then the second, and a third, and tossed every one of them aside. The books ended with the joyful union of lovers, safe in worlds of their own making. I'd thought that those worlds, the book worlds, were the truer ones. Now with safety, love, joy, all at such a distance, that seemed less certain. Maybe *The Pirate Lover* was just a lie, spun to comfort the gullible. This thought was so horrible that I fell asleep in order not to think it anymore.

Nights when I was alone in the warehouse apartment I sank into my largest armchair with a book or a pile of *Good Housekeeping* propped on my belly, crumbs from whatever I was calling dinner in a halo around the pages. Ladies' magazines had an inflexible seasonal pattern that was soothing when it wasn't annoying: "Best Christmas Ever," "Start the New Year a New You," "Thanksgiving Side Dishes," "Best Brownies Ever," "Lose Ten Pounds," "You and Your Teenager." Then there was "Can This Marriage Be Saved?" which also seemed to cover the same territory it had when I first met it. Every marriage began to seem riddled with the same rot, every hopeful piece of advice too flimsy to hold the crumbling thing together. I revisited the books that I'd read by Mrs. Daniels's fire, watching Jane Eyre commune with spirits that urged her to flee temptation, feeling oddly soothed when the Cyclops ate a few more of Odysseus's men, and I revisited Electra once more as she made her way through the break in the wall and fell into her chained lover's arms.

I tried on the possibility that I might never feel safe again. I missed Lilly. I played checkers with Annie. I comforted Jane and Snyder. I longed for something that was related to but not Charles Helbrun III. I didn't mention Charles Helbrun's proposal of marriage to anyone. I knew what they'd say, and I didn't want their voices mixed up in my own thinking.

"Let me think," I said to Charles when he called. "Give me time."

A practical man, an accommodating negotiator, he agreed to wait for my call and leave me to think. I had surprised him. I promised not to take too long.

I woke up in the big stuffed chair that sat in front of the apartment's biggest window, again. A plate with the one remaining piece of toast on it sat on the floor at my feet. I'd been reading, watching streetlights, looking for circling cars or figures looking up at my windows. I might have refused Max's advice to never stay here alone at night, but that didn't mean I wasn't watching for him. Waiting. I'd nodded off and when I regained consciousness I was tipped over on one side, the cushion under my face wet from drool.

A shower and three cups of coffee and I was off to work. I let a catering service representative and a consultant I talked to on the telephone think I was Lilly without correcting them. The consultant had called to discuss the seminar Lilly had hired her to run: "Love and Romance—Their Links to Sales." My secretary left at the normal time but I kept on until around eight. I walked up the stairs to my apartment thinking about the way Max Luhrmann's sentences tended to have solid-sounding ends. I decided I would try not to think about anything: not Lilly, not the growing disorder in my apartment, not Max. But you can't control your mind. The triangle of exposed throat.

That night a storm whipped tree branches against the windows of the upper-floor apartment and I fell asleep in the chair, again. In the morning I walked through my usual routine: coffee, shower, clothes, keys, coat. I had an appointment with a new sales manager and so, instead of walking down the inside stairs to our offices I headed out the back door and the outside landing, the quickest way down to my car. I swung open the door and turned to lock it.

Hanging smack in its center was a little tail of blond hair, streaked through with a subtle highlight or two, bound at its root with the silver clip I'd given Lilly for her seventeenth birthday.

NEAVE

Move to the Rubber Duck

The officer who answered the call told me that cutting hair and putting it on a door was not a crime. I hung up and paced the apartment like an animal for perhaps an hour. Then I took the step I was probably waiting to take all along: I called Max. He hadn't needed anybody to explain that ponytails nailed to doors were a very bad sign. He'd put me in his car and driven us to the police department, where he represented our concerns because at this point I wasn't driving safely or speaking clearly. The uniformed officers at the desk suggested that someone had left part of a wig as a joke. Max then jumped over the divider and headed toward the door labeled PRECINCT CAPTAIN.

A very large patrol officer stepped into Max's path. He was thickly muscled and about half a foot taller than Max. He moved deliberately, sure of himself, planting himself and crossing his arms. "You can't come back here, bub." Max stepped around him and shifted his weight quickly to evade an arm when the patrolman flung one out to stop him. He turned to face the cop who was advancing on him.

"You are not going to touch me," Max said quietly. "I am not going to touch you." He took my arm and led me past. "Excuse me," he said coolly as we brushed by. We reached the back of the station unmolested, moving through a little pool of quiet all around us.

Ten minutes later the precinct captain had called in a detective and was agreeing that when somebody left a human ponytail on a door, that was bad. He was not reassuring. The husband, we told him, hadn't been found or questioned, or, as far as we knew, even looked for. "It's different now," he told us. "The meat was a clear threat. You should avoid being alone in your apartment for a few days, Miss Terhune. We'll nose around. Keep in mind that you actually don't know who left it." He asked us for every employer or address we knew for Ricky. He asked for a list of any employees who'd been fired or had quit abruptly. He asked about enemies. Did I have enemies?

Max was tightlipped as we walked to his car. "You can put some things together to last you a few days," he said as he turned the ignition. "You don't have a choice anymore, Neave. If you won't go to the *Rubber Duck*, we're heading for your sister's house."

But there was that clear image in my mind of Ricky trailing me to Jane's, parked in a dark car outside her home, watching Annie move through the lighted rooms of her home. "I'm not going to Jane's."

"Then your brother's."

Again, I imagined Snyder opening the door and finding Ricky Luhrmann standing there, possibly with a large blunt weapon in his hand, some spittle at the edges of his mouth. "No," I said. "Not Snyder's either."

"Then that's it. The *Rubber Duck*."

I could see the thick hank curving away from the nail. The silver clip. "I don't know."

"Neave. The ponytail."

I was so tired—so flattened and beaten and scared. I could feel Max feel all those things on me and gather himself to bear down, right now, while I was vulnerable. He'd seen my face when I put that hank of hair in a brown paper bag to take to the police station. He'd seen the shaking hands and blank eyes.

We didn't speak as we walked back up the stairs to the door, where a few strands were still snarled around the nail. We stood on the iron grate landing and looked at the silky twist of hairs. Something dark lapped up inside me.

"Max, what was your sister's name?" I asked. "The one who died when she was little."

"Pansy."

"What did she look like?"

"A pansy. A pretty little happy thing."

I plucked the stubborn remaining hairs from the nail and held them up over my head until a breeze took them.

"All right," I said finally.

"You'll move to the boat?"

"I'll go there tonight. Maybe tomorrow. I don't know about further than that. It's no guarantee, Max. If somebody wants to find me, all he has to do is follow me when I leave the office at the end of the day and trail me to the boat."

"He won't go near you during the day when you're surrounded by people. He'll stay away until he can be sure the staff is all gone, but you're going to start leaving before the office empties out—leaving when you're still surrounded by people. He'll wait until after hours before he cruises by, expecting you to be alone. If your car's gone, he'll wait for you to come back. But you won't come back because you'll be safely asleep on the *Rubber Duck*. You'll get to the *Duck* a different way every night. Different routes. Sometimes you'll take a bus. When you drive, you make the rearview mirror your best friend. You think anybody's following you and you can't shake them, go to your sister's. Not the boat. I only wish I could tell you to come to my apartment, but we know he's got a close enough interest in my comings and goings to make me an undesirable backup plan."

I looked at him. "People tend to find what they look for," I said.

"You don't have to help them by standing still in an obvious place. I don't think the first thing he'll think of is a slip in a Charlestown marina. Please, Neave."

"Okay."

"Tonight. We'll move some of your things and you'll stay on the boat."

I agreed, too close to the hanging ponytail to resist him.

I followed him to the *Rubber Duck* at her slip in Charlestown and let him lift me over the rail into the boat. He left me in the snug cabin. I lay down on the bunk with the soft bumping slap of the water beneath and around me. The refrigerator was stocked according to Max Luhrmann's idea of need: coffee, milk, bread, bologna, peanut butter. I waited for sunrise and when it came I boiled water in the little electric heater and made myself toast, which I smeared with peanut butter.

Charles would be angry if he knew I'd moved to this boat and not told him about it. I thought about anger being his first probable response. Charles Helbrun was most comfortable when he was in charge, and this, in many circles, made him terrifically attractive. People, powerful people, asked him to sit on their boards specifically because of his ability to radiate power, to engage and persuade and control. He had money and respect. When he was with me he listened to me with care. He had introduced me to the universe where men wore English suits and women wore Parisian scents and everyone knew how to order wine: a world of complete safety. Many beautiful women had pursued him without success. As his wife, no social door in the city would be closed to me if I wanted to walk through it. No policeman would dismiss my concerns as frivolous. No day would end alone with a peanut butter sandwich and a Mars bar. There would be no watching my rearview mirror for pursuers. I would be watched over; I would be listened to; I would be treated carefully by powerful people.

If I said no to Charles, I might never marry. I could live out my entire life alone. If I said yes, I could walk down an aisle in flowing white silk, Janey wildly happy and Annie in a puffy pink dress, me with my gaze fixed on Charles: handsome, clear-eyed, disciplined, faithful Charles, waiting for me at an altar. I could have that.

I screwed the top back on the peanut-butter jar and rinsed the coffee cup. I left the *Rubber Duck*, walked to a bus stop in the nacreous six a.m. light, and went directly to the office. The moment I reached my desk I picked up the phone and dialed his number. It was barely daylight but I knew his habits. He'd been up for an hour already and was probably on his third cup of coffee, strategizing, laying out his day. He picked up immediately.

"I am honored that you asked me, Charles. But I won't marry you."

NEAVE

The Rubber Duck

Ruga brought it to my attention that I was scaring the Be Your Best staff. "You act crazy, you cancel meetings, you don't get orders in, and you look like you rolled in hay. All the time. Look at your nails, all bitten and raggy. Look at your hair! You act like the company's going down the tubes so they look for new jobs." She stood me in an inconspicuous space to observe the office movements at strategic points of every day so I could see a little gang leaving early, taking long lunches, spending time on the telephone—rats thinking the open water was a better bet than my particular ship. This year's sales conference was so close and here I was, nominally in charge, alienating friend and foe, leaving the office for long stretches without explanation.

"Look," Ruga said with a shrug, "you wish this to happen? What are you thinking?"

She was right. I had to straighten up.

A week after I'd started going to the *Rubber Duck* I went to the parking lot behind our building and found all my car's tires slashed, flattened right down to the pavement. I didn't need to wonder who had done it. Max had been right. Ricky had been here, maybe been here night after night, and not found me. Tonight he was determined to keep me from leaving. I felt the rush of something like cold water in my chest. I scanned the street. I walked around the block, looking. There was no sign of him; no dark figures of any kind sitting in cars for no apparent reason. But the tires hadn't been slashed for no reason. I called Snyder.

"Snyder," I said, "I need a favor."

"What's the favor?"

"Oh, for chrissakes. How many favors do you owe me? What difference does it make what the favor is?"

"Fine. All right. What do you need?"

"I need a ride someplace. And then I need you not to mention where you take me to anyone. Not even Jane." I named a street corner about a half mile from Be Your Best and told him to meet me there. I called a garage to have them put the car on a flatbed and haul it off to get new tires. I put a change of clothes in a bag, pushed my hair under a hat, settled a large pair of sunglasses over my face and walked out of the building with the last salesgirl to leave. I walked quickly to the block where I expected to find my brother. He was waiting.

"Why is all this so secret?" he asked. "Is something wrong with your car?"

"Just give me a ride, Snyder." I directed him to the docks in Charlestown, taking a discursive route and checking the rearview mirror regularly. Nothing. When I got out of the car I looked Snyder directly in the eyes. "You won't mention where you dropped me off to anybody. Anybody at all."

"How will you get back to the office tomorrow?"

"There's a bus I can use. You don't have to worry about it. I can trust you on this, right, Snyder?"

He nodded soberly and I believed him.

I walked down the quay to the *Rubber Duck*, stepped over the side, and unpacked some of my old defenses against confusion and fear: books, cookies, and a magazine or two. More recently I had added Milk Duds to my arsenal. I stretched out on the tiny bunk and picked up *Ladies Home Journal*, flipping to a "Can This Marriage Be Saved?" column describing a wife's supposedly flirtatious behavior around other men, a party ending with her slipping out with her husband's handsome brother. . . . Confronted with her own secret desires, the wife offered a couple hundred words of apology that looked to me like nothing but a description of the husband's shortcomings. He had been so distant, so indifferent to her intellectual and spiritual needs. The attractive brother had made her feel noticed for the first time in so long. . . . I could hear exactly what Lilly would have said to this one: "Get a job," she'd say. "She's an idiot, and the husband is a bore. She's dying of boreism with that man."

I opened my old copy of *The Odyssey* and a yellowed paper dropped to the deck. I picked it up and opened it: Boppit's commendation from the armed forces for service above and beyond the call of duty. How could it have been here all along when I'd flipped through this book so often without seeing it? I would give it to Jane. Maybe I'd frame it first. Now I lay it open beside my rocking bed and felt grateful about Boppit, and sad about his untimely death beneath our old Chevy's back wheels. He'd been a brave dog. A good dog.

I thought about the way Boppit seemed to be confused when his ears flicked up, because they were so uneven. I listened to the slap of waves on the tires tied to the dock. I fell asleep.

I was in a rocking place, someplace where the floor moved. I was pursued, running! I was so frightened I could hardly breathe, and I struggled to run faster. I was in a labyrinth of dark wooden corridors, tiny doors on either side of the narrow passages I rushed through. I heard the thing behind me, the heavy, lumbering animal steps, the sounds it made when it breathed. Somewhere above me I heard barking and a voice. Lilly's voice! I turned around to retrace my fleeing steps and find a way upward, to the voice and the barking. Endless walls and closed doors and the thing behind me so close! And what was hanging from the doors like little tails? Were they bundles of hair? I had to find the door that would lead upward and away. Then I was not running through the narrow corridors but struggling in the water, everything dark around me and a hand on my arm, pulling me down. I resisted, kicked and pulled until I realized that I was having no difficulty breathing or seeing even though I was submerged. In fact, the water moved against my body in the most wonderful way. I turned to see what or who had pulled me here. The sensations of water against my chest, my legs . . . how lovely!

But then something broke through the wonderful sensations, something loud and assaultive. Rifle fire? Cannon? *BANG! BANGBRSCHHKKKKK!*

"Neave?!"

I struggled through the gelatinous sleep, upward to the voice, found myself sitting in a narrow bunk in a neat cabin whose door was wide open and filled with a spiky silhouette. I looked around. I was not deep in watery space but in the little cabin of the *Rubber Duck.*

"Neave?"

The silhouette was speaking to me: Max Luhrmann, wearing pajama bottoms, his hair standing out mostly to the left of his head and his feet bare. My eyes adjusted and I saw his face pink up, possibly in response to my scrutiny. I couldn't tell.

"I'm awake," I said uncertainly. "I'm awake, right?"

Max nodded. "Of course you are."

"The explosion. There were gunshots or something."

"That was just Charlie Healey setting out at an ungodly hour with a backfiring engine. He's two slips down from the *Rubber Duck.*"

I quieted myself and listened. There it was: the liquid sound of a small boat chugging off into the harbor. "Max, where did you come from?"

"The lab owns another research vessel at this dock. It's got a bunk. I thought . . ."

"What? That Ricky would come here and shoot me?"

"No. Yes."

"You've been sleeping two boats down and waiting for him?"

"No. Yes."

"What exactly did you think you'd do if he managed to follow me and showed up?"

"Stop him," he said.

He spoke matter-of-factly and he looked sure of himself. He held something that looked like a tire iron in his hand. I noticed the muscles along his forearm, the curving lines running up to the upper arm. He saw my eyes run from his hand up to the shoulder and back to the tire iron. He tucked the weapon behind a hip, a bit out of sight. "Well. I guess I'll head back."

His pajamas had slipped down enough to expose the curve of a slender hip. He was close enough for me to smell sleep on him and metal and rope. Just a hint of toothpaste. I crossed the two feet of cabin that separated us, slipped a hand behind his head and pulled it down. He let me. I kissed him.

I was entirely sure of this: he kissed me back. His free hand—the one without the tire iron—made its way around me. He drew the whole length of me against him for just a moment and then, as if a switch had been flicked, his entire body stiffened and then he stumbled, actually stumbled, back and away. I waited, the two of us frozen in place so close to each other that I could still smell the sleep on him. The toothpaste. I kept my feet where they were but tipped the rest of me an inch, maybe two, closer to him. He'd kissed me, really kissed me, before he pulled away.

"I'll just go back," he whispered. He whacked the back of one heel against the door on his way through, recovered, twisted quickly, and caught his elbow on the doorway before disappearing back to his watch post.

He didn't want me. Or did he want me? There had been the kiss, the whole body pressed against me, but then the stiffening, startled rejection.

Nothing I had known about desire was anything at all compared to what was burning its way through me now. He had kissed me back. Hadn't he? Wasn't that what I'd felt before he stumbled backward?

Which was truer: the kiss, or the rejection of the kiss?

I spent what little was left of the night pacing back and forth between the cabin's miniature refrigerator and miniature door, five steps either way, weighing the two against each other. In the end I decided to go with rejection. I lost my nerve, or I came to my senses—it wasn't clear which—but I decided that I'd have to behave as if the moment were an aberration, an inauthentic moment of distress. He'd recoiled from me: I saw no other way to save myself any dignity.

I hadn't known that desire could feel like something slashing into your chest and pressing all the air out of your lungs. The skin of my body felt charged and light, expansive and tight at once—it couldn't contain what I felt. If I'd known how to get out of my own skin I would have blown myself open to get some relief. Why would anyone want this? How had anyone in history survived this, much less longed for it, written poems and novels and songs about it? All this time I'd thought I'd understood my books, understood Electra's Marais dress, understood what the women at our conferences were buying and selling and hoping for.

I'd understood nothing.

LILLY

What You Go With

I was so confident. I could turn him around; it wasn't that bad, blahblahblah. But somehow it surged past the place where I could control him. It started to snowball. *Neave is interfering, Neave poisoned your mind against me; Neave is ruining everything. Who put that bitch in charge? Why does she think she's got all this power?*

Because she did have all that power. She co-owned Be Your Best. She was my sister. But don't think for a second I ever said that to the man. I let it go. Now, of course, I see how dumb that was, but back then all my experience told me that I could smack unproductive ideas out of his head with a bottle of Champagne, some interesting underwear, and a little commonsense talk. I'd been telling myself this would be the same as other times. It would go away. She's ruining nothing, I said to him. So what if you don't like her? Lots of people don't like her. She's not likeable. Also, Neave Terhune is not the boss of me—and neither are you.

He started insisting that I break off from Neave and have my own business—get her out of my life. Our lives, he said. Neave, I reminded him, is my business partner, my sister. She and Annie are the ones who love me more than anybody else on Earth, including him. When those words hit the air, "including you," I saw the truth of what I'd said. He didn't love me best. Neave and Annie did. Janey and Snyder did. He didn't support me. Be Your Best did. I saw that he wanted to take all these things away from me, and when I looked at him then I felt something go dark. He hated my sister. He felt nothing at all for my daughter. Ricky saw me feel it. He knew I was considering things from a new distance and I felt the whole weight of what I was to him shift.

He said he had something in mind for Neave, and I reared up and turned on him. I said bullshit you do, and he said I should buzz off about things that he knew more about than me. I felt things between us start to spin.

I had to slow this down, get control again. I said we should go away, get out of town and cool down a little. Maybe check into some little romantic joint in Vermont. I fell back on the strategies that had always given me a firm grip on him before, but "before" was gone. We were in a different place, further out than any lingerie could reach and pull us back. I was trying to find a way forward was all; my repertoire of strategies was more limited than I'd known. If I were Neave I maybe would have come up with a fresher strategy. But I'm not Neave.

He said okay. I had this sweet little inn in mind when I put on the turquoise suit with the nipped waist and snug skirt to meet him. That suit used to make me feel like I was mistress of my destiny. I knew what my ass looked like when I was walking away in that suit. From Where I Am Now I see that your destiny is a tough thing to steer, even with the help of Chanel and the right shoes, but I'd built a whole career on that kind of thinking and I wasn't prepared to give it up that morning.

We'd stopped for a cup of coffee. We were getting back in the car. He'd twisted the conversation back to Neave, how she was probably a little dyke who poked in our business, his business. I knew then that something had to be made clear, some line in the sand had to be drawn right there. I told him to shut up. I told him if he ever bothered her, he'd never touch me again. If he so much as made a vague threat against Neave I wouldn't waste my time complaining to him or his brother, Max—I'd get on a witness stand and I'd say whatever had to be said. I would positively take care of his ass if he stepped over that line.

Whose line? Ricky said.

The way he said it. Not just calm, but happy someplace that'd been rooted in him for a long time.

He stayed happy, all the way through the hard work of making me dead. He used a tire iron, and then he used saws. Maybe I shouldn't have been, but the truth is, I was so surprised. Why are we surprised when the thing that was coming at us all along finally reaches us?

Then he put me in the water, all in different places. He'd thought about this, apparently, and was ready with a plan. Some of me was dropped off on Cape Ann, other parts went to a lonely pier in Lynn, and the last of me went off a deserted dry dock in Chelsea. Off I went, drifting, sinking, turning, rising. It's not easy parting ways with your body. For that first little while it felt like being blind and deeply confused.

Then I was here, Where I Am Now, which you can imagine was strange, but less strange somehow because the dog was here to greet me. I was so grateful to see anything or anybody familiar, even if it was Boppit. I knew him right off.

We got more comfortable with each other. He'd try to explain things to me.

"You're close to where you were," he'd say. "It feels very different at first, but then if you look over your shoulder, you see it all curving behind you. And ahead. Only the thinnest little film of something in between you and that other place. There's not so much distance between as people think. Twist around here and take a look."

I did, and there right in front of me was Annie, following Jane up a flight of stairs, chattering, looking preoccupied, serious but not unhappy. I felt a wave of relief. Then Annie vanished and I saw Neavie. She was lying on a little bunk in a boat, a pile of Mars Bars wrappers at her elbow, an open magazine in front of her. Something had dribbled down her blouse and her hair looked like a hedgerow. It was as bad as Boppit had tried to make it.

"Oh my God!"

"You aren't kidding." He nodded. "And she's been raging around, scaring your staff, insulting your vendors, disappearing from work and not telling anybody where she's going."

"She's got good reasons to act like that."

"We all do, sugar. You have to step over it. She's got to order the panda-bear incentives for the Christmas gift orders, nail down the conference trainer schedules. Neave's been letting things slide with only weeks to go before the company's sales conference. Some of the staff think the ship is going down and they're taking four-hour lunches and looking for other jobs. She needs some help. I'm going to get you to her so you can help her."

"The conference . . ." I murmured. Suddenly I was in Neave's head. I could see a pink platter being struck out of Janey's hands, lemon cake and pale icing sprayed in an arc on the stairs behind her. "What's happening?" I whispered.

"You're seeing something Ricky's already done from inside Neave. You're sliding around."

"Ricky . . ."

"Yes. He has her in his sights; worse, he's in her head. You don't necessarily have to be dead to get inside somebody's head, Lilly. We have to do something about that blouse. And the purse: look at that ink-stained baggy old thing. Good lord above. They're horrible. A monkey would have made better choices."

"So what?"

"Lilly, these are our jobs: Keep Neave from driving the business into the dirt. Keep Ricky away from Neave."

"How do we do that?"

"Oh, we've been doing it. You know parts of their minds that nobody on Earth but you knows. You help get us in. I concentrate it into a kind of real. We're already there, just not as much there as we need to be."

Boppit saw my expression and sighed. He said, "I'll try to describe it. We'll call it dreaming for now. When Ricky thinks of her, if he's heading to Neave's apartment when she's alone, I feel it. I dream myself into his mind. I suggest that he is very, very thirsty; how had he ever gotten so thirsty? And here's a bar that he suddenly needs to go into to get a beer. He thinks, Just one. Just a few minutes. He gets to her apartment and she's gone, because I dreamed her into her car and off to the docks while I was dreaming Ricky into a bar. I put an impulse in her to go now, now, now! You do it too."

"I don't feel myself doing it," I said.

"Lilly, when I go into Ricky's mind, you're there with me whether you know where you are or not. Do you ever feel like something's sliding down your spine, something pulsing and whipping around?"

"Yes."

"There you go. That's Ricky. Soon when you travel into a mind, it'll run in your head like a newsreel. You'll get better at it."

It already sort of did run in my head. It didn't feel real, but when it happened its moving parts could give me a shock of recognition.

"I know," Boppit said, though I was sure I hadn't spoken out loud. "It will feel familiar even though it also seems like it hasn't happened yet, or never happened in the past."

"If we can dream him away from Neave, why can't we make Ricky forget about her and go away?"

"We're just pushing a few things into his path. We're not changing his nature."

"Isn't there something more we can do?"

"We're going to work on her accessories."

"Accessories? I thought we decided that a good pair of shoes doesn't protect you from much in this world."

"Sometimes they just tip the balance the littlest bit, and Neave needs us to put a thumb on the scale for her."

"No offense to you, Boppit, but you're not the first thing that would come to anybody's mind if they needed heroic intervention. And we both know what came of my thinking I could control Ricky Luhrmann. We're all wrong for this problem."

"Yet we are here. And Ricky has not once been behind Neave when she drove to the *Rubber Duck*."

"You said she'd be able to see us, Boppit. When's that going to happen?"

Mr. Boppit laced his arm through mine. "Just stay with me. Concentrate. We'll get there."

"Where is 'there'?"

"We're close. It's what I told you: We think of her. She thinks of us."

"Then what happens?" I asked.

"She'll see us."

"Even if that's true, what good will it do us, or her?"

"We'll be in her universe, in her time. From there it'll be easier to turn her attention back to Be Your Best and away from Ricky Luhrmann. We stay alert, on guard, keep watch for him, and we think her into safer places. We push her back into a life where she isn't sitting in a pile of crumbs looking like every psychopath's ideal victim. Then we're going to get her a good haircut."

I'm no crier, but I started crying then.

"Now, now," Boppit said gently. "Don't despair. I'll take the purse. You take the hair. We'll go from there."

It was what we had, and that, in the end, is what you go with.

NEAVE

Lilly and Boppit Break Through

I woke to full sun shining through the *Rubber Duck*'s cabin windows and across the legs of a young man sitting on the tiny cabin refrigerator. He wore marine whites—formal military except for a Chanel silk scarf at his throat, and a pair of high heels on his feet. He grinned happily and his tongue kind of lolled a bit to one side as he closed his mouth again. The expression was distinct, idiosyncratic, unmistakable.

"Boppit?" I whispered. He nodded, and the gesture summoned up the idea of a wagging tail. I glanced at his feet.

"At last! You see me. What about Lilly?"

"Lilly? Do you know where she is?"

"Of course I do. She's sitting at the end of your bunk."

"I don't see any Lilly."

"Look harder, honey."

I looked. There was just a dark blur in the air, maybe, at the other end of the bed. Then it was like a purple foggy mass, then the purple solidified into my favorite blouse—purchased sometime around 1941 and borrowed by Lilly Terhune for a special date. The blouse never returned. But Lilly, my Lilly, seemed to be sitting three feet away from me wearing it now. She smiled at me and lifted one hand in greeting. A lit cigarette balanced between her fingers.

"See me now, Neavie?"

I opened my mouth but I couldn't make any sounds come out.

Lilly nodded at Boppit and grinned. "You were right! She sees me."

Boppit smiled. "Of course I was right. The truth is, though, I'm relieved. It took so long." He turned to me. "Neave, snap out of it!"

"You aren't there and I don't see you. I'm fine."

"You're fine," Boppit said, "and you do see us. We'll just sit here for a while until you calm down."

I looked down at his feet, the high heels peeping up beneath the cuff.

"Aren't those our mother's favorite pumps?"

"They were." He lifted one leg and tipped the toe of the shoe toward me so I could appreciate the instep. "The woman had terrible taste, but these shoes—the mysterious exception."

"I was shopping with her when she bought them," Lilly explained. "I forced them on her."

"Well, of course." Bop nodded. "That would explain it."

"You chewed those pumps to Kingdom Come and she locked you in the garage," Lilly said.

"She did." He laughed. "Remember that, Neave?"

I said, "What are you?"

"Exactly what we look like." Boppit tilted his head toward me, the tongue managing to look like it was hanging over an incisor even though it wasn't.

"Lilly, are you . . . ?"

"Alive? No, sweetie. I'm something different."

"But . . . different, meaning dead? The ponytail . . . it meant what we thought it meant?"

"It did."

"I don't understand what's happening, Lilly."

Boppit broke in. "Understanding is overvalued. You have to get dressed, Neave. You have to get to the office."

"I'm not just confused. I'm. . . ." I stopped talking because I didn't know what I was. Surprisingly, though, whatever I might have been, it wasn't scared. In fact, I felt something in my chest open up that I could honestly call happiness. How strange, I thought.

Lilly was already rooting through the suitcase I'd left by the door. "Where's your makeup?"

"Home."

"Okay. Let's head to your apartment and get you polished up."

"Lilly, if we can find Ricky we can get him arrested. Do you know where he is?"

Dead Lilly smacked the table in front of us. "Forget him and pay attention to the conference, which is, by the way, coming at you like a freight train. You've got to get that last additional clause on the trapeze contract nailed down. I've been looking forward to that act for months."

"You're not looking forward to anything anymore. You're dead." I turned to Boppit. "Why are you wearing that uniform?"

"Everyone else asks me why I'm wearing high heels."

"What a surprise."

"You don't have to be like that. The uniform is what I am. To my mind the shoes don't contradict the uniform, thematically speaking. The day you found me? I wasn't looking for garbage those afternoons I spent tipping over trash cans. I was looking for a Qualicraft soft vinyl tortoise-shell upper, preferably with acrylic Art Deco heels. When I was with your family I kept a stash of my favorites in the back of the garage. And I was waiting for you."

"Tell me, really, what you are," I asked.

"I am what I am, sweetheart." His tongue popped between his teeth and his eyes closed into slits like they did when we rubbed his belly or when he was especially pleased with something and he looked very pleased right now.

"Up and at 'em, Neave. I've been looking forward to giving away a powder-blue convertible at a blowout sales conference since the day we sat on the floor of the warehouse and split that bottle of beer. That was a perfect little half hour, sitting on the floor talking about diamonds and robin's-egg-blue cars and everything that was going to happen to us. It did all happen to us. And it's going to keep happening, only just to you."

I was responding to my dead sister and my profoundly changed former pet as if they were real, which my mind told me they were not. Boppit stood up and plucked my purse off the side table where I'd left it, turning it upside down and dumping its contents out. "This thing?" he said briskly. "Into the trash."

"But that's my everyday purse . . ."

Lilly stood up. "Time for a new everyday. You can't carry that ink-stained sack around and be who you have to be now. People will be looking at you to figure out what to wear, looking to you to tell them what to do. You have to be me now as well as you. Your hair? No woman who wasn't in the middle of a nervous breakdown would let whatever happened to your hair happen. You're heading a cosmetics company—not a cattle ranch."

"Nothing's wrong with the hair. And it's possible that I am in the middle of a nervous breakdown. I mean, look at you. Look at me, talking to you."

"Up and at 'em," Lilly said.

"No. No, I'm not going up and at 'em with you, because you are dead."

"Dead is not as absolute a condition as you've been led to believe."

"I've never set up and run a conference by myself. You're the face of the company. Not me."

Dead Lilly snorted. She lit a new cigarette. "Me and the dog are going to get you a new face." When she flicked the ashes they just pinged into space before they hit the deck. I looked more closely at her. I reached out and tried to take some of the purple silk sleeve between my finger and thumb but it dissolved when my fingers reached it. Lilly was here and not, the shirt a firmly rooted memory and an illusion.

"I loved this blouse," I said. "It disappeared after you borrowed it for a date with Danny Rominowski. Is that a cigarette burn on the sleeve?"

"Yup. Doesn't it look terrific on me?" She stood, held her arms out and turned so we could admire the effect. "No wonder I borrowed it." Lilly lit her next cigarette on the last one, which faded into air when she flicked it away.

"Mommy swore those things would kill you."

"Well, she was wrong." Lilly leaned forward. "Ricky beat them to it. The new trapeze contract's filed under some spare stockings in my top drawer at work. And some stuffed panda bears are shipping tomorrow. I think."

"What do we need panda bears for?"

"They're an incentive for the new Christmas gift packages we're offering. You get a panda with every complete package purchase. We're attacking those slumping December sales head-on. It'll be fabulous. We won't have enough of 'em."

"Really?"

"Really. Call Betty and tell her where it is. She can forge our signatures. She does it all the time."

I closed my eyes and leaned back. I tried to breathe very slowly. "If you're not real, and I'm sure you're not real, go away," I whispered. "When I open my eyes you'll be gone."

I opened my eyes and they were still there. They were staring at me and they didn't look pleased.

"Gone, gone, gone," I whispered.

"Real, real, real," Boppit whispered back.

"The blouse wasn't enough to convince you we're here?" Dead Lilly asked. "What about my knowing where my spare stockings and the circus contract are?"

"You must have told me about the contract and the stockings before you disappeared and I forgot but it's in my head. You're a memory."

"I can show you where the shirt ended up," Boppit broke in. "I know exactly where it was all those months you looked for it."

"No, you can't, and if you could I wouldn't care."

"Let's see if that's true." Suddenly I wasn't on the *Rubber Duck* but moving up a flight of stairs. They were the stairs we'd climbed in our childhood house to get to the unfinished closet in my bedroom, the row of old snowsuits and outgrown clothes hanging like a barricade between my secret reading place and the rest of the world.

"This is just in my head," I whispered.

"The head is such a large place." Boppit hummed, skimming along beside me.

We flowed down the hall and into the bedroom we used to share. There was the closet, the row of coats and leggings that our mother had started hanging up here sometime in 1931. Boppit pushed aside a plaid shirt of Snyder's and a poodle skirt of Jane's. There it was—a blanket and lamp and crumbs from the cookies I'd stolen right off the baking sheet one rainy afternoon in 1938, *The Pirate Lover* sitting at the top of the nearest pile of books.

"That damn book." Boppit sniffed. "How many women have come to grief because they read too many pirate stories at impressionable ages? Why do you think Mrs. Daniels tried to keep it away from you?"

I tried to pick it up but it melted away when I touched it. There were the vinyl shards from Mom's favorite record, shattered in that spasm of rage sometime in the winter of 1939 and swept into a corner but never removed. She'd kept her records in a cherry cabinet and relied on them when she felt blue. If you found her dancing alone in the living room, you'd know it was a bad day.

Lilly peered down at the record label. "You had a temper. And Mommy had a talent for provoking you."

I felt bad about "My Sweet Little Headache." I'd felt bad about it a minute after it was in pieces. I'd felt bad about it while watching my mother look for it. Once again Mom had been right—resentment had been the poison I'd drunk, hoping it would kill the other fellow. I said, "I don't want to be here, Lilly."

"I want to show you the blouse."

"It's not here."

"Of course it is. I put it here myself." Dead Lilly jammed her hand between two storage bags and there it was, a run of purple silk and the hard knobs of pearl buttons. They still looked like there was a tiny lightbulb inside each of them; they were still the milky silver blue they'd been when I first touched them in Jordan Marsh's designer label section in ladies' on the second floor. Lilly had told me about pearls starting their lives as little bits of irritating sand that refuse to get spit out by their oyster. I thought of that every time I touched those buttons. I looked at the record shards. I looked at the worn stolen book that had been my company all those secret hours.

"What a little firetrap this closet was," Lilly observed. Thank goodness you never took to smoking. You'd have burned the house down. Remember my handing you your first cigarette? . . . 1941. We opened our bedroom window."

True. We'd leaned out the window and blown the smoke away from us so Snyder wouldn't smell it and rat us out to Daddy. Kents. I'd gotten sick in the bushes in the backyard.

"Lilly, I'm so happy to see you, but you make me very nervous," I said to my dead sister, who was, improbably, both holding the purple silk blouse and wearing it. "You understand, right? Thank you for visiting but maybe you could just go away now. Mr. Boppit too."

"Can't, doll. The conference. The company. Your future. Look at you, missing meetings, ignoring phone calls. Look at your hair, for God's sake. Nobody knows where you are half the time. He'll find you. And you'll be alone."

I didn't have to ask her who she meant. "He'll move on."

"Oh, sweetie." Boppit sighed. "He won't, but you have to. Otherwise your feelings are going to rip you up like a vulture working on roadkill. We're here to save you from yourself. From him. Help us."

"Saving me from myself?"

"Stop looking for Ricky. Accept that sometimes you don't get any kind of justice."

"Tell me what you are," I begged the two figures that flanked me now. "Tell me what you want from me."

"We already did," Mr. Boppit said.

"I think I'm in trouble," I said.

"You might be, honey." Dead Lilly nodded. "I'm afraid you really might be."

THE PIRATE LOVER

Fire Ship

"It's time," Basil announced to his crew, a strangely exhilarated and cheerful crew, considering that their captain and possibly all of them faced eternity in the next few hours. Still, an almost festive excitement reigned. Men had spent the last four watches working with Chips the carpenter to cut out the shapes of pirates, complete with hats and cutlasses. These they nailed along the rail of the xebec. Every deck was caulked with tar, every piece of rigging sluiced with oily slush—the frying remains from a hundred dinners. All the powder that Basil Le Cherche felt they could spare without making themselves entirely defenseless had been carried to the xebec and set amid tarry rags. When it was as much a floating bomb as it could be, he stood on the quarterdeck and addressed them.

"I've said only volunteers will serve, and each and every one of you volunteered. I can't take each man jack with me, and you must accept that." They knew what was what: this fire ship would be aimed at the heart of the enemy's ships, set alight, and left to blow Judge Henri Le Cherche and his convoy all the way to the judgment of God. But to get the ship close enough before it was lit and abandoned, a small crew would have to risk their lives. Basil Le Cherche would stake his own life on the plan—he himself would lead the group who steered the fire ship into her final moments on Earth.

Electra had risen up against him again in the privacy of the captain's quarters, once more demanding to accompany him and once more being denied. She drew his hand to her breast, guided his fingers beneath the rough sailcloth to the silk of her own skin. They kissed, both of them knowing that it was perhaps the last time they would touch each other.

When the evening sun held itself just above the horizon, the *Cat* and its accompanying handmaiden, the xebec, skimmed out of the hidden inlet where the judge's convoy had not been able to follow and made a direct assault on Henri Le Cherche's superior forces. The sun lit them in silhouette, making the xebec's rails look as if they were lined with men eager to make a boarding-party assault.

"Are they mad?" Henri Le Cherche's first lieutenant laughed. "They give us every advantage. Such a pity that men with such fighting spirit will all be dead so soon."

The judge himself watched the approach with initial exhilaration. But Henri Le Cherche had not survived among the thieves and criminals with whom he associated as long as he had without a coward's feral sense of self-protection and a liar's feel for a lie. Surrounded by men who readied for hand-to-hand combat with the xebec's crew, he said nothing but ordered his pinnace to splash down and take him to the ship at the farthest edge of the convoy. "Watch for my signals," he ordered. "I will command from the rear."

Onward the attackers came, closing at five knots on a stiffening wind from the west. The *Cat*'s crew shook their reef and dragged a sail behind them beneath the surface of the water to give the appearance of striving for every bit of speed so the slower xebec could pull ahead and do its work without drawing suspicion. And it did. Basil Le Cherche and his small group lit the slow fuse at the bow, slid into a gig that they lowered over the aft starboard side so the xebec itself hid their retreat from the enemy, and began their mad row back to the *Cat*.

Waiting. Waiting. The xebec closing fast and then inside the very convoy, close enough so the wooden images nailed to the railing were plain at last and the enemy saw they had been deceived, cries of "Fire ship! Fire ship!" all too late and then a massive explosion—spars, rigging, and body parts spread over three square miles of sea.

The *Cat*'s crew did not cheer, for though they had succeeded and they had the captain and his small crew back aboard, the terrible loss of life was sobering to them. Only the ship at the very edge of the convoy—the ship now carrying Henri Le Cherche—was intact.

"Captain!" cried an upper yardsman, pointing toward this sole undamaged ship. "She runs!" Indeed, Henri Le Cherche had ordered the ship carrying him to turn and run, leaving her distressed comrades to fend for themselves. Basil Le Cherche ordered his clearest-eyed lookout up to the mainmast yard with a glass. "Do you see Judge Le Cherche aboard her, Bill?" he called.

"Yes, sir! I see him!"

Basil Le Cherche turned to his first lieutenant, his expression satisfied and disgusted at once. "Set a course to pursue. I hardly needed the confirmation. No other man would order a ship away while his men drowned and burned in the wreckage behind him. Two points to the east," he bellowed. "Man the pumps and douse the mainstay sail and the foresail!" This old trick caught every whisper of wind and the crew knew their captain well enough to jump to the task. There was blood in the air, every man jack eager to board and take the escaping schooner. "We will have him by sunset if this breeze stays with us!" he cried, and a cheer from the sweating crew answered him.

"This time, my love," Electra whispered in his ear, for she had come up behind him and stood so close he could smell the salt on her warm skin. "This time I will board with you—for that is the schooner that carries his slaves—the women who have been taken into bondage, and they will trust and follow me before they trust any man. I am necessary to you!"

He looked at her and smiled. "My warrior witch, you are indeed necessary to me, but in this battle you will serve from the decks below. The surgeon needs steady hands and a hard head, and I hereby make you his assistant for you have both. There will be bloody work in his sick bay before we are done."

"Below the water line in that dank little corner? But I shall see nothing of the battle!"

"You will see it through its most eloquent annotations, my love—the bodies that are carried below. You are not being banished to an insignificant backwater. You may find yourself in the bloodiest corner of the battle before we are done. I remind you that I am your captain, and I command your service there."

He pulled her to him and pressed his lips to her throat. "Perhaps one day we will face an enemy side by side, my love. Be patient with me, and remember that I love you more than life itself."

NEAVE

Mr. Boppit and Lilly Dress Me for Success

They got to work on me, Dead Lilly and Mr. Boppit, and I got used to them. More than used to them. They herded me into a hairdresser's chair and on to the office and the meetings I'd been missing. When I walked into the offices in my newly polished form I felt the staff come more alive, stiffen like a sail that's caught a breeze.

Boppit and Dead Lilly hovered over my shoulder, giving me orders, making suggestions, invisible to everybody but me. I stopped muttering to them under my breath because they ordered me to stop it. I discovered that I trusted them. I did what they said. *Reassure your employees*, they'd insisted. *Return those telephone calls. Watch your tone. Smile. Don't throw things.*

Be Your Best was still in good hands: It was in Dead Lilly's and Mr. Boppit's hands, and more masterful guidance would be impossible to find. Two hundred and thirty-seven salesgirls were checking in to the hotel in six days. The circus troupe was negotiating with operations at the hotel to get the trapeze rigged in the main conference room. Speakers and trainers were gathering their notes and checking the schedules. Brochures on new products and colors were printed and sitting in bound cubes in the office. I was making meetings on time, answering the telephone, actually—weirdly—beginning once again to care. I did what they told me to do. "You have an empire to defend!" Bop would say, tugging me toward one task or another. I walked around speaking to people and the people I spoke to talked back, which I took to be proof that I didn't look as deranged as I knew I really was. I got myself a new purse and this simple action seemed to clarify and lighten my entire mind. Boppit picked it out, standing invisibly by my side at Filene's.

Lilly had always done the opening-night speech. She was the reason why every year salesgirls got in their cars and drove to this conference, often over the objections of the children and husbands left behind to turn all the laundry pink and suffer cold-cereal dinners until their mothers returned. These travelers had come to be reminded that they changed the lives of every woman they touched as a representative of Be Your Best. They wanted to see welcome notes and blue flowers in their hotel rooms. They wanted to hear tinkling crystal at dinner. They wanted to see the advertising layouts for new inky evening-wear eye colors that Lilly had talked me into, darker and sexually bolder than what we had now. She'd sat by my side and told me what to wear at the meeting with the directors when we were planning the new colors. Grapevine chatter said that half the sales directors were talking about the new Neave Terhune to their girls in the field.

The salesgirls who would be in the conference audience wanted to hear more about the new strategy to fight weak sales in December, historically the darkest month for Be Your Best because every spare dime in customers' purses went to Christmas. Boppit and Lilly described their battle plan for that: the Christmas Collection of Special Gifts for Him and Her, with every order accompanied by the adorable Be Your Best stuffed panda. "Tell the Directors that the December strategy is brilliant, that they themselves are astounding, and everything's going to be spectacular!"

I did. I was their superhero. More meetings with design and manufacturing, and voilà—shipping possible by November 15. We had a hundred Christmas Collection and adorable panda prototypes ordered to be ready to show off at the conference itself. By the end of that day every bit of energy had been wrung out of my body and my head lay facedown on my desk.

Boppit stepped up to me and brushed a hair from my shoulder. "It'll be fine. New colors. New products. You're hitting your stride, Neavie!"

"It's you and Lilly. Not me."

"No, kiddo," Boppit said, tugging me upright and straightening the seam line of the sleeve at the shoulder. "It's you."

Boppit, Dead Lilly, and I had gone over the catering menus, the opening speech, the training-session schedules, the motivational games, the entertainment, the presentations on new products, and the final dinner and award presentation. "Now the last but not least task," Boppit said. "Wardrobe."

They lifted me up and escorted me into my bedroom, dropped me on the bed, and began rummaging in the closet. When they stepped out, each of them had an outfit in hand. "Here," Mr. Boppit said. "We'll have to plan the outfits over the course of the entire conference so they build and reinforce the effect they make."

"I don't plan, Boppit. I just get dressed."

"Exactly." He nodded. "We're here to do something about that."

We had deflected attention from Be Your Best's vanished creative leader, Lilly Terhune. When an article in the *Boston Globe* used the word "disappeared" next to the words "glamorous business tycoon Lilly Terhune," Dead Lilly was delighted to be described as a glamorous business tycoon but determined not to have being dead get in the way of her perfect sales conference. "Get on the telephone, Neave," she said. "Call the directors and any influential salesgirls you can think of and talk up the new stuff—hint about the circus extravaganza. Let them hear that everything's on target. Be sweet. Let them know they're fascinating and smart and their voice sounds so good-looking. They're all talkers, and they'll talk."

I found that when the need arose and was clearly defined, I could flirt. Only a handful of attendees canceled.

The opening address was Lilly's trademark performance. "The trick is to look like exactly what every salesgirl on the floor wants to be,"

Lilly told me. Mr. Boppit stepped around her and walked into my closet. "We'll start with the shoes, because they are the foundation to any look," he said briskly. "People who know what's what look at the shoes first." He kicked my feet. It hurt, which astounded me.

"I can feel you!" I gasped. Up until this point Boppit and Lilly had been like the air. What was this dog but debris from my exploded confusion and grief, after all? Yet when he kicked me, a solid *whummp* argued against his imaginary state. "What's happening here?"

"You haven't noticed. Yesterday I offered you a cigarette," Lilly said.

"So?"

"You smoked it," Lilly said. "We're less distant to you . . . more solid."

I bent to take the shoes off, and when I got upright again Boppit whipped down my zipper. "Off," he demanded briskly. "Now, then." He turned to the closet. "Nothing in here will work. Except . . . perhaps this Ben Zuckerman suit. Look at this, Lilly."

She blew a series of smoke rings. "Love it. Of course, I should. I picked it off a rack in Jordan Marsh in 1952 and wore it the next day. Passed it off to Neave when my closet got too full. But that's too sober for opening night. We'll use it for the day-two sessions."

"Right," Bop said, flicking it with one finger. "So—Neave, show me anything else in this closet that Lilly picked out or passed down."

I obliged. We stood shoulder to shoulder and looked over a lineup of about six dresses, two skirts, four blouses, and a clutch of belts. Boppit did a hard five-minute assessment, then stepped forward with perfect confidence and started laying out entire ensembles, one by one. "For the welcoming speech we need something splashy yet not intimidating; glamorous, but not so glamorous that the audience can't imagine themselves in it. So—isn't there something a little more . . . frivolous yet still elegant in there? Oh my God!" he cried, leaping out with his prize in his hands. He held out a silk broadcloth sundress, snug through to its tiny waist with a wide midnight-blue belt cinching everything above a skirt that must have had twelve yards of fabric in it. Red and aquamarine camellias flowed over the skirt's white background. Boppit held it to his waist and turned so it moved like a current around him. "So, so perfect! A Molyneux frock! And you are not wearing one of those pointy-cone brassieres under it. We want you to look like you've actually got breasts. The pointy look will be so outré in five years. We are placing you at the head of that vanguard."

"How do you know what will be outré or not?" I ask.

He rolled his eyes at me and handed me the dress. "Again with your narrow idea that things only go in one direction. What have you got in the way of underwear that accommodates strapless?"

"I don't think I've ever worn strapless."

"Then why is this dress here?" Boppit demanded, swinging a silk sheath up off the bed to consider. "Lilly, this one was yours too?"

Dead Lilly nodded. "It's last season, Bop," she warned.

"Dovima was wearing this thing in the *Vogue* March issue so who the hell cares if it didn't go down the runway last week." He whipped around to consult with Lilly. "This is perfect for the awards dinner. What should we do about the underwear?"

They located the appropriate underwear in the dresser that Lilly'd used when we lived together. She and Boppit yanked open the drawers and found strapless brassieres, corsets, garter belts, stockings—some still in their pearl-finish boxes with filmy tissue paper.

"Now, the shoes . . . something delicate, reserved but lightheartedly sexy." Boppit hummed, bent over and digging through the closet like a terrier. "Look at this pitiful collection. My God, you wear Buster Brown," he whined, dangling a brown penny loafer between his thumb and forefinger. "Yet you are in the fashion business. This is just too strange." He held the shoe up to show Lilly. "This kind of footwear might work if it were worn with an air of irony." He looked at me doubtfully. "Do you think you can manage ironic?"

Maybe. Maybe not.

"We'll say not," Boppit said.

"Here." Dead Lilly drew me to a full-length mirror. "Look at yourself, Neavie."

I did. "Oh," I said softly. "Oh." And I started to cry, because something about the image in the mirror was more like Lilly Terhune than Lilly herself. Dead Lilly stood behind me and patted one shoulder. Mr. Boppit patted the other. "We can stand up there on that stage right behind you, Neave. Nobody'll see us. Just you. Slip on these pretty little patent heels—a woman can convince anybody of anything in those shoes. Now let's get your final conference plan-of-attack-meeting outfit ready, because those people will be in your office in an hour and you're going to walk in there and tell them exactly what's going to happen."

"You can do it." Dead Lilly nodded at my reflection in the mirror as if it were truer to me than the flesh. "Look at you. So ready."

On the opening day of the conference when I first stepped to the front of the room, a thick, soft silence greeted me. Some of the more clueless salesgirls were still looking up expecting Lilly Terhune to sweep up to the lectern. But it was me. I looked out at them and it was as if I were suddenly looking out of Lilly Terhune's eyes, believing the things Lilly believed—that selling Be Your Best cosmetics was a public service on the order of providing drinking water and electricity.

"Tell them they are continuing practices that civilization has honored for as long as there has been civilization," Boppit had said to me as we prepared. "Remember that before lipstick existed in that beautiful twist tube, the Mesopotamians applied jewels to their lips. The Egyptians used potted dyes. Cleopatra crushed carmine beetles to get the red she wanted."

"Are you speaking from direct observation or something else?" I asked.

"You know, I'm not sure," he said. "I only know I know it."

When the moment came, I stood at the podium and looked out at the sea of hopeful faces, all those bow lips and shining flip hairdos beaming back at me, and I felt myself pulled toward them. I started talking. I told them that Be Your Best couldn't make anyone fall in love with anybody all by itself, but it could help women remember the selves that could command true love: their best selves. I believed every word that I said. I could feel them believe me back in waves of scented energy.

So much desire! How could I have worked by Lilly Terhune's side and built this business and felt so little of what was flooding that room just then? I told my rapt audience that I had something to show them. Cued, my two most beautiful, fur-coat-clad staffers drove directly onto the stage in a powder-blue convertible whose license plate read BYBEST. They raised their hands to wave at the crowd, and a spotlight caught the diamonds in the bracelets at their wrists. The winners of these trophies, I sang out, would be announced at the closing-night candlelight dinner. But Be Your Best treasured each member of its sales force!

This was the catechism of Lilly's conferences. Every single woman who attended must leave with something beautiful, even if it was just a powder-blue clutch or a blue cut-glass necklace. Every single one of them was going to sit down to a candlelit dinner and be waited on by handsome young men. Every single hotel room had a welcoming card with an inspiring message propped against its vase of blue hydrangeas. "It's our job to make them feel beautiful," Lilly had said. "Cherished. Important. It's what they're selling, so they damn well better know what it feels like."

On closing night the trapeze act had pulled two hundred screaming women to their feet. The Cadillac had been driven away; the diamonds had been awarded. The conference had been declared fabulous. That night I drove to the *Rubber Duck* and lay down on its bunk. Eventually I peeled off the French bodice under the silk suit that Dead Lilly had jammed me into that morning. I pried off the heels that Mr. Boppit assured me, as he shoehorned them onto my feet, looked like glass slippers. I lay down feeling more exhausted than I ever had in my entire life.

"Hard work, letting someone else inside you," Mr. Boppit said to me. He'd appeared at the end of my bed. He was scratching himself briskly behind one ear, his mouth open and his tongue resting on the lower teeth. "Hardest work in the universe." I looked at him and thought, I feel so tired I might be dead—Dead Me, in heels.

"No, no," he said, bouncing onto the end of the bed. "You're just Neave, changing. That's all."

LILLY

He Sees Us

Boppit was right. Whenever Ricky Luhrmann thought about her, whenever he started to drive in the direction of Be Your Best at the end of a workday when he might have followed Neave's car to the *Rubber Duck*, we dreamed him away from her. We concentrated. We slowed him down. By the time he was parked in the street, looking up at her apartment windows, she was halfway to the docks. She still followed Max's instructions to watch the rearview mirror and take a different route every time, to pretend to drive to Janey's or Snyder's if she even suspected someone was following. Sometimes she took a bus. I got better at it. The concentration now was like dreaming. We'd dream Ricky Luhrmann asleep or dream him into a bar when Neave crossed his mind, and he'd find himself so tired or angry or drunk that he was seriously slowed down. He'd get to her apartment and find himself too late to follow her. We'd dreamed her into her car and gotten her on the road already. Ha!

"Will we be able to do this forever?" I asked Bop. "Keep him and her apart?"

"I can't say."

"She's so different, Boppit. She looks like dynamite. She's taking charge at the office, and everybody's treating her like . . ."

"You."

"Yes."

But it wasn't working completely and it couldn't work forever. When our concentration flagged, we could feel Luhrmann circling. Once or twice his car had even driven slowly past Be Your Best early in the evening while staff were still around. He was like a circling raptor.

"I put her in all this danger," I said at one point. "I did this!"

"Don't waste time feeling sorry for yourself, Lilly Terhune. Aren't you dreaming alongside of me, concentrating, keeping him away? Haven't we made Neave larger and stronger? She's absorbed you. When she has to face whatever it is she'll have to face, she'll be bigger."

"So she will have to face something? It's definitely going to happen, even though we're protecting her?"

"I suspect so."

"But we'll be there when she needs us?"

"That's not always the way it works."

"You said you were here to protect her, that you've always protected her."

"I have, Lilly. That's how I know that it doesn't always end well. I'm just a dog in the world, and it's a wicked, wicked world."

So we kept on, eating bologna sandwiches with her on the *Rubber Duck*, talking about things like what food we'd bring to a desert island if we could only eat that one thing for the rest of our lives. We waited. We concentrated. We dreamed.

Max kept the *Rubber Duck* schedule and watched Neave's movements as carefully as we did. She didn't know that he'd kept up the habit of sleeping two boats down with a crowbar under his bed when she was on board the *Duck*. He tried to never pass her on the docks, to never let her see him climbing into the other department boat. Any conversation about the schedule or what was stocked in the *Rubber Duck* pantry took place over the phone during daylight hours. They avoided actual physical interactions with each other. They pretended the kiss never happened while all along neither one of them stopped thinking about it. That's how it works. You lie to yourself.

Things got so peaceful that we let our guards down. Maybe we concentrated a little less. Actually, we did concentrate less. Then one morning maybe twenty days after the conference we were standing in front of the Be Your Best building, Boppit distracted by a bag of clothes one of the secretaries had tossed into a Dumpster.

"That woman is an absolute clotheshorse and she has impeccable taste," he argued when I said I didn't want to tip myself rear-end up into a trash can with him. "You don't walk away from an opportunity like this—I don't do this regularly anymore, Lilly. I'm discriminating and that woman's castoffs are worth a serious look."

He didn't even glance over his shoulder to see if I was behind him, because he was too preoccupied by what he was imagining in that bag. I wasn't behind him. Today the sun was bright, the office staff was streaming in and out the door looking purposeful, and all was right in our universe. Then some little clang rang inside me. It vibrated somewhere in my stomach—low in my stomach—and I whipped my head around to find out what had set it off and the ringing feeling pulled my eyes right to him.

He was in a parked car only feet from Be Your Best, watching the front door. He had a hat on and sunglasses, but it was him. His head was at that Ricky angle. His hands rested on the wheel and I saw a flash of wedding ring. I'd picked that ring out. I started walking toward him. The dog had tipped himself into the Dumpster at this point, pawing through the clotheshorse's bag, but at almost the exact moment I felt the clang inside myself, Boppit's head popped up and he let the bag go. He slid down from the Dumpster and moved to my side. He'd felt it too.

"There," he said. We were already both looking in the same direction. "He's so close," Bop whispered. He started walking, and I walked right beside him because it felt like that was the right thing to do, all the way to the front of Ricky Luhrmann's car. "Did you feel a weird kind of clang just before you saw him?" Boppit asked. "I thought I felt something clangy, kind of warning-ish." Boppit was holding a shoe from the Dumpster bag. He tapped it thoughtfully against the knuckles of his free hand. "He's never been this close, I mean, parked right here at the door."

"What does that mean?" I asked.

The dog shook his head back and forth in the *I can't say* way. We were planted directly in front of the car's grillwork. I didn't expect Ricky to be able to see me, but I wanted to see him. We'd walked through the Be Your Best offices by Neave's side a dozen times without a single reaction from anyone there, so I stood right in his line of vision and looked at him, sure he'd see nothing.

At first he stayed focused on the door of Be Your Best, shifting for a better view when someone came or went. He was waiting for her. Then he began to get uneasy, glancing around, trying to find the thing that was making him nervous. Boppit was leaning on his hood, looking straight through the windshield and directly into the man's eyes. Ricky took off the sunglasses and rubbed his hand over his eyes and forehead, hard. He peered out his windshield, right past Boppit, who was almost directly in his line of sight, and to the left—to me. And then everything in his face changed because he saw me. There was no doubt about it.

He gunned the engine and drove right through us. I got twisted in a kind of sucking whirlpool of Ricky Luhrmann. Boppit was more collected, more quickly, than I was. He stood there breathing pretty normally but I was staggering, choking in the middle of the street.

"You scared him, that's for sure," Boppit said soberly.

"How could that happen? How could he see me?"

"I have no idea," Boppit said.

"I know the man and I think I know where he's going to go with this. He'll try to get his head around the idea that he hadn't seen me at all. But he's going to fail. Then he's going to look for something to hurt because he's going to feel scared and he needs some relief."

"Why wasn't he that clear to you when you were alive?" Bop huffed. Then, "Something's shifted, Lilly. Something's going to get settled." Boppit lifted his hand to show me the peep-toe swing-strap sandal he'd carried off from the Dumpster. "I'm going back to get this one's mate. Look at this shortened vamp." He held the shoe in silhouette so I could appreciate it. "Slim lines, beautiful wax finish on the leather. Not pigmented or veneered in any way."

"Boppit, what can we do? Are you saying that what we're doing isn't working anymore?"

"Maybe."

"Maybe? Is that secret code for 'yes'?"

"Maybe."

"Boppit, how long are we going to be here, with Neave, as well as Where We Are Now?"

"Oh, we don't control that. " He lifted the shoe. "Isn't this color brilliant! How could a woman just toss these away? What is wrong with the world?"

"I don't know, Bop," I said. "It's a mystery."

It was a dark moment for me, truly.

BOPPIT

Snyder Gives Her Away

It was Snyder who undid all the layers of protection we'd put around her, Snyder who led him to her. Days, Neave was surrounded with colleagues. Nights, she had managed to evade him by sometimes using buses instead of her car, by keeping an erratic schedule, discovering different routes every night. Night after night he had arrived at the warehouse apartment hoping to follow her wherever she went. Night after night she was already gone when he got there.

All he wanted was to find her alone, no little niece or brother or hulking brother-in-law. No witnesses whatsoever. Could the sister be bullied into telling him where she was? Maybe. But there was that husband, that Todd guy. Todd was large. Ricky considered the boyfriend, that Helbrun guy, and dismissed that idea too. Touch a guy like Helbrun and you'd fall into a nest of lawyers.

But the brother, comic-book boy. There we go. The brother was a weak link. Kick a few grains of sand in his face and he'd do whatever you told him to do. And the brother was alone quite a bit in that studio of his. Very easy to find.

By this point Snyder's studio had three telephone lines and a part-time assistant who answered the phone and mounted and framed posters.

The Snyder Terhune Fantasy Art Company didn't have a sign over the door because most of its sales were done at gallery shows and through the mail, but a person just had to call the number in the phone book to get directions and that's what Ricky did. He lingered outside the door until the assistant was gone for the day and the brother was alone. Ricky knew a little about Snyder. He knew Snyder was nervous, that he ran to his sisters when he got scared. Ricky was confident that he could pull off the scaring part. Then the brother would run to Neave. Ricky congratulated himself, very pleased with the plan. He climbed the stairs to the studio, swinging open the door that the last assistant had left unlocked. Snyder froze into a block the instant he saw Luhrmann.

"What's wrong, little man?" Luhrmann asked, crossing the room and positioning himself within a few inches of Snyder's face. "No cause for concern. I'm not here to cause trouble. I'm here to find out where my wife is."

"Lilly? I have no idea, Ricky. We've been trying to find you, to ask you." Snyder took a firm grip on the glass cutting table so Luhrmann wouldn't see his hands shake.

"I'll bet you did," Ricky said quietly. "But I'll bet your sister Neave convinced my wife to disappear on me. I'd like to talk to that sister of yours."

"She's at work every day. She's not hard to find."

"She's hard to find if a person wants a more intimate conversation. Some privacy. Tell your sister that I think she's hiding my wife. Tell her that's not a smart thing to do."

"She doesn't have any explaining to do to anybody. And we don't know where Lilly is. You're the one with explaining to do!"

"I don't think so, Superboy. You just tell Neave that me and her need to have a chat. In private. Tell her that for me." He smiled.

"I can't help you, Ricky," Snyder said. "I don't think Neave has anything to say to you."

Snyder stood as tall as he could and held on to the table. He kept hanging on to it while Ricky Luhrmann sneered, said he could bide his time, and walked slowly out of the studio, closing the door quietly behind him. Then Snyder rushed to the window and watched the man step out of the building, go to his car, and drive off.

But then poor Snyder made the mistake that Ricky had hoped he would make. He'd watched the car pull out, reach the corner, and turn. He stood there another ten minutes to assure himself that Ricky was gone and then he scrambled down the stairs so fast he kept himself from plunging headfirst to the first floor only by hanging on to the banister. All he could think was that he had to tell Neave what had happened. He was too distracted, too frightened, to consider that Ricky might have simply circled the block and parked someplace where he could have a view of Snyder's departure, which is just what Ricky had done. Despite decades of exposure to advertisements for spy-mirror tubes and gadgets that made it possible to see around corners, Snyder had no idea how to spot someone following him. It was easy for Ricky Luhrmann to trail him all the way to the Charlestown docks and pull into a parking place that gave him a narrow but clear view of the boats. There he sat, watching while Snyder ran down the quay, calling her name, watching Neave open the cabin door and calm him, watching her usher him into the cabin quickly so he wouldn't attract attention.

Then he drove away, satisfied that when the time was right, he knew exactly where to find an isolated Neave Terhune.

THE PIRATE LOVER

Attack

Closing, closing, coming up into the wind with the enemy schooner directly in her path, the *Cat* made quick work of the chase. They were driving directly into Henri Le Cherche's path, apparently intending to board his last intact ship, the *Terrible*.

"Sir!" cried Basil Le Cherche's lookout. "There are women aboard the *Terrible*—I see them being pushed belowdecks . . . some very strangely dressed women!"

"His little flock of custom whoremaster pleasers," Basil answered. "His slaves. Aim above the waterline—I intend to kill him but not sink a ship crammed to the gunwales with helpless prisoners. Arm the boarding party! Top yardsmen first and behind them lower deckhands—snipers into the rigging! Gun crews continue ongoing fire—sweep their quarterdeck until the moment we cross. Mr. Hortense," he said, turning to his lieutenant. "I leave you in charge until my return." With that, Basil Le Cherche drew his sword and positioned himself at the rail with his eager hands poised at his back, ready for the leap onto the enemy's deck.

As they came within yards of the *Terrible* a lucky shot smashed through her mizzen topgallant. It swept downward, pulling the *Terrible*'s spanker and mainsail along with it and coming to rest at last on the deck of the *Cat*—a bridge to the enemy ship. "Now!" Basil Le Cherche cried as he sprang up and over, onto the deck of the *Terrible*. His slashing drive took the hand off his first attacker and in the pressing chaos he struggled to break free of the crush of men—to hunt madly amid the blistering confrontations all around him, to find his enemy, his nemesis, his brother.

The collision of the fallen mast onto the *Cat* and the feral cries of the boarding party all pulled Electra Gates up from the sick bay and onto the deck. She had ignored the angry, protesting surgeon, plaited her hair into a sailor's pigtail, jammed a hat on her head, and pulled a heavy cotton middy over herself to make her figure more square. Now on the deck itself she bent before the guns and blacked her face with their powder, the better to move unrecognized. Holding fast to a dagger, determined to find and free the women she knew were battened down belowdecks on the *Terrible*, she stepped to the rail of the *Cat*, balanced there above the pitching black water for an instant like an otherworldly creature about to fly. And then she sprang.

Her landing was hard, much harder than she had imagined it would be, and as an enemy ran toward her with a sword raised, Trotter lunged forward and delivered a blow to him, saving her life. He yanked her to her feet. "Get onto your bleeding feet, you fucking swab, or they'll slice you to ribbons! Watch your fucking back, boy!" he cried, pushing her behind him and facing yet another attacker. She whirled, then pushed herself toward where she hoped to find the main hatch. Just as she reached it another attacker lunged toward her, bludgeon in hand, and without engaging her mind at all, she slipped under the man's line of attack and thrust her dagger upward into his rib cage, directly to the heart. When he collapsed on the hatch she rolled the body to the side, pried the hatch open, and dropped down into the black depths of the enemy ship.

There she found exactly what she'd expected to find—a dozen figures, all young, some too young to have yet entered into womanhood, all clustered around a single guttering taper. They gaped at her, she gaped in return, so strange did their costumes seem as they stood with the sound of battle just above their heads. Flounces and bows, boys' trousers and wigs, pants and bodices of many descriptions made of many materials. All against the bulkhead, bottles were lined up—each one corked and sealed with wax, each one holding a scrap of cloth or paper. She pulled the cap from her head and released a flood of shining hair. They saw her stare.

"Bottles, miss," one said at last. "For messages. We put them under our clothes and drop them in the sea when we're allowed to go to the head. It's all we could think to do. All we had the power to do, for we're helpless, miss. Helpless."

"What do the messages say?"

"Each and every one the same, though it might be in different words: 'Save us!'"

Electra looked at the girls and smiled. "Well, saving is a sport that is open to all, is it not? And the game is afoot, my loves. Rip the skirts away from yourselves so your movement is free, for if you ever hope to see freedom yourself, you will need to be quick and willing to swing a club! Are you willing to fight for your own liberty?"

A guttural group cry answered her. All but one of them rose up and ripped clothing from their bodies, wigs from their heads. This last creature, a youngster dressed as a boy, purple and green bruises covering half her swelling face, fell to her knees and began to pray. Electra fell to her own knees before the terrified girl. "What is your name, child?"

"Polly," the child whispered.

"Polly, you will not be used as you were before—ever again," Electra promised.

"Will I die?" the girl murmured.

"Perhaps. But you will never be used again."

This promise, along with Electra's own commanding presence, was enough to bring the tiny creature to her feet. She stepped forward and joined the group of former captives. Electra turned, raised her dagger, and cried out for them to follow. They flowed behind her in a stream that broke into waves when they reached the deck. Once there they separated, stripping weapons from the fallen and turning on the crew of the *Terrible* with an energy that matched the slave ship's name. And Electra led them.

Into the bloody chaos they moved, and their presence stunned both the men of the *Terrible* and the *Cat*. The shock the girls and women generated worked entirely to their advantage—a man falling away in surprise is an easier man to kill than one who stands ready, and the women's momentum had an almost manic force. Men who towered above them by more than a foot, who outweighed them by as much as fifty pounds, found themselves falling away before this awful assault. Within moments a concerted rush led by the first mate and a gunner from the *Cat* pressed the men of the *Terrible* toward the hatch, driving them beneath where once the women had been held prisoner. Electra herself locked the hatch.

Her eyes swept over the blood running through the scuppers and the bodies of those who had fallen. When her searching eyes at last found their object, he was giving orders to secure the prisoners and take the *Terrible* to London as a prize to be condemned by the Crown. As she approached her lover she saw him reach out to grasp a railing, begin to stagger, lose his balance. Blood streamed from a cut over his left eye. A pike thrust had opened a thigh. She reached him, ripped his shirt from his back, and tore it into strips, binding the thigh and head.

"You cannot be here," he said, his voice full of wonder. "You are a spirit."

"I am flesh and blood," she answered him, taking his hand and pressing it against her. "Feel the beat of my heart and the warmth of my flesh. Know that both belong entirely to you." Basil did not answer but continued to regard her with wonder. "Basil," she said. "Your brother? Does he live?"

"You are safe, little witch. He no longer lives, though the memory of his last moments will be forever engraved on my body." Basil touched first his temple and then his thigh. "Remembrances of him," he said softly.

"The rest of his convoy?"

"Without him to lead and protect them with his connections, they will sink back into the dark places from whence they came."

All around them Basil's men were ordering the deck, pushing the dead over the side, fishing the broken mast and readying the *Terrible* to sail. Electra's eyes were drawn to a body so small it looked like a bundle of clothes. She stood and approached it, knelt over it. Polly lay quietly, her expression as calm as if she were merely sleeping. Not a mark was visible on her body, and only when Electra touched her and the body fell to its side did she see the crushed back of the skull.

"No one will ever use you again, Polly," she said softly. She drew a sailcloth gently over the corpse's face. "I promise you."

NEAVE

It's Done

The police officially stopped looking for Lilly Terhune. There was no body so there could not be a murder charge. No address or telephone had ever been found for the husband, who officially remained un-interviewed. *I don't mean to upset you, ma'am*, a young officer had offered at the end of his last meeting with us, *but missing people tend to end up being missing people*.

Charles Helbrun III had called me every day through the entire month to give me yet another chance to reconsider my error and agree to marry him. I thought he called more in shock and irritation than disappointment. I felt sorry to lose the things that had come with him: the way he looked so in charge of things that I could just lean into him and relax, the respect that radiated toward him wherever he went, the beautiful dining rooms and powerful people he moved among, the way he looked when something caught his interest. But I wasn't sorry enough to marry him. I knew I didn't desire him, because I now knew what desire was, and I wasn't willing—not anymore—to choose what Charles Helbrun III had to give.

The conference success rippled outward. AP wires ran photos of salesgirls on trapezes. Be Your Best got profiled in five major city newspaper business pages. Within three months the sales force grew by

20 percent. I'd never been busier in my life. Meanwhile Lilly's old office stayed just the way it was when she walked out the door for the last time expecting to come back soon. People stopped looking over my shoulder for her, stopped hesitating about coming to me for answers to what used to be her questions.

Oddly, the people I felt most comfortable with were Mr. Boppit and Dead Lilly. In her first weeks here in my world, Dead Lilly had left Boppit and me sometimes to go to Janey's. That's where Annie's new life was, and Lilly needed to see it. No one in that household saw her stand by her sleeping child at night. No one could touch or smell or hear her as she leaned against a doorjamb in their kitchen at dinnertime.

"Lilly'll be all right," Boppit said to me. "She just needs to get the idea of Annie being there and being happy in her head." Boppit was right. Eventually Lilly spent less time there, more with me and Bop.

"Maybe," my dead sister said to me when she rejoined us after a visit to Annie, "maybe how this is all happening is what's best. I was a C-plus mother. Janey's an A. A-plus, maybe." This was true, but even a dead person can have her feelings hurt, so I didn't agree out loud.

In the last couple of days I'd noticed that Boppit and Dead Lilly were unusually restless. They couldn't sleep, which kept me awake. If it was moonless, we'd wander onto the *Rubber Duck*'s deck for a while before returning to the cabin to toast bread. Bop and Dead Lilly would lean on the minuscule counters or sit on the tiny table, getting in my way and offering opinions while we buttered toast and looked into the black-mirror middle-of-the-night windowpanes. I loved the phosphory snap of a match as Dead Lilly started another cigarette. We'd make our way through pots of coffee and entire loaves of bread. We talked about love. They thought I'd done the right thing, turning Charles down.

"You didn't love him," Boppit said.

"And he didn't love her." Lilly nodded.

"He thought he did." This from Boppit. "But what did he know?"

Lilly sighed. "So handsome. And all that money. You know, he would have been happy spending the rest of his life with you."

"But she wouldn't have been happy giving the rest of her life to him," Boppit said. "He would have bored you sooner or later, Neave."

"Maybe I would have bored him," I said.

"No. He didn't want enough from you to be bored by you."

"In your own way," Dead Lilly said to me, "you're actually greedier about love than I ever was.'"

"One more?" I had the knife in one hand and a piece of bread poised above the toaster coils. Maybe this would be enough, I thought: me and Dead Lilly and Boppit running the company days and toasting bread nights, Annie secure and happy with Janey and Todd, Snyder hamstering away with his fantasy art. I could live like this, couldn't I?

"It's not like I'm alone. I have you two now," I said. "I have Annie and Jane and sometimes in a pinch I can even count Snyder."

Bop stopped and fiddled with a strap on his platform Mary Janes. He was in a youthful mood, he'd said when I saw them and asked why he picked them up in the first place. He was being sentimental. "For now."

"What do you mean, 'For now'? How long is 'now'?"

"Don't you worry about it."

But from where I stood at the moment it looked worrisome. I'd become somebody who needed them. "Do you mean 'Don't worry because we aren't leaving for decades,' or 'Don't worry because worrying is a waste of time'?"

Boppit said, "We mean 'Don't worry.'"

I had an uncomfortably sharp view of myself sitting there in the middle of the night, talking to a uniformed dog in shiny Mary Janes and a figure that I accepted as my dead sister.

"Shhh," Boppit said suddenly. His ears popped up and his expression got focused, though not on anything in the room. He whined softly.

Dead Lilly set a buttered crust down. Her expression was more serious than I'd seen it since she first arrived, her eyes black as the panes of glass behind her.

"We have to leave you for a bit," Boppit said soberly.

"You're not leaving me for good, are you?" The idea of their disappearing was so much more terrible than the fact of their having come to me in the first place. "Please don't leave."

Boppit's eyebrows had popped up in that worried, protective look he used to have when he lay by my bed and kept watch in our childhood room. "We're not exactly in charge, Neavie."

I reached out to touch his uniformed arm, but when my hand got to it, the fabric had no substance. Only the day before I'd touched it and felt sturdy cotton. Now my hand floated through the arm and I jerked it away. He and Lilly got dim, then wispy.

I tried to settle in without them. More tired than I'd known I was, I almost immediately fell into a state I wouldn't so much call being asleep as being unconscious. And in this state I had what in other times in my life I would have called a dream: Max Luhrmann and I were on Mars, with the whole lightless universe as a background. Hunched behind us were Bop and Lilly. I could feel their feelings. There was a touch of ferocity about their mood: They were on guard; they were a little frightened. In the dream Dead Lilly put her arm around me and I could hear her thoughts. She was thinking "Goodbye," and every part of me rang like an alarm had gone off in my chest.

I swam up from the dream and looked frantically around for Lilly and Boppit, who were not there. I wanted to wake up like I had when I was twelve years old and be greeted with Boppit's direct gaze and thumping tail. His eyes would catch whatever streetlight made its way into the room and I would lie down again, and sleep. But he was not here with me now.

I searched around the side of the bunk for something to read. The usual pile lay by my side: a few magazines, my copy of *The Pirate Lover*, a spare copy of *Jane Eyre* I'd picked up at a used bookshop. The one I'd read with Mrs. Daniels lived on a shelf in my apartment. This backup edition was an old-fashioned blocky thing bound in Moroccan leather, designed more to take up a lot of space on a library shelf than to be read. It weighed upward of six pounds and had a spine as thick and horny as wood. Some deeply stupid editor had decided to illustrate it with sighing maidens and flower-choked weddings. When I'd first found it I'd hefted it up and flipped through hoping to find drawings of scenes I had imagined with Mrs. Daniels: the pacing, feral wife in Mr. Rochester's attic, the lightning-shattered chestnut tree where Rochester had first kissed Jane, the flames spiraling up his bedroom curtains. Nope. I'd bought it anyhow. Now it lay open in front of me to a page with an insipid young woman playing a piano. She was smiling flirtatiously, tipping her head and batting her eyelashes in a way that Jane Eyre would find contemptible. This improbable ninny was looking up at a slender man, who smiled goofily back, just as Rochester would never smile. I sighed, flipped the page, and fell asleep for the second time that night.

When I woke again my bunk was rocking. A low throb worked its way right through the wood and into my body. I reached for the light, flipped its switch. No power in the cabin, yet through its window I saw that a dim light shone on deck. Someone had disconnected the generator from the cabin. The *Rubber Duck* was moving, chugging almost silently along at no more than two or three knots, but moving.

"Boppit?" I whispered hopefully. "Lilly?" No answer. I was alone, except for whoever or whatever had untied the *Rubber Duck* and pointed her out to sea. As my eyes adjusted I found that enough light came through the windows for me to navigate around the cabin. The *Rubber Duck* hit a wave head-on, dipped down, and rose up. I pushed the blankets back, noticing that my hands were shaking. I swung my legs over the side and went to the door. The latch was locked or jammed, immovable.

"Hello!" I yelled. "What's going on?" But my body had already told me what was going on. The inside of my chest was filled with something electric, churning.

"Ricky?" I called. "What do you want?" Silence. Only the thrumming, low-level gears, the occasional slap of a wave on the hull. "Ricky!"

I sat down on the bunk and worked on getting my breathing under control. When he opened the door, and it seemed pretty certain to me that he would eventually open the door, it would be easy for him to pin me in a corner in this tiny space. The cabin windows were too small for me to squeeze through. I had to break the door latch and get to the deck, where I'd have more freedom of movement, more of a chance. I scanned the room for some heavy object to bring down on the door's jammed latch handle.

Was that sound another engine? I climbed up to one of the windows and listened. Something was chugging toward us, bumping against the *Rubber Duck*'s hull, no one speaking but I heard a busy flurry of ropes tying another boat to our side. Just at the outside edge of my range of view I saw a shape heaving itself over the rail and onto the *Rubber Duck*'s deck. And there was Ricky Luhrmann's bulky darkness beside the first silhouette, not helping it over, not stopping it, not moving at all but talking.

"What a surprise," Ricky's voice said, not sounding at all surprised. "You hid your car, didn't you? Clever boy, making me think that tonight there was nobody around. But look at you now, all hero rescuer. All you need is a cape."

"You've been drinking."

"Very possibly."

"Ricky, let's just take the boats back. If anybody notices they were gone, we'll just say you took it out for a ride because you were drunk and you weren't thinking straight. We'll forget all about it."

Ricky's creaking laugh cut through the door so clearly I stepped away from it. He must be standing within inches on the other side. He said, "No. I don't think so, Max. I think we're just going to play this out."

"I'll turn us around."

Footsteps, scuffling, the *bwuppp* of a body against the bulkhead. Then I couldn't hear anything for a few minutes. I climbed on the tiny refrigerator and tried to see them through an open ventilation hatch. The wind had thickened and it whipped a loose canvas on the lifeboat across my line of view, obstructing everything.

"Ricky, you don't know what you're doing."

"Yes I do. I'm going to teach the cunt little sister to mind her *p*'s and *q*'s, to leave me alone, to stay away from me and my business. That includes talking to my brother, talking to the police, asking questions, calling my old boss, hunting me down like it's her business, her right.

It's not. I've been thinking about things I could do that would make it clear to her. There are lots of things. The meddling little bitch needs to know I don't sit back and do nothing if she messes with me."

"I think she knows that already."

"But it didn't stop her, did it? She kept at it. A few minutes with me, here in the quiet, nobody around to hear a thing, and I'm sure she and I will come to an understanding. Get back in your boat and go home, Max. I'll return her in the morning when I'm done with her. And she won't say anything to anybody because I'll tell her exactly what will happen to her if she does. And you won't say anything to anybody because that's what you do."

"It's not what I'm going to do."

"People don't change. You've always been a not-say-anything kind of guy. You did nothing then. You'll do nothing now."

"What do you mean I did nothing?"

"You left me alone with her. You came home and there she was, just a little floating thing in the bathtub. Oh, my. How did it happen, Max? Such a tragedy! And when the horrified parents got home we were all so mortified for you, the boy who was babysitting when it happened. Because it was your fault. And you know why? Because you left me alone with her. You went across the street to play basketball. *Only be gone for ten minutes*, you said. Who can drown in six inches of water? That's what you said to yourself. We'd left her alone in the bath a dozen times and all was well. But not this time. You knew better. You left her even though you knew what I was. That's why you're to blame."

"Ricky, you loved Pansy. Why would I think that you would hurt her?"

"I didn't plan it. I just wanted to play, push her head under for a second. I didn't expect it to feel like it did." Ricky's voice was unfolding, getting bigger. "Everyone blamed you. Even you blamed you."

"Neave!" Max shouted out, suddenly sounding panicked. "Are you all right?"

"I'm all right!" I yelled. "The latch is jammed! The lights won't go on in here!"

"Let me take the helm, Ricky. This harbor's clogged with islands."

"Oh, I studied the charts. We'll be past Spectacle and out into the open water in a few minutes. There's the green harbor light. Almost open ocean now. Nobody will hear a thing. Get in your little boat and go back, Max. There's nothing you can do here. I'm a man of my word. I'll bring little sister home when I'm done with her."

I tried, again, to force the cabin door latch. I scanned the dark cabin, looking for anything solid and heavy, but nautical rooms tend to be designed with things bolted down against the natural movement of a boat in water. There was my pile of candy wrappers, a glass and a fork, magazines, the books. And there was a wooden box that I knew held a brass compass. I opened it, plucked the gleaming thing from the gimbals and leveled it, brass-back first, at the latch. One hard blow and the handle rattled though it didn't give way. Two more and I was rewarded with the sound of a screw or bolt dropping onto the deck on the other side of the door. I grabbed a pencil and pushed it into the old-fashioned iron casing, poking until I heard a satisfying clink. I pushed at the now broken latch again and felt it yield.

Then the door was yanked open so abruptly that I fell forward, out of the cabin and into the firm grip of Ricky Luhrmann. "Got it open at last, sweetheart?" He wound my collar and the back of my pajamas around one hand like a fabric rope and dragged me to the railing, where he pulled the pajamas snugly around my throat. He turned me around so Max could see my face. We stood there like statues, Max and I disheveled and in pajamas, Ricky drunk enough for his balance to give way a bit when the boat hit larger waves. Even slightly drunk, though, he was shockingly strong, and his grip tightened if I so much as shifted my feet an inch.

"Look," he said with a laugh. "It's a pajama party." Max stood perfectly still. I could feel him being quiet so that Ricky would keep talking, be distracted into a drunken false moment and drop his guard. Max caught my eye. *Wait*, his look said. *It'll come*. Ricky's tone was conversational. He said, "You know, Max, I've been listening to you go on about currents and snarks and tracking the junk that goes overboard for years. If I were to slip, and accidentally knock little sister over the rail, I bet I could tell you where she'd end up."

"Really?"

"Her head'd be the first thing to go. It'd wobble off in a week, faster if I snapped it before her tragic loss of balance. Then the ankle joints give way. That's why you find so many feet on beaches. I expect a shark'll snip off something. You told me once about a guy in Australia catching a fourteen-foot tiger shark that vomited up a bird, a rat, and a whole human arm, which still had identifiable fingerprints and a tattoo so the police were able to identify the guy. His murderers were found but released—an arm's not a body. You taught me that. And you need a body to accuse somebody of murder. Cut up a body—no murder!"

"That was in 1935."

"The law's still the same now, though, isn't it?" The engine kept softly chugging and the sea opened up around us. "I could put images in your head, Max. Things you don't want there and you'll never get them out. Just think."

"I have been thinking, Ricky."

"Remember your telling me about the poet Yasayori? You said that a thousand years ago he was banished to a remote island by his emperor. He wrote hundreds of poems on little wooden planks and threw them into the sea, hoping some would reach his parents. One washed up near the palace and a guy took it to the emperor, who loved it. He sprang that guy—sent a boat right out to fetch him back to civilization. I remember every single thing you've ever said to me. Can you imagine having your head refuse to let anything just go? It fills up. It's like this enormous pressure, pushing, pushing, pushing."

I had gone utterly still, struggling not to telegraph any sensation at all to the man with the firm grip on my neck. He kept talking. "Let's say a shark gets one arm, and the torso lands on a beach in Ireland. That would be almost a year from now, wouldn't it? Do I have the times and currents right?"

"Pretty much."

"The way you're looking at me right now, Max? It's how Mommy used to look at me. She knew. She knew what I was."

"That must have felt terrible, Ricky."

"No. It's a warm buzz. I'd stare at her until I could feel it, like I'm staring at you now. I can feel it starting. Feels great. Nothing in the world like it."

"Let her go." Max took a step toward us and Ricky twisted me around, tightening the grip and reaching behind his belt. When he brought his hand in sight again it held a knife. Max stopped.

"You understand that I have to discipline her. You can't let them just do what they do. Then they think they can do whatever they want. You have to control that. Correct them."

Max's eyes flicked to the left and I understood that to mean that a moment had come, that Ricky's attention had lost its focus. I lifted my heel and drove it upward behind me as fast and hard as I could. I connected exactly where I'd aimed, and Ricky fell back. Max charged forward and into him, catching his shoulder and spinning him to the deck. Ricky rolled away. I saw the gleam of the blade but Max kept moving directly into him and when they came down together Ricky had laid open Max's thigh from hip to kneecap.

But I was free, and I knew the toolbox was only yards away. As Max crumpled onto the deck and Ricky scrambled to his feet, I flipped it open and pushed aside a caulking tool. A double-bladed bolt cutter lay beneath it. Also a bolt. Ricky straddled Max, breathing hard. He raised the hand holding the knife high, looking blind now with something that might have been rage but wasn't. He was happy.

Max swiveled his head, searching for me, and there I was, one hand gripping the five-pound metal tool, the other holding a bolt. I stood behind Ricky and to his right. I flicked the bolt into the shadows behind Ricky, to his left. His head twisted around to follow the sound. I closed on him and brought the bolt cutter to bear in a hard, fast sweep.

I caught him in the jaw. The blow whipped his head back and

around, and the body followed the head. I'd heard bone crack. He hit the rail and I could see his eyes go wild when he understood what was about to happen to him. His arms flailed out in a panic and he managed to get a loose grip on the rail with his right hand. I brought the bolt cutter down again, heard cracking bone again. The broken hand flew up and away from the rail. He went over.

Max struggled to get to his feet and grab the tumbling body but he slipped in his own blood and fell again. To my astonishment I saw him try to throw his good leg over the rail and follow Ricky into freezing water that would give him about two minutes before hypothermia killed him. I knocked him down, yanked his T-shirt over his head, and started ripping it into strips to tie up the thigh.

"You can't go after him," I said grimly. "You can't, and I won't."

"He'll drown!"

"Hopefully. Maybe the propellers will catch him when he rolls under the hull."

I had to keep pushing Max back down on the deck while the *Rubber Duck* chugged along steadily at three or four knots and I gained enough pressure around the thigh to stop the bleeding. By then we were beyond the place where Ricky had gone in, and even with starlight the ocean surface was all glistening black skin broken by lacy chop. A human head bobbing above that great expanse would be almost impossible to find. Clouds had thickened and the wind had picked up. The freshening wind, the waves, the chugging engines swallowed any hope of hearing a man calling for help even if he were still alive and yelling, which was unlikely. He was lost. Still I did what Max insisted we do and turned the boat around. We flipped on searchlights and swept the water carefully, left to right, close to far, right to left. Nothing. What was left of Max's pants leg was soaked through with blood, red where the wound seeped and then began to openly bleed again, purple and crusty farther from the cut. His hands whitened, and then his face.

"You're going to bleed to death if you don't lie down," I insisted. The *Rubber Duck* lurched and he lost his balance. Max was not a small man and I had a firm grip on him. We came down on the deck in a tangle, me on top of him, holding him down.

"Enough," I said. "Max, I gave him a massive whack with that bolt cutter. He's been in freezing water for a long time. He's not alive, and you won't be alive for long either if we don't stop that bleeding. We're going in."

Max could navigate around the islands as easily as around the furniture in his office, and he guided us back past Graves, past Spectacle, then Peddocks and Georges and Thompson, back to Charlestown and the docks. We cut the engines and tied up.

"Don't move any further," I admonished him when I'd gotten him to the end of the dock. "Stay right where you are. I'll get a car and swing back to pick you up."

Twenty minutes later we were in a white-curtained examination area in Mass General's emergency room, Max's pants scissored away and three interns swabbing, stitching, and setting up a transfusion. Then a gunshot wound drew them away and Max and I were alone.

"Did you know?" I asked. "About what he did to your sister, I mean?"

"No. I couldn't know that."

"So you called it an accident?"

"I called it my fault. My parents called it an accident, but that was only because it was less horrible to think it was an accident than anything else."

"You said your sister'd been left in a bath by herself lots of times. Didn't you wonder? Didn't you think that Ricky . . . ?"

"I don't know. I know I left the house for a few minutes of pickup ball. I know I told Ricky I'd be right back. I was gone maybe twenty minutes. I know that."

"He said you knew what he was," I said. "Did you?"

"Sometimes you can't know what you know," he said. "You know that."

I did.

We sat side by side for another half hour, waiting for a doctor to return and decide what to do with him next. I said, "Max, what happened tonight on the *Rubber Duck*, nobody's going to blame us. And nobody's going to find Ricky's body."

Max had managed to get blood in his hair as well, and now it stood out from his skull, matted where it had congealed and dried. I patted a clump of it down. I slipped my fingers along the bloody line he'd left on his cheek, down to his throat.

"Justice is done," I said to him.

Before our hospital stay ended, we laid out the facts of the evening's events for the authorities as thinly and plainly as we could. The interrogators looked at Max's condition and asked him if he wanted to press assault charges against his brother, which made him laugh, not in a sane-sounding way. The staff left again, a nurse saying that Max would have to be admitted for the night because he needed another transfusion. *Stay put*, she said as she walked away.

"Thank you," he murmured. "For saving me. For getting me here."

"You're welcome."

Max Luhrmann looked as ravaged and windblown as a man coming from a storm at sea, which I guess is exactly what he was.

"Neave?"

"What?"

"You are so beautiful."

The words sent a little electric trill through my chest. "Max, you took that painkiller the nurse gave you? The little white one?"

"Yes. It's why I can say what I think. It doesn't mean I don't think it."

I looked at him so carefully, so afraid I'd see a man who was too drugged to say what he meant. The man I saw looked entirely like himself, only bleeding and disheveled and a little slowed by the painkiller. He looked like he was in charge of his mental faculties.

He said, "You're in my head almost all the time."

I was still wearing the bloodstained pajamas I'd driven to the hospital in. My hair was jammed in a lumpy ponytail. I'd found a pair of old sneakers on the boat and slid my feet into them. There were holes in the toes. One of my hands lifted like the movement was its own idea and went to his lips. He stayed very still and then, slowly, put his hand on my neck. I pulled his whole body directly, entirely, against mine. I drew his head down and kissed him. He kissed back. I pulled away.

He reached for my hand and caught it. He pulled me onto his gurney. "Again," he said. So I kissed him again.

NEAVE

Message in a Bottle

Ricky Luhrmann's body was never recovered. They stopped looking when no trace of him surfaced over a ten-week "search." Now he is a missing person who is missed by no one. Nothing will ever mark a grave or commemorate a date. His feet could be on a beach in Ballybunion and his head could be on its way to Reykjavik. Nobody has been accused of his murder because there is no body. There is only Max, who thinks that if he hadn't walked out of the house that afternoon when he was ten and Ricky was eight and a little sister played in the bathtub, that everything could be different. He's looking for something that will explain his brother.

I'm not. The world has Ricky Luhrmanns in it and sometimes there's no explanation for what they are. They hurt people because it feels good. If Ricky Luhrmann had been fished out of the water and dried off, he would have gone and gotten a piece of wire and wound it around my neck. Then he would have nailed my hair to Max's office door.

Max sold the *Rubber Duck* out of the hydrography department and bought a science research vessel he found in Woods Hole named *Boogie Woogie*. The oceanography department used it for salinity and current tracking, recreational fishing, and (unofficially) for parties. Six months after Max and I became lovers I was along on a party-boat ride on the

Boogie Woogie to celebrate Charlie Healey getting a paper published in *Scientific American* magazine. His subject was MIBs—messages in bottles—which everybody had told him was not only an unpublishable topic but an embarrassing one for a serious researcher. After three or four beers, Charlie cornered me and repeated most of the article verbatim. I'd been the only one at the party who hadn't glided out of his path when he'd come at them, so I learned that the American, British, and German navies had been tossing MIBs into the ocean for more than a hundred years, using them to track currents—the first human-made drifters to bob along the entire Northwest Passage. "Cast thy bread upon the waters, for thou shalt find it after many days," Charlie said drunkenly, poking me in the shoulder with the hand that wasn't holding a beer. "Ecclesiastes. Biblical flotsamology." He told me about an alcoholic preacher named George Phillips who put anti-drinking sermons into forty thousand bottles and pitched them into the Pacific. They reached Mexico, New Guinea, Australia. Fifteen hundred people who'd found them wrote to Phillips—lots of them promising to stop drinking. Those sermons inspired a Capt. Walter Bindt to start throwing bottles that he called Gospel Bombs anywhere he sailed—sometimes fifteen hundred of them in a single voyage. Then he told me Daisy Alexander's story.

"Daisy was a Singer Sewing Machine heiress who moved to London and started putting messages in bottles and tossing them into the Thames. When she died, nobody could find her will. That's because it was in a bottle. Twelve years later a newly bankrupt restaurant owner named Jack Wurm was walking on a beach in San Francisco, wondering if he should kill himself. He found the bottle, broke it open, and unfolded Daisy Alexander's will. It said, 'To avoid all confusion, I leave my entire estate to the lucky person who finds this bottle and to my attorney, Barry Cohen, share and share alike. Daisy Alexander, June 20, 1937.' The estate was worth twelve million dollars. The Singer family challenged the will in court and lost. Doesn't that make you feel better about the way the universe works?" Charlie laughed. "Isn't the universe wonderful and weird?"

Yes, I thought. It could be.

"All you have to do is bend over and pick up the bottle!" he went on.

I turned to Max, who was behind me listening to somebody going on about harmonics and the music of the gyres. I said, "Max, will you marry me?"

THE PIRATE LOVER

Pirate Wedding

The enemy of my enemy is my friend, they say, and oh how many enemies Judge Henri Le Cherche had made in his short and brutal life. News of the battle between the brothers spread from the closer shores to the villages, the towns, and the cities where the judge had acted directly or through his many layers of subordinates to have his way: sexually, legally, financially. He had ruined countless lives, and now that the judge was dead and far beyond revenge they closed ranks against him and appeared in courts to say that Basil Le Cherche—a man holding a letter of marque and no pirate at all but a noble servant of his country—had been attacked by his brother Judge Henri Le Cherche's forces, who sought to take his prizes for themselves. Thief! Thief and whoremaster, they cried, for the women who had followed Electra Gates up and out of the darkness of their prison appeared also in those courts, dressed demurely with their hair bound modestly, describing Henri Le Cherche as a monster who had essentially purchased them into slavery.

Invitations came cautiously, and then in a rushing stream. Society waited and gauged its response against its most powerful members and when one of the royal family requested Basil Le Cherche's presence at a ball in his honor, all Paris opened its doors to him. He declined the invitations. They had not invited Electra Gates, whose status was much more vulnerable to scandal than any man's—and he would go to no palace, nor any hovel, that did not welcome her.

"You know they will not invite a woman whose presence could compromise their wives' reputations," she said to him. "You are a hero, but I, I am consort to an adventurer—I am fallen."

"I will force the issue!" he cried. "Every door in society must open to you, or I will seclude myself!"

She laughed. "Basil, do you think I care what the bejeweled harpies of society do or think? You should move about freely if you choose—but I am free to avoid the world, and I treasure that freedom. You must accept these invitations and remain in the world. You have shipyard managers to bribe if you are ever to set sail again, politicians you must encourage to sign the documents that make you free to go where you will. Remember that you have men to help or hinder. Be sure that if I wished to go somewhere, do something or be something, I would see it done. I will go where I wish, or not. You need clear no way for me."

How could any man or woman resist her? he thought. This woman who only a few months ago had been an obedient girl—an offering on the table of the season's balls, something set on her mother's hook to cast into pools of wealthy men. That young woman was gone, and here in her place was a creature who could embrace both battle and lovemaking, and the only opinion in the world besides her own that swayed her was his—because he was hers, chosen with the full freedom of her heart and soul, given to him with the surging fullness of her own desires.

"I do what you will me to do," he told her. "But know that I will brook no disrespect towards you—anywhere from anyone."

"Their opinion does not move me and it should not concern you, Basil. We are not of their kind, and will be gone from them soon. We have a ship. Two hours in Shelmerston's port and you can put together the best crew afloat. And then, perhaps the West Indies. The Sargasso. Spain."

He laughed. "Say the word, little witch," he said, "and we set our sails to please you."

"We will circle the Earth together, Basil Le Cherche. We will be each other's world, complete unto ourselves."

He pulled her into his arms. "If you say so, Electra Gates," he said, "it shall be."

In the next weeks no visitors but Madame de Lac came to the rooms she and Basil had taken while the *Cat* was being refitted. Electra had not seen Madame de Lac since the night of the ball, but she was not surprised to see her card. She told Trotter to admit her. Madame de Lac had never had much interest in the moral issues that any sexual affair presented, and Electra's ostracization from polite society meant nothing to her. She was married, wealthy, and, perhaps most important, she knew the secrets of virtually anyone in Paris or London who could harm her. They would have nothing to say to her visiting a fallen woman.

"You are a fool, Mademoiselle Gates, but I understand. I too was a fool for the briefest time. A little window that closed before I could leap through."

"You refer to my relationship with Basil Le Cherche?"

"Of course."

"And what was this little window? The one you declined to leap through?"

"I loved someone once. I let him go."

"Are you saying that you regret it, Madame de Lac?"

"Do you serve tea in this house, Mademoiselle Gates? I long for one of those cinnamon cookies from the new shop that everyone is raving about."

Electra understood this to mean that her interesting, and interested, guest was willing to speak frankly but she was gathering herself, flushing the servants from the room before she spoke openly. The servants, in this case, were Basil Le Cherche's bosun, and Trotter, his personal valet, who followed him on shore as well as at sea. Electra smiled. "Trotter and Joe discovered that little shop within an hour of touching foot on land. Sugar is their siren call. I'll send them off to lay waste to its riches. Again. They've been there three times this week—most excellent servants." She rang her little bell and sent them off, their departure leaving an echoing silence for the minutes before Madame de Lac spoke again.

"The world can be an ugly place, Mademoiselle Gates, and I know you have seen some of its darker corners. I knew Henri's habits very, very intimately." She opened her light silk coat to expose the soft flesh. A jagged red scar sliced down and around one perfect breast. Electra gasped. The jacket was buttoned again.

"Henri Le Cherche did this?"

"No. Another of his kind. There are many of his kind, my dear, as I suspect you already know. Mine happened to be one who loved a sharp blade. He was my first and I hope only complete lapse of judgment."

"Was this the man you were in love with?"

"He was."

"Did someone help you . . . escape him?"

"I destroyed him myself."

"I am sorry," Electra whispered.

"Perhaps I am, too, but not very much. From him I learned to recognize any number of monsters—all kinds of monsters—and most of them expressed their hatred of the world through their relations with their women. Strange. Yet they are fairly legion among us, hiding sometimes behind judge's robes and sometimes in ragged simple oilcloth cloaks. We walk among them, and they hate us."

Electra waited quietly. She knew that what Madame de Lac said was true, but she also knew that it was not the only truth.

Her visitor went on: "I know you know this about the world. Yet you are not held captive by fear. You do not withhold trust. You are free of cynicism and loneliness. I am not."

"You could be the same."

"I cannot. You have experienced something that I no longer believe I ever will know. I no longer even seek it."

"What is that, Madame?"

"You fell in love. And you fell in love with a man who was worthy of it."

"Madame de Lac, I have heard of your lovers, who are legion. You are married to a rich and powerful man. You seem to seek love with a passionate intensity."

"Many of them are the kinds of conquests that a woman collects as amusements or insurance—decent men who can offer protection from the monsters, so to speak. Others, men that are not merely conquests . . . I have hoped to change, to love one of them. But I cannot. To change, one must cast aside self-protection, all the while knowing what could happen if one does. I live surrounded by luxury and flatterers. But I live deeply alone."

"Madame de Lac, I remind you that your life is not over. You speak as if from the grave."

"You are young. You do not understand the binding quality of decisions that have been reinforced with decades' worth of other very small, apparently insignificant decisions. They gather momentum and carry you so far that you cannot go back. I am not saying I regret my life, Electra Gates. I am only looking at the beginning of yours with great interest."

The cookies arrived, carried in by a grumbling Trotter, who dropped the tray between them and left.

"I take it your man is not familiar with the niceties of pouring?" Madame de Lac said, one eyebrow arched. "Yet he understands a mistress's desire for privacy—a valuable skill in any servant. Allow me." She served them. "Electra, I see your mother's card sits on the table in the front hall."

"It does."

"I take it from your tone that you did not receive her."

"My mother understands nothing. Speaking with me would only upset her more."

"Perhaps. But pity is seldom wasted and you might offer some to her. Like many before her, she can only see a daughter who betrayed her mother's highest hopes for her. She does not see the daughter who is faithful to her own self, her own hopes. The woman lacks courage, but so do most of us. And after all, my dear, you are in love—you glow in the wake of what it has brought you—and you can afford a little generosity to one who has never known such a state. Pity her."

So uncharacteristic were these compassionate words from Madame de Lac that Electra took them to heart and the next time her mother came to her door, Madame Gates was admitted. She entered weeping, clutching her bosom. "I have tried to forgive you," she cried. "I have suffered, and I have wondered, and I cannot understand. And you know this but do not care!"

"No. I do not."

"Because of you I have been shamed and impoverished—I live on the crumbs of the few who allow me into their homes simply in order to pity me!"

"Reject their pity. Scorn them," Electra advised, her eyes narrowing.

"You think that is a simple matter without money? Heartless creature! Soulless wanton vixen!"

"Wanton, perhaps. Heartless and soulless, no. Mother, I have access to a great pool of material wealth and can easily divert a stream of it toward you. An excellent address, some beautiful clothes—these things will silence most of the harsher judgments directed at you now."

Her mother was stunned by this unexpected turn in the conversation—confused and hesitant now where she had been so sure of her feelings only a moment before. "You are changed," she said at last. "I hardly know you."

"Basil Le Cherche and I are to be married, Mother, at the spring flood. We sail for the West Indies the very night we wed, and it is possible that you and I will never see one another again. I never meant to hurt you," she added gently. "But I must be free to be what I am. All that I am—and that involves Basil Le Cherche."

"Nothing will dissuade you? You mean to marry this man?"

"Yes. I do."

And so she did, swathed in white silk, her train streaming behind her like another sail as she stood by Basil's side on the *Cat*'s quarterdeck and they swore before the world to love and cherish each other for the rest of their lives. Celebration spilled over the entire city and its harbor, for those who were grateful for the removal of Judge Henri Le Cherche from the face of the Earth sailed alongside, their rigging crowded with cheering men, and as they slipped from their moorings and into the great channel, a stream of accompanying ships fired a thirty-gun salute before unfurling pennants that signaled "Success in Battle."

Just before they sailed Electra moved to the rail with a wax-sealed bottle. She cradled it like a live thing and when her lover asked her what she was doing she told him she was thinking of Polly. Who is that? he asked. Just a girl, she answered. And what was in the bottle? He smiled, amused at her little diversion. Nothing, she said. But she had written down the story of how love had cracked open the borders of her life and admitted more feeling and valor than she had believed the human frame could bear. Someone would come upon it, perhaps someone like Polly whose life had led her to believe that there was only darkness or monsters beyond the edges of their dreary rooms, their daily habits. Electra made up a prayer for the occasion and cocked her arm: *Let such a seeker find this stoppered bit of blown glass and be changed.*

And so they sailed for the West, toward their future—whatever they would know or understand of eternity that could be understood within the limits of the body, that mysterious portal through which we must move to understand joy.

NEAVE

Reader, I Married Him

The wedding: mythic ritual made of white lace, pink frosting, and tossed bouquets. I know the clichés but I never bought into the particulars. That's a little girl's dream and I am a grown woman.

I was married aboard the *Boogie Woogie* in a bathing suit, accented with a white towel wrapped loosely and knotted at the waist. Max wore a bathing suit too, a towel draped across his shoulders like a cape. We swore to be each other's until death separated us, pulled off our towels, and jumped over the side for a swim. Most of the guests joined us.

Max's entire oceanographic department was there. Ten of my sales directors and Ruga Potts were there. Janey and Snyder hugged each other and Jane cried. Annie was told not to dive off the back of the boat. She waved at us, promised she would not die, and jumped. Ten anxious seconds later she surfaced howling and splashing, terrifically pleased. Todd hoisted her back onto the boat. She flung herself off again, this time into a small crowd of doggy-paddling flotsamologists. I watched Todd assess Annie's situation, decide she was safe, and turn to look at Jane. His face said that she was the gravitational center of the universe, which of course to him she was.

Ruga Potts was suddenly at my side. "That one," she said, tipping her chin toward the splashing and howling Annie, "disobedient."

"Sometimes," I responded.

"Good. The obedient ones, when the men with guns come, they are the first to get shot." Ruga swayed just the tiniest bit. "She will not be easy to shoot." She squinted at some empty space to the right of me, and then brushed at my hip. "Dog hair?"

"Are you drunk, Ruga?"

"I am." She swiveled on her heel and looked at me happily. "You are very beautiful today. The bathing suit, so perfect."

"Thank you."

"My wedding dress was blue, like the robin-bird egg."

"I didn't know you were married."

"They killed him." This revelation silenced me completely. Ruga lifted the glass to her lips and sipped, unperturbed. "It happened to so many. Yet I am here, alive."

"Yes."

"Sometimes the men with guns win, my love, but sometimes we defeat them and stand in the sun with a glass of Champagne." She sighed. "Look at you in your beautiful bathing costume." She watched the horizon for a moment, and then the wedding scene all around us, splashing flotsamologists and flirting salesgirls, Annie perched on the bow with a plastic crown on her head and a wand that had appeared from somewhere, Todd and Jane holding hands on the bridge. "So lovely." She sighed. Ruga lifted her glass toward Max, who was just about to jump off the quarterdeck. "Good legs," she observed. She looked at me and I felt my face heat up, which made her laugh. "Blushing! So we have both beaten the men with guns."

We had. Ruga clinked her glass against mine and lifted it. "To love," she said. "To beauty. To hope. To employment and a lipstick that does not melt. All things yield to them. Maybe not right away. But sooner or later, which we know for a fact because we are here now."

I never told Max about Dead Lilly and Mr. Boppit. They were at my side the day he said he wanted to marry me more than he wanted anything on Earth. They stood beside me, invisible to the gathered celebrants, when I put Annie's plastic tiara on my head and marched onto the deck of the *Boogie Woogie* to say I would. They were at my side the week before the wedding.

The moment I said "I do," Bop and Lilly started to lose their density and color. By that day's nightfall they had vanished. I have never seen them again.

And what of *The Pirate Lover*? The route to our highest hopes tends to run right through some dark, booby-trapped places. A girl needs a map and a light to steer her; she might need a flamethrower or a cannon as well. She might need a pirate lover. For now the dogeared little paperback is in a box at the back of a closet. But when it's time, I'll pass *The Pirate Lover* on and let Annie make of it what she will.

WHY I WROTE THIS BOOK

I met my first romance novel at the Talkeetna Roadhouse, where my daughter and I were staying the night. Most of Alaska and hundreds of tourists pass through this jumping-off town to the Denali National Park, and many left books behind for the Roadhouse lending library. Here they sat over the coffeepot on a shelf that ended in a few bear spray canisters, also on loan to travelers who'd forgotten theirs. Almost every battered paperback on offer was a romance.

I'm a New Englander, who until this visit had no experience with romances. I'd read the novels my teachers had given me, which were never romances, and I read addictively. But I was bookless when we got to Talkeetna, so I plucked one from the lending library shelf and took it to bed. My ignorance was dispelled; I was entranced.

When I got home, I headed to a library and got myself a big stack of books with titles like *The Moth and the Flame*; *Dirty, Willing Victim*; and *Too Tough to Tame*. The nice young man at the checkout counter saw my selections, leaned forward, and very discreetly offered to let me jump a waiting line of 248 (yes, really) people who wanted to read *Fifty Shades of Grey. I just happen*, he whispered, *to have a recent return right here under the counter. If you're interested.*

Well, of course I was interested. I took them home and entered

Romancelandia. Brio! Bad guys with mansions and castles! Great sex! Silliness! Sadism! Dominance. True love. Submission. Salvation. It was clear to me that under the heaving bosoms and wands of pleasure there was something elementally true going on.

In Romancelandia, sex and power were tangled, even interdependent. But wasn't that the way it really was? Weren't they also linked in *The Taming of the Shrew*, in *Wuthering Heights*, in the evening news reports of recent domestic murders? I hadn't read *Fifty Shades of Grey* or *Too Tough to Tame* until I started all this, but when I did, the struggle to control the lover or be controlled seemed like an old story, recast to play out in billionaires' luxury condominiums or wooden ships on stormy seas.

And here's where I thought the thought that became this novel: If someone set a romance plot side-by-side with a "real" story about love, would the struggle to dominate or be subordinated be the same in both worlds? Would both narratives suggest that a power struggle was central to sexual satisfaction? To love? Would both stories slip over a line and become deadly, or would they describe someone's salvation? In other words, are romances true?

The novel is a romance about romances. It takes place in two settings: Romancelandia, and the post-WWII world of emerging cosmetics industries. Its heroines discover that the forces of evil often have a magnetic, sweet, bluntly sexual pull. They allow themselves to be pulled, and find that when they reach the edge of what's safe and known, there's an almost overwhelming urge to jump. Pleasure and danger—they're an indelibly bound combination familiar to any hiker who plucks a dog-eared pink paperback to carry into the woods along with her bear spray. That's romance.

Bring on the pirates.

ACKNOWLEDGMENTS

Thanks to my editors, Amy Einhorn and Caroline Bleeke, who were never wrong. Thanks to Bill and Liv Blumer at Blumer Literary for standing firmly by this book's side (as well as mine). Thanks to Terry Grobe, Pat Mulcahy, Judy Karp, and Mark Feldhusen for reading and responding in ways that shaped the work. Information about the cosmetics industry is taken from written accounts of the business, particularly the parts of it shaped by Mary Kay Cosmetics, Elizabeth Arden, Madame Helena Rubinstein, and Charles Revson. Thanks to Sarah Wendell and Candy Tan for their *Beyond Heaving Bosoms: The Smart Bitches' Guide to Romance*. The Jerry Weist collection informed some of the fantasy art descriptions. May his remains end up, as he wished, on Mars.

RECOMMEND

THE ROMANCE READER'S GUIDE TO LIFE

FOR YOUR NEXT BOOK CLUB!